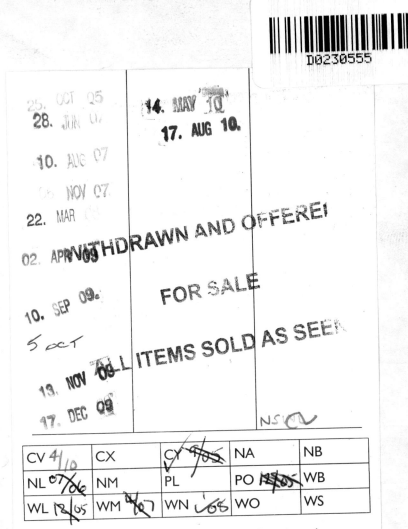

By Julian May

Voyager

Ironcrown Moon

THE BOREAL MOON TALE:
BOOK TWO

JULIAN MAY

HarperCollins*Publishers*

Voyager
An Imprint of HarperCollins*Publishers*
77–85 Fulham Palace Road,
Hammersmith, London W6 8JB

www.voyager-books.com

Published by *Voyager* 2005
1 3 5 7 9 8 6 4 2

Maps by Richard Geiger

A catalogue record for this book
is available from the British Library

ISBN 0 00 712322 1

Typeset in Meridien by Palimpsest Book Production Limited,
Polmont, Stirlingshire

Printed and bound in Great Britain by
Clays Limited, St Ives plc

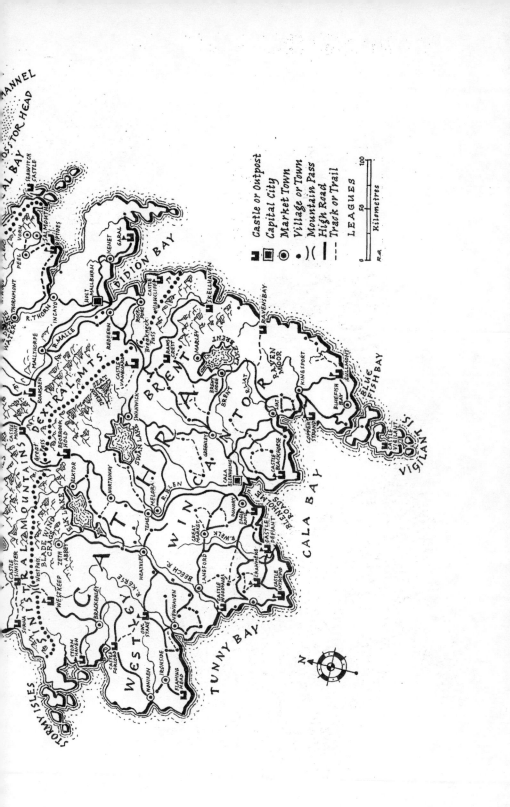

FINAL VERSE OF THE BLOSSOM MOON SONG,
AN ANCIENT CATHRAN BALLAD

Down in the waters, cold and deep,
My true love has gone to eternal sleep.
Long will I wait for his returning,
Hoping, my heart afire with yearning.
In Blossom Moon, in Blossom Moon, it will never be.

PROLOGUE

The Royal Intelligencer

An unexpected thing happened last night.

As is my habit, I had been working long hours on my Boreal Moon Tale, struggling along despite cramped fingers, dimming eyesight, and the daunting magnitude of the writing project I had set myself at a time when most old men are content to doze and dream. But I have more reason than most to wish my story told to the world – most specifically to the inhabitants of High Blenholme, island of my birth, whose official Chronicle will no doubt be turned all arsey-versey by my mischievous revelations.

I had laid aside my quill after describing the chain of improbable events leading to King Conrig Wincantor's establishment of the Blenholme Sovereignty, thinking this would be an appropriate place to break the narrative and end the first book of the tale. It was very late and bracingly cool, as nights tend to be during midwinter months in southern Foraile, and the air was laden with the sweet scent of moth-jasmine. Oddly – though I did not fully appreciate the fact until later when I went outdoors – the night was almost completely silent. The usual sounds made by nocturnal birds and insects were absent and the murmur of the nearby Daravara River was muted.

After sanding the final closely written parchment sheet, I added it to the rest and locked the manuscript in the copper box that preserves it from the mice and palm roaches that would otherwise make a meal of it. I rose from my desk, paused to work the worst knots from my aching muscles, and blew out the bright flame of the brass desk lamp, plunging the room into near-darkness. A faint illumination came from the lantern that my peg-legged housecarl Borve leaves lit at the far end of the hall to guide me to bed. That was usual. What was *not* usual was the odd flickering glow coming through the window that looked northward toward the river. The crescent moon had set early and thick foliage made it difficult to see outside. My first thought was of wild-fire, since the light was too ruddy and fitful to be starshine. The rains were late this year and the scrubby hills above the jungle valley were tinder-dry. I made haste to the door, slipped outside onto the veranda, and went down the short flight of steps into my riverside garden so as to have a clear view of the opposite shore.

The northern sky was ablaze with immense rippling curtains and thrusting beams of scarlet, green, amethyst and flame-gold, so bright that they dimmed the stars, so active and intricate in their movements that every instinct of the beholder seemed to affirm that this was no mere natural phenomenon, but the work of elemental living beings.

I knew who they were, what they had been – those shining abominations who had fed on pain!

The people of High Blenholme gave them various names: the Beaconfolk, the Coldlight Army, the Great Lights. Their domain is the far north, the arctic barrens and the island in the Boreal Sea from which I had been banished. Never had I seen the Lights during my enforced sojourn on the southern mainland. Early on in my exile, when I had cautiously ques-tioned my manservant Borve about folkloric beliefs in this part of the world, he made no mention of terrible sky-beings in the local pantheon of demons and demigods. Yet here they were, transforming the night of subtropical Foraile into a facsimile of the incandescent heavens above the northland. Was it possible that I was dreaming? I hardly thought so, but it would not be the first time that nightmares provoked by the evil ones among the Beaconfolk had tormented me.

Still less did it seem they should be able to manifest themselves here, so far south! Their once-mighty powers were circumscribed now, pent-up and curtailed so that the pain-eating predators among them might no longer slake their obscene appetites upon humans and other ground-dwelling beings. And yet I seemed to feel something reaching for me, grasping my poor pounding heart with claws of ice and slowly – so slowly – tightening its grip. The chest spasm was tentative and entirely bearable, but my feeble old legs now refused to support my body and I subsided onto my knees, eyes still locked onto that dreadful blazing sky.

I have said that the night was strangely quiet. I was aware of this anomaly almost at the same time that I realized it was not quite true. A ghostly sound was discernible at the very limit of audibility, a sibilance that ebbed and flowed like surf, all the while overlaid with a complex rustling that almost resembled speech. I had first heard its like some sixty years ago, as I lay dying on the Desolation Coast of Tarn. The Coldlight Army had blazed above me then in all its awful strength, jeering at my mortal frailty, ridiculing the notion that a pathetic creature such as I might be able to frustrate its devilish entertainment.

'But I survived in spite of you!' I managed to croak, shaking a fist at them. 'I used your own twisty rules of magic to thwart your schemes. Do you want to know how? It's simple: I never told you my true name! I'm Snudge, but I'm *not* Snudge. What d'you think of that, Lights?'

Above me the luminous draperies and glorious colored beacons flared in response to my puny effort at defiance. The faint crackling sound intensified momentarily and I felt a crushing agony behind my breastbone. The pang subsided almost at once and I slowly exhaled, sagging back onto my heels and then sprawling sideways to rest against the trunk of a small tree, eyes shut tight.

Was the pain really of their doing, or was my aging heart simply giving out at last as I dreamt of my old enemies? I waited motionless, in fearful anticipation of a more violent attack that would finish me; but none came, and at length I relaxed, reassuring myself that the lethal capabilities of the Lights were indeed extinct. They could do me no serious harm. I, Deveron Austrey, called Snudge, would live.

When I opened my eyes, I saw that the sky was empty except for the rich expanse of southern stars.

The grand scheme to unite the four disparate realms of High Blenholme into a single Sovereignty was conceived by my first master, Conrig Wincantor, later to be nicknamed Ironcrown, while he was still very young.

Growing up as Prince Heritor of Cathra, the richest and most powerful of the island realms, Conrig idolized his remote ancestor Emperor Bazekoy, the towering personality who first vanquished the great Continental nations of Foraile, Andradh, and Stippen, then set out to wrest control of Blenholme from the Salka and the other nonhuman monsters who had inhabited the place since the dawn of time. The year that Bazekoy's conquering army sailed up the River Brent marked the beginning of the Blenholme Chronicle.

After a long and glorious life, the emperor chose to return to the island to die – influenced, according to legend, by a dream of Great Lights. Over a thousand years later his remains, interred in Zeth Abbey, were destined to play a strangely influential role in the life of Conrig's father, King Olmigon of Cathra – as I have already described in the first volume of this Boreal Moon Tale.

Conrig's own reign began in Chronicle Year 1128, with a triumph and what seemed to be an appalling tragedy. A great sea-battle and a climactic storm in Cala Bay resulted in the defeat of King Honigalus Mallburn of Didion and forced that ill-fated monarch to accept vassal status in Conrig's new Sovereignty of High Blenholme. As a condition of Didion's surrender at Eagleroost Castle, in a move that stunned most of the high nobility of Cathra, Conrig divorced his Tarnian wife Maudrayne Northkeep – presumed by him to be barren after six years of turbulent marriage – and pledged to wed Princess Risalla, the younger half-sister of Honigalus.

Although I was only sixteen years of age at the time, I was already closely attendant upon Conrig and serving un-officially as his Royal Intelligencer by virtue of my secret wild talents. Thus I was one of the horrified witnesses who saw Maudrayne calmly put her name to the bill of divorcement, then throw herself off the castle battlements into the wintry sea forty ells below.

I was also a member of the large party who subsequently combed the ice-covered shore rocks for Maudrayne's body. My uncanny seekersense was then extremely powerful; nevertheless I was unable to detect any trace of the poor suicide. In the days that followed, both the Brothers of Zeth and Conjure-Queen Ullanoth of Moss utilized their magical talents to hunt for the woman Conrig now termed the Princess Dowager, scrutinizing not only the shoreline but also the interior regions of the island, on the improbable chance that she had somehow survived. The searchers found nothing. It was decided that the body must have been carried far out into Cala Bay, to be lost in the frigid depths.

After a month of official mourning, Conrig quietly married

Risalla Mallburn. His profound condolences had been
dispatched to Tarn, Maudrayne's birthplace and the only
island nation not yet accepting the Edict of Sovereignty. Tarn's
ruler, the High Sealord Sernin Donorvale, reacted with
predictable fury to his favorite niece's public humiliation. In
the year following her presumed death, Sernin rebuffed
Conrig's demands that Tarn join Cathra, Didion, and Moss
in a unified High Blenholme, even when the Sovereignty
'reluctantly' cut off trade with his corner of the island, leaving
Tarn at the mercy of rapacious mainland merchants and
pirates. Forced to purchase food and other needful commodi-
ties from the Continent at inflated prices, the once-wealthy
domain grew more and more impoverished and vulnerable.

The injurious effects of the Wolf's Breath volcanic erup-
tions – which had caused widespread crop failures on the
island, shut down Tarn's all-important gold mines, and
precipitated the political upheaval that inspired Conrig's
scheme of unification – were now only a bad memory.
Eastern Didion recovered from the famine that had devastated its largest cities. Its pragmatic ruler, Honigalus, rebuilt
the capital city of Holt Mallburn that had been devastated
by Conrig's invading army. He regained the trust of Didion's
independent-minded timberlords, whose cooperation was
vital to the restoration of his country's shipbuilding industry,
paid off the war reparations demanded by Conrig by building
a new fleet of naval vessels for the Sovereignty, and did his
best to keep a lid on his fiery younger brother Prince Somarus,
who remained implacably opposed to Conrig's hegemony and
considered Honigalus a traitor for having capitulated.

In the tiny kingdom of Moss, which enjoyed First Vassal
status in the Sovereignty thanks to Conjure-Queen Ullanoth's
magical assistance to Conrig during the war with Didion,
things were apparently tranquil. The queen's insanely ambitious younger brother Beynor, who had briefly occupied the

throne until his imprudent ventures into high sorcery incurred the displeasure of the Beaconfolk, had fled to the desolate Dawntide Isles to live with the Salka monsters. Whenever she gathered strength enough to pay the pain-price to the Beaconfolk, Queen Ullanoth made use of a powerful magical tool, the moonstone sigil Subtle Loophole, to keep watch on Beynor . . . and to observe other events transpiring here and there about High Blenholme. Part of this intelligence she shared with her sometime lover, High King Conrig. The rest of it she kept to herself, while she quietly pursued thaumaturgical studies and pondered the possibility of seizing control of the Sovereignty herself when the time was ripe.

Early in the spring of 1130, when most Tarnian ports remained icebound and the majority of that nation's fighting ships were still hauled up ashore, High Sealord Sernin learned that a large fleet of freebooters had set sail from Andradh on the Continent, intending to seize Tarnholme and the other important port cities of Goodfortune Bay – the only section of the Tarnian coast that remained reliably unfrozen in winter. Poised in the mountains above Tarnholme to re-inforce the sea invasion was a ragtag but formidable army of insurgent warriors loyal to Prince Somarus, led by robber-barons of western Didion.

Facing an impossible situation, Sernin and his Company of Equals swallowed their pride and sought aid from the Sovereignty, pledging fealty in return. Conrig agreed only after Tarn bowed to draconian conditions. The High King dispatched his new navy to beat off the Andradhians, and commanded his Royal Alchymist to bespeak the hedge-wizards attending rebellious Prince Somarus, warning of nasty consequences if his fighters pressed their attack on Tarn.

The Continental freebooters were soundly defeated at sea, while the prince's outlaw Didionite land-force scuttled back

over the White Rime Mountains into the wilderness of the
Great Wold, never having unsheathed their swords.

While these events transpired, I myself grew from a youth
into a man. My wild talents ripened with maturity, known
only to my royal master Conrig, to his brother Stergos who
had become the Royal Alchymist, and to a handful of other
trusted intimates of the High King.

During those early years of Conrig Ironcrown's reign, my
duties were important but rather humdrum. I spent most of
my time spying on Cathra's quarrelsome Lords of the
Southern Shore, holders of the original fiefdoms established
under Bazekoy over a millennium ago. This group of affluent
merchant-peers, who had played only a minor role in the
establishment of the Sovereignty, remained a continuing
thorn in the High King's side because the ancient laws of
Cathra made it difficult for the Crown to increase taxes on
their considerable revenues. Also, unlike the rest of the
nobility, the Lords of the Southern Shore possessed the immemorial right to veto changes in the Codex of Zeth, the charter
affirming the rights and privileges of Cathran aristocracy and
defining limits of regal authority – including the succession
to the throne. It was the Codex that specifically excluded
anyone possessing the least whiff of magical talent from
Cathra's kingship. This rule dated from Bazekoy's time, and
prevailed in Tarn and in Didion as well. Only Moss, youngest
of Blenholme's nations and founded by a brilliant sorcerer,
was an exception.

Less than a year after Conrig's second marriage, High
Queen Risalla gave birth to a strapping son who was named
Bramlow. Unfortunately Lord Stergos, the Royal Alchymist,
almost immediately determined that the child had moderate
arcane powers. In a move that surprised and bewildered his
Privy Council and loyalist nobility, the High King pressured

the Lords of the South to amend the Codex so the boy could be named Prince Heritor in spite of his talent. The lords refused, backed up by the powerful Brethren of the Mystic Order of Zeth, who inflamed the sentiments of the common people against the king's dubious proposal. In the end, Bramlow was consecrated to the Order as an acolyte, the inevitable fate of windtalented royal offspring.

Excepting Conrig himself . . .

Oh, yes. My royal master was himself possessed of an all-but-insignificant portion of magical aptitude, imperceptible to the scrutiny of the Brothers. His urgent push to amend the Codex in Prince Bramlow's favor was actually an attempt to safeguard his own position as High King of Cathra and Sovereign of Blenholme, in case his great secret should be revealed.

I, with my own undetectable 'wild' powers, had discovered Prince Heritor Conrig's puny talent by accident years earlier – and almost paid for it with my life. Instead, the prince decided to make me his personal snudge, or spy. Later, I inadvertently betrayed my master to his older brother Stergos, who kept the perilous confidence in spite of serious misgivings.

Ullanoth of Moss, the beautiful young sorceress who later became that nation's Conjure-Queen, also knew about the king's talent, but had motives of her own for not disclosing it. Only two other persons had found out Conrig's secret: his first wife Maudrayne, whom he believed to be dead, and her friend the Tarnian High Shaman Ansel Pikan, who was very much alive. So far, Ansel had also kept silent. But he remained a potential threat who might possibly betray Conrig and precipitate the dissolution of the Sovereignty. Killing the powerful shaman was no easy option. The only person who might be capable of doing the deed, Ullanoth herself, demurred for fear of offending the touchy Beaconfolk, who were the source of her powers. She did counsel Conrig with the obvious solution to his dilemma: sire a 'normal' son as soon as possible. Then, if worse came to worse, the attainted High King could abdicate in favor of the infant Prince Heritor and make use of an obscure point of law to declare himself regent, preserving his grip on the Sovereignty for at least twenty years, until his son's majority.

Two years after Bramlow's birth, in 1131, High Queen Risalla was delivered of healthy male twins who were named Orrion and Corodon. Lord Stergos and the other Brothers of Zeth who examined the babies pronounced both of them free from magical talent. Orrion, the elder by half an hour, was affirmed as Prince Heritor.

Unfortunately, the Brethren were mistaken in their assessment of the twins – as I learned to my dismay when I first beheld their tiny faces. As with their father Conrig, I was able to perceive that the infant boys had the faint but unmistakable spark of talent in their eyes. It was my clear duty to inform the king, but perhaps understandable that I should have delayed making the dire announcement. Knowing about Conrig's own hidden talent had already placed my life at grave risk; if I confessed to knowledge of his newborn sons' taint as well, who knew what my liege lord might do?

As it happened, I was spared the unwelcome task by none other than Queen Ullanoth, who had scried the little boys from a distance with the powerful moonstone sigil named Subtle Loophole. After confirming her discovery, she did not hesitate to tell Conrig the truth about the twins. She advised the dismayed king to keep the matter secret, continue pressing for a change in the law of succession . . . and beget still more offspring. In appreciation of the Conjure-Queen's wholehearted pledge of silence, Conrig doubled the annual benefice already vouchsafed to her loyal but needy little realm in exchange for magical services rendered.

Thus it appeared, as the fateful summer of 1133 began,

that most of the problems that had threatened to undermine
Conrig Ironcrown and his fledgling Sovereignty were well
under control. The realm of Cathra enjoyed unprecedented
prosperity. Thanks in part to my own underhanded activities, there was a welcome respite in the intrigues and machi-
nations of the Lords of the Southern Shore. High Queen
Risalla was happily pregnant again. Didion's fractious robber-
barons were quiet, licking their wounds following yet another
failed small insurrection by Prince Somarus. Embittered Tarn
seemed finally resigned to its vassal status and paid its exor-
bitant taxes without a murmur. The Continental nations had
apparently shelved their expansionist schemes for the time
being and were content to engage in orderly trade. Even the
Dawntide Salka monsters were lying low, not having raided
the shore settlements of Moss for over a year, thanks to fierce
storms created by Conjure-Queen Ullanoth and a sharp retal-
iatory strike on the islands by the Sovereign's navy under
Lord Admiral Hartrig Skellhaven.

I myself was a contented man that year, celebrating my
twentieth birthday and entry into adulthood on the second
day of Blossom Moon.

As part of the great Summer Solstice festival a few weeks
later, I was initiated into knighthood together with fifteen
other armigers from all parts of Cathra, becoming Sir Deveron
Austrey. We received the accolade at the traditional ceremony at noon on Midsummer Eve. To my surprise, I was
not made a simple Bachelor like the others but was created
a Knight Banneret of the Royal Household in recognition of
my confidential services to the Crown. The commander's
honors included a velvet purse containing a hundred gold
double-marks, twice the boon vouchsafed to the Knights
Bachelor; a smallish fortified manor house called Buttonoaks
with a freehold of six hundred goodly acres, situated in the
rolling hills below Swan Lake, which was supposed to provide

me with a decent income and a place to live when I was not
needed at the palace; and the services of two armigers rather
than one, together with an apprentice windvoice who would
ostensibly enable me to communicate with my superiors via
the arcane network of Zeth Brethren. (My own windtalents
were, of course, a state secret.)

After the dubbing ceremony, High King Conrig kindly
suggested that I quit the court for several weeks and visit
my new demesne, which lay less than three days' easy
journey to the north. With the realm at peace and likely to
remain so for some time to come, the king anticipated no
immediate need for my particular services.

I agreed to the idea eagerly and made ready to leave at
once, glad of the chance to avoid the elaborate Solstice
banquet and the many entertainments that would take place
over the next several days. I found the pomp and splendor
of court festivities tedious. In my rôle of Royal Intelligencer,
I often moved among the great ones of the Sovereignty; but
I had been born a commoner of low estate, the son of a
palace harnessmaker, and preferred more modest pleasures.

I invited a close friend, Sir Gavlok Whitfell, to accompany
me on my tour of inspection. He was another who esteemed
the simple life and was glad of a chance to spend time in
the country. Together with our youthful attendants, Gavlok
and I left Cala Blenholme city about the sixth hour on Solstice
Eve, heading north toward the Swan Lake region. My
armigers Val and Wil, and my windvoice Vra-Mattis, newly
come to the palace from Vanguard and Blackhorse duchies
and Zeth Abbey respectively, were still unfamiliar to me. But
they all seemed to be biddable lads and I looked forward to
getting to know them better.

I was in a fine humor, anticipating exploration of my
manor in the company of congenial men. For a short time
at least, I would answer to no master but myself.

ONE

The great outdoor feast in the Cala Palace gardens had come to its conclusion by the tenth hour of Solstice Eve. While servitors dismantled the banquet boards, re-arranged the chairs and benches, and laid out the hardwood dancing floor with its flower-decked standards and strings of twinkling lanterns, the throng of high-born guests slipped away to chambers of ease inside Cala Palace to refresh themselves before the music began.

In the royal retirement room adjacent to the great hall, High Queen Risalla sat at a dressing table enduring the attentions of her personal maid, who was rearranging her hair. The Sovereign himself rested on a padded long chair, seeming to be lost in deep thought. He had hardly exchanged a dozen words with the queen since they had left the gardens. The room was warm and he wore only his black undertunic, hose, and soft ankle-boots, having shed his ornate overrobe of black tissue velvet with white gold ornamentation. His valet was busy daubing spirits of wine on a grease spot on one of the sleeves.

'Sire,' the queen said, 'I have a special request to make of you.'

Conrig frowned absently. 'What is it, madam?' He had significant concerns of his own this evening, following a brief confidential talk with Earl Marshal Parlian Beorbrook towards the end of the feast. And there was also Ullanoth's impending visitation . . .

'I'm concerned about our children. With so many special events going on today, I had no time to look in on them. Your Reverend Brother dosed the boys with a physick he declared would surely cure them of their catarrh, and it's true that Bramlow and Corodon seemed well on the road to recovery yesterday. But I'm worried about little Orry. He's so much more delicate than the others.'

'Send a page to inquire how the lad does,' the preoccupied king said, only half listening.

Risalla waved the maid away, rose from her stool, and came to stand beside her husband. She was a woman of five-and-twenty whose face often seemed bland and plain in repose; but when she was animated, as now, her cornflower-blue eyes glowed with a disconcerting vigor. For the festivities she was attired in a high-waisted gown that revealed nothing of her six-month pregnancy. It was made of violet silk, embroidered about the low neckline with a pattern of vine leaves picked out in gold thread. A chain supporting a single large diamond pendant hung at her throat. Her honey-colored hair was dressed in a high coil of braids adorned with tiny twinkling sprays of gold wire and amethyst brilliants. A delicate golden diadem, yet to be pinned into place, waited on the dressing table.

'No, husband,' she said firmly. 'Sending a page won't do. I insist on going to the nursery myself, before Orrion and the others are put to bed. Do come with me! You haven't visited the children all week.'

'It won't be long before the dancing begins,' Conrig objected. 'We have to step out first, as well you know. And after that we must prepare for the special visitation of the Queen of Moss.'

Risalla's lips tightened in determination. 'The housemen are only beginning to put up the lanterns around the dance ground. There's ample time.' She took his hand, drawing him to his feet. 'Surely the Prince Heritor of Cathra is deserving of your sovereign attention.'

Something flickered in Conrig's dark eyes. But then he let a slow, wintry smile soften his face. He was a tall man and well built, still youthful in appearance at thirty years of age, fine-featured with a short beard and hair the color of ripe wheat. The famous iron crown, originally the rusty top hoop on a small cask of tarnblaze but now polished and given a handsome blue-heat finish, lay unobtrusively on his brow.

'Dear madam, you defeat me once again. We'll surprise the little rascals at their supper, and I don't doubt that we'll find all of them in good fettle, save for their disappointment at having to miss the Solstice celebration.' He said to the valet, 'Trey, summon my escort. And carry on scraping off that splash of gravy while I'm gone.'

'Thank you, sire – dearest husband.' Risalla spoke with every evidence of humble diffidence before adding in a drier tone, 'After all, it's not as though the dancing could begin without us. And Conjure-Queen Ullanoth is a very patient woman . . . or so I've heard.'

Conrig Wincantor, Sovereign of High Blenholme, stood with his wife outside the closed door to the royal nursery. A look of contained chagrin stiffened his features. Shrieks of childish laughter, furious shouts from an adult female, and the sounds of smashing crockery were audible through the thick oaken planking. The household knights of the royal escort kept straight faces with difficulty, while the two palace guards on duty in the corridor came to attention and smote their polished cuirasses in salute.

Inside the nursery, there was a jarring thud and someone

began to scream hysterically. A shrill voice cried, 'I'll catch him!'

'Oh, my,' Queen Risalla murmured, with a sidelong glance at the king.

Conrig scowled and addressed the senior door guard. 'What the devil is going on in there, Sergeant Mendos?'

'I 'spect it's the monkey, Your Grace,' said the guardsman, his countenance wooden. 'Little Prince Bramlow commanded that it join them for supper. Viscountess Taria's abed today with a megrim and the younger ladies and the nursemaids haven't a lick o' sense among the lot of 'em, so they agreed. Silly wenches thought it'd be fun to see the wee beast sit down at table with the royal lads. Cheer 'em up, like, since they couldn't attend the festival. I said it was a bad idea –'

'Bazekoy's Bones!' growled the king. 'Where's the creature's keeper?'

'Gone away, sire. The young ladies made him leave. He didn't want to let the monkey off its chain, y'see, and Their Graces insisted.'

'Fetch the stupid cullion,' Conrig snapped. 'I'll teach him to tend to his duty!' He hauled the door open and entered the nursery, followed by the queen. The knights of the royal escort tactfully remained in the corridor.

The large suite of rooms housing the royal children was illuminated by mellow twilight entering through open casement windows. On a food-splattered but otherwise empty table in the center of the supper area stood a sturdy boy some four years of age: Prince Bramlow, the oldest son of Conrig and Risalla. He was barefoot, wearing a red nightrobe as befitted an acolyte of Zeth, and held a bunched tablecloth in his hands as he stared keenly up at the unlit iron chandelier overhead.

A monkey the size of a large housecat sat on one of the candle-arms. It clutched a bowl of strawberries and chittered with evil glee as it pelted the human inhabitants of the room

with well-aimed pieces of fruit. The floor around the table
was littered with capsized furniture, broken plates, cups,
spoons, and scattered cushions – all commingled in a soggy
mass of spilt porridge, slices of bread, mashed berries, and a
pool of milk spreading from a cracked pitcher.

Two very young ladies-in-waiting huddled together behind
a wooden settle, weeping, their fine clothes rumpled and
splashed with berry juice. A third noblewoman, somewhat
older, stood with her back to the far wall. The giggling two-
year-old boy struggling in her arms was Prince Heritor Orrion,
who seemed to be in good health. His twin brother Corodon
jumped up and down and squealed with laughter. A pair of
nursemaids approached the table, glaring up at the monkey.
One maid brandished a broom and the other held a clothes
basket at the ready.

'Here goes!' Bramlow cried out to them, shaking the tablecloth he held. The piece of fabric billowed, soared from his
hands like a living thing, and wrapped itself neatly about the
simian vandal, who tumbled into the waiting basket with a
muffled howl. The two younger princes clapped their hands
and cheered. Bramlow hopped off the table, bowed formally
to the king and queen, and stood there grinning as the
triumphant nursemaids carried the struggling captive out of
the room. The unencumbered ladies-in-waiting made deep
curtsies and waited, their faces now full of dread. The woman
holding Prince Orrion set him on his feet at a gesture from
the queen.

Risalla said, 'Nalise, Erminy, Vedrea, you may leave us.
Wait outside until you're summoned.' The ladies fled, closing
the door behind them, and the queen regarded her sons with
a sad expression. 'You children have been very wicked.'

'Yes, Mama,' the three of them chorused. The younger
boys looked frightened and stood close together, hand in
hand. They were not identical: Prince Heritor Orrion was

slightly smaller than his twin brother, plain-featured and sandy-haired like Bramlow, while Corodon had his father's striking good looks and hair so fair it shone like silver.

'Wicked,' Conrig repeated in a terrible soft voice. 'But especially you, Bramlow. And you know why.'

The older boy lifted his chin. 'Yes, sire. It was bad to use talent to catch the monkey. But –'

'Only an ordained Brother of Zeth, dedicated to the service of the realm and pledged to harm no human person, may use overt forms of windtalent. A child who uses overt talent for vain or silly reasons commits a serious sin.' Conrig's voice deepened and Bramlow winced. 'A *royal* child who dares to exhibit overt talent in front of others, reminding them that one of our ancestors tainted the blood by mating with a nonhuman, comes very close to committing treason. Even though you're still too young to go to Zeth Abbey and begin your arcane studies, you are old enough to know right from wrong in this important matter.'

The boy dropped to his knees on the dirty floor. 'I'm sorry, sire. Really, really sorry.'

'You will be punished, Bramlow. For one week, you'll remain alone in your room, with only bread and milk to eat. A novice Brother will guard you. You are forbidden to windspeak Uncle Stergos or any other talented person, neither may you scry nor perform any of the other kinds of subtle magic that are usually allowed to you. The watching Brother will know if you disobey.'

'I – I promise I'll be good.' Tears gleamed on the four-year-old's face. 'Please don't punish the monkey!'

'The animal will be confined to its cage for a sennight,' said the king, 'and its keeper will receive a sound thrashing. Keep in mind that it is your fault that they suffer. Now retire to your room and pray for forgiveness until the midnight sun touches the horizon. Then go to bed.'

'Yes, sire.' Bramlow rose up, bowed, and trudged away into an inner chamber.

When he was gone the queen spoke to the twins. 'It was very wrong of you to ask the ladies to bring in the monkey without its chain and collar. A monkey isn't a person. It can't be trusted to behave. Do you understand this now?'

Corodon smiled slyly. 'Bram said it be great fun. It was!'

'But wrong.' Orrion's face was solemn. 'We sorry, Mama.'

Queen Risalla gathered the boys to her, kissing them. 'How do you feel today? Do you still cough and sniffle?'

'No, Mama. All well now.' Corodon beamed.

'And did you eat supper before the monkey spoiled the food?'

'Some porridge,' Orrion mumbled.

'Monkey took strawberries,' Corodon said. 'We didn't get none.'

'Didn't get *any*,' the queen corrected him. She rose to her feet. 'The ladies will make you milksops to eat in bed. No strawberries for you tonight. That will be your punishment. Now bid your father goodnight.'

Conrig lifted and embraced each boy gravely, looking deeply into their eyes before kissing them. The infinitesimal glint of talent was imperceptible to him, as it was to the Zeth Brethren and every other adept save Conjure-Queen Ullanoth and possibly Snudge – who'd never said a word about it, curse him!

Talent. That blessing and curse was present in all three of his offspring. But Risalla was once again with child, and if God pleased, Conrig would know tonight if the unborn was a normal-minded heir and the Sovereignty secure.

Much later, as the time of Ullanoth's visitation approached, Conrig and Risalla waited in the king's private sitting room in the royal apartments. The draperies were drawn against the still-bright sky, but open casements admitted both cool air and the sounds of laughter and dance-music rising from the gardens. Risalla had changed into a summer nightrobe of fine primrose-colored lawn and reclined on a cushioned couch. The hypnagogic draught prepared by Vra-Stergos, which she had swallowed only a few minutes earlier, was already making her drowsy.

'I still don't see why this examination is necessary.' The queen did not bother to hide her resentment. 'You required no such thing of me when I was pregnant with the other children.'

'Ullanoth has fashioned a new spell,' Conrig prevaricated. 'It will not only tell us the sex of our new child, but also whether or not it has talent.'

'Talent!' Risalla's tone was uncommonly peevish as she drifted between wakefulness and sleep and her usual invincible self-control dissolved. 'What does it matter if this babe shares poor Bramlow's arcane abilities? You have your precious heir to the throne in Orrion, and there is always Coro in case . . . in case . . .' Her eyes closed, but she gave a start and was wide awake again. 'In case of misfortune – may heaven forfend. I don't see why I must sleep during this procedure, either. Why shouldn't I know what Ullanoth does to me and to the child in my womb? I *hate* the notion of her casting a spell on us! I hate her, God forgive me, though I truly know not why.'

Her vehemence startled Conrig. He was fairly certain that she was unaware of the longstanding liaison between him and the sorceress, and the queen's temperament was ordinarily so coolly dutiful and tranquil that she seemed as incapable of jealousy as she was of sexual passion. In contrast to his mercurial first wife Maudrayne Northkeep, whom Conrig had adored until he came to believe that she could not give him children, Risalla Mallburn kept close custody of her emotions. It had never occurred to him to ask if she loved him; he deemed it sufficient that she was gently mannered, reasonably attractive, intelligent, fertile, and a princess royal of Cathra's traditional antagonist, the vassal nation of Didion.

'The Conjure-Queen will do nothing to outrage your dignity,' Conrig reassured her. 'She will only look at the child in a special way, without even touching you.'

'I still hate being in her power. Helpless.'

'Perhaps it's your Didionite heritage that makes you uneasy. You have a natural distrust of magic, due to your people's hostility to the sorcerers of neighboring Moss. And it's only natural that you should still resent Ullanoth's rôle in Didion's . . . submission to the Sovereignty.'

'Our defeat!' Risalla sighed and her eyes slowly closed again. 'To say nothing of the shame that most of our warriors died not in honest battle, but as the prey of bloodsucking tiny monsters, commanded by your good friend, the Conjure-Queen. All Didion knows that she invoked the Beaconfolk as well as the spunkies to ensure your victory. And so do many of your own nobles, here in Cathra. They believe you are in league with the Lights.'

'Madam, you don't know what you're saying.' He tried to speak calmly – for, after all, she was hardly conscious and Gossy had assured him that she would remember none of this tomorrow. Yet he had no doubt that Risalla spoke now from deep conviction, freed by the alchymical potion from the constraint of prudence that usually governed her tongue. It was no surprise to Conrig that the barbarous Didionites should believe him to be in thrall to Beaconfolk magic. But if it were true that his own people gave serious credence to the notion . . .

'Who among the Cathran nobility has spoken so perfidiously?' he asked her. But she only turned away and seemed to sleep.

There came a sound of hesitant knocking. The king rose from beside his wife's couch and opened the door. The corridor was empty except for his elder brother Stergos, the Royal Alchymist, attired in splendid crimson vestments in honor of the festival. Although he was five years Conrig's senior, he appeared to be much younger, with a clean-shaven round face and curly blond hair that always seemed slightly disordered. Tonight he was obviously ill at ease and his brow was dewed with perspiration.

Stergos whispered, 'All's well with Her Grace?'

Conrig nodded and the alchymist came quickly into the apartment, closing and locking the door behind him. 'I bespoke Ullanoth in Royal Fenguard castle not ten minutes ago. She can ascertain nothing through her ordinary scrying, but if the unborn possesses talent, she will be able to Send to it as she does to you and me. First, let me make certain that your lady sleeps.' With great care, Stergos lifted one of the queen's eyelids. The iris with its dilated pupil had rolled upward. 'Good. Now we must distance ourselves from Risalla if the experiment is to work. Let's go into the queen's sitting room.'

They passed through Conrig's great bedchamber and Risalla's adjacent one into the spacious solar where the queen and her ladies were accustomed to sew, read, and break their fast. 'We should be at least twenty ells away from her,' Stergos said, 'so our own talent is incapable of giving substance to the Sending.'

'What then?'

'I am to bespeak the Conjure-Queen that all is in readiness,' said his brother, perching on one of the chairs near the cold fireplace. The king took the other one. 'She will attempt the Sending, while we pray she does not succeed. If Ullanoth walks through that door, it means that the babe's talent permitted her to materialize beside Risalla.'

'And I'm futtered once again,' Conrig murmured bitterly.

'Damn it, Gossy! If I could but convince the Lords of the South to do away with the impediment, then I'd be safe and so would my sons . . . What a king young Bramlow would make! Bold as a hawk and sharp as a varg sword! You should have seen the little rogue get the better of that bloody pet monkey this evening.' He described the scene in the royal nursery, and Stergos had to smile in spite of his nervousness.

'I punished the lad harshly,' Conrig admitted. 'A week's confinement on bread and milk. He must learn self-discipline if we ever hope to have the talent restriction lifted. The Lords of the South will never yield if they envision a wizard with overt powers sitting one day on the throne.'

Stergos ventured, 'Shall I windspeak the Conjure-Queen now?'

'Wait just a moment.' The king casually covered his mouth with his hand. 'I must ask your advice on another matter before we converse with Ulla's Sending. She almost never uses the Loophole to eavesdrop now because of her considerable pain-debt, and if we guard ourselves from scrier's lip-reading our speech should be secure from her.'

'What is it, Con?' Stergos had drawn the hood of his crimson cloak over his head so that his face was concealed.

'I had disquieting news from Parlian Beorbrook tonight at the feast. You know he's just come down from an inspection of our Wold Road outposts in western Didion.'

'Don't tell me Prince Somarus is up to his old tricks!'

'No. As far as the earl marshal can tell, the bastard's laying low for the moment somewhere in the Lady Lakes region. Beorbrook's news concerns something far more serious: a rumor that Maudrayne may be alive, hiding somewhere in Tarn. A traveler from Donorvale said that the rumor has spread like wildfire over the past two weeks among the fishermen's taverns of the north-western shore, and thence to the low dives of the Tarnian capital.'

The hooded figure of the alchymist had given a great start as the king spoke his first wife's name. 'Saint Zeth preserve us – it's not possible that Maude lives! The conjoined minds of the Brotherhood searched the entire island, virtually inch by inch, and failed to scry any trace of the Princess Dowager. Even Ullanoth's Subtle Loophole detected nothing – and the sigil supposedly can oversee anyone, anywhere in the world.'

'So the Conjure-Queen says. But her close scrutiny took place four years ago, shortly after Maude was thought to have drowned. At the time, Ulla admitted that her search might have been thwarted by Red Ansel Pikan. The magical capabilities of the Grand Shaman of Tarn are unknown to her. He might have been able to block the action of the Great Stone. The painful search effort so debilitated Ullanoth that she was forced to avoid using Loophole for many months. Since then, as far as I know, she has made no further attempt to look for Maude.'

'What are we to do, Con?' Stergos's voice was taut with shock. He and the king had found and read Maudrayne's secret diary after her presumed death. In it, she had revealed not only that she had conceived Conrig's child, but also her knowledge of her husband's arcane taint. 'If the princess lives and has birthed a son not possessed of talent, you are undone! She knows your secret and could divulge it at any time, with Ansel to testify to the truth of it. Even if your twin sons by Risalla are accepted as normal, the law says that Maudrayne's boy must inherit your crown if you are deposed.'

'*If* she lives! And *if* she tells what she knows and produces the normal-minded male child. Here is where I require your advice, Gossy. Would it be wise for me to once again enlist the Conjure-Queen in the search for Maude? I'm reluctant to do so, since it would give Ulla even more power over me than she has now. I feel I'd be jumping from the hot griddle into the fire-pit.'

'My God, yes. Her ambitions . . . Con, you know I've never trusted the woman.'

'Yes, yes,' the king said impatiently. 'Nevertheless, her Loophole probably holds out the best chance of locating Maude and any child she may have had.'

'Perhaps not, if Red Ansel still keeps the Princess Dowager under his protection. But even the most powerful sorcery has limitations. For instance, Maudrayne and her child could not live permanently inside a spell of invisibility woven by Ansel. Such an existence would be insupportable to the healthy human temperament. Furthermore, a high-spirited woman such as Maude would never consent to be immured within some impregnable magical fortress for years upon end.'

Conrig gave a short mirthless laugh. 'No, not Maude! She'd take her boy hiking on the tundra and sailing in her yacht on the arctic waters. She'd teach him to ski and to hunt elk and icebears and sea-unicorns. And if she does these things, there are bound to be local people who know about it. In my opinion, she might be sought and found by a clever and talented spy – such as my Royal Intelligencer, Snudge. What do you think, Gossy?'

Stergos hesitated. 'If Maude is hiding in Tarn, she would surely be protected by the magic of more than one of the local shamans. Ansel would hardly spend all of his time shielding her. He has other responsibilities. Deveron Austrey would have a special advantage over the lesser northern adepts, since his talent is imperceptible to all but the most powerful. Furthermore, he's impossible to windwatch, so they would be able to observe him only with ordinary eyesight. But what will you do if Deveron does discover that your former wife is alive, and has a son?'

'That . . . can be decided later. But I believe there's only one solution to the problem.'

'For the love of God, Con, tell me you would not –'

The king cut off his brother's horrified protest. 'Say no more! This rumor may prove to be entirely false. We will not discuss the fate of the Princess Dowager now.'

'As you please, sire.'

Conrig said, 'I gave Snudge permission to leave Cala Blenholme and visit his new estate following his initiation ceremony. He said he'd ride out at once. You must bespeak him, ordering his return.'

'Very well. I'll take care of it as soon as we finish here.' Stergos threw off his vestment hood. 'We should delay no longer bespeaking the Conjure-Queen.'

'Do it then,' Conrig said.

The Royal Alchymist let his head sink into his hands and called out silently on the wind. After a few minutes had passed, he opened his eyes and said, 'She will make an attempt to Send immediately.'

They waited, straining their ears, fearing the sound of approaching steps from the room where Risalla lay, but hearing only the distant sounds of music and revelry outside in the gardens. At length Conrig leapt to his feet.

'I can't stand it any longer. I'm going in there –'

'That won't be necessary.'

The sweet woodsy scent of vetiver wafted into the room. A silhouette was standing in front of the tall undraped window, completely enveloped in a deep-green cloak. Ullanoth's Sending had flashed into existence with no warning. A hand, pale as milk and wearing a ring of carved moonstone on one long, graceful finger, emerged from the folds of cloth and extended itself toward Conrig.

He hastened to take the hand, brushing the back of it with his lips. He carefully avoided any contact with the ring, which was a powerful sigil named Weathermaker. 'Gracious Queen, welcome.'

Ullanoth of Moss unfastened her cloak and handed it to the

High King as though he were a simple lackey. Except for the purplish shadows about her eyes, her face was as lovely as ever, framed by shimmering long hair that mimicked the pearly interior of certain seashells. Her gown was the same unadorned green samite as her cape, and her belt was gold, with a hanging purse. Around her neck hung a golden chain with a curiously carved small translucent pendant that glowed in the dim room like wan foxfire – the Great Stone named Sender, the third major sigil that she owned. Its power, invoked only at the cost of terrible pain now that her debt to the Lights was so heavy, enabled Ullanoth to inhabit a magical simulacrum of her natural body, in which her soul might travel anywhere in the world while her true flesh lay senseless. The Sending was no vaporous ghost, but rather a warm and solid replica with a full palette of physical sensation, able to carry from its point of origin all clothing and other accoutrements worn or held by the original. It could not, however, draw sustenance from food or drink at its destination, nor could it carry back any foreign object. And if the Sending remained in existence for more than a few hours, the true body would begin to deteriorate mortally.

There was another important limitation to the Sending that only the most advanced arcane practitioners were aware of: it could materialize only near a talented person, from whom it drew magical substantiation.

'Then Risalla's unborn child is free of talent!' Conrig cried joyously.

Ullanoth nodded. 'Yes. Tonight, I've used Vra-Stergos as my substantiator. Let us go to your wife now and determine whether the babe is male or female.'

The three of them went into the room where Risalla lay, but after a few suspenseful moments Ullanoth stepped away from the sleeper's couch and shook her head. 'Alas for your hopes, my king! Your wife carries a healthy girl, without arcane talent as all of her sex must be, unless they are of far northern human blood . . . or doubly descended from the Green Ones.'

Conrig groaned. 'If the laws of Didion prevailed here, the lass might reign as their great Queen Casabarela did! But Cathra reserves its crown for male issue, and so must my Sovereignty.'

'Unless the law is changed,' Stergos put in with a hopeful smile.

'Don't be a fool, Gossy,' the king exclaimed. 'Why should the Lords of the South agree to change it now, when all save we three believe there are two legitimate male heirs to the throne? We can only hope for a better outcome to a future pregnancy, and meanwhile pray that no enemy learns the secret of my poor sons and I.'

'There are only two enemies,' Ullanoth said, 'that need concern you now.'

Conrig and Stergos regarded her with open dismay, each thinking that she must have heard the rumor about Maudrayne and her son.

But the Conjure-Queen went on to say, 'My little brother Beynor knows nothing of your own talent – not yet. But he's up to some kind of mischief with the Salka. I've been too indisposed to spy on him closely with the Loophole sigil of late, but my ordinary scrying reveals him to be in a state of unusual excitement. I've told you that Beynor spends his time studying the historical archives of his monstrous hosts in the Dawntide Isles. I cannot read lips well, and the Salka have erected magical barriers that dim my unaugmented oversight of their citadel. But I believe that Beynor may have made some important discovery. And he may have shared it with your old enemy, Vra-Kilian Blackhorse, the former Royal Alchymist.'

'But how?' Stergos demanded. 'Our wretched uncle was deprived of all talent by the iron gammadion before being

confined to Zeth Abbey. Kilian is unable to speak on the
wind himself, nor can he receive any windspoken communication from another. And no humans dare set foot on the
Dawntide Isles, so there can have been no written message
from Beynor delivered to the abbey.'

'My brother may have been cursed by the Lights and
stripped of his sigils,' Ullanoth said, 'but he still retains the
strong natural talents he was born with. One of those is the
ability to invade dreams. When we were young children, he
used to torment me until I learned to shut him out.
Fortunately, that defensive ability comes readily to those who
are adept at the arcane arts.'

The king nodded thoughtfully, remembering that Snudge
had also told him once of being harassed by Beynor while
sleeping. 'So you believe your brother communicates with
Kilian through dreams?'

'Zeth Abbey is well-shielded from windsearching, but I
have been able to follow Beynor's mental footsteps, as it
were, to that place many times. I doubt there is any other
person residing in the abbey who would be of interest to
him.'

'Beynor and Kilian!' Conrig mused. 'What common cause
could the two exiles share nowadays? And yet they did
conspire against me as I prepared to invade Didion . . .'

Ullanoth had learned some years ago that both villains
shared knowledge of a mysterious hidden trove of sigils. But
she was unware that the King already knew of its existence.

'I shall have to warn Abbas Noachil about this at once,'
Stergos said. 'He's very old and ill, but he can order the
Brethren to take special precautions against Kilian's escape.'

'That would be prudent.' Ullanoth turned to Conrig.
'Unfortunately, Beynor has also attempted to invade the
dreams of some person residing here in Cala Palace. I learned
of this only two days ago, as I scried him on the parapet of

the Salka island fortress and followed his windtrace. I don't
know who his intended target was, only that the dreamer
successfully repelled Beynor's effort.'

'God's Teeth!' Conrig exclaimed. 'Could the bastard have
been trying to enter *my* dreams?'

'Were you aware of any such assault?' Ullanoth asked.
When Conrig admitted he could recall no such thing, she
smiled. 'Then you're very likely safe. Your talent, meager
though it is, would probably have alerted your sleeping mind
to any attempt at forcible entry. Were you an untalented
person, however, it's possible he might have invaded you
without your being aware of what was happening.'

'This is a troubling piece of news,' Stergos said. 'If Beynor's
target was not the High King, then who might it have been?'

'I don't know,' she said. 'Dream-invasion is an uncommon
talent. Certain members of Moss's Glaumerie Guild have used
it in the past to gather information from the minds of ordinary folk, or as a means of subtly coercing dreamers into
some activity. More often than not, the invasion fails of its
objective unless the dreamer is predisposed to cooperate, is
very young, or has impaired willpower.'

'Will you continue to oversee Beynor's footprints on the
wind,' Conrig besought her, 'and warn us if he attempts some
wicked ploy among the residents of Cala Palace? I would
deem it a great favor.'

'You ask the impossible. My surveillance of my brother is
sporadic at best because I am so drained of strength. I only
undertake it to protect myself and my kingdom from his evil
designs.'

'Then what can we do?' Conrig asked.

'Nothing except be on guard.' Ullanoth took her cloak
from Conrig's hands and wrapped it about her once again.
'It's time for me to leave you. I dare not let my Sending
remain here any longer, for I feel myself growing very weak.

Be assured that I'll notify Vra-Stergos promptly if I should discover anything that you should know.'

'Thank you for examining the unborn babe, my dearest queen.' Conrig made a formal inclination of his head. 'I regret that your pain will be endured to no good outcome.'

She touched his cheek. 'We are with one another so seldom now that I welcome the opportunity to be here – even if it can only be in a brief Sending. Consider a voyage to Moss this summer. You can easily contrive an excuse.'

'It's a wonderful idea. You'll be hearing from me.' He bent over her hand again, and a moment later she disappeared.

Aghast, Stergos whispered, 'Surely you would not go to her!'

Conrig's smile was grim. 'No more than I would dive head-long into the steaming crater of Mornash volcano. But let her have hope.'

The Royal Alchymist spoke anxiously. 'You know what Kilian must be after.'

'I know. But the Darasilo Trove can't be easy to get at, else our uncle would have had his minions seize it years ago . . . or you and Snudge would have located the bloody thing yourselves.'

'But –'

'Brother, we'll consider the matter tomorrow, when Snudge returns. He knows more about that cache of sigils than anyone else we can trust. For now, I think you and I should carry Risalla to her bed. Then you must bespeak Snudge ordering his return and warn Abbas Noachil to put Kilian and his three cronies into close confinement. Meanwhile, I'll seek out Earl Marshal Parlian in the gardens and ask his opinion of this fine mess. One thing is certain: I was much mistaken in telling my Royal Intelligencer that this would be a peaceful summer.'

Stergos had given all of the Brothers in the palace permission to set aside their usual duties and enjoy the Solstice
entertainments. So he was surprised to find three red-robed
figures standing outside the great door that led to the
Alchymical Library, engaged in earnest conversation. He
vaguely recognized them as visiting scholars, associates of
Prior Waringlow who had come down from Zeth Abbey
several months earlier to do research on some historical
project or other.

'Why are you tarrying inside the palace on such a beautiful night?' he asked them, unfastening a large iron key from
the ring he wore on his belt. To reach his own rooms, he
had to pass through the library.

The Brothers bowed in respectful unison. One of them
said, 'We had hoped to do some studying, Lord Stergos, but
found the library locked. Perhaps you'll admit us –'

'Nonsense! Go listen to the music and have a cup of wine.
Your work can wait.'

'Certainly, my lord.'

Stergos watched them go, trying to recall their names. But
thoughts of what he must say and must *not* say in the
upcoming wind-conversation with Vra-Mattis, the novice
Brother assigned to Snudge, distracted him, and he gave up
the effort as he fitted the key into its massive lock.

TWO

Drumming. Drumming. Drumming.

Dom dom t'pat-a-pat pom . . . dom.

The sound coming from the little hut beyond the byre was soft but still audible in every room of the arctic steading's main house, repeating the same simple percussive figure, continuing hour after hour for nearly two days, longer than ever before. Sometimes the beat would falter, the timing spoiled because of inattention or the fatigue of the drummer's aged wrists and fingers; but after a painful pause the rhythmic sound always began again.

Dobnelu the sea-hag was having a particularly difficult time crossing the barrier this time. She could not recall how many false starts she'd made. Even a single mistake in the three thousand measured patterns of drumming meant going back to the beginning, but it was unthinkable that she abandon the effort. Not even her dire premonition about the woman and the boy who were her special charges must tempt her to give up. Red Ansel Pikan and Thalassa Dru were waiting beneath the ice. Needing her.

And so was the One Denied the Sky.

Dobnelu could only join them in the starless world by

means of the drum-trance, a ritual not especially difficult for Tarnian shamans in the prime of life, but an excruciating ordeal for a woman whose years numbered over four score and ten.

Dom dom t'pat-a-pat pom . . . dom.

Eyes shut tightly against the brightness of Midsummer Eve, resolutely gripping the bone drumsticks in her gnarled hands, Dobnelu the sea-hag forced herself to go on.

The maidservant Rusgann and the boy were somehow able to sleep through the maddening sound of the drumming, but Maudrayne Northkeep always remained conscious of it, even when she slipped into and out of a troubled half-doze. In disjointed prayers, she begged for an end to the infernal noise.

At last, as always, the end did come. The drumbeats ceased abruptly after a single climactic *DOM*. There was a sudden silence, broken only by the bleating of a goat in the meadow. The hag had succeeded in opening the door to that other place again. She'd entered and so left her prisoners free of her supervision for at least a day, perhaps even two.

Maudrayne pushed aside the opaque curtain of her cupboard-bed and descended on the stepstool, naked except for the ornate golden necklace with the three great opals that she never took off, her Uncle Sernin's precious wedding gift that she had worn on the night she cast herself into the sea. The air in the shuttered little room was fresh and pleasantly cool, thanks to the sod roof of Dobnelu's sturdily built home. Outside, under the endless midsummer daylight, it was probably rather warm. Perfect for what she had planned.

After putting on her clothes, she tiptoed to the partly open door leading to the large central chamber, the combined kitchen and sitting room where her serving woman and the boy slept. The hourglass on the mantelpiece indicated about three in the morning. Little Dyfrig's nook was wide open and he sat unclothed on the edge of his bed, watching his mother with solemn, intelligent eyes. Neither Maudrayne nor her son needed much sleep in the summertime: their Tarnian blood saw to that. But Rusgann Moorcock was a southerner, and she'd demonstrated that she could sleep through a tundra-deer stampede. Her bed-cupboard's curtains were shut.

'No more magic drum,' Dyfrig whispered to his mother. His hair had the same tawny golden color as that of his father, and he also possessed Conrig's handsome features and unusual dark brown eyes. A moon earlier, the boy had celebrated his fourth birthday.

Maudrayne put a finger to her lips and beckoned him. He slipped to the floor noiselessly and joined her at the kitchen's single small window. Leather-hinged at the top and held open by a hook and eye fastened to the low ceiling, it was covered with a screen of black gauze to exclude biting midges. Outside, bright sun shone on the meadow and reflected from the island-strewn expanse of Useless Bay beyond the drop-off into the fjord. A distant iceberg with multiple spires, like a dazzling white castle, hovered on the horizon off Cape Wolf.

Maudrayne pointed to the sea-hag's holy hut at the edge of the steading and spoke softly into the boy's ear. 'Eldmama Nelu has drummed herself into an enchanted sleep again. Her body will stay in the hut for a few days now, while her spirit soars away northward to the icecap of the Barren Lands to talk to the One Denied the Sky and the other witches and wizards. Now that she's gone, we can leave the farm without her permission and go wherever we please! Would you like to walk along the seashore today and have a treasure hunt?'

He squealed with excitement. 'Yes! Yes! Maybe we can find whale bones, or scales from a mirrorfish!'

'Shhh. You'll wake Rusgann –'

Curtain-rings rattled and the maid's homely face popped

out of her enclosure. 'I'm already awake, Your Grace.' A lanky body modestly clad in a homespun shift emerged. 'And you know very well we're forbidden to leave the steading circle without Dobnelu along to protect us from danger.'

Ignoring the servant's admonition, Maudrayne went to the larder, where she gathered rye bread, cheese, a small crock of goosegrease flavored with wild herbs, and some sweet cranberry cakes. 'There's no danger,' she insisted. 'None at all, except from our own misadventure, and we'll take great care not to lose our footing on the cliff trail or be caught by the rising tide. Now dress yourself, Dyfi. Visit the backhouse and wash your hands, and we'll be on our way. We can have a picnic breakfast on the beach.'

The boy threw his clothes on and darted outside with a joyful shout, slamming the door. The maid Rusgann lumbered over to her mistress and stood, fists on hips, scowling in disapproval. 'Your Grace, the spells protecting us extend only to the ring of white stones around this house and the outbuildings. If we venture outside the magic circle, the Beaconfolk could do us harm. Or some windwatching scoundrel of the king's might scry us!'

'Do you know what day this is, Rusgann?' Maudrayne was serene and smiling. Her long auburn hair, freshly washed and hanging free as she stubbornly insisted upon wearing it, shone like burnished copper. 'This is the Solstice Eve, a very lucky day. No wicked sorcerers or monsters – not even the Coldlight Army – can harm human beings today.'

'Huh! I never heard of such a thing.'

'That's because you're Cathran-born. We Tarnians know more about dark magic than you do. As for windwatchers – none of them know we're in this godforsaken spot except Ansel, who brought us here. No one who matters even knows we're alive! So I say we're in no danger. And today my son and I will leave this dreary steading and walk free for hours along the sunny shore without a cranky old witch dogging our heels.'

She wrapped the food in a cloth and put it into a basket, together with a long kitchen knife, a leather bottle of mead, and two wooden cups. There would be plenty of good water from freshets trickling down the cliff face. 'The only question is, will you accompany Dyfi and me on our holiday, or stay behind and sulk?'

The maid was hauling on her garments. 'It's not safe, Your Grace! There's others that could find us here besides magickers. Like that blue fishing vessel that tarried offshore two tennights ago. Dobnelu said the crew peered at the steading with a spyglass! The old woman was in a rare tizzy about it. It seems that plain eyesight isn't hindered by her shielding magic. The fishermen could have seen you out by the byre.'

'Please God, they had! For I recognized the lugger as one belonging to Vik Waterfall of Northkeep Port, where my own family's castle lies. And since catching sight of it, I've thought of nothing but how we might use such a boat to get away from here.'

'Oh, no, Your Grace!'

'Stop calling me that, you stupid creature! The only one here worthy of such an honorific is my son.' She turned away, and her next words came through gritted teeth. 'And I'll see Dyfrig gets the crown he deserves . . . if I don't die of vexation and melancholy first, trapped in this loathsome place.'

The sturdy maidservant persisted in speaking her mind, as was her habit. Rusgann's fierce loyalty had never equated with submissiveness. 'My lady, you owe it to the lad to keep him secure. To obey High Shaman Ansel's instructions and those of the sea-hag. Life here's boring, I'll give you that, but Mistress Dobnelu and the shaman know what's best for you.'

'Lately, I've had my doubts.' Maudrayne stared out the

window at the desolate grandeur of the fjord and the high tundra above it. The snow that had blanketed the windswept plateau was finally melted now, leaving outcroppings of pink and grey granite and patches of vivid green grass tinged with the purple, yellow, and white of short-lived arctic wildflowers.

Rusgann sniffed. 'I suppose doing housework and taking care of farm animals is a hard life for a high-born lady like you –'

'You silly thing! That's not it at all!'

'Well, what, for pity's sake?' the maid muttered. 'We have a snug place to stay, plenty of food to eat, and magic to keep your enemies at bay.'

'We've been here for four years, Rusgann, hardly ever leaving the stone circle. I have only a small child and you and that senile witch for company, with infrequent visits from Ansel when he can spare us the time. God knows I'm used to northern winters that are eight months long, but not the isolation we have to endure here in this miserable hovel!' Maudrayne gestured in disgust at the modest kitchen, which was neat and clean enough now thanks to her own efforts and those of the maid. 'My family's castle at Northkeep is a cheerful place, full of people. When I lived there we weren't forced to stay inside during the long winter nights – not even when the Coldlight Army prowled the sky. My brothers and cousins and I played in the snow and went visiting and bathed in the hot springs. There was singing and feasting and games and bards telling wonderful tales. And in summertime we sailed and hunted and fished and gathered berries and went exploring. This wretched steading might as well be a prison. And Ansel won't even tell me how long we must stay here.'

'He said we must remain until there's no danger to you and the lad. How can you dispute the wisdom of that?'

She stamped away from the window with her blue eyes blazing. 'And just when will the danger be over? When Dyfrig is a man full-grown? When his damned father is dead? All of life is fraught with peril, yet we don't spend our time hiding safely under the bed!'

Rusgann made a helpless gesture. 'You seemed content enough to stay here earlier.'

'When I believed we had no other choice. When Dyfrig was a baby who couldn't understand the need for prudence and secrecy. But he's four now, and wise beyond his years. He needs teachers and companions of his own age. If he's forced to spend his entire childhood here, his spirit will be stunted – just like those tiny winter-blasted birch trees up on the tundra that never grow more than two handspans high. I can't let that happen to my son! Surely there are better ways for Ansel to secure our safety. Why can't we live under the protection of my brother Liscanor at Northkeep instead of in this cramped farmhouse?'

'You could ask the High Shaman that question when next he visits us. But in the end, you have to trust his judgment.'

'I used to think Ansel was my loyal friend, whose only interest was our welfare.' Maudrayne spoke in a low voice and her expression was disillusioned. 'Lately I've come to believe he may have other reasons for keeping us confined here that have little to do with our physical safety.'

'I don't understand.'

'When last he came, just after the ice breakup, Ansel and the sea-hag were whispering together in the kitchen, thinking that little Dyfi was napping in his bed-cupboard. You and I were mucking out the byre. The boy heard Ansel say, 'We must make certain he remains king. He's the only one strong enough to hold them back. Without him, we have no hope of liberating the Source.' The boy was clever enough to remember the strange words exactly – and he asked me about them.'

Rusgann's brow wrinkled in puzzlement. 'I suppose Ansel was speaking of High King Conrig.'

'Yes. Both Dyfrig and I threaten him – but especially me, since I know a great secret of his that would cost him his throne. Perhaps Ansel hopes to eliminate this threat by keeping us out of the way.'

'But who is it who must be *held back* by King Conrig? And what in Zeth's name is the Source?'

'I know not which particular enemy Conrig's Sovereignty must hold in check. He has so many! As for this Source, the last time Ansel spoke of it was after I jumped from the parapet of Eagleroost Castle into Cala Bay. As he rescued me, he spoke mysteriously about what his Source would think if my unborn child and I had died in the icy water.'

'My lady, I still don't know what you're talking about.'

'From other things old Dobnelu has said, I've come to believe that Ansel's Source might have something to do with the person the hag visits during her long trances. Perhaps they are even the same.'

Outside, Dyfrig was calling. 'Mama! Come out! Let's have our picnic. I'm hungry.'

Maudrayne Northkeep, who had been wife to Conrig Wincantor and Queen of Cathra, picked up the basket and headed for the door. She looked over her shoulder and said to Rusgann, 'I believe that Ansel and Dobnelu and this Source may be playing some deep magical game. To them, Dyfrig and I are nothing but pawns on their arcane gameboard – and so, evidently, is my former husband, the Sovereign of Blenholme. But I'll be no one's gamepiece willingly, and neither will my son. This is the last summer we'll spend here, Rusgann. We're going to escape.'

The handmaid's mouth dropped open in consternation.

Maudrayne laughed. 'Don't stand there gaping, woman. If you're coming to the shore with us, step lively.'

She sailed out the door, and with Dyfrig skipping at her side went through the outbuildings toward the flowery meadow, where honeybees and boreal warblers foraged, and a herd of goats and sheep with their young grazed the fresh grass. At the edge of the enchanted circle, Maudrayne told the boy to wait while she went to the holy hut nearby and looked inside.

The place was windowless, but light entered through a smokehole in the roof. Dobnelu lay unconscious on a rickety cot, her discarded magic drum beside her. She was a small person who could not have weighed seven stone, dressed for the ritual in a tattered blue silk robe that had once been magnificent and costly. Her head had only a few wisps of white hair and the skin of her skull was so translucent that blood vessels seemed to cover it like a netted cap. Her eyes, large and black and smoldering with arcane energy when she was awake, were shuttered by crinkled lids. Her mouth hung slightly ajar, showing a few stumpy teeth. From time to time her lips moved soundlessly.

'Where do you journey?' Maudrayne whispered. 'Whom do you talk to?'

The former queen's hand stole into the basket where the sharp kitchen knife lay and she fingered the long blade. It would be easy to take the sea-hag's life while she was entranced and helpless. But would such a deed be justifiable, even to permit their escape? The old woman was terrible-tempered and imperious but without real malice. She had opened her home to three refugees at Ansel's request (complaining loudly all the while), but had treated little Dyfrig with unfailing kindness, so that he came to love her and called her Eldmama Nelu. Maude and Rusgann she had used as domestic slaveys and farmhands, berating them mercilessly when they were clumsy or negligent. But she had never punished them with her magic.

I cannot kill the witch, Maudrayne realized. Nevertheless, I won't rest until I find a way to escape without doing her serious harm.

She left the hut and closed the door behind her. Rusgann was waiting with Dyfrig, carrying her own cup and an extra bottle of mead. Maudrayne put the things into the basket, handed it to the maid, then led the way through the pasture to the steep path down the cliff.

After the picnic breakfast was eaten, the three of them embarked on the promised treasure hunt along the narrow fjord beach. Good food and plenty of drink had cheered Rusgann so that she put her former misgivings aside. The bay waters sparkled under the bright sky. Kittiwakes, fulmars, and other birds nesting on the rough rock walls and sea-pinnacles made a raucous din. Green sedges, cliff-ferns, and tufts of white starwort grew in sheltered high places, while some deeply shadowed stretches of shingle above the tide-line were still heaped with slow-melting slabs of ice driven ashore by the winter westerlies.

The tide was receding. They hiked along the emerging sands and slimy boulders below the fjord cliffs for hour after hour, finding all sorts of interesting things: colorful agate pebbles, net floats, shells, the skull of some small animal, and a freshly dead mirrorfish two ells long from which the boy gleefully scraped a heap of huge, gleaming scales. There was even a chunk of white quartz with embedded metallic specks that might have been gold. Maudrayne carried all the treasures in the basket, along with the remains of the food.

Dyfrig raced ahead tirelessly, pursued by laughing Rusgann. After a while the two of them were lost to Maudrayne's sight behind a jutting promontory at the end of the fjord beach.

She brooded as she hurried to catch up with them. Escape from Dobnelu's steading was not going to be easy. The sea-hag was a vigilant guardian except when she was sunk in one of her trances or stupefied by strong drink, as happened when changing weather made her bones ache. The drumming happened only at irregular intervals, so they would probably have to rely on ardent spirits to disable Dobnelu's wind-searching ability. Fortunately, Rusgann was an expert distiller of malted barley liquor, and there was plenty left from last year's batch. However, tempting the old woman to over-indulgence without arousing her suspicions would be tricky.

As the raven flew, Northkeep Castle and its surrounding villages lay only sixty leagues to the south-east, on Silver Salmon Bay; but to get there traveling overland was virtu-ally impossible. Away from the shore, this region of Tarn was a trackless plateau of rolling tundra and bogs. Game would be the only food source unless they waited for the berries that ripened at summer's end. Maudrayne was an experienced hunter, but without a bow and arrows, she could take birds and animals only by means of inefficient snares. Nor was the upland wildlife entirely innocuous: even if they managed to evade the bears, snow-lions, and wolf packs, biting midges might well eat them alive.

Following the shoreline meant fewer insects and preda-tors, and the tidepools were full of mussels and crabs and stranded small fish. But the irregularity of the coast route more than doubled the distance to the castle, and the going would be appallingly hard, especially for a small child. South of Dobnelu's home fjord, the shore was jumbled rock and saltmarsh, rather than easily traveled sand. Below Useless Bay lay another broad inlet with a river delta and treach-erous flats that could be crossed only by means of ski-like mudshoes. The final obstacle before Silver Salmon Bay and the settled lands held by her elder brother, Sealord Liscanor, was a precipitous headland so sheer that it could only be climbed with the aid of ropes.

No, only an idiot would think of escaping on foot. The terrain was too difficult and the journey would take too long.

Dobnelu – or Ansel himself – would be certain to find them with windsight long before they reached Northkeep Castle. Only one course of action had any real chance of success: escaping the same way they had arrived – by boat.

Fishermen came only rarely into Useless Bay, fearing its treacherous shoals as much as the sorcery of the infamous sea-hag who dwelt there. But the sighting of Vik Waterfall's lugger – and Dobnelu's warning about the sailors having a spyglass – had given Maudrayne an idea. The next time a boat appeared offshore, she'd try to signal to it from a place out of the old woman's sight. She'd proffer the valuable opal necklace, and use handsigns to tell the crew what she wanted and where and when to pick her up. If she was lucky, one of the men might recognize her, even though ten years had passed since she sailed her sloop-rigged yacht among the fishing fleet in Northkeep Port, before going south to become the bride of Conrig Wincantor . . .

She had almost reached the end of the rocky point that separated the long fjord beach from the next cove, into which Rusgann and Dyfrig had evidently vanished. She paused for a moment, setting down the basket and looking out to sea, past the numerous barren islands and shallows that gave the bay its discouraging name, to the distant open water where the great iceberg drifted. As a proficient sailor in northern waters, she knew that with cautious navigation and a fair wind, even a small craft might reach Northkeep in a little over half a day. Given a few hours' head start, even if Dobnelu woke from her drunken slumber and bespoke Ansel of their escape, he would never catch them at sea unless he conjured up a storm that risked killing them.

And Ansel doesn't want us dead, she said to herself, else he would have left us to our fate long ago. No, our deaths would somehow spoil his great game.

Mulling the possibilities, Maudrayne made her way around

the end of the promontory, climbing among huge granite boulders veined with white quartz and overgrown with thick mats of slippery seaweed. This part of the shore was unfamiliar. In their abbreviated outings with the old woman, she and the boy had never gone so far away from the steading. When the tide turned, the easily traversed sections of these rock piles would probably be submerged, and Maudrayne was beginning to be concerned about getting back safely with Rusgann and Dyfrig ahead of the flow.

The next cove was small and extremely steep-sided, with a towering islet poking up amidst a welter of exposed reefs a few hundred ells offshore. The boy and the handmaid were nowhere in sight, perhaps concealed among the many large rocks at the base of the cliff. She was ready to call out to them when she caught sight of something that brought her to a standstill with her heart pounding.

Barely visible in its anchorage on the far side of the high island was a single-masted fishing lugger with a blue hull. It was almost certainly the same boat that had cruised past two tennights ago.

Dear God! Was it possible that Rusgann had signaled Vik Waterfall to come ashore?

In her haste, she tripped and fell, spilling the contents of the basket into a tidepool. She muttered an oath and hurried to retrieve only the important things – the knife and the finely made wooden cups – thrusting them into the capacious pockets of the peasant apron that was part of her everyday garb at the steading. Unencumbered now, she scrambled over the rocks as fast as she could. Some of them were house-sized or even larger, with narrow gaps between them that had to be threaded with care. She was still unable to see much of the cove shoreline ahead, but she was encouraged by the occasional sight of footprints on patches of wet sand. Dyfrig and Rusgann had certainly come this way.

At last she came out onto the narrow beach, and pulled up short.

About twenty ells away, a leather coracle was drawn up on the strand, one of the lightweight watercraft with whale-bone frames that the smaller Tarnian sailing boats often used as tenders. Two men stood near it, hailing her approach with eager shouts. Rusgann sat on the pebble-strewn sand a short distance away from them, with her back pressed against a half-buried boulder and Dyfrig huddled against her skirts. The maid's hair was disheveled and her face distorted by fury.

The older of the two men came striding toward Maudrayne, and her heart sank as she realized that he was not her affable old acquaintance Vik Waterfall but rather the latter's younger brother Lukort, a character notorious in former years for his violent temper and unsavory dealings. Eleven years ago, the Waterfall clan had banished him for stealing lobsters from the traps of other fishermen. Yet here he was, wearing a skipper's cap, in charge of his brother's boat.

Lukort Waterfall was sinewy, straggly-bearded, and not very tall. His eyes, almost as pale as a wolf's, were close-set under bushy brows. He wore a vest of pieced and embroidered sealskin, canvas trousers cut off at the knees, a belt with a tarnished silver buckle, and high seaboots. His companion was a burly, oafish-looking youth with a soup-bowl haircut, a heavy jaw, and cheeks as smooth as a girl's, clad in a homespun tunic and trews of undyed wool. His huge feet were bare.

'Princess Maudie!' Lukort exclaimed, doffing his cap with a flourish and bowing deeply. 'You took long enough gettin' round the point. We feared you had a mishap.'

'Mama!' Dyfrig screamed. 'Run!'

Before her shocked mind could react, Lukort rapped out a command to the younger man, who darted to the boy, wrenched him away from Rusgann, and clapped a big hand over his mouth.

The maid sprang to her feet shrieking, 'You stinking whoreson, let him loose!' The youth fetched her a casual blow in the stomach with his fist and she fell moaning to the stony sand.

His mouth temporarily freed, Dyfrig again cried, 'Run away, Mama!'

'Don't move!' roared Lukort. A split second later his tone was wheedling and conciliatory. 'Be easy now, princess. My son Vorgo and I won't hurt the wee smolt and we won't hurt you . . . So he's *your* boy, is he? Well well! Yon wench said he was hers! A liar as well as a foulmouthed hellcat, ain't she?'

Vorgo smirked, keeping a firm hold on Dyfrig as he wriggled. Rusgann struggled to her feet and stood a few feet away from the pair. Her face was unreadable.

'I know you, Lukort Waterfall,' Maudrayne said in a stern voice. 'How dare you mistreat my child and my servant?'

'The twitch needs to be taught good manners. Got a nasty mouth on her. As to the lad, no one's mistreatin' him. We just don't want him runnin' off afore you and me have a chance to talk business.'

'Business?' Her mind was a turmoil of conflicting emotions. 'What kind of business?'

'The world thinks you be dead, princess. Your brother Liscanor was in a black rage when the news come to Northkeep. He tried to talk the other sealords into makin' war on Conrig Ironcrown to avenge the insult to you and your family. Nothin' come o' that. Tarn had too many other troubles, and now we're part of the Sovereignty whether we like it or not.' He shrugged. 'But here you be, alive – thanks to the God of Heights and Depths! – and with a fine young son to boot. Imagine that! How old would the little fella be? About four, eh?'

She said nothing, feeling the hairs at the back of her neck creep with apprehension. The crafty devil had guessed who Dyfrig's father must be.

Lukort murmured something to Vorgo, who hoisted the child to his shoulder and strode to where the coracle lay. He cut off a piece of line to bind Dyfrig's wrists, put him into the skin boat, and cast off, heading for the lugger anchored behind the small island.

The skipper beckoned to Maudrayne. 'Come closer. No need to keep shoutin' one at t'other. Don't worry about your lad. I told my son to take special good care o' him.'

She came slowly toward Lukort, stopping well out of easy reach. It would not do to underestimate the cleverness of this villain. She spoke to the maid. 'Are you badly hurt, Rusgann?'

'Nay, my lady. The young lout only punched the breath out of me. The lad and I came on the two men here when we rounded the point. Dyfi was all happy and excited, but I warned him he must say nothing at all until we knew they intended no evil. This Lukort was polite enough at first, asked if I knew the Lady Maudrayne Northkeep who lived nearby with the sea-hag. Said he was one of Lord Liscanor's subjects, come to see if you were being kept here against your will.'

Maudrayne turned her gaze to the fisherman. 'Two tennights ago, you saw me at Dobnelu's steading through your spyglass.'

He nodded, all joviality. 'And wasn't it a great shock, seeing a queenly redheaded beauty carrying a milkpail from the old hag's byre! Us seamen give Dobnelu's fjord a wide berth accounta her curses. But nothin's to stop us peepin' at the place as we sail on by. I studied through the glass and nigh jumped out o' my skin when I realized 'twas you: Ironcrown's wife that was supposed to be drownded in Cathra, alive and well and back home in Tarn. I pondered it for days, wonderin' what to do.'

'Wondering how he could turn his discovery to profit!' Rusgann growled.

'And did you tell others of what you'd seen?' Maudrayne inquired.

'Only a few good mates who know to keep their gobs shut. Needed advice, didn't I, to figger the best way to outwit the sea-hag.'

Maudrayne said, 'I'm surprised you dared risk her wrath, setting foot on this forbidden shore.'

A look of low cunning spread over the skipper's face as he took from his shirt a small pouch hanging on a string around his neck. 'Got me special charms for that. Vorgo, too. Cost every silver mark I owned to get 'em from Blind Bozuk the shaman. This here lets us cross the hag's magic circle of stones without her knowin'. Bozuk said it'd only work on Solstice Eve, when the fires of sorcery burn wan in the midnight sun. We waited till the time was ripe, then sailed back here in my lugger *Scoter,* keepin' far out from shore. We came into Useless Bay with the centerboard up, mostly using sweeps to drive the boat. Mortal hard work it was rowin', but we stayed clear of the shoals and made it to this cove, outta sight of Dobnelu's steading. We was all set to go afoot along the fjord and creep up to the farmhouse, when the wench and the lad come along.'

Rusgann said, 'I was fool enough to say you were following us along the shore, my lady, when I thought the men might be friendly. This one started whispering to that blockhead son of his. The lackwit blurted out something about hiding behind a rock and grabbing you when you appeared. I tried to run with Dyfrig then, but they caught us and knocked me down.'

'And now you intend to kidnap us, Lukort Waterfall?' Maudrayne said contemptuously.

'*Rescue* you, princess!' The fisherman's voice was laden with false reproach. 'First I figgered to take you back to your brother, hopin' he'd give me a nice reward.' The yellowish eyes shifted. 'But now I reckon if I took you and the boy down south, some others – say, your uncle the High Sealord Sernin – might be even more grateful for your return.'

'I see.'

Others! Sly Lukort knew full well that Conrig Ironcrown was the one who would pay a fortune for her and the child . . . alive or dead. And if it were not to be the latter, she'd have to think fast.

'Here comes Vorgo back with the coracle, so let's be off, princess. Your boy's waitin' for you aboard *Scoter*. She's a fine craft, a legacy from my late brother, may the fishes eat his eyeballs. You'll ride easy in her.'

'How many in your crew?' Maudrayne asked casually.

He chuckled. 'For this sailin', just me and Vorgo. *Scoter* needs five men when we're haulin' in fish, but you're a catch easier to handle, eh?'

Only the two of them. So the plan that had sprung into her mind might work. 'You'll take my maidservant also, of course. She is very dear to me and to my son.'

Lukort's face hardened and he shot a rancorous glance over his shoulder at Rusgann. 'Not bloody likely. The big wench stays.'

'I beseech you not to leave her here with the terrible sea-hag. Look – I'll give you a fine reward if you but reconsider.'

She pulled the splendid necklace of opal and gold out from her dress and made as if to unfasten the catch at the back of her neck.

'Swive me!' the fisherman gasped, undisguised greed widening his eyes. 'That's a beaut! Fire-stones the size of quail eggs.'

'The clasp is stuck. Come help me open it. The bauble is yours in payment for Rusgann's passage.'

'Huh! I reckon it's mine anyhow!' And he was on her as

fast as a heron striking, laughing in malicious triumph. He took hold of the pendant stones and gave a painful tug. She was aware of his wiry eyebrows and foul breath and the bits of food caught in his beard as she pulled the kitchen knife from the pocket of her apron and drove it into his throat just to the side of his windpipe, severing the great bloodvessels of the neck as she'd done many a time hunting, when putting a downed and wounded game animal out of its misery.

Lukort uttered a bubbling croak and, staggering, caught her by the hair. She yanked the knife free and an amazing jet of blood shot from the wound, soaking the two of them as they fell in a tangle of flailing limbs. With him struggling beneath her, she stabbed him again, this time taking him between the ribs. She screamed, 'Rusgann!'

The maid rushed forward, a granite stone the size of a turnip in one hand. She used the other to pull Maudrayne aside and smashed the rock into Lukort's crimson-smeared face. Kneeling beside him, she struck again and again and again until there was nothing human left of his features.

'Stop,' Maudrayne said at last. 'He's dead, bled out like a stuck deer. But take care, his boy Vorgo is coming back in the little boat.'

'Dad!' wailed the big youth, his lumpy countenance full of horror. He sat as though paralyzed in the coracle, which drifted in the shallows a dozen ells away. 'Dad!'

Maudrayne rose slowly to her feet, a figure tall and hideous with gore, holding the red-stained knife high. 'Now for you!' she howled, wading into the sea. The youth stared at her in disbelief, then threw himself over the gunwale of the skin boat and began to thrash away frantically in the direction of the lugger.

Maudrayne took a few more steps in pursuit of the swimmer, shouting threats, while Rusgann splashed to retrieve the empty coracle, which she deftly flipped onto the sand.

'Well done,' Maudrayne said. 'Oh, well done, my dearest friend!' She came ashore.

'Are you hurt, my lady?'

'Scratches and bumps. The bastard didn't get my necklace, but he left a smart welt trying to steal it.'

Rusgann used her drenched apron as a wash-clout on both of them, removing the worst of the blood, until Maudrayne said, 'Enough. We can finish cleaning ourselves on board the lugger. Poor Dyfrig must be terrified and we must go to him.'

They launched the small craft and climbed into it, after helping themselves to Lukort Waterfall's filleting knife and belt wallet. A great mob of ravens and gulls had suddenly appeared and were wheeling in a cloud above the body, ready to begin feeding. The noise they made almost drowned out the sound of a distressed human voice.

'It's that poor dolt, Vorgo,' the maid said, 'wanting us to pick him up. He knows he'll never make it swimming to the fishing boat. The ice-cold sea water is sapping his strength.'

'Go back to shore!' Maudrayne shouted to the youth. 'Go back! If you strip off the soaked clothes draining your body heat, you may live.'

After a momentary hesitation, the floundering swimmer changed direction and headed toward land.

'The air's warm,' Maudrayne said to Rusgann with a grim smile. 'He knows the way to the steading, and he has his own pouch of magic trinkets to give him access to the sea-hag's house. Mayhap Dobnelu will let him stay when she awakes. With us gone, she'll need a new slavey.'

THREE

The prisoner in Zeth Abbey filled the hours of Solstice Eve with his usual quiet activities. In the early morning, before the sun made the enclosed garden too hot, he pulled weeds, and carried endless cans of water from the well in his strong arms so that the roses would not flag, and gathered whatever things Brother Herbalist had requested. Then, after eating alone in his little apartment as became one banished from the routine of the Brethren, he retired to the great library to study. His choice of materials sometimes surprised the librarian, but Father Abbas had decreed that all things were to be at his disposal, as though he were still a Doctor Arcanorum in good standing in the Mystical Order of Saint Zeth.

After supper, as he often did, he held conversation in the bee-yard with his three friends; the clouds of busy, harmless insects ensured that no unwanted person would overhear their scheming. When the night-bell rang, he took to his bed more eagerly than usual and slept, and dreamed . . . and opened his mind to the invader.

Kilian. Vra-Kilian Blackhorse. Do you hear me?

'Finally, Beynor! I'm relieved to hear from you at last. You really should have contacted me earlier. I was becoming concerned. But never mind. My men in Cala Palace are ready. By the end of Midsummer Day, if all goes as I've planned, they will have escaped from the city with the Trove of Darasilo! I hope that matters go similarly well with you.'

There's a serious problem. I need you to postpone the Cala mission. Just for a short time.

'Impossible. My agents were given their orders months ago. By now all the arrangements are in place. It's imperative that the attack occurs early tomorrow, while those at the palace are sleeping off the previous day's festivities.'

Kilian, I need more time to complete my research here at the Dawntide Citadel. A week at the most. I've laid my hands on a document in the Salka archives that could be vitally important. But translating it is no easy matter. When I skimmed the thing, I could understood only about one word in five. But I deciphered enough to know its tremendous significance. It dates from before Bazekoy's Conquest!

'I couldn't stop the Cala mission from proceeding, even if I should want to. Vra-Garon has been sent off to Elkhaven on business by Abbas Noachil, and is also carrying out an important assignment of mine. He won't be back here until tomorrow. There's no one else at Zeth Abbey whom I can trust to windspeak my agents, and it's too late to send them a message by conventional means.'

Kilian, I could windspeak your men and tell them to hold off. It wouldn't be easy from this great distance, but I could do it. They'd listen and obey if you give me their signatures and the command password now, instead of waiting until –

'No! You'll bespeak and windwatch them only when the trove is safely in my hands. Do you take me for a fool?'

You misunderstand –

'And don't think you can circumvent my safeguards against your coercive talents by invading my agents' dreams!

You'll never countermand my orders that way. The Brothers were trained in my own somnial defensive techniques before they ever left the abbey. No one can speak to them in dreams unless they consent. But I daresay you've already found that out for yourself, or you wouldn't be trying to trick me!'

Kilian, please believe that I'd never betray our agreement and try to seize the trove for myself.

'Of course you would, my boy. Neither of us has ever trusted the other. That will never change until we've successfully divided Darasilo's sigils, and overcome the obstacles that now prevent either of us from utilizing their sorcery.'

Just listen to me. Let me explain why I need more time. I don't want to offer our bargain to the Salka until I learn more about the Unknown Potency's effect upon the Beaconfolk themselves. The stone does more than liberate sigils from the Lights' control and abolish bonding. I'm certain of that. This ancient document tablet that I've found may reveal why the Potency was created in the first place. There's something in it about an intention to sever the Lights' ability to meddle in the affairs of earthbound beings such as ourselves.

'Depriving us of Beaconfolk sorcery altogther? I don't much like the sound of that!'

I'm more interested in the possibility that the tablet might confirm what we've only assumed must be true – that the Unknown's power may enable me to utilize liberated sigils with impunity!

'And so you shall. I thought you were already convinced of it. If the Lights lose their ability to feed on the pain of sigil-wielders, if they're compelled to deliver sorcery without demanding a price, there is no way they can harm you. Their curse is effectively annulled.'

I must make certain. What good will my half of Darasilo's Trove do me if the curse still holds good? I'll tell you one thing: if I can't have mine, I won't help you get yours. And neither will I free you of your iron gammadion!

'Calm yourself.'

Once I leave Dawntide Citadel, I'll never have access to these Salka archives again.

'Then take the tablet in question along with you when you go. Puzzle out its contents later, on the voyage to Didion.'

I can't take the bloody thing away. I can hardly lift it. It's a stone slab the size of a cartwheel, jam-packed with inscriptions, and if the monsters knew I'd stolen it they'd probably slaughter me out of hand . . . or do worse.

'Copy the wording.'

I haven't the proper materials to make a rubbing, and there's too much on the tablet to simply write it down. The only parchment available in this benighted place are the fragile sheets I make myself from baby sealskin. I have only a few of those left.

'Don't forget that Darasilo's Trove includes two arcane books written in the Salka tongue, in addition to the large collection of inactive stones. The books' subject matter deals with sigils, beyond a doubt. I could tell that from the illustrations, even though I'm unable to read the Salka language. One of those books may very well contain the information you seek.'

Why should I take a chance? I'm going to postpone leaving here until I translate the tablet. That's final. You do as you please and be damned.

'Beynor, you've forgotten the other important reason why we dare not delay. The king of Didion and his family will begin their progress upriver from Holt Mallburn on the day after the Solstice, as they do every year. There's only one suitable spot for our ambush – just below Boarsden Castle at Boar Creek, where there are fierce rapids and an exceptionally deep eddy. It will take the royal party no more than six days to reach that point in their voyage, making the traditional stops along the way. Six days, Beynor! Barely enough time for you and the Salka assassins to get there and organize yourselves, since they won't be able to swim at full speed once they're in the river. If our amphibian friends aren't in place, ready to attack, we'll be forced to revise the Didion part of our scheme drastically – or abandon it altogether.'

Getting the Salka to kill King Honigalus and his family is a needless complication, Kilian. I've said that from the beginning.

'And I've told *you* why it's an absolutely essential step in the destruction of the Sovereignty.'

Well –

'Pull yourself together and keep your mind concentrated on the great goal that's finally within our grasp! I've done what I promised to do, putting my agents into Cala Palace without getting caught. Your task dealing with the Salka has been more difficult, I'll grant you, but you're the bravest, most audacious young man I've ever known. This is why I've been willing to place my own life and hopes in your hands. Listen to me, Beynor! We may never love one another as father and son, yet we are bound together by our mutual ambition more closely than by any tie of blood. Only together can we exploit Darasilo's Trove. Only together can we dupe the Salka into assisting us to bring down Conrig's Sovereignty. Only together can we rule.'

Damn your eyes!

'Bless yours, my boy – and may you use them to see straight ahead and avoid distractions! I have every confidence in you. Don't let me down.'

. . . Very well. I'll arrange to meet with the Four Eminences immediately.

'Excellent. I know you'll convince them. Put your mind at ease.'

Huh! That's hardly possible – given that I must shortly confront a pack of inhuman brutes who may well decide to torture me in creatively gruesome ways, rather than strike a bargain.

'Salka minds work more slowly than ours and are deficient in imagination. It's more likely that the monsters will pretend to accede to the proposal while planning to break faith with you later. We can deal with that easily enough. Don't take it amiss, but it's a good thing that the Salka think you a pathetic failure, cursed by the Lights, with only a few puny magical powers left. The arrogant boobies are bound to underestimate you and let their guard down.'

You state the facts with tactless candor, for one who was once first counselor to a king and now lives in disgrace, under a deferred sentence of death, stripped of all magical talent by the iron hanging around your neck.

'Don't be so touchy. Neither of us can afford wounded pride. Together we may possibly rule the world. Apart we're doomed.'

No more word games, Kilian. It's time for me to go.

'Before you do, we must discuss your sister. My agents in Cala Palace will do their utmost to disguise their real objective. But if Conrig suspects that either of us might have caused the trove to be stolen, he might pressure Conjure-Queen Ullanoth to put us under close observation. Even worse, he could ask her to trace my agents. No ordinary talent is able to scry the moonstones, but her Subtle Loophole sigil can.'

Conrig would never let the Conjure-Queen know about Darasilo's Trove. He'd be afraid she'd covet it for herself.

'I suppose you're right. But the king might use some pretext –'

Ulla hasn't spied on me with Loophole since the incident last year that nearly cost her life. I've been assured of this by Master Kalawnn himself. That particular sigil is the most powerful one she possesses, and the price of its conjuring is tremendous. Unless Conrig tells her that we might have stolen a secret hoard of inactive moonstones, she'll refuse to endanger her health and sanity by using Loophole to watch us or my men.

'She's bound to find out about the trove sooner or later.'

That's why I intend to have the Salka attack her. I've worked out a plan –

'I agree we should make her demise one of our earliest priorities . . . but only after the death of Honigalus! You must convince the monsters to kill him and his heirs first, Beynor. The circumstances are ideal and such an opportunity may never come again. The destabilization of the Sovereignty is absolutely crucial to our success. But that won't happen unless Conrig loses his hold on Didion. Do you understand?'

Yes. Honigalus first, but then Ulla dies.

A sigh.

Return to your peaceful slumber, Kilian – as I do my best to tiptoe scatheless through the nightmare I inhabit here. Should I manage to gull the Salka, I'll pop back into your dreams to inform you how the matter went. If I fail, remember me as you study Darasilo's worthless collection of baubles – and think of what might have been.

The brightness and warmth of the endless midsummer daylight hardly penetrated the dank chambers of the great Salka citadel that crouched on the highest point of the Dawntide Isles. After four years of exile in the awful place, Beynor always felt pierced to the bone by cold, no matter how many furs he piled on. He was one-and-twenty years old now, and had enjoyed excellent health when he first came; but he knew he could not survive here much longer. The citadel was an abode fit only for nonhuman grotesques. It drained his bodily strength and weakened his innate talent more and more with each passing day. If he must risk every-thing now in a bid to restore his lost fortunes, then so be it. He carried a whale-oil lantern as he descended a slippery flight of steps to a corridor that extended well below sea level. The widely spaced jars of luminous marine plankton used by these Salka to illuminate the lower precincts of their refuge gave too meager a light to accommodate human vision. Even the smoky flame of the lantern was inadequate, and Beynor cursed as he threaded his way among numerous stinking black puddles, fed seawater (and noxious little swimmers) by perpetual leaks in the tunnel ceiling.

At length he reached the anteroom outside the presence chamber of the great trolls known as the Eminences. Six gigantic Salka guards holding granite battlehammers stood before double doors faced with slabs of carved amber and wrought gold. The hanging bowls of glowworms were larger here, giving plenty of light, so the young sorcerer discarded his sputtering lantern, strode forward with as much fortitude as he could muster, and spoke in the harsh tongue of the monsters.

'I am Beynor ash Linndal, rightful Conjure-King of Moss and honored guest of your people, come for an audience with the Eminent Four.'

Slowly, the amphibians inclined their crested heads and studied him with a gaze like banked smoldering coals. They beheld a man tall and slimly built, having an intense narrow face and long pale hair that had gone stringy in the dampness. His eyes, which seemed at first to be black, were actually darkest green, with a glimmer of exceptional talent in their depths. The regal garments Beynor had worn when fleeing his lost kingdom had long since fallen to rags; and since his nonhuman hosts were unfamiliar with clothing, he had fashioned with his own hands a suit of pieced sea-otter fur, along with a voluminous fox cloak and sturdy boots of seal hide. The sole emblem of monarchy he had brought from Moss, the Royal Sword in its heavily bejeweled scabbard, was girded about his loins.

Saying nothing, the guards stepped aside and swung the chamber doors wide open. Beynor entered and the doors clanged shut again. He stood with his hands steepled in the Salka gesture of submission, biding his time until he should be recognized by the Eminences.

The beings who awaited him in the fantastically orna-
mented undersea cavern lolled on stubby-legged golden platforms, heaped with seaweed, that served them as couches.
They were unattended and conversed among themselves in
voices like muted thunder, apparently paying no attention
to the human newcomer. A low table containing dishes and
flasks of outlandish food and drink stood within tentacle-
reach. Behind the dais rose a huge mosaic made from multi-
colored bits of amber and gleaming pearl-shell, depicting a
legendary Salka hero. His flexible arms brandished twin
obsidian axes, his saucer eyes glared fire-red, and his fanged
mouth gaped in a silent roar. The image was framed by
amber-bead curtains and lit with hanging crystal globes
containing lively phosphorescent organisms.

Like the champion in the mosaic, each Eminence wore
around his thick neck a softly glowing greenish-blue carving
suspended from a golden chain: moonstone sigils of the minor
kind that drew magical power from the Beaconfolk at the
cost of pain to the wearer.

The Eminences were not royalty, but rather ruling elders
chosen by their people for strength of character and proficiency
in their separate fields of endeavor. Three of them – the First
Judge, the Supreme Warrior, and the Conservator of Wisdom
– Beynor had never seen before. As a mere human sorcerer,
even one of royal blood who had come bearing a marvelous
gift to ensure his welcome, he had been beneath their notice
during his enforced stay in the Citadel of the Dawntide Isles.
The only one of the Four familiar to Beynor was Master Shaman
Kalawnn, pre-eminent adept of his race, who had been an inti-
mate friend of the late Conjure-King Linndal. Unaware that
Beynor had murdered his father, Master Kalawnn had agreed
to give the deposed young ruler sanctuary after the Great Lights
cursed him and stripped him of all but one of the sigils he had
used to secure the throne of Moss.

That single remaining magical moonstone of his, dull and lifeless as it had been since it was first fashioned over a thousand years earlier, rested now on a spindly gold tripod to the right of the dais. Its presence was presumably a tribute to the human who had finally returned it to its original owners. The sigil's name was Unknown Potency, and it was the most celebrated thing of its kind ever made, priceless at the same time that it was deemed supremely dangerous.

For long centuries following the damnation of the stone's Salka creator, the precise manner of the Potency's activation and operation had been forgotten by other members of the amphibian race. The person who made it – supposedly to be used as the ultimate weapon against the conquering hordes of the Emperor Bazekoy, although the monsters were not certain of this – had in the end failed to empower it.

Never brought to life, dreaded more than cherished, the Unknown Potency had become an enigmatic symbol of extinct Salka glory. Over the centuries, learned thaumaturgists among the monsters believed that the sigil might hold the key to unimaginably great magic surpassing that of the Beaconfolk. But none had been brave enough to test it, for fear of the Great Lights' capricious wrath.

About a hundred years earlier, through subterfuge, the Unknown Potency and six other notable sigils had passed from the Dawntide Salka into the hands of an extraordinary human wizard named Rothbannon, who used some of the stones to establish himself as the first Conjure-King of Moss. Although Rothbannon did eventually learn the spells that would activate the Unknown Potency, he and his descendants were disinclined to make use of the dubious sigil – as had been Beynor himself, even when the security of his throne was at stake and the fickle Beaconfolk turned against him. As the Great Lights repudiated and cursed the young king, they unaccountably left in his possession the 'dead'

Unknown Potency, at the same time forbidding him to make use of it, or any other sigil, on pain of instant annihilation. But the Lights had not stopped Beynor from handing over the Unknown to the Salka.

Nor had they prevented him from engaging in studies concerning the nature of the cryptic stone while he lived in the Dawntide Citadel under Kalawnn's protection . . .

'We give you leave to approach us, Beynor,' the Master Shaman now said, 'and to speak to me and my august colleagues about your researches.'

He came forward, and without preamble pointed to the Unknown Potency on its golden tripod. 'Eminences, I've discovered what this thing does.'

The leaders uttered undignified whoops of astonishment. The Supreme Warrior, who was the largest and most physically imposing of the Four, surged up from his couch and slithered across the dais with astonishing speed. He plucked from its resting place the small object resembling a hard translucent ribbon twisted into the form of a figure eight, and held the thing high while bellowing into Beynor's impassive face.

'*You* have discovered the operation of the Unknown Potency? The secret that eluded the most learned of our shamans for over eleven hundred years? How dare you say such a thing? You're lying!'

'I studied your own archival tablets, Eminence – documents that have lain neglected in the bowels of this citadel since the defeated remnant of the Salka host took refuge in these forsaken isles. The work was very difficult, even though I am fairly fluent in your language. But I persevered. I succeeded. And now I propose to share my hard-won knowledge of the Potency with you.' Beynor paused. 'As is only just, I ask something in return for my labors.'

'Now we come to the heart of the matter!' exclaimed the

Supreme Warrior, with a vicious clash of teeth. 'He intends
to trick us in some fashion, as the wretch Rothbannon did!
Kalawnn – explain how this miscreant was able to pry into
our sacred archives. How long have you been aware of this
alleged discovery?'

'Calm yourself, Ugusawnn,' the Master Shaman replied
equably. 'I myself gave Beynor leave to investigate the
Unknown Potency's history not long after his arrival. Why
not, since our own scholars seemed unaccountably tepid in
their reaction to the precious sigil's return? As to Beynor's
discovery, he told me of it just hours ago, saying he had
finally marshaled sufficient evidence to support his hypoth-
esis. I commanded him to wait on us Four without delay
and explain everything.'

'And now the insolent groundling thinks he can barter his
so-called knowledge!' roared the Warrior. 'I say he should
be tortured until the truth is wrung out of him!'

'The journeyman is deserving of his wage,' said Beynor,
who seemed unfazed by the threat. 'Forgive my saying so,
Eminences, but your shamans – with the shining exception
of Master Kalawnn – are a timid and lazy lot, fearful of arcane
matters outside the range of their limited experience. They
flatly refused to help with my researches, so I undertook
them alone, working for four years under conditions inimical to human good health. Eventually I uncovered the
Potency's secrets. It may no longer be called Unknown,
Eminences! I know its true nature. And while the Great
Lights have forbidden me to empower it – or any other sigil
– they have not constrained you Salka. I'm willing to show
you how to bring the stone to life. What's more, with my
help, this one small moonstone can restore to you your lost
homeland on High Blenholme island, avenging your defeat
by Emperor Bazekoy.'

'Astounding, if true,' said the First Judge. He was a rotund

personage who snacked on tidbits from the refreshment table
as he observed Beynor through shrewd, half-closed eyes.

The ancient Conservator of Wisdom whispered, 'If there
is the least chance that the groundling does speak the truth,
we must weigh his proposition.'

'I am truthful,' Beynor stated. 'And I'll reveal everything
I know if you pledge to help me attain my own heart's goal.'

The Supreme Warrior gingerly replaced the precious piece
of moonstone on its golden stand and loomed over the young
man. Two boneless arms as thick as beech trunks, each having
four digits armed with daggerlike talons, reached out in
menace as the Salka general spoke with ominous gentleness.
'You'll tell what you know without making demands, carrion-
worm, or I will first disjoint your limbs piecemeal, then slowly
slice open your belly and consume your throbbing entrails
while you watch with dying eyes.'

'That will do, Ugusawnn,' said the Conservator of Wisdom.
He was an individual of wizened stature, plainly infirm and
weighted with years, but his red eyes burned with an
authority that quelled the Supreme Warrior like an upstart
child. 'Please resume your place. I will question the former
Conjure-King of Moss myself.'

'Huh!' said Ugusawnn. But he crawled obediently back to
his slimy kelp couch as the Conservator beckoned for Beynor
to come closer.

'It pains me to speak loudly, groundling. But listening to
lies pains me even more. Do you swear by your human God
to tell me the truth about the Unknown Potency, on peril
of damnation to the Hell of Ice?'

'I do indeed, Eminence.'

But not all of the truth . . . no more than I told it to Kilian!

'Then say first what favors you seek in return for your
discovery.'

Beynor took a breath. 'My principal desire is vengeance

upon my evil sister Ullanoth and her accomplice Conrig Wincantor, the Sovereign of Blenholme. They conspired to humiliate me and steal my throne, and are ultimately responsible for my losing the friendship of the Beaconfolk. To achieve the ruin of these two persons I would renounce all hope of ever ruling Moss – or any part of High Blenholme Island. Instead, I offer to restore your original homeland to you, after which I intend to pursue my own destiny on the Southern Continent.'

'He *offers* Blenholme to us!' the Supreme Warrior scoffed. 'As though he ruled it rather than Conrig's Sovereignty.'

'The Unknown Potency can enable your army to destroy both the Sovereign and my sister,' Beynor said. 'With my help.'

'Tell us how,' the First Judge demanded, picking his glassy teeth with one talon and examining the result with a frown.

'Before I do that, I require tangible proof of your goodwill. It's only just, Eminences – and my request isn't difficult to fulfill. As a first step in subverting Conrig's Sovereignty, I believe we must undermine his control in the region where the island is most vulnerable: the vassal kingdom of Didion. Didion is a keystone state whose lands adjoin those of the other three realms. It is susceptible to a Salka sea invasion from the east, the west, and most especially from the north, through the Green Morass. Its king, Honigalus, is a weakling, but he is unswervingly loyal to Conrig.'

'What has this to do with us?' the Conservator hissed impatiently.

'As the first step in achieving my revenge, and your reconquest of Blenholme, I ask you to help me assassinate Honigalus, his three children, and his wife, who stand in line to the throne. If this is done, the king's younger brother will inherit – a hothead prince named Somarus who is violently opposed to the Sovereignty. I'm very well acquainted with Somarus and his ambitions. He's highly susceptible to my coercion. And if this princely creature of mine were perceived by neighboring Tarn to be a legitimate heir to the throne and not a fratricidal usurper – as would be assured if *Salka* were clearly seen to be responsible for his brother's death – then Sernin Donorvale and the Sealords of Tarn would have no scruples about allying with Didion in an attempt to throw off Conrig's hated dominion. The Sovereignty would be plunged into chaotic war, making it easy for your own army to seize the advantage.'

'It sounds like a clever scheme, if somewhat convoluted.' The Conservator of Wisdom spoke wistfully. 'But history has shown that our fighters have not the physical agility nor the military competence to withstand human beings on land. This is why most of us have remained in the Dawntide Isles for these many centuries, only venturing to attack the groundlings on rare occasions, from the sea . . . and why the Salka who still dwell in Blenholme's Little Fen and the northern estuaries inhabited by humans live furtive, inconspicuous lives.'

Beynor said, 'The high sorcery of the *Known* Potency will make you superior to any weapon humanity can wield, be it natural or supernatural.'

'Tell us how this can be,' said the First Judge. He uncorked a flask and poured a viscous fluid into a gold cup, sniffed it, and took a tentative lap. His tongue was purple, and nearly the length of Beynor's forearm.

The young sorcerer strode to the golden tripod and cupped his hands beneath the inactive sigil. 'Look upon it, Eminences! Apparently naught but a finely carved little stone ribbon, twisted to resemble a figure eight. But a finger slid along its surface discovers that the thing has but a single side and a single edge! A twofold wonder . . .'

'Do not touch the Potency!' the Supreme Warrior bellowed. 'Never touch it again!' Beynor froze but did not flinch. After a moment, he let his hands fall to his sides and withdrew from the tripod, smiling.

'Continue,' said Master Kalawnn, with a reproachful glance at his colleague.

Beynor nodded. 'Properly conjured, this small object defies the Beaconfolk's control of their own sorcery. *It forces them to yield up arcane power through moonstone sigils without causing pain to the conjurer.* The mere touch of the living Potency liberates any other active sigil from the Lights' control, as well as from the control of the former owner. A liberated sigil retains its efficacy, without exacting the former pain-price. Think what this might mean to wielders of minor-sigil weaponry such as flame-stones and stunners.'

'Incredible!' Kalawnn exclaimed.

'Not at all, Master. I've also discovered that the Potency can instantly activate dead sigils without the usual agonizing ritual, whether the Lights will it or not. You Salka might also use the Potency to safely empower newly fashioned Great Stones. Just imagine what ten Weathermakers could do to Conrig's army and navy! Or even one Destroyer . . .'

'At the present time, we are unable to make new sigils,' Kalawnn admitted, shaking his ponderous head. 'All that we have left are those minor stones brought to the isles by the refugees fleeing Bazekoy.'

Beynor kept a lid on his elation with difficulty. The chief sorcerer of the Salka had confirmed what Beynor and Kilian had previously only deduced to be true: the monsters would already have used Great Stones as weapons against humanity if they had owned any.

'Still,' Beynor said, 'the Potency can be a great boon to you. Even the lesser sigils conjure more powerful sorcery than talented humans are capable of. King Conrig's alchymists and warriors will flee in terror before your conquering magic!'

The Supreme Warrior gave a skeptical grunt. 'That remains

to be seen. In my opinion, if we have only minor stones to assist us, humans might retain a strong advantage – especially on land – as they did in Bazekoy's day. Even our Great Stones did not deter his warriors for long. They slew the sigils' owners from afar with their arrows, then were able to smash the dead stones before we could retrieve and reactivate them. Only three Great Stones ever came to the Dawntides, those that Rothbannon took away from us. They eventually were handed down to you. In your incredible stupidity, you misused them, and now only this Unknown Potency is left.'

'A more prudent course is open to us,' the Conservator of Wisdom said. 'As Kalawnn observed, we lack the ability to make new Great Stones *at the present time*. But that situation could change.'

Beynor forced himself to speak nonchalantly in the face of this shocker. 'And how might that come to pass, Eminence? Nothing I've studied so far in your archives tells of the origin of moonstone sigils.'

The Conservator turned to the Master Shaman. 'Colleague, please explain matters to this groundling protégé of yours. My voice grows weary.'

'Thousands of years ago,' Kalawnn said, 'our people discovered that a certain precious mineral had the power to conjure the magic of the Coldlight Army. The mineral was never abundant, and obtaining it was a difficult and dangerous business. With the passing of time and the changing climate, the two sources of the mineral, known as the Moon Crags, became inaccessible to our people. Indeed, the very location of the smaller crag has been lost – we know only that it lies atop a mountain – while the larger crag is situated deep within the Barren Lands of the far north, in a place now colder and more inhospitable than it was in ages past.'

The Conservator said to Beynor, 'If the Unknown Potency

does indeed have the power you describe, we might undertake a special effort to reach the Barren Lands Moon Crag
once again. It might take a number of years to accomplish
the task. But if we fashioned powerful new Great Stones and
activated them through the Potency, then our victory against
humanity would be certain rather than problematic. The
Lights would have no way of betraying us, as they did so
perfidiously when Bazekoy first threatened our homeland.'

The other Eminences murmured in agreement. Beynor
stood like a statue, fighting the nausea swelling inside him.
He'd been so certain that they were ready to acquiesce to
his scheme – and now this!

Well, there remained one bargaining tool that could mend
the situation. Mentioning it now might lead the Eminences
to suspect – rightly enough – that he was planning treachery
after the action in Didion; but he had to risk it.

'It's understandable that you feel you must hold off
reclaiming your heritage until you obtain Great Stones,' he
said carefully. 'However, I might point out that there are
three other Great Stones already in existence that could be
used to further the Salka cause without delay. In my opinion,
these sigils alone would enable you to secure a strong initial
foothold on High Blenholme while your valiant shamans
simultaneously undertake the Moon Crag quest.'

Kalawnn said, 'I presume you refer to those owned by
your sister, Conjure-Queen Ullanoth, which supposedly came
to her as a gift from your dead mother, along with four minor
stones.'

'Hmm. I'd forgotten about those,' the Conservator said.
'The young witch was said to have found them hidden among
the roots of a swamp tree, after being guided by a dream.'

'That's so,' Beynor said. 'The important sigils are called
Sender, Weathermaker, and Subtle Loophole. My sister rarely
uses their high sorcery these days, since she has accumulated

an enormous pain-debt employing them in the service of her lover, King Conrig.'

'She uses them against us!' Ugusawnn snarled. 'In our failed attack last year, the Conjure-Queen employed her Loophole sigil to see us coming, and smote our landing force with a great storm conjured by Weathermaker. After that, even with the queen disabled by pain, human ships attacked these very isles. Our fighters were crushed like fishlice!'

'I'm aware that recent Salka assaults against Moss were repelled.' Beynor gave the Supreme Warrior an apologetic shrug. 'Forgive me, Eminence, for saying that the actions were poorly planned, using insufficient numbers of warriors who relied upon brute strength rather than appropriate magic.'

The huge eyes of Ugusawnn gleamed like baleful rubies. He bared his crystalline teeth at Beynor, and each was twice as long as a man's hand. 'Do you know a better way to fight the Conjure-Queen and her allies?'

'Suppose your forces were equipped with numbers of Concealers and Interpenetrators. I know your people possess such minor stones, as well as many others, but they are reluctant to use them because of the price. Liberated by the Potency, these sigils can assure victory! If you mount a stealthy attack on Royal Fenguard from the upstream side, using my special knowledge of the castle's defenses in that area, you could penetrate the fortress walls and move about under cover of invisibility. Queen Ullanoth's Great Stones would be yours before she or her ally King Conrig realized what was happening . . . because, with the Potency, you would not have to kill the queen before taking her Great Stones for yourselves.'

The First Judge was aghast. 'What are you saying?'

'As you are aware, Eminence, a living sigil will ordinarily burn or even kill an unauthorized person who ventures to seize it. Even if the bonded owner is separated from the sigils, the owner can often command it from a distance – perhaps causing great harm or mischief. But a moonstone liberated by the Potency is severed from its former owner at once. Recall what I said: a liberated stone becomes re-bonded pain-lessly to the Potency wielder without the usual lengthy and painful ritual.'

The Conservator of Wisdom spoke with heavy sarcasm. 'It is good that we need have no fear that *you* might manage to appropriate your sister's three Great Stones for yourself, Beynor of Moss!'

'Alas, no, Eminence,' Beynor lied. 'The curse of the Beaconfolk places them beyond my reach forever. But not beyond yours.'

'All this sounds like a splendid course of action,' the Supreme Warrior sneered, 'but in my opinion it has as many holes as a sponge. It relies too much on this groundling's help and I don't trust him. We can't even be sure he's told us the truth about the Potency.'

The Master Shaman said mildly, 'Beynor is the son of my departed friend, Conjure-King Linndal. He has never given me reason to doubt his friendship toward the Salka people. He returned the Potency to us without condition. We know for a fact that he is incapable of using sigil magic himself. His assessment of the situation in Moss coincides with my own knowledge of Ullanoth's affairs. I think we should consider the proposal to invade Moss very carefully. That isolated corner of High Blenholme would provide us with a perfect staging area for the main attack upon the rest of the island. Numbers of our people already reside in Moss's fens and in the swamps along its principal rivers. And I agree with Beynor that the Conjure-Queen's three important sigils would immediately give us an enormous advantage over human enemies.'

'Then let's go against Moss right away!' said the First Judge, hoisting high his golden cup for emphasis. 'Why muck about with this assassination of the Didionite king? What benefit is that to us?'

'It gains you my gratitude,' Beynor said in a loud, cold voice. 'And it's a sure method of fatally weakening Conrig's Sovereignty. If you kill Honigalus, I promise to help activate the Potency immediately afterwards and help you attack Moss. If you refuse me, I won't share my knowledge with you.'

'I say we should simply put this presumptuous tadpole to the torture,' growled the Supreme Warrior, 'He'll tell us everything we need to know about the Potency inside of an hour. Once our search parties are equipped with liberated minor sigils that the Lights can't meddle with, we'll locate the Barren Lands Moon Crag in short order. We won't need this snotty groundling's help to reconquer Blenholme if we have plenty of new Great Stones. No human force could stand against us!'

'Bazekoy's did,' the Conservator said bleakly. 'Remember that.'

'Because the Lights betrayed us,' the Warrior thundered. 'They allowed him to win – perhaps for their own perverse amusement. This time, the situation will be different.'

'Doing things my way would be so much more efficient, Eminences,' urged Beynor. 'I can speed your conquest because I'm human. I know human strategy. I know human weak- nesses and strengths. And more than anything in this world, I want to destroy Conrig Wincantor and my sister Ullanoth.'

A prolonged silence fell over the chamber.

'How strange,' mused the First Judge, as he licked the last mucilaginous drops from his cup, 'that Conjure-Queen Ullanoth should have discovered a hidden cache of sigils so fortuitously – although we know that many such must have been secreted away during our long retreat from Bazekoy's host. I wonder if other lost Great Stones might be located using her Subtle Loophole, that most puissant tool for wind-searching? If we owned a liberated Loophole, then it would be unnecessary for us to launch a long and arduous expedition to the Barren Lands Moon Crag.'

Beynor felt his gorge rise anew at this terrible possibility, which had never occurred to him. What a catastrophe if the monsters located and took control of Darasilo's Trove before he could steal it away from Kilian . . .

But the Conservator's next words wiped away Beynor's dismay and kindled fresh hope. 'It seems to me that the young sorcerer's proposal to help us seize the Conjure-Queen's sigils has considerable merit. We should not reject it lightly.'

'I agree,' said the Master Shaman. 'Furthermore, torturing the human as Ugusawnn urges can produce unsatisfactory results. Humans have such frail bodies compared to our own.'

'If I die under the Supreme Warrior's ministrations before telling you the secret of the Potency,' Beynor said reasonably, 'you will have thrown away any chance of abolishing the pain-yoke of the Lights, or regaining your ancestral island home.'

'He's right,' the Conservator said. 'And this assassination that he demands as a goodwill gesture doesn't seem particularly difficult.'

'It would be quite a simple matter,' Beynor said, 'requiring only a small force of Salka warriors. Perhaps only a score. I would have to lead them myself, since I'm familiar with the River Malle and the type of vessel carrying King Honigalus and his family. I also know the best escape route. As soon as the fighters and I return to Dawntide Citadel, I'll show you how to activate the Potency. You must choose who among you will bond to the Great Stone –'

'It must be Ugusawnn,' the Conservator said. 'He is the most suitable person. Aside from his undeniable fighting prowess, his own sigil enables him to communicate with us across long distances, so we always know how his ventures are faring.'

The Supreme Warrior's enormous glowing eyes widened in gratified surprise. 'Do the other Eminences concur?'

The Judge and the Master Shaman nodded.

And Beynor thought: Perfect! My principal opponent is disarmed!

'Ugusawnn will also lead the assassination party into Didion,' the Conservator said, 'with the human sorcerer serving as his guide. This will not only enhance the possibility of success, but also make certain that the action proceeds without . . . unexpected developments.'

The Conservator meant Beynor's escape. But he already had worked out a simple plan to get away from the monsters. 'I would be honored to have such august company on the expedition,' the young sorcerer said humbly.

The Supreme Warrior glowered at him. 'Precisely where are these royal murders to take place?'

'At a point on the River Malle near Boarsden Castle, where the barge is most vulnerable to attack from the water,' Beynor said. 'The spot is some six hundred leagues from the Dawntide Isles. Honigalus and his family will be there six days from now.'

'So soon?' the Judge said.

'Our strongest swimmers could get there easily if we left at once,' Ugusawnn said. He shot Beynor a look of distaste. 'But I don't know how we'll manage to transport the groundling sorcerer without drowning him. I'm not even convinced that it's a good idea for him to go along on this mission. What if he's killed? We'd never empower the Potency then.'

'It would be up to you,' the Conservator said wearily, 'to keep him secure.'

'Do you still intend to oppose this scheme, Ugusawnn,'

Kalawnn asked, 'even when we would make you Master of the Potency?'

'I don't oppose it. But I do mistrust this tricky groundling with all my heart and soul!'

Beynor said, 'I know an easy way to transport me to Didion. When the Master Shaman so graciously offered me sanctuary, I came here from Royal Fenguard in my own barque, *Ambergris,* which was a gift to me from the Didionites after I did them a great favor. The ship is in a sad state of neglect now, careened in one of the coves below the citadel. But her boats should still be sound, and they are of a common type that would be inconspicuous on the River Malle. I can cross the sea in one of them, dismasted and towed along at speed by your force. When we reach Mallmouth Harbor, I'll step the boat's mast, hoist her sail, and go innocently up the river – pulled more slowly and inconspicuously as needed by my Salka guardians.'

'Is this practicable, Ugusawnn?' the Conservator inquired.

'It would probably work.' The Supreme Warrior spoke without enthusiasm. 'But I'd rather leave the groundling here. Let him instruct me in the details.'

'I won't agree –' Beynor began to say.

'Silence!' The Conservator of Wisdom gave the command in a voice that was suddenly resounding and steady. 'Beynor of Moss, step back from the dais and wait by the doors while we Four confer.'

Beynor obeyed. Numbed by the ordeal, he now felt no anxiety nor sense of anticipation as the great trolls murmured interminably among themselves. At long last the Conservator called out, 'Beynor, come and stand again before us, and receive our decision.'

Kilian. Vra-Kilian Blackhorse. Do you hear?

'Yes, Beynor.'

We've won. A small Salka force will leave for Didion within a few hours, taking me with them. They'll be led by their Supreme Warrior, a surly savage named Ugusawnn. After slaughtering the royal family, we're supposed to return to Dawntide Citadel, where I show the Four Eminences how to activate the Potency. They've decided to bond it to the Supreme Warrior. He intends to lead an attack on Royal Fenguard immediately, snap up Ulla's sigils, and conquer the world for the Salka.

'Heh heh heh! Brilliantly done, my boy. What a pack of simpletons!'

I'm supposed to believe that Ugusawnn will take me along on the invasion of Moss. But I'm fairly certain he intends to kill me as soon as he's sure that I've properly activated the Potency.

'It would be extremely vexing if the monsters did polish you off.'

Ugusawnn is no fool and he has serious doubts about me. Still, it should be easy enough to give him the slip once he and the others have taken care of Honigalus. They have no suspicion that I'm able to impel a small boat with my talent – as if that weren't one of the first tricks a Mossland magicker learns! Once I'm safely away in Didion, I'll windspeak the Eminences the revised version of the bargain. And we pray that they swallow their outrage and agree to it.

'Why shouldn't they? The alternative is custody of a useless dead sigil. How could the Salka possibly suspect that the Potency bonds to no one? That it can be snatched away from this Supreme Warrior and used by anyone at all without causing harm to the taker?'

Such a thing would never occur to them. I wonder why the Potency's creator made it thus? Not too sensible, was it? Not that I'm complaining!

'Consider this: If the Potency doesn't bond to its activator, then it doesn't die when the owner does. Unlike all other sigils, the Potency might very well be immortal.'

Interesting – and unsettling, too. God of the Depths! How I wish there were some way of reading that last archive tablet! We need to know why the Potency was made, and why its reputation has always been so dire.

'After we wipe out the Salka with Darasilo's Trove, you can return to their citadel and find out.'

Perhaps . . . Kilian, this conversation must end now. The Supreme Warrior is expecting me to join him. We're inspecting the small boat that will carry me to Didion.

'Good luck, then, Beynor. May you have a safe voyage.'

I'll see you in your dreams.

FOUR

Snudge and his companions broke the first short day of their northward journey shortly before the eleventh hour after noon. The cavalcade had arrived at a little village called Swallowmere, some sixty leagues north of the capital, where there was a tavern of unpretentious but promising aspect. The horses were tired by then, but the young travelers weren't – not on Solstice Eve, when every man of spirit save those constrained by holy orders was expected to celebrate High Summer.

The Green Swallow Inn proved to be well stocked with extra food and drink for the occasion. Crowded with friendly locals, it featured a three-man band of peasant musicians and plenty of lasses to dance and flirt with. Snudge, his armigers Valdos and Wiltorig, and Sir Gavlock and his squire Hanan joined wholeheartedly in the roistering.

Meanwhile Vra-Mattis, the apprentice windvoice assigned to Sir Deveron by the king, eschewed worldly pleasures as befit a novice in the Mystical Order of Saint Zeth. The night was very warm, so Mat put off his robe and settled down in the inn's forecourt in his undertunic. He ate a good supper of mutton-dumpling stew and strawberry tarts, rested his saddlesore muscles, and finally fell into a doze on a heap of clean straw, bothered not a whit by the convivial racket coming from inside the tavern.

Some time later, in the wee hours, the novice was jolted awake by an urgent windspoken message from the Royal Alchymist Lord Stergos, intended for Sir Deveron. Its portent was so grave that Mattis hastened to seek out his master without even donning his robe. The interior of the inn was now jam-packed with funseekers, many of them so taken by strong drink that they could barely stand. Skirling pipes, a squawking fiddle, a thumping tabor, laughter and song fairly shook the rafters.

Mattis found his master grinning owlishly as he stomped and shuffled in a drunken round-dance with three cavorting farm-girls. From the sidelines, Sir Gavlok hoisted a cannikin of rustic rotgut and cheered, ignoring the frantic novice who bellowed into his unresponsive ear.

The dance finally ended to raucous applause and Mattis rushed to take Snudge by the arm and pull him in the direction of the inn's front door. Gavlok trailed along after, protesting his friend's evacuation.

'Sir!' the novice cried. 'Sir Deveron, can you understand me?'

'Unhand me, knave,' Snudge mumbled. 'Wanna dance!' He tripped over his own feet and fell to his knees in the dirt courtyard. 'Feel sleepy. Time f'bed.'

'Sir, please listen!' Vra-Mattis attempted without success to haul his master upright. 'I've received an important wind-message from the Royal Alchymist. His Grace the High King commands you to return to the capital immediately.'

'Booger the king. Booger Stergos. Go 'way.' Snudge rolled onto his face.

The dismayed windvoice appealed to the other young knight, who now seemed to be almost sober. 'What am I to do? We dare not wait until he's slept off his carouse. Lord Stergos insisted that we leave here at once.'

Gavlok nudged his collapsed friend with his foot. 'Commander! Arise! Duty calls!' The only response was a muffled curse. Inside the inn, the music had started up again more loudly and off-key than ever. A fat man staggered out the door and spewed in the shadows.

'Poor Deveron,' Gavlok mourned. 'His very first holiday. Alas – he was having such a fine time, too! But I fear, Brother Mat, that drastic measures are now called for. Assist me, if you please.' Together, the two men began to drag the inert Snudge across the courtyard toward the stables. A courting couple fled at their approach.

Sir Gavlok Whitfell was aware that Deveron Austrey frequently undertook secret missions for King Conrig, but knew nothing of his friend's arcane talent. Formerly armiger to Lord Stergos, Gavlok had been knighted a year earlier than Snudge and was now assigned to the Royal Alchymist's Guard. Although he was nobly born, the fourth son of a distinguished Westley family, he was too introspective and sensitive to be an enthusiastic warrior. Lord Stergos valued the gangling, fair-haired young man for his intelligence, his unswerving integrity, and his self-deprecating sense of humor – as did Snudge.

'We do this for Sir Deveron's own good,' Gavlok declared to the windvoice, as the two of them reached a horse-trough with their burden. They tipped Snudge into the water with a great splash, then hauled him out and sat him down in the straw, coughing and spluttering.

'Whoreson!' Snudge croaked, lashing out with feeble fury at the friend who was divesting him of his sodden garments. 'I'll b-broil your b-bollocks for this!'

'No doubt,' Gavlok replied. 'But first you must listen to Vra-Mattis, who has a message for you from the king.'

'What?'

Mattis told him. Snudge groaned piteously. 'Shite! My head spins like a whirry – whirligig. A 'mergency, you say? What sort?'

But the novice had not been entrusted with further information, and Snudge knew with woozy certainty that there was no possibility that he himself might bespeak the Royal Alchymist and learn more. His own windtalent had been totally extinguished by ardent spirits, as had most of his other mental faculties. In fact, he was nearly paralytic.

'Gavvy,' he whispered, sinking to the ground again and holding his swollen head in his hands. 'Gavvy, old friend. I muss – must lay a great 'sponsibility on you. Can't hang two thoughts together myself. D'you think you can get the lot of us on the road? Fresh horses, o'course. Clean clothes, too. Our three squires are swizzled as swineherds, lyin' in a filthy heap somewhere inside.'

'I'm none too sharp myself,' Gavlok admitted, 'and I'll need your fat purse to make the arrangements. But count on me.'

'Good man.' Without another word Snudge curled into a ball and began to snore. Overhead, the sky was already pink at three in the morning of Solstice Day, and Cathran songbirds were singing their dawn chorus, oblivious to the merry-making inside the inn.

He woke with his head clanging like an anvil, riding through a town where well-dressed inhabitants stared at him as he passed. Now and then, someone would snicker. He discovered that he was lashed to the saddle so he would not fall, and he was mounted not on his fine black charger but on a scruffy roan nag with a hogged mane. The beast plodded along on a lead-strap behind another rider who wore a dusty crimson robe. To the rear was a drooping figure on a third horse, with a lead attached to Snudge's cantle-ring.

'Mat?' Snudge's mouth felt like the inside of an old boot and his eyes seemed clogged with sand.

The robed figure looked over its shoulder at him. 'Ah. Finally awake? Very good.' He called out to someone riding ahead. 'Sir Gavlok, my master has come round.'

Gavlok made some unintelligible reply. Snudge muttered to the novice, 'What – what's the hour? And where are we?'

'This is Axebridge, a village along the River Blen some fifteen leagues above the capital. I have relatives here. It's about the ninth hour of morning. We'll stop soon for brief refreshment.'

'Never have I had a worse hangover,' Snudge whimpered. 'I'm nearly blind with headache and perishing of thirst.'

'I'll make a remedy for you soon,' Mat said cheerfully. 'Alchymical studies have a practical side, thanks be to Saint Zeth. A concoction of strong ale, raw egg, garum, and ground pepper will quickly banish your blue devils, sir.'

The party turned off the high street into a lane and proceeded to a prosperous-looking cottage where a large chestnut tree gave welcome shade from the hot sun. There Gavlok assisted Snudge to dismount while Vra-Mattis helped the three moaning armigers.

'This is Mat's cousin's house,' Gavlok said. 'I'll pay the goodwife well to prepare food for us, which we can eat when we're back in the saddle. But first, we'll fetch you and the lads that healing draft.'

Leaving the stricken men sitting on the grass and drinking from skin waterbottles, the tall skinny knight and the bandy-legged little novice went to the cottage door and spoke at length to someone inside.

Valdos Grimstane, who at sixteen years of age was Snudge's senior squire, said faintly, 'I think I may die, Sir Deveron.'

He was a grandson of Duke Tanaby Vanguard, and it was a mark of Conrig's esteem that such a high-born youth had been assigned as armiger to the newly belted Royal Intelligencer. Valdos was pleasantly ugly and usually of a ruddy complexion, but at the moment his face was cheese-green and his eyes so bloodshot that their true color could hardly be discerned.

'No, you won't die, Val,' Snudge assured him. 'You'll gather your wits as speedily as you can, for something has caused the High King to cancel our country holiday and summon us all back to the palace posthaste. I know not why.'

'Bazekoy's Biceps! You have no hint at all of what's up?'

'None. But I suspect it's no trivial business.'

'What a disappointment for you, sir, not to see your new manor house after all,' said the junior armiger. A year younger than Valdos, his name was Wiltorig Baysdale. He was a native of the Southern Shore, a distant cousin of the Lord Treasurer, Duke Feribor Blackhorse, and uncommonly good-looking and tall for his age. He had curly blond hair, grey eyes, and an ingratiating manner that Snudge had found to be a bit cloying. But perhaps the lad was only overeager to please.

'I daresay Buttonoaks will wait, Wil.' Snudge sighed. 'I've been assured that my steward is a very competent fellow . . . How do you feel?'

'Seedy, sir. I've never been drunk before. It seemed great fun last night, but I've never had such a headache. I could swear that nails are being pounded into my skull.'

'Ah, ye poor mite,' came the mocking voice of Gavlok's squire, Hanan Caprock, a burly youth who came from the wild mountain lands above Beorbrook Hold. 'Imagine that – your first hangover! Must be a quiet life down in Blackhorse Duchy . . . when the local peers aren't murdering each other or plotting treason against the Sovereign. I suppose you'll be a virgin, too, eh?'

Wil's face went crimson. His retort was surprisingly cool.

'That's none of your business. And I advise you to stifle your crude remarks in future, or you'll regret it.'

Hanan's hooded dark eyes narrowed. 'Oh, I will, will I, pretty one?'

'That's enough!' Snudge said testily. 'Hanan, you've a mouth on you like a potboy. Apologize at once, or Sir Gavlok will hear about this. I won't have my men baited.'

The older squire climbed to his feet and bowed elaborately to Wiltorig. 'I ask your pardon, Baysdale. And I apologize to you, also, Sir Deveron. I'm a highland ass who never learnt fine manners! So why don't I trot off and see if my master can use me for donkey-work?' He slouched toward the rear of the cottage, where Gavlok and Vra-Mattis had disappeared along with the woman of the house.

'I'm surprised Sir Gavlok tolerates such a lout,' Wiltorig remarked with disdain.

'His choice of squire is not your concern.' Snudge stood up and eased his sore joints. 'And so long as Sir Gavlok rides with us, you'll be civil to Hanan, even under provocation. Is that clear?'

'Yes, sir.'

Snudge was weary of the armigers' callow chatter and felt a need to organize his own befuddled thoughts. 'I'm going to stretch my legs in yonder orchard. There's probably a well behind the house. You two water the horses. They're very thirsty.'

'How do you know that, sir?' Wiltorig asked with studied innocence.

Snudge was taken aback. The lad's tone seemed oddly pointed. 'Any competent horseman can tell!' he snapped. 'Obey me.'

He cursed himself for the possibly revealing slip of the tongue as he moved away into a grove of cherry trees that were already setting fruit. One of his lesser gifts was the ability to coerce and control horses, and he was also uncannily aware of the animals' physical needs and afflictions. When he was a young boy, the talent had brought him special treatment in the royal stables from grateful grooms. Eventually, it resulted in his first fateful encounter with Conrig Wincantor, which had forever changed his life.

But why had the armiger Wiltorig posed his question so oddly? Was Snudge being overly imaginative – or had someone primed the boy to watch for evidence of wild talent? *Duke Feribor Blackhorse?*

Snudge felt a queasy stirring in his belly that had nothing to do with his hangover. The formidable Lord Treasurer was a childhood friend of King Conrig, one of his closest advisers, and in a perfect position to have put forward his young relative as an armiger candidate. Snudge, wrapped up in the excitement of his investiture and the unexpected holiday, had thought nothing of the coincidence until this moment.

His physical discomfort forgotten, he thought about it now. And berated himself for never having put together certain facts about the duke.

Feribor, accused by persistent rumor – which the king flatly refused to countenance – of having poisoned his first wife, as well as orchestrating the death of his feckless older brother Shiantil so that he might inherit the Blackhorse dukedom . . .

Feribor, who now stood first in the line of succession to the Crown of Sovereignty, should Conrig's offspring be debarred . . .

Feribor, suspected of colluding with the scheming Lords of the Southern Shore, and completely exonerated of any wrongdoing after a too-hasty investigation in which the Royal Intelligencer played no part . . .

Feribor, Lord Treasurer, whose tax-gathering irregularities came under scrutiny when other members of the Privy Council pressed the issue, only to be forgiven his 'mistakes' by a Sovereign who refused to believe his old Heart Companion would cheat the Crown . . .

Feribor, nephew to the deposed Royal Alchymist and convicted traitor Kilian Blackhorse, who might have been told by his uncle of the hidden Trove of Darasilo – and Snudge's role in revealing its existence to Conrig . . .

Feribor, who might have long suspected that the shadowy young royal henchman Deveron Austrey was a wild talent dangerous to his own ambitions, whose late armiger Mero Elwick had murdered three of Snudge's companions and narrowly missed killing *him* – probably following his master's orders . . .

Did the devious duke still want Snudge dead? Had Feribor assigned young Wil Baysdale to complete the job botched by Mero? The latter had failed because he coveted the sigil named Concealer, Snudge's secret possession. Mero had been a greedy fool, and his vain attempt to seize the moonstone had brought about his own death.

If Wil *was* newly cast in the role of assassin, there was almost nothing to be done about it – at least for the present.

If I tell King Conrig my suspicions, Snudge thought, he won't believe me. Even worse, he might mention my mistrust to Feribor – which could provoke the duke into taking immediate action against me. And what if Wil hasn't been ordered to kill me at all? What if he's under orders to report my activities to Feribor?

Spying on the king's spy!

I must discuss this matter with Lord Stergos as soon as possible, Snudge decided. The Royal Alchymist had always been a sympathetic mentor to him. If anyone could overcome Conrig's misjudgment of the Lord Treasurer, it was his beloved older brother . . .

The cherry orchard was bounded by a wooden fence, which Snudge climbed, now painfully aware of an overfull bladder. Beyond was a strip of stony ground that ended at a bluff overlooking the River Blen and the broad valley leading to the sea and the sprawling city that had been renamed Cala Blenholme by the Sovereign. After relieving himself against a boulder, Snudge stood shading his still-bleary eyes against the blazing sun. A rampart of towering white clouds loomed on the southwestern horizon, no doubt the advance guard of a thunderstorm that was certain to disrupt the Solstice festivities in the capital. It was a moment before Snudge realized that a narrow pillar of jet-black smoke was also rising from the skyline.

Rising from the exact location of Cala Palace.

Lord Stergos! his mind screamed on the wind. *What's happened?*

There was no reply.

Before knighthood was conferred on him, Snudge had been accustomed to conceal his secret activities by posing as one of the anonymous young armigers or footmen attached to the retinue of some trusted noble, who would be under royal orders to visit the place or person under investigation. The cooperating peer was of course aware that Snudge was the king's spy; but he had no notion that the young agent possessed arcane abilities exceeding those of most Brothers of Zeth. In this situation, it had been relatively easy for Snudge to slip away from his fellow-retainers, perform his clandestine duties, and bespeak his findings directly to Lord Stergos, who would pass the information on to the High King.

Once Snudge was dubbed Sir Deveron, however, a new arrangement became necessary. A Knight Banneret had far more authority and status than a mere squire or even an ordinary knight, and was potentially more useful to his royal master. But he was also more conspicuous. Snudge rated two armigers of his own, and soon would employ servants who would expect to attend him closely. In time, he could expect to command other knights and men-at-arms. His privacy was diminished, and he was bound to find it more difficult to exercise his wild talents secretly.

Conrig did not intend for his intelligencer's arcane gifts to become common knowledge, but neither did he wish to be constrained in his ability to stay in close contact with him. The solution was to assign a personal windvoice to Sir Deveron Austrey, who would act as official liaison between him and the throne.

This was by no means an unusual privilege: many senior royal officers had ordained Brothers of Zeth in their retinues, and so did other important personages. Sir Deveron's apprentice windvoice Vra-Mattis Temebrook was a more modest symbol of privilege, but he was bright, highly talented, and at eighteen years of age eager to escape the gimlet eye of the Palace Novicemaster. In time, if Mat proved loyal, Snudge thought he might consider sharing his great secret with him. But for now he intended to use the young Brother cautiously, and urge Lord Stergos to do the same –

Unless some evil thing had happened to the Royal Alchymist. Why hadn't he responded to Snudge's call? It was up to the apprentice windvoice to find out.

Back at the cottage, Snudge found Gavlok and the others preparing to depart.

Vra-Mattis held out a cup to him. 'You still look unwell, sir. Drink down this hangover cure. It'll do you a world of good.'

Snudge quaffed the dose with a shudder. 'More ails me than a thick head.' He called the others to gather around him. 'During my stroll I came upon a vantage point overlooking the Blen Valley and the distant capital. I regret to tell you that a great fire seems to be raging in the vicinity of the palace.'

The armigers cried out horrified queries, but Snudge shook his head. 'Be silent! Vra-Mattis, withdraw from us and attempt to bespeak Lord Stergos for information. If you can't attract his attention, call upon his assistant, Vra-Sulkorig, or any other of the ranking Brethren who may be able to reply.'

The novice wasted no time in speech. He moved behind the trunk of the big chestnut tree, seated himself on a root, and covered his head with the hood of his robe in order to concentrate.

Snudge issued more orders. 'Valdos, see if the goodwife has such a thing as a tall clothespole. We're going to ride at speed from here on, with you bearing the royal banner, and we have no lance to tie it to . . . Wiltorig, unpack our mail shirts and helmets and lash them to the saddles where they may be easily donned if needed. Hanan, do the same for Sir Gavlok and yourself.'

The armigers rushed to obey.

Gavlok said, 'We should be able to reach Cala in an hour. These horses I bought at Swallowmere may not be handsome, but they're tough as flint. Is there aught that I can do?'

Snudge replied in a low voice. 'I may ask a great boon of you later. For now, only stand by me as a friend.'

'With all my heart, Deveron. But I'm no great shakes in a fight, you know –'

'Oh, sirs!' cried Vra-Mattis, rising up from his tree root and calling out to the two knights. 'A terrible calamity has occurred at the palace. There's been an attempt to kill Lord Stergos! His apartment and the library have been almost completely demolished by several tarnblaze explosions and a great fire.'

'Is he dead?' asked Snudge.

'Nay, sorely burned but expected to survive. I bespoke Vra-Sulkorig, who says that your speedy return is now more needful than ever. The Royal Alchymist demands to speak to you and will take no remedy for his pain lest it send him to sleep and prevent him from giving you a special command. But he will tell no one what this command might be – not even the High King.'

'I see.' Whether it was Mat's disgusting potion at work, or his own brain's energy rising to the occasion, Snudge now felt clear-headed and revitalized. 'Then the King's Grace is unhurt?'

'He and the rest of the royal family are safe. The fire is confined to the wing of the palace where the Zeth Brethren reside. Sadly, numbers of them have been killed or injured. You're aware, of course, that the devilish substance tarnblaze cannot be put down by magical spells. The conflagration is being fought with water pumped from the river and the palace moat. It still burns strongly, and the roof-timbers are collapsing.'

'Tell Vra-Sulkorig I'll try to attend him and Lord Stergos inside of an hour. Bid him have the City Guard clear the West River Road approach so we won't be delayed. By now, there must be panicky crowds as well as gawkers on the streets surrounding the palace.'

Mattis nodded and covered his head again.

'All is in readiness, Deveron,' Gavlok announced, 'whenever you wish to ride.'

A few minutes later they were all in the saddle, galloping back onto the highroad with the squire Valdos leading the way, holding the crown banner of the Sovereignty and shouting, 'Make way! Make way for the king's men!'

FIVE

'My lord, I'm here. I grieve to see you so wounded.'

Snudge bent low over the bandaged face of the patient lying motionless on a bed in a room adjacent to the king's suite. Only the hazel eyes were uncovered. They were partially open, with their lids blistered and lashes seared away, and darted aimlessly from side to side as if vainly seeking someone. Snudge felt his heart contract. Was the poor man blind?

'My Lord Stergos, are you awake?'

Is it you, Deveron? The response came in unsteady wind-speech.

'The skin around his mouth has been terribly burned,' High King Conrig whispered. He sat on a stool beside his suffering brother, his own countenance a mask of anguish. 'He may not be able to answer.'

Snudge said covertly, 'He bespoke me. But I dare not let these other people hovering round about him know that we can converse mind-to-mind. Send them away. Lord Stergos is in great pain. He may slip into unconsciousness at any moment.'

Conrig climbed to his feet and addressed the crowd of

red-robed physicians and alchymists. 'All of you, leave us. Sir Deveron and I will confer privately for a few minutes and pray over my brother.'

The Brothers reluctantly filed out of the sickroom and closed the door. A subdued roll of thunder announced the approaching storm.

Snudge said, 'Lord Stergos, do you have a message for me? It's safe to use windspeech. The others have gone away.'

Ah . . . Mustn't compromise your secret, Deveron. Especially not now.

'No, my lord.'

All of them think . . . the explosion was attempt on my life. Even Con! Not true. I believe . . . someone demolished my quarters to get at the Trove of Darasilo. You remember Kilian had it. We never found . . . impossible to windsearch sigils . . . we thought he hid it somewhere in palace . . . he'd never entrust it to another.

'I agree,' Snudge said. 'Shall I tell His Grace about this?'

'Here!' Conrig protested. 'There'll be no secrets kept from me!'

Tell him.

'Sire,' Snudge said firmly, 'in matters of high sorcery, you must always be guided by the judgment and wisdom of your Reverend Brother. However, he's given me permission to tell you his concerns. Do you remember the secret trove of inactive sigils and the two magical books that I discovered in the rooms of the former Royal Alchymist, Kilian Blackhorse?'

'Yes. Our search after Kilian's arrest turned up nothing, so I assumed they had been lost. Gossy said so, too. If the things had turned up, he planned to destroy them to keep them away from that cunning little bastard, Beynor of Moss. He and Kilian were cooking up some conspiracy together.'

'Your brother believes that the sigils were hidden somewhere in the Royal Alchymist's apartment by Kilian, before Lord Stergos himself took up residence there. He also thinks that the tarnblaze assault was an attempt to uncover the items so that they might be stolen away.'

Conrig nodded. 'So we can presume that either Beynor or Kilian himself was responsible for the explosion?'

Beynor . . . exiled among Dawntide Salka. No way to escape. Queen Ulla assured us. But Kilian . . . friends at abbey . . . The windvoice trailed away.

Snudge said, 'Lord Stergos thinks Beynor couldn't have done it himself. He's a virtual prisoner of the Salka on a remote island in the eastern Boreal Sea. Kilian is confined under house arrest in Zeth Abbey, but he has many friends – as we know too well – whom he may have converted to his cause.'

Conrig was on his feet, clenching his big fists. He began to pace back and forth. A flash of lightning lit the room, followed almost at once by a crash of thunder. 'Damn that scheming wizard! I knew I should have lopped off his treacherous head. But our mother couldn't bear losing her precious brother!'

Queen Mother Cataldis was a gentle but steel-willed woman. Neither Conrig nor Stergos could bring themselves to oppose her.

Three visiting Brothers . . . scholars . . . outside library yesterday when all the others were away at the Solstice Eve feast.

'Lord Stergos says there were three suspicious Brothers of Zeth working near his apartment yesterday,' Snudge said. 'By the library.'

The High King bent over the bandaged man. 'Gossy! Can you tell Snudge their names?'

Can't recall. Ask Dean of Studies, Vra-Edzal.

Snudge reached for a wax tablet and stylus that lay on a bedside table beside a tray of medicines, wrote the name down, and handed the tablet to the king. 'This man will know, sire.'

Deveron . . . examine my rooms. See if there really is a hiding place . . . empty. Those unholy tools of the Beaconfolk must not reach Kilian . . . Aah! The pain . . . very bad.

'Never fear, my lord. I'll do as you say. If Darasilo's Trove has been stolen, the thieves can't have gone far yet. We'll catch them.'

The sigils and books must be destroyed. You know what Kilian and Beynor would do with them. Even my dear brother might . . . Promise me!

'I promise, my lord.'

The pain . . . the pain . . . No more, Deveron. Summon the doctors and I'll take the poppy draft. God have mercy on me . . .

'What's he saying?' Conrig demanded.

'He's finished speaking. He wants the doctors. He's in agony.'

Conrig strode to the door and shouted for the medical attendants to return. They flocked back, and several of them lifted the burn victim, parted the ointment-smeared bandages covering his mouth, and administered the narcotic draft that had been refused earlier.

'You must leave him now, Your Grace,' one of the doctors said. 'He will sleep for many hours.'

Conrig scowled, but he finally turned away and beckoned Snudge to follow. When the two of them were alone in the corridor, the king asked sharply, 'What did you promise Lord Stergos you would do?'

'Pursue the mysterious Brothers,' Snudge said evasively, 'presuming they stole the sigils and the books.'

'If those three are the villains who burned poor Gossy,' the king said with quiet menace, 'they shall have their own close acquaintance with flame.'

'Perhaps they're still hiding in the palace. But it's more likely that they escaped in the confusion and fled the city. A search must begin at once, sire. You'll need to summon this Vra-Edzal. He can provide the names and descriptions of the three, and perhaps even arrange for drawings of their faces. This would greatly assist both the windsearchers and the untalented hunters. The Lord Constable, Earl Marshal

Parlian, and the other members of your Privy Council will have to know about this.'

Including Duke Feribor Blackhorse, who might have played a key role in the disaster! But there was no way of proving that, nor even any chance now of discussing the possibility with Stergos.

'Hmm.' Conrig looked away, thinking. 'I must decide how much to tell my counselors. Unfortunately, we can't avoid giving out some sort of description of the stolen trove. But it should be as vague as possible – old books of great value only to alchymists, and a few small stone carvings. We'll offer a large reward, but make it seem that the most important consideration is capturing those who wounded Stergos and destroyed the library. All of the searchers will be sworn to secrecy. Others will learn soon enough about this damned collection of moonstone sigils, but we must keep their dread capability secret. Only you and I and Stergos must ever know of that.'

'Not the Conjure-Queen?' Snudge asked softly. 'Her Subtle Loophole would readily scry the location of the stolen things.'

'God forbid! If Ullanoth found them before we did, it could bring on a catastrophe far worse than the one we already face. You do understand that, don't you, Snudge?'

'Yes, sire. I was not sure *you* did.'

'Impudence . . .'

'However, you face something of a dilemma here, sire. I think Queen Ullanoth is bound to learn something about the theft before long. News of the palace fire will spread from one end of the island to the other. Fortunately for us, there's no easy way for her to get her hands on the trove, even if she scries its location. Her Sending is unable to take back anything to its point of origin. She'd have to come after the trove using her natural body. That would be quite difficult for her, given the situation in Moss and her present state of physical frailty.'

'What are you driving at? What's the dilemma?'

'If the thieves aren't captured in short order, you may be forced to ask for her help. To prevent the trove from falling into the hands of Kilian or Beynor.'

'God's Eyes! Of course. One of them certainly planned the theft.'

'Or both,' Snudge said. 'This is what Lord Stergos believes. He asked me to inspect the scene of the conflagration. Perhaps I might find some useful indications.'

'The burned-out wing can hardly be cool yet, but the oncoming rainstorm will take care of that.' Outside the corridor windows it had grown very dark, and the lightning and peals of thunder were now almost continuous. 'When you finish, come to my study. We still must talk of the reason why I called you back to the city.'

Snudge let his chagrin show. 'How remiss of me! This terrible disaster wiped all thought of the other matter from my mind.'

'We'll talk of it later.' Conrig turned abruptly and strode away.

Snudge started off in the opposite direction, intending to go to the knights' lodging in the Square Tower where he had left Gavlok and the others. He was going to need help searching the ruins, and he already felt deathly weary. The anguish emanating from the mind of Lord Stergos had deeply affected his own humor. It was a troubling aspect of his wild talent that he was only beginning to come to terms with. There were other considerations as well, but they didn't bear thinking of now.

And neither did his motive for not telling King Conrig all that he had promised Lord Stergos.

Snudge, Gavlok, and the three squires armed themselves with iron-shafted pikes, donned waterproof military cloaks and heavy boots, then set off to begin the miserable task of poking through steaming rubble. A torrential deluge now beat down upon the palace. Since the damaged wing had largely lost its roof and was open to the elements, the rain had quenched the last of the flames. Most of the firefighters had withdrawn.

When Snudge's party arrived at the ruined library they found Vra-Sulkorig Casswell himself. He had put off his robes in favor of waxed-leather hunting garb, and was supervising the removal of an incinerated human body from among the fallen stacks.

Stergos's principal assistant bore the symbolic title Keeper of Arcana, but his actual duties were administrative. He was an austere, balding man in early middle age, more pragmatic than mystical. The king's brother was over twenty years his junior, and had relied on Sulkorig's greater experience to govern the scores of Zeth Brethren assigned to various palace duties.

As Gavlok and the armigers began a cautious tour of the gutted library, Snudge explained to the Keeper why he and his men had come.

Sulkorig nodded brusquely. 'Looking for clues, are you, Sir Deveron? Then you'll find this interesting.' He held out something in his gloved hand. 'We found it with these sad remains.'

Snudge took the muck-encrusted, faintly gleaming object, bent down, and rinsed it in one of the myriad pools of rainwater. It was a solid gold gammadion pendant on a matching chain, one of those worn by every professed Brother of Zeth. On one side, the pendant was engraved with the voided cross emblem of the order. On the other side was a name. Snudge had to strain to read it in the gloom:

VRA-VITUBIO BENTLAND – C.Y. 1108

'The name of the owner and the date of his ordination,' Sulkorig explained. 'He was one of those heroes who attempted to rescue the Royal Alchymist after the tarnblaze explosions took place.'

Snudge pocketed the pendant. 'I'll give this to His Grace. He'll surely wish to commemorate the bravery of this man, who gave up his own life for Lord Stergos. Can you tell me anything about him?'

Sulkorig watched stoically as two white-faced young novices finished loading the nearly fleshless, contorted corpse onto a litter and covered it with a sheet. 'Take him to the old laboratory and lay him out with the others, lads. You need do no more work today.'

'Yes, Brother Keeper.' The pair shuffled off with their grisly burden.

'Vra-Vitubio was a visitor to Cala,' Sulkorig said to Snudge, 'one of three historians come down from Zeth Abbey to do research in our library. I myself know little about him, but doubtless his companions can tell us all that the High King requires for the commemoration.'

'Doubtless,' Snudge said through clenched teeth. 'Do you know the names of the others?'

'Vra-Felmar Nightcott and Vra-Scarth Saltbeck. It appears that they were also among those who tried to rescue Lord Stergos, but were unable to find him in the smoke. Neither one was seriously hurt.'

'Would you do me the great favor of windspeaking the two right now, and ask them to present themselves to Lord Telifar, His Grace's secretary?'

Sulkorig's brows rose in surprise, but he pulled off a glove and covered his eyes with his hand. After a couple of minutes had passed, he regarded Snudge with a puzzled expression. 'Neither man responds. I consulted our infirmarian, and they are not among those recuperating from injuries.'

'I didn't think they would be! Vra-Sulkorig, you know that I am the king's man, and that I undertake to perform certain privy services for him. I must tell you something now in strictest confidence. His Grace suspects that those two Brothers and their dead comrade were responsible for this terrible conflagration.'

'My God! Why should they do such a thing?'

'In order to steal certain valuable arcane objects belonging to Lord Stergos. I was not in the city at the time of the disaster. Please tell me what you know of the sequence of events here.'

The first explosion had occurred at about eight in the morning, at a time when most residents of the palace were still sleeping off the night's festivities, so as to be well rested for the events scheduled later on Midsummer Day. The Brothers were free to do as they chose, but many of them – including the Royal Alchymist – attended the usual communal breakfast in the refectory at the sixth hour.

Stergos would ordinarily have gone to his office at the far end of the cloister wing after eating and dealt with his correspondence. But on this holiday, with the scribes and secretaries excused from duty, he told his assistant Sulkorig that he would return to his own quarters for a time, since he had much to meditate upon. When the first tarnblaze explosion blew open the outer door of the Alchymical Library, Stergos was among the stacks, searching for a book dealing with the thaumaturgical history of the Salka race.

The concussion toppled many of the free-standing book-shelves. One of them caught Stergos by the lower leg, trapping him. He began to cry for help and became aware of agitated shouts in the exterior corridor. Then, as he later told Vra-Sulkorig, red-robed figures moved into the smoke-filled chamber. As yet there was no widespread fire. A reassuring voice called out from not far away, apparently trying to locate him among the jumble of fallen stacks. Stergos answered, but heard nothing further for some minutes save the tolling of the alarm bell mounted outside the library door and a single youthful voice – perhaps the bellringer – screaming for help.

What happened next was so appalling that Stergos nearly fainted from shock. First came a sound of persons running. The smoke, which had the typical sulphurous stench of tarn-blaze, had thickened and it was getting harder for him to breathe. Then a tremendous blast emanated from his own rooms on the far side of the library, causing more shelves to crash and shaking the edifice to its foundations. He'd left the apartment door open when he came out to fetch the book, and even through the smoke he could see a huge gout of flame belch out of his sitting room and set the library furnishings – and his own clothing – afire.

He cried out with the last of his strength, then succumbed to oblivion until he awoke in the King's Suite and bespoke his story to Sulkorig, who later pieced together certain missing details by questioning witnesses.

Earlier, the novice who had been hauling hysterically on the bell cord was joined by another young Brother with more initiative. Shortly before the second explosion occurred, the two of them decided to attempt to rescue the unknown victim who was trapped in the library and calling out. They pulled down arras from the corridor wall and wrapped themselves, as protection against the fire within, and together plunged into the smoke.

Instantly, they were bowled over by two Brothers dashing *out* of the library and crying, 'Run! Run for your lives!' Then came the horrendous second blast, and the fast-spreading inferno. In a small miracle, the roaring flames seemed to diminish the thickness of the smoke momentarily. The two rescuers caught sight of Stergos engulfed in fire. They used an arras to beat it down, then dragged the Royal Alchymist to safety.

By then the corridor was thronged with men in red robes, members of the Palace Guard trying without success to restore order, and a few servants bearing containers of water, who doused the burned man and his scorched saviors.

'Everyone on the scene assumed that the two Brothers who had emerged from the library a few minutes earlier were would-be rescuers who lost heart and fled,' Vra-Sulkorig concluded. 'Someone recognized them as they pushed through the crowd and tried to ask them questions. But they were coughing and moaning, and soon vanished amidst the commotion. By then the flames had spread to other parts of the cloister wing, and the residents were fleeing.'

Snudge stood over the spot where the corpse had lain. 'Do you see, Brother Keeper? He had come only a few ells from Lord Stergos's apartment door. He must have been the last one to run out of there before the second explosion happened. The fireball roasted him in mid-stride.'

'Blessed Zeth,' Sulkorig muttered. 'May heaven grant him mercy.'

Snudge suspected there was scant chance of that.

'Sir Deveron!' The armiger Valdos called out from somewhere inside the ruined apartment. 'You must come in here and see this! But beware. Some of the roof beams are sagging and may collapse at any minute.'

Snudge entered, trailed by the Keeper. Fallen timbers lay everywhere in precarious tangles, some still smoldering in spite of the continuing downpour. Blackened and broken containers of ceramic or glass had survived, but all of the furnishings were ashes, and the beautiful hardwood floor that he remembered from his clandestine invasion of Kilian's quarters four years earlier was entirely burned away, leaving the same flagstone underpavement that was visible in the library.

Valdos stood just inside the doorframe of what had been

the Royal Alchymist's bedroom. The rear wall, made of closely fitted granite blocks, bore an irregular stain of yellowish-white at least five feet in diameter, surrounded by a halo of soot.

'I believe that the second explosion involved two bomb-shells, set off simultaneously,' Vra-Sulkorig noted. 'In my early life I was a soldier, and I've seen such things before. Perhaps the fire-raisers had intended to blast open the door to Lord Stergos's apartment. When they found it unlocked, they used both bombs inside.'

But Snudge's attention was elsewhere.

In the middle of this room, where the bed had once stood, was a square area of newly exposed floor that measured some three ells by four. Instead of stone, it was covered over with rusted iron plates that were bulging and distorted by heat. At one end, a pair of plates on hinges had dropped open like trapdoors, revealing a hole partially clogged by debris from the fire. Stone steps led down from the bedroom level into a kind of cellar . . . or crypt.

'Codders!' Snudge whispered.

He crossed the room with the greatest care, squatted gingerly, and peered into the opening. The underground chamber was about three ells deep and awash at the bottom with water in which floated bits of burned material. At the far end were two sizable objects of roughly hewn stone with heavy lids. They looked like tombs. In front of them stood a warped iron framework like a skeletal cabinet or chest that still held a few slabs of charred wood.

The iron thing had a tantalizing familiarity.

Then he knew what he must be seeing. Using his pike as a staff, he descended the steps into the crypt.

'It was the remains of Kilian's small oaken storage cabinet, sire. The one I had discovered in his sanctum, bound with iron bands and fitted with the peculiar lock that almost defeated my attempt to pick it. Its doors – or what was left of them – were wide open.' He reached into his belt-wallet and placed a discolored metal mechanism on the king's desk. 'I found this in the dirty water down around the tombs. But there was no trace of the sigils that had been stored in that cabinet – more than a hundred of them – nor the small moonstone medallions that were fastened to the covers of the two large books that I left behind with the sigils.'

Conrig took up the lock and turned it slowly in his hands. 'Someone knew how to work it,' Snudge said. 'It's undamaged. And open.'

The draperies of the study windows were drawn against the grey twilight and the wrenching sight of the ruined library and cloister wing across the quadrangle gardens. It was around the tenth hour after noon and still raining steadily, although the thunder and lightning had passed.

'So now we are certain,' the king said. 'The trove is gone. Stolen.'

'I fear so, sire. I learned some time ago that the two ancient books were transcribed in the Salkan language. Like the smaller one that I took away, they contained pictures of different sigils. I can only presume that the books held expanded descriptions of their varied uses, along with spells of activation.'

'Including that of your own Concealer sigil that was . . . lost during the assault on Mallmouth Bridge?' The Sovereign's tone was dry.

'I never noticed, sire. Since the larger books were illegible to me, I paid them scant attention. Concealer was certainly depicted in the smaller book, which had much of its content written in an old version of our own tongue. That's why I stole it. But Concealer's activating spell, like all others in the little book, was written in Salkan. And I must emphasize that correct pronunciation is absolutely critical for bringing a sigil to life. I was told by Beynor himself that saying the words wrong would anger the Beaconfolk and cause them to kill me. So he pretended to coach me – while actually plotting my death. Lord Stergos and I believe that Kilian also knew the peril of mispronouncing the spells. This was why he formed an alliance with the Crown Prince of Moss and agreed to share the stones, in exchange for Beynor's expertise in the Salkan language. The Glaumerie Guild knows how to bring sigils to life, and Beynor belongs to the Guild, as do all members of Moss's Royal Family. Kilian evidently had no suspicion that there might be another, simpler way to activate sigils – merely by touching them to the moonstone disks mounted on the book covers.'

'You never told me that.' Conrig looked at Snudge narrowly,

For good reason, Snudge thought. There was more to the brief activation process as well, which he would never divulge to the king. 'It slipped my mind, sire. And of course I was forced to give the little book to Ansel Pikan shortly after I took it.'

'God only knows what *he* might have done with it! You and Stergos were both fools not to have kept it safe.'

Snudge said nothing. The Royal Alchymist would have destroyed both the book and the Concealer if he had been able to. He believed their magic to be inherently evil and corrupting to the user. Belatedly, Snudge had come to the same conclusion. For this reason he had hidden Concealer away after the Battle of Mallmouth Bridge, telling the king it was lost in the fray. He had not attempted to use it since.

Conrig's brief flash of anger vanished and he smiled. 'Ignore my ill temper. I fret about my poor brother. Although the leeches say he'll recover, he will carry terrible scars.'

'Then his sight was spared? I was afraid –'

'God be thanked, his vision is normal in spite of the burns

about his eyes.' Conrig poured amber malt liquor into his favorite cup, which was silver with a gold-lined bowl and a great amethyst set into the stem as a talisman against poison. 'Will you drink with me?'

'I thank you, sire.' Snudge took a crystal goblet from a sideboard and accepted a small amount of the spirits.

'Please be seated,' Conrig said. Both of them tasted the malt, which was smooth and fiery. 'I have a mission for you, one that will take you far from Cathra.' He held up his hand as Snudge attempted to speak. 'No, it has nothing to do with the pursuit of the thieves, although it may be possible for you to join the hunt for them as you journey north on this other matter. I already have three thousand men searching for the fugitives, and pictures of them provided by Vra-Edzal were transmitted by wind hours ago to every corner of Cathra. By tomorrow, the local adepts will have drawn up numbers of posters with images of the two rogue Brothers and nailed them up in every city and town.'

Snudge nodded and waited.

Conrig said, 'As for this special assignment: there is no other person I can entrust it to, for it involves a challenge to my own perilous secret.'

'Your talent.'

'Aye, my accursèd talent, that would deny me my Crown of Sovereignty –'

'And perhaps give it to Duke Feribor,' Snudge blurted, 'unless the Queen's Grace should be delivered of a normal-minded son.'

Conrig sighed. 'She carries a normal child, but it is a girl. Queen Ullanoth was kind enough to confirm this fact for me.'

Snudge lowered his eyes at the disappointing news.

'At yesterday's feast,' the king went on, 'the earl marshal told me of a very disturbing rumor that apparently circulates in north-western Tarn among the local fishermen. It popped up only recently, and its gist is that my first wife may still be alive.'

'Sire, that can't be!' Snudge exclaimed. 'I windsearched for Princess Maudrayne myself when she flung herself from the parapet at Eagleroost – and for months thereafter. The Brothers of Zeth also combined their talents to sweep the entire island for traces of her. So did the Conjure-Queen, using her Great Stone Subtle Loophole.'

'Ansel's sorcery probably could have concealed Maude from all of you with ease. Tarnian shamans are the most powerful natural talents in the world. Consider also the disturbing fact that her personal maid Rusgann Moorcock unaccountably vanished without a trace. The woman was devoted to Maude, as if she were her own sister . . . And there's worse, which I've never confided to you.' He took a deep pull of the malt liquor and hesitated.

'Your Grace?'

'Ah, shite,' muttered the king. 'You must know. Stergos and I found Maude's diary. In it, she wrote that she knew of my talent and would not hesitate to expose it if I persisted in my amorous attachment to the Conjure-Queen. She also wrote that she had told Ansel my secret. And the diary held still another surprise: Maude was pregnant with my child.'

'Great God! And yet she said naught to you!' Snudge was both baffled and horrified. 'She signed the bill of divorcement. And was willing to take her own life and that of the unborn babe . . .'

'A woman of fierce Tarnian passions. How we once loved one another, Snudge! But for six years it seemed she could not conceive, and the shame of it made her anxious and short-tempered. Meanwhile, I was absorbed in the struggle with my late father and the Privy Council, and had small time for the loving attentions that such a high-spirited woman demands of her mate.'

Snudge had only taken a few sips from his goblet, but he now downed a generous swig. A sense of foreboding had begun to grip his heart. He knew Conrig's terrible dilemma concerning Maude and the child – and feared what his own role might be in its resolution.

The king said, 'The Princess Dowager is capable of a hatred as deep as her love once was. If she lives, and if her child lives and is a son, he is my legitimate successor. He was conceived in wedlock. The divorce is irrelevant. Add to this Maude's knowledge of my talent –' He shook his head, tossed down the last of his drink, and refilled the cup.

Snudge said, 'You wish me to go to Tarn and find out the truth. But that may be impossible, if she's protected by Ansel's sorcery. Even though my windsearching talent is considerable, it has limitations that I'm only beginning to understand. I met Red Ansel Pikan and he's more powerful than I can ever hope to be. Furthermore, he's in league with some supernatural entity he calls his Source, who guides him like a puppet. We know so little of the shamans of Tarn, sire! They're said to be directly descended from the Green Men, who shared this island with other inhuman monsters before Bazekoy's conquest –'

'Anent that point, let me tell you something else you may not know!' the king hissed. 'Green blood also taints thee and me, Deveron Austrey – and every human being possessed of talent, for this is how our magical abilities were instilled in us!'

'Oh, sire –'

'But that matters naught. The only important thing is that you find Maude and her babe – if they do live – before their existence is revealed to the world. And when you find them, do what must be done to protect me and my Sovereignty from the danger they pose.'

Snudge held the king's gaze. 'You wish me to slay them.'

'I did not say that. If you're able to eliminate their threat in another way, then do so. You are my sworn man, Deveron Austrey. Do you accept this charge?'

Snudge set his unfinished drink on the polished wood of the royal desk and rose to his feet. 'I will carry it out as best I can, Your Grace.'

'That's no answer.' Conrig's voice was low and harsh.

'It's mine, sire.'

Their eyes remained locked, but the Sovereign of Blenholme was the one who finally blinked and looked away. 'I fear her more than Kilian and Beynor,' he whispered, 'more than Ullanoth, more than all the scheming rebels of Didion and Tarn and the Southern Shore combined.'

'I know. Let me see what I can do.'

Conrig sat still, staring at nothing. Then he gave a small start and seemed to pull himself together. When he spoke it was with his usual forcefulness. 'Tomorrow, seek out Parlian Beorbrook and tell him your mission. I trust the earl marshal absolutely – as must you, since he also knows of your talent. Ask his advice. He understands the barbarians of the north country better than any man in Cathra, since he and his family have defended our border against them for nearly three hundred years. He may be able to lend you guides from his troop of Mountain Swordsmen to assist your penetration of Tarn. Whatever else you need, you shall have.'

'I desire that my friend Sir Gavlok Whitfell may accompany me on this mission, along with our armigers and Vra-Mattis, my apprentice windvoice. Gavlok and Mattis, at least, must know at the outset that we seek Maude and her child. The squires can be kept in ignorance until we reach Tarn. Since Lord Stergos is too ill to receive windspeech from me or Mat, I recommend that Vra-Sulkorig, the Keeper of Arcana, relay messages in his place. He will also have to be taken into your confidence – at least partially.'

'Very well, but none of these people must ever know of *my* talent, even though we have to tell them about yours. The danger posed by a son of Maude to the Cathran succession is sufficient justification for your search.'

'I'll be prudent when reporting, sire.'

'As you make your way north, I also desire you to wind-search for the two thieves. Your natural ability along that line is probably greater than that of anyone else in Cathra.'

'But Cathra is a large nation,' Snudge protested, 'and we can't be sure which route the two outlaws have taken. If they head directly to Zeth Abbey and Kilian, I might have a chance of scrying them out. But perhaps they went in some other direction entirely, or even escaped in a ship. They might be under orders to hide the trove in some remote spot where Kilian will retrieve it later.'

'Let's hope not,' the king said, looking glumly into his cup.

'Your Grace, you must think about the wisdom of asking Queen Ullanoth for help. There's danger – but if she finds the two men with her Loophole, you can send pursuers straight to them. You don't have to tell her what the villains stole – only that they attempted to kill Lord Stergos. As soon as the trove is located, it must be destroyed. This is the only safe course. Lord Stergos knows it, and so do you. Inactive moonstones can be crushed without danger and rendered useless. We may presume that the book-medallions can be destroyed in a similar manner, and the pages burnt.'

Conrig groaned at the prospect, and Snudge knew that his niggling suspicions about the king were correct. He still toyed with the notion of using the things himself.

'I must think about what to do,' Conrig said. 'If Ulla somehow seizes the trove . . .'

'That's why the stones must be smashed and the books burnt, sire,' Snudge emphasized. 'To keep them from her, from Kilian, and from Beynor.'

'Yet I must be sure in my mind that I've made the right decision. I'll take one more day to think on it further, for I'm so weary now that my wits fail me. Leave here tomorrow at an early hour, but only after conferring with Earl Marshal Parlian. Travel to Tarn via the Great North Road and the Wold Road through Frost Pass. Break your first day's journey at Teme, and I will then tell you my decision about consulting Ullanoth. You may go now.'

Snudge bowed. 'Very well, sire.' He turned and started for the door.

'One final thing,' the king said. 'I know you told me that your Concealer sigil was lost. I'm also aware of your deep misgivings about moonstone magic. But if it should happen that your sigil were found . . . I'd be most grateful if you'd use it once again in my service.'

Snudge stiffened, but he refrained from turning back to meet the king's eyes. 'I doubt it will ever be found, Your Grace. But be assured I'll do everything in my power to carry out my duties faithfully.'

SIX

The darkness was not absolute. The outcroppings of frost mottling the cave walls had a faint glow, and the auras of the three visitors outlined their subtle bodies in dim colors that changed with the fluctuation of their emotions.

He himself was visible only by reflected light, a shapeless, eyeless hulk chained to the rocks with gemlike fetters of bright blue-glowing ice. His enemies had forced him to retain the Salka form he had assumed during the Old Conflict, since it was capable of physical suffering. And so he had suffered in both body and spirit for over a thousand years, while denied the sky.

But the foe could not take away his great oversight or his voice, which kept hope alive as one helper after another failed in strength or was struck down. These latest three souls were among the best he'd ever found. He'd cherished them specially and sustained their human fragility while they implemented his instructions. Because now, after what had seemed an interminable series of failures and setbacks, it seemed that there was a real chance he might finally succeed in severing the unnatural link between the Sky Realm and the groundlings.

Did you bring the small book?

'It's here.' Ansel drew the ancient volume from his belt-wallet and set it down on the rime-encrusted cavern floor. The disk of moonstone fastened to its crumbling leather cover was lifeless, but still capable of drawing down the power of the foe. 'There remain the two books hidden in Cala Palace, Rothbannon's transcription from the Salka archives, and the archival tablets themselves, sequestered in the vaults of the Dawntide Citadel.'

Thalassa Dru, have you brought contributions from the Green Men and the Worms of the Morass?

'I have only a few this time, unfortunately, and all of the lesser sort.' She emptied a pouch containing a dozen dead moonstone carvings onto the floor next to the book.

Still, this is a worthy effort. Every stone that is obliterated weakens the link . . . And you, my dear Dobnelu. What do you have?

'I have gleaned three minor stones from the sea. And this, which one of my friendly wolves discovered deep in the wilderness of the Stormlands and brought to me.' The hag tossed the lesser sigils onto the heap, but the fourth she held up before the featureless dark face of the One Denied the Sky. It was a small wand carved from pale stone, covered with minute lunar symbols. 'I've never seen one of these, Source, but I believe it to be a Destroyer, perhaps a relic of the Barren Lands phase of the Old Conflict.'

Ah! So it is! Blessings be upon you, Dobnelu, for ridding the world of one of the most evil of the Great Stones, and thus confounding the Pain-Eaters. My souls, you have all done very well. Now shield your eyes, while I unite with the Likeminded and dispose of these abominations.

The humans pressed their hands to their faces. A dazzling burst of light illuminated the enchained hulk of the One Denied the Sky for an instant. Then the cave was restored to its former state of tenebrous gloom. The book and the sigils were gone, as usually happened. But something else had occurred that caused the auras of the three humans to flare amber and sea-green with surprise.

'Your chains,' Ansel exclaimed.

The two women echoed him in a wondering chorus. 'Your chains!'

The blazing sapphire color of the transparent ice manacles pulsed and then slowly faded, as though the links were being filmed over with grime. After a moment the internal luminescence once again increased, but it was significantly duller than before.

'Their radiance diminishes,' Ansel breathed, hardly daring to believe it. Can it be that their strength also grows less?'

'Are you still tightly shackled?' Thalassa Dru asked.

The huge form shifted, straining at the links, but to no avail. *Alas, my souls. I'm held fast, as always.*

'But this must mean something,' Ansel said.

True. I think it's necessary that I consult immediately with the Likeminded about this strange occurrence. Forgive me, but we must forgo our usual hours of meditation and discussion. Perhaps when you come to me the next time, I'll know more . . . Dear souls, I thank you for once again enduring the ordeal of crossing. Now return to your own world.

'Farewell,' said Thalassa Dru, and vanished.

'Farewell,' said Dobnelu the sea-hag. But instead of disappearing, her fragile form staggered as if from a blow, and her aura flared violet and flame-red, betraying sudden fear. 'I cannot go back! The way is closed to me. Why? Source, what has happened?'

Ansel opened his arms to her and embraced her, while gazing at the Source with stunned disbelief. His own corona had dimmed and reddened.

The thing manacled by ice stirred, and its utterance was full of sorrow. *I did not see it happening! I was distracted. Oh, my poor dear Dobnelu! Your entranced body has died.*

The violet of her aura deepened and she spoke in a tremulous wail. 'While my subtle body remains alive . . . trapped
here in this netherworld beneath the icecap? Oh, heaven
help me! I didn't think such a thing was possible.'

'It isn't,' Ansel said. His face was now a raging furnace.
'Unless the death wasn't natural. Source! Have the Pain-
Eaters done this?'

No. Now I perceive the truth. Share my envisioning, souls.

'Good God – and the miserable maggot laughs about it!' The
High Shaman of Tarn held the old woman tighter, clenching
his teeth to forestall a volley of curses at their bad luck. His
fury burned, drowning the crone's emanation of stark terror.
'One of Blind Bozuk's damnable charms allowed this to happen,
Dobnelu. I saw the thing clearly, hanging about the stripling's
neck. Both Bozuk and the murderer will pay for this.'

'What will happen to me?' The hag moaned.

*Don't despair, dear soul. There is a remedy, although it will not
be easy to employ. Ansel, you must go to the steading as quickly as
possible – in your physical body, of course. This is not an occasion
for subtlety.*

'I left my boat anchored in the lee of Cape Wolf. It won't
take long for me to get to the fjord. But are Maude and the
child in danger as well?'

*Not from him . . . Go now. Bring the body-husk back to me, and
be very cautious during the crossing so that it is not lost.*

He nodded, released Dobnelu from his embrace, and
vanished.

She stood there forlornly. What remained of her aura was
so dull a purple as to be nearly brown. 'It seems colder. And
I suddenly feel very tired. May I be seated, Source?'

*Your vital energies are dwindling. It's to be expected – but in
order to protect you from true death, I must change you for awhile.
Don't be afraid. If all goes well, you'll awake later in your own
home, quite restored.*

'And if it goes badly, will I die?'

Don't think of that. Only come and touch me.

She cringed. 'You always forbade it before this.'

Now it's necessary. Come. Hold out your hand, close your eyes, and let me take care of you.

The dead-black tentacle with its glowing blue chains reached out to her. She lifted her bony old hand and squeezed her eyes tight shut.

With a faint ringing sound, a tiny emerald sphere no larger than a pea fell to the cavern floor.

The One Denied the Sky was alone again. He picked up the sphere with great care, turned about, and pressed it into the ice of the wall behind him. It sank in until it was deeply embedded, joining scores of other glimmering little objects, all of them shining hopefully green.

There is a remedy. If it works, you'll live. If it fails, you'll also live, my poor human soul.

But what a life.

The slow-witted youth named Vorgo Waterfall had sense enough to follow the sarcastic advice of the bitch-princess who had slain his father. He floundered back to shore, stripped himself naked, and lay on a flat rock in the midsummer sun, shuddering and blubbering, until the encroaching tide forced him to move further inland. After his blood warmed and his skin dried, he wrung out his woolen shirt and trews and put them back on. They weren't too uncomfortable. He still had his belt and his sheath-knife and the little charm-sack hung round his neck on a string. But nothing else – not even boots.

His father's body had boots. Maybe other things. It was awash now, rolling a little with the wavelets that had appeared along with a rising wind. The thought of touching a dead man made his flesh creep with superstitious fear, and for a long time he held back, watching the ravenous, noisy mob of birds that dived and pecked, dived and pecked.

Finally he ran at them through the shallows, throwing stones and yelling at the top of his lungs. Some of the birds flew away, but others attacked him with such viciousness that he was afraid they'd get his eyes. So he gave up, sobbing, and ducked his head in the water to wash away the filth they'd splattered on him, and the blood.

What am I going to do now? he asked himself. The lugger had long since gone away, its escape from the shoaly bay assisted by the rising tide. The bitch-princess hadn't even bothered rowing with the sweeps. She'd just hoisted the sail and jibed out through the reefs slicker'n eel slime!

Cursing monotonously, Vorgo Waterfall trudged along the shrinking beach. He knew he wasn't clever. Dad'd told him that often enough, sometimes with a curse and a smack on the ear. 'But you be a crafty one, Vorgo,' he'd also said. 'You got a nose for the main thing, like a cur pup. You can do lots worse than follow that nose o' yourn.'

Right now, his nose was leading him back the way the women and the boy had come, toward the sea-hag's steading. The tide was half-high, and in many places the going was hard, even dangerous, until he rounded the point and came to the fjord beach. There all he had to do was slog on. He tried to come up with a plan. Dad always had a plan. But now the bitch-princess who would have made them rich was gone. Only the sea-hag was left.

She was a witch, a very powerful one. All of the fishermen of the north-west shore knew that it was death to enter her fjord. But why should that be? He thought hard about it as he tramped and waded along. Why didn't she want visitors? Other magickers were glad to sell their potions and amulets and spell-dollies to orn'ry folk, but not old Dobnelu. Why?

Maybe she had gold hidden in her house!

He touched the bag of charms hanging at his throat. What was it they were supposed to do? Make him invisible once he entered the circle of magic stones? Fend off the sea-hag's sorcery? He couldn't recall. But the charms had to be strong, because Dad had paid a lot for them, and they were good only on Midsummer Eve.

So he had to get on with it. Find that gold!

He climbed the cliff path, crossed the meadow, and stopped at the boundary of stones – ordinary looking things with nothing special about them at all. He clutched the charms and held his breath as he stepped between them, but nothing happened.

Am I invisible now? he wondered. No way to tell. There was a tiny hut not far away, near the vegetable garden. He decided to start looking for the gold inside it. People often hid things under the floor of sheds.

When he pushed the door open he gave a yelp of fear and froze in his tracks. The sea-hag herself was in there, lying on a low cot! She didn't move but he could hear her raspy breathing. He was amazed at how small she was and how frail. The sorceress who'd terrorized the entire coast of Tarn was just a little old bag of bones dressed in a ragged robe!

Why, he could wring her neck like a chicken . . .

Vorgo bent over her and very carefully touched the hag's sunken cheek. She slept on, so he screwed up his courage and did it, and she never squirmed or cried out or even opened her eyes, but only ceased to breathe. He let go of her and lurched away. Sweat ran from his hair into his eyes and he was shivering in spite of the day's heat.

Dead! The awful sea-hag was dead, and her treasure was his for the taking. All he had to do was find it.

He searched inside the farmhouse for four hours.

But he found no gold, no money, no jewels, hardly anything

of value at all save a dented silver cup and a string of agate
beads and a finely wrought little dagger with a carnelian
pommel. Frustrated and furious, he kicked a wooden bucket
across the kitchen. Now what? He'd have to hunt more
carefully, try the byre and the hen coop and the backhouse.
But first he'd have something to eat from the well stocked
larder –

The outside door opened.

Standing there was a robust man of medium stature, clad
in a simple brown deerskin tunic and matching gartered
trews. He wore crossed baldrics with many small bulging
compartments, and on his breast was a massive pectoral of
gold inset with Tarnian opals. His hair and beard were as red
as fire-lilies and his deep-set black eyes glittered with unshed
tears.

'Did you do it?' he asked.

Vorgo had heard of him: all Tarn had, although few had
ever seen him face to face. This was Red Ansel Pikan, the
Grand Shaman, leader of nearly all the other magickers in
the sealords' realm, the most famous wizard of the northland. Too shocked to speak, the youth stood stock-still with
his mouth hanging open.

The shaman lifted a small baton of carved unicorn-ivory.
There was a soundless flash. Vorgo gave a despairing wail
and his legs folded under him. He knelt on the scrubbed
wooden floor with his hands clasped in entreaty. 'I didn't
kill her! I never did!'

He felt a frightful pang of agony in his right ear. He shrieked
and writhed as something small fell from his head, bounced
off his shoulder, and smashed into white shards on the floor.

Ansel's black eyes had grown enormous and they held no
pity. 'Tell me your name. Explain what you're doing here.
If you lie to me again, your *other* ear will freeze solid and
fall off. More lies will cost you your nose and your lips –'

'No!' Vorgo howled. 'I'll tell!' The sordid tale poured out, disorganized and half-coherent; but Ansel understood it well enough. Dobnelu's physical body had been casually slain by a half-wit, barely sixteen years of age for all his brawny build, corrupted by his venal father, hardly knowing right from wrong.

He sighed. 'So the princess and the maidservant and the boy sailed away in your boat?'

'Yes, my lord.' Vorgo hung his head and bawled. Strings of snot leaked from his nose.

Ansel's eyes lost their focus and he windsearched the sea south and east of Useless Bay. Found her almost at once, handily steering a fishing smack under a louring sky. What a woman! Rusgann and Dyfrig were with her in the cockpit. The maid was honing a long kitchen knife with an oilstone. Maude wore an even larger blade on her belt. They had tied up their skirts to simulate trousers, donned tattered oilskin jackets, and wrapped their heads in grubby kerchiefs.

They'd reach Northkeep in late tomorrow, with the wind light and fitful.

Here's a pretty mess, Ansel thought. I must take Dobnelu's body to the Source without delay. The tricky crossover is bound to take hours, and only the Three Icebound Sisters know how long I'll have to tarry in the cave once I do arrive. Meanwhile, Maude is giving me the slip as nicely as you please! I can't becalm her with the weather brewing up as it is, and I certainly can't capsize the boat with a windblast. So she'll take refuge with her brother Liscanor at the castle. And he'll use his resident windvoice to inform High Sealord Sernin of the news about Maude and her son – and a talented Sovereign sitting on Blenholme's throne. The gaff will be well and truly blown – and how will Conrig Wincantor survive to play his part in the New Conflict?

Shall I abandon Dobnelu and transport my subtle self to

Maude? I could subdue her and the others and sail their boat back to the steading. *But she might arrive at Northkeep before I finish the drumming ritual and am able to transport myself.*

Shall I carry on trying to save my friend and let the Source sort out the others? *He's not omnipotent. Once Maude lets Conrig's cat out of the bag, it's out to stay.*

God of the Heights and Depths! Is there any other way I can salvage this situation? *Why not bespeak Liscanor's wind-voice, scare him silly, and command him to keep his mental gob shut?*

'Workable!' Ansel Pikan exclaimed out loud.

'M-my lord?' the wretched youth mumbled. He sat slumped on his heels. A thin trickle of blood from his amputated ear stained the shoulder of his shirt.

Ansel had nearly forgotten the murderer's presence. Time to deal with him.

'Vorgo Waterfall, you have committed a grave sin by taking a human life and you must atone for it. You are young, however, and sadly lacking in brains. And as it happens, I can use you.'

'Me?' The dullard slowly lifted his head.

'You. I'm going to attempt to bring back the woman you slew. Restore her life. It may take a fairly long time. If she does return, I want her to find her house and her livestock just as she left them. So you will stay here and take care of them as if your own life depended upon it. *Because it does.* Do you understand me, Vorgo?'

'You're not gonna kill me?' Dawning hope.

'Not if you work hard. Can you do that?'

'Oh, yes, my lord!'

'I can't promise to let you go, even if the sea-hag lives. She's a very old woman and needs help to survive in this place. You'd have to stay with her until her natural death occurred. Natural, Vorgo! It could take years. After she passed on, I'd come and take you back to your people in Northkeep Port. What do you say? It won't be an easy life, and if you can't bear the thought of it, I'll just freeze you to death right now. You won't feel a thing.'

'No! No! Please, I'll do it. Anythin' you say.'

I'll have to spell every task out for him three times over, Ansel thought in resignation. But first, I'd better bespeak Liscanor's windvoice – and any other near to Northkeep.

'Stay here and beg God's forgiveness. I'll be back in a moment to tell you what to do.' The shaman stepped outside the door and closed it behind him.

Back in the kitchen, Vorgo wiped his eyes and nose with his sleeve. Only now did he truly understand his great good luck. He wasn't going to die! Instead, he'd feed ducks and herd goats and sheep and hoe the sea-hag's cabbages. It would be lots easier than gutting fish or mending nets. This house was much larger than the squalid cottage on the waterfront he'd shared with his evil-tempered father. Probably fewer rats, too. And the larder was crammed with food and barrels of homebrewed ale and jugs of malt. Not bad at all!

He'd worry about the sea-hag coming back to life later.

Meanwhile, there was still her treasure to hunt for . . .

The rain began late the next day when they were still a league out of port, and Maudrayne was glad of it. With no darkness to hide them, she had been concerned about being recognized. Lukort Waterfall's lugger *Scoter* would be familiar to every sailor and fishmonger in Northkeep, and she had wondered if it might be safer to moor it in some secluded spot, go ashore in the coracle, and push on to the castle by some roundabout route afoot.

The misty rain and the false dusk brought on by the low-hanging clouds made that unnecessary. Boldly, she steered straight for the castle's deep-water landing stage. A few other returning skippers hailed her, but she deflected their interest in the time-honored fashion of the trade by growling, 'No luck,' and adding a salty curse on fickle fish.

Torches burned on the castle landing. Two large schooners and a single tall fighting frigate, Liscanor's beloved *Gayora*, were tied up there, along with a score of smaller craft. For some reason, the slip where she'd always berthed her own sloop-rigged yacht in days gone by was empty, so she guided *Scoter* in with easy competence while Rusgann tossed the bow line to a boy who had been sitting on the dock, fishing, indifferent to the gentle rain. No one else was in sight. They were probably all celebrating the holiday.

'Can't tie that old tub up here,' the urchin said with a grimace of contempt. He was about ten years old, dressed in rags, with bare feet. He had already caught a pair of fat speckled rockfish. 'Sealord's guards be along to send you packin' afore I get 'er snubbed to a cleat.'

'Make that line fast!' Maudrayne commanded in a no-nonsense voice. She rummaged in Lukort's confiscated wallet and held up a silver penny. It was probably more money than he'd seen in a year. 'Then fetch the watch commander quick as you can, and this will be yours.'

'Aye, cap'n!' He obeyed, then ran away.

'Get Dyfrig,' she told the maid, and hopped onto the dock with the stern line to secure it. Her son had gone below to the boat's tiny cabin when the rain started, and now he emerged rubbing sleep from his eyes, staring up at the immense curtainwall and looming towers of Northkeep with something akin to fear.

'Where are we, Mama?' he said.

'This is the castle where I was born. Now it belongs to my dear brother, who is your Uncle Liscanor.' She released her bound-up skirts and stripped off the concealing headcloth. Her long auburn hair gleamed in the torchflame, spangled

instantly with tiny drops of rain. For a final touch, she pulled
the spectacular opal wedding necklace out of her dress and
arranged it on her bosom. Then she jumped back into the
boat.

'Now listen to me carefully, Dyfrig.' She crouched to meet
his eyes. 'We must once again play the game where you
pretend to be Rusgann's son. We do this because, for the
time being, I don't want anyone in the castle to know who
you are.'

'Not even Uncle Liscanor?'

'Not even him. I'll reveal our secret to him later, but probably not tonight.'

'All right, Mama.' Dyfrig looked at her askance. 'Are there
wicked men inside the castle, like Lukort and Vorgo?'

'None so evil as those two villains,' she reassured him,
hoping that she told the truth. 'Only men and women who
talk too much – who might carry tales about you if they
knew you were a crown prince. Without meaning to, they
might betray our great secret and put us in danger. So while
we're in the castle, you must call Rusgann "mama" and stay
close to her always. Try not to talk to me at all. The child of
a servant wouldn't do that. But if you must, call me "my
lady". Can you remember that?'

He smiled in a somber manner that was anything but child-
like. 'Yes, my lady.'

She kissed his forehead. 'Well done.'

'Here come the guards,' Rusgann muttered.

They heard the tramp of studded boots, along with the
excited cries of the dockboy.

Maudrayne leapt back onto the dock. Rusgann handed up
Dyfrig to her and followed more decorously.

'There they be, just like I said!' The dockboy came dancing
impatiently ahead of a squad of four guardsmen, then skidded
to a halt with his eyes like saucers. 'Mollyfock! They be

wimmen – and a wee brat!'

The sergeant, a grey-bearded veteran, strode up to Maudrayne with his hand on the hilt of his sword. 'Now then, what's all this? Who do you think you –' His mouth snapped shut like a trap. He stood silent, his gaze sweeping her from head to toe, before whispering, 'My lady Maude?'

Maudrayne nodded regally and smiled. 'So you remember me, Banjok. It's been many years since last we met, and so much has happened.'

The younger guards obviously had no notion who she was and stood well back, their expressions uncertain. That suited Maudrayne. She said to the sergeant, 'Please say no more at this time – especially not my name.' She pulled her oilskin jacket closed to conceal the necklace. 'Only take us to the sealord at once. I presume he is here?'

Banjok looked dazed. 'Yes. He's within, with Lady Fredalayne, presiding over the Solstice Day feast for the Line Captains and their families. It was moved to the great hall because of the rain. Please follow me.' He turned and marched off.

The urchin thrust himself forward, blocking Maudrayne's way. 'Hold on! My penny!'

She had to smile at his determination. 'What is your name?'

'Eselin. Some day I'll be a Line Captain and eat with the sealord!'

She handed the coin to him. 'It will happen, Eselin, if you make it happen.' Then she walked away into the rainy evening, trailed by Rusgann, Dyfrig, and the three silent guards.

Once they were inside the walls, Banjok dismissed his men, warning them to say nothing about the odd visitors if they valued their sword-hands. After the three retired to the guardroom inside the gatehouse, the sergeant led the women and the little prince into an antechamber called the Peace Room, just off the great hall. The dinner guests who came armed left their weapons and shields there, hung on wall pegs, according to the Tarnian custom. The place had a few padded benches but no other furniture.

Banjok locked the outer door that gave onto the corridor along the wall of the central keep. 'Wait here. It may be a short time before the sealord is able to leave the high table.' Banjok opened the heavy inner door and slipped quickly into the hall, from which loud sounds of music and conviviality emanated.

Rusgann sat Dyfrig on a bench, told him to stay there, and led her mistress to the opposite side of the chamber. 'Now let's be sure I understand what's going on here,' she hissed. 'Do you intend to tell your brother what's happened since your supposed death?'

'I'll say Red Ansel saved me from drowning, and brought me and my beloved maid to the sea-hag's steading to keep us safe from Conrig Wincantor, who wanted to put me under permanent house arrest in Cala so I wouldn't make trouble. I'll tell Liscanor that I know a terrible secret about Conrig that could cost him his Sovereignty, but I won't reveal what it is. Not yet.'

'Any more than you'd tell me,' Rusgann grumped. 'I suppose I was the pregnant one who delivered a boy-child.'

'Of course. Your hair is fair, like Dyfrig's. It'll work if you can keep people from questioning him. Pretend he's sick, or numbed by the ordeal of our escape.' Maudrayne shrugged out of the damp oilskin jacket and dropped it onto the stone floor. She took a comb from her belt-purse and began to work on her snarled hair.

'What do I say about the escape?' Rusgann asked. She retrieved the discarded oilskin and hung it on a peg, then took off her own.

'More or less the exact truth. I couldn't bear to live with the hag any longer. I planned to signal to a fisherman and bribe him to take us away. But Lukort Waterfall had already spotted me through his spyglass and come to kidnap me and hold me for ransom.'

'So we killed him, and left his son Vorgo to the sea-hag's mercies, and we sailed away, and here we are – bashed and bloodied, but safe!' Rusgann's plain face shone with unholy relish.

'Not really. There's still Ansel to worry about. I'll ask Liscanor to protect us from him, demand that we be allowed to stay here in Northkeep. But if Ansel wants to take me away, there's nothing my brother can do. He can't go up against the Grand Shaman of Tarn. He's a brave man, but he's afraid of Ansel. They all are.'

Rusgann put her finger to her lips. 'Keep your voice down. You'll frighten the boy.'

Dyfrig was leaning tiredly against the wall, looking very small in his oversized rainjacket. But his dark eyes were fixed on the women and he was doing his best to listen in.

'Sorcery!' Maudrayne's tone was full of loathing. 'What a curse it is! But how many people are willing to believe that? Not many, when magic can give you power over other persons, or secret knowledge that's even more valuable. Even Ansel's been corrupted by it! I thought he was my true friend, but all along he planned to use Dyfi and me in some bloody cosmic scheme.'

'Now, my lady, you don't know that for sure. You might be misjudging the man.'

'We'll find out when he walks straight through the locked gatehouse door of Northkeep.' Maudrayne gave an ugly little laugh. 'And I doubt we'll have long to wait. The sea-hag never stays entranced for longer than two days. She'll bespeak Ansel when she wakes up and finds us gone, and he'll know we went to Northkeep. Where else could we go?'

Rusgann frowned. "Twould be best if your brother put you aboard that fine big warship of his right away, and sent you to the High Sealord at Donorvale. Doesn't Lord Sernin have a passel of strong-minded wizards loyal to him? Would Ansel dare oppose all of them – and the Tarnian council of sealords as well?'

'I don't know.' Maudrayne was thoughtful. 'You're a wise woman, Rusgann. It's a plan worth considering. If I told Sernin the truth about Dyfrig . . .' And the greater truth about Conrig! 'I'll ask Liscanor to bid his windvoice bespeak Sernin at once.'

Maudrayne embraced the maid, then went to sit beside Dyfrig, trying to draw him close to her. He pushed her away. 'You shouldn't be doing that, my lady. I'm only a servant boy.'

Her face went white and she sprang to her feet. For the first time in months, she burst into tears.

Rusgann gathered her mistress into her arms and held her as she sobbed, and it was thus that Sealord Liscanor discovered them when he arrived a few minutes later.

She sipped from a cup of soothing bearberry tea and huddled near the peat fire Liscanor had kindled in the little south-tower sitting room, waiting for him to return with news of the windvoiced conference with Sernin Donorvale. Rain tapped on the small glazed window. The sky was almost black.

After a brief, emotional reunion with his long-lost sister in the Peace Room, Liscanor had summoned his wife, sworn her to secrecy, and entrusted Rusgann and Dyfrig to her care. Kind Lady Freda had tried to put Maudrayne to bed as well, but she refused to rest until she had conferred with her brother. The two of them slipped up a back stairway to the secluded little tower chamber where the sealord conducted

his private business. There she told him what she wanted
him to know. But over an hour had gone by since he left
her alone, and she was becoming very worried. What could
be taking so long?

When the door finally opened and she saw his face, she
knew it was nothing good.

'Come, sit here and tell me.' She poured him a cup of tea
from the steaming pot on the hob.

Liscanor Northkeep had the same bright auburn hair as
his sister, but otherwise they were unalike. She was beautiful and regal in demeanor, even in her torn and dirtied
peasant garb, while he had a body like a barrel, arms so
heavily muscled that they hunched his shoulders, and a
pitted, truffle-nosed face that was almost ogrish in its spectacular homeliness. Only his voice belied his unsightly
appearance: it was deep, resonant, and cultured.

'Maudie, my dear, there's magical mischief brewing,' he
said, shaking his head. 'My windvoice, Kalymor, told me he'd
been forbidden by the High Shaman to bespeak any message
of mine to anyone. I threatened him with a beating and then
with banishment, but he wouldn't budge. He said Red Ansel
would do worse to him if he disobeyed, and no other shaman
in the demesne of Northkeep would transmit messages for
me, either. They're to keep silence for a tennight!'

'I suppose it was to be expected,' Maudrayne said, resigned.

But Liscanor's sea-blue eyes glistened with triumph.
'There's more than one way to skin a hare, Sister! On the
outskirts of town lives a renegade hedge-wizard called Blind
Bozuk, who owes no allegiance to Ansel and his high-flown
kind. He sells love-philtres and fake talismans and other
rubbish to gullible souls, but he's also a genuine wind adept.'

'I know of him. He supplied Lukort Waterfall with charms
to counter the magical defenses of the sea-hag.'

'I rode out myself to this rogue's hovel and gave him ten

gold marks to bespeak a message to our Uncle Sernin. While I stood there, Bozuk contacted his great and good friend Yavenis, an outcast witch of Donorvale. She supposedly delivered my message to the High Sealord in person.'

'Supposedly,' Maude said. 'What was the message?'

'It was simple and discreet: "Come at once to Northkeep in your fastest ship, with your most trusted men."'

'Ah. Very good.' She ventured a smile.

'We'll set sail ourselves at once in my frigate *Gayora,* and rendezvous with Sernin on the high seas. Then you shall tell your two great secrets to both of us.'

'I think I must tell them to you now.' She had made the decision on the spur of the moment, prompted by a growing certainty that Ansel was going to intervene somehow, and she would never reach Donorvale. 'Someone must know, in case something happens to me . . . and to my dear little son.'

'Son!' Liscanor exclaimed. 'Great God, are you saying –'

'The fairhaired lad Dyfrig is not the child of my servant. He's mine – the first-born son of Conrig Wincantor and heir to the Sovereignty according to ancient Cathran law. Furthermore, this High King who has forced Tarn into vassalage reigns under false pretences. He is a man having arcane talent, ineligible to sit his throne.'

Liscanor stared at her in thunderstruck consternation, deprived of speech.

'My servant Rusgann is a witness to Dyfrig's birth. She and many others in Cala know I was a faithful wife who never cohabited with any man save my husband. Dyfrig is the very image of Conrig. The king's talent will be much harder to prove, since it is extremely meager and imperceptible to the usual methods of detection. My own testimony would not suffice, and the Conjure-Queen of Moss, who also knows about it, may refuse to speak. But I suspect that Lord Stergos, Conrig's Royal Alchymist and his brother, must know the truth as well. He is a man of scrupulous honor, who would keep Conrig's secret only passively, by not volunteering the information. If he were put under solemn oath and questioned, he would not lie.'

The stalwart sealord's face was ashen and he was wringing his hands like a woebegone maiden. 'Oh, Maudie, this is awful news indeed! I hardly know what to say! I'm only a simple northcoast sea-dog and these are state secrets of the most devastating kind –'

'Guard them with your life, then. But never hesitate to reveal them to Uncle Sernin and the Company of Equals if I cannot.' She rose from her seat. 'Now we must leave Northkeep without delay. There's more than Ansel to be concerned about. That villain Lukort Waterfall was probably planning to sell me to Conrig Wincantor. Who can say whether he told the magicker Blind Bozuk about me when he purchased charms from him?'

Liscanor looked guilty and ashamed. 'God help us if I've placed you in danger, Sister. I never thought of such a thing when I went to the whoreson, thinking how clever I was. Forgive me!'

'Dear Liscanor, there's nothing to forgive.' She kissed his weather-roughened cheek. 'How long before we can sail?'

'Less than an hour. I've already given orders to prepare the ship. Her officers were all here at the feast, and her crew resides in town.'

'Then let's fetch my son and my servant, and get on board without further delay.'

It was after midnight when they left the castle and went on foot to the berth where the frigate was tied up. Seamen and housecarls in castle livery were still carrying chests and kegs of supplies aboard, and dozens of shadowy shapes were moving on the upper decks and in the rigging. Rain slanted sharply down, blown by a chill wind. It was very dark.

Liscanor went to confer with the officer who stood at the foot of the gangplank, then quickly returned. 'I'm told that the cabin being prepared for the three of you is not quite ready,' he said. 'I must go aboard *Gayora* and do a final tour of inspection. It's no place for you, with men rushing about on last-minute ship's business. Why not wait in that covered area, beside the large warehouse nigh to the curtainwall? It's dry there, and the torches give plenty of light. I'll send one of the ship's boys for you as soon as I can.'

He went off, cloak flapping like the wings of a very stout bat, and Maudrayne and Rusgann moved over the wet cobblestones into the sheltered place. The maidservant carried Dyfrig's well-wrapped body over her shoulder.

'He still sleeps?' Maudrayne asked, lifting her son's hood.

'Never woke, even when I dressed him in the new clothes Lady Freda gave us. He was too sleepy to eat much, and so was I. Can't say I'm happy to set out to sea again on such a raw night, but it's for the best.'

'I hope so . . . Solstice Day is over. Such a terrible, eventful day! And no sooner do we reach a place of safety, than we must leave it.' Her eyes roamed over the other vessels and small craft tied up at adjacent slips. 'Lukort Waterfall's boat *Scoter* is gone. My brother must have had it moved across the harbor basin to the fishermen's wharf to divert suspicion. Still, numbers of people must have seen us bring her in besides the dockboy Eselin. One of them might have talked about us to Blind Bozuk, even if Lukort didn't.'

'You've got no good reason to think Lukort told the magicker about us,' Rusgann said crossly. 'Stop worrying.'

'Perhaps the hedge-wizard wouldn't sell Lukort the special charms unless he told why he wanted them. Sneaking into the sea-hag's steading is hardly the usual thief's job-of-work! Information about me would bring a pretty sum from

Conrig's Tarnian spies. You could trust a person like Bozuk to know who they are.'

'We'll be away from here soon, my lady. Then Bozuk's tittle-tattle won't be worth two groats in a dungheap.'

The sound of clopping hooves echoed among the warehouses, almost drowned out by the increasing noise from the ship. 'Someone's coming,' Maudrayne said. 'There. A covered wagon drawn by two mules. Perhaps it's the last batch of supplies that my brother's been waiting for.'

They watched the wagon's approach without curiosity. Then a small figure came rushing down the ship's gangplank and trotted toward them across the wet pavement.

Rusgann heaved a sigh of satisfaction. 'About time! Here's the ship's boy.'

He was about twelve years old, clad in oilskins, and bowed smartly from the waist. 'My ladies! Sealord Liscanor bids you kindly come aboard, for we cast off immediately.'

The muleteer had drawn up a few ells away, and after setting the brake on his rig, climbed down and approached them with a casual wave of his hand. He wore a waterproof hooded longcoat slit up the back, and all that could be seen of his face was teeth gleaming in a wide grin.

'What do you want, my man?' Maudrayne asked irritably when he blocked their way to the ship. 'We have no time for you.'

'Maudie, Maudie. You have all the time in the world.'

She opened her mouth to scream for help, but no sound emerged. In fact, she was frozen to the spot in mid-gape, like some ridiculous statue. Rusgann and the ship's boy were similarly immobilized.

Red Ansel Piken lifted Dyfrig from Rusgann's unresisting arms, carried him to the covered wagon, and stowed him inside.

No, Maudrayne thought. No, no, no. Not after we have

come so far and endured so much!

The huge castle and the rainswept dock with its flaming torches seemed to fade to a foggy blur as tears of rage and helplessness filled her eyes. She strained to cry out as Ansel returned and led Rusgann away, docile as a sheep, and assisted her into the wagon. Maudrayne was powerless against the shaman's sorcery just as she'd always been. He'd do whatever he wanted with them. Use her and poor little Dyfrig any way he chose.

He came to her and took her arm, and she was able to walk but could not speak. Across the gleaming stones, up a short ladder, and into the back of the wagon she went. It was filled with straw and numbers of bundles. Rusgann and Dyfrig lay covered with blankets, apparently asleep. Ansel soon had her bedded down as well, then closed the tailgate, put the ladder inside, and laced shut the canvas cover.

He returned to the paralyzed ship's boy, who was still poised in an attitude of confusion. At Ansel's touch, the lad looked about wildly. Only gibberish came from his mouth.

'Your power of speech will return once you're back on the ship,' the shaman said. 'You're to tell Lord Liscanor that the two women and the child are safe aboard in their cabin. You'll remember nothing at all of me or what happened here. Now go.'

Ansel went back to the wagon and climbed into the driver's seat. After arranging his coat to keep the worst of the rain off, he released the brake, cracked the whip over the mules, and set off for the road that led east, away from the sea and into the Stormland wilderness of Tarn.

SEVEN

'Arise, Kilian Blackhorse. Arise and don your robes. By order of Abbas Noachil, you must leave this chamber and accompany us to a more secure accommodation.'

His second dream of Beynor had hardly faded, and he woke with difficulty. Someone was shaking his arm. He opened his eyes and saw the forbidding face of Vra-Ligorn, the Hebdomader or superintendent of discipline at Zeth Abbey. He was at first unable to stir, as sometimes happens when one is roused from deep sleep. Then the blankets were stripped away and he was hoisted to his feet. Two husky Brother Caretakers manhandled him into his clothes. Two more held heavy staves and lighted lanterns, even though they had opened the opaque drapes to allow the early morning twilight of Solstice Day to enter his bedroom. The caretakers of the Order of Zeth wore brown robes. Although they possessed talent, it was too weak to generate important magic, so they devoted themselves to serving the ordained Brethren through manual labor or domestic duties.

Kilian found his voice at last. 'Vra-Ligorn, where are you taking me?'

'To a cell on the sump-pit level, my lord. And you must submit to being chained while we convey you there.'

The last remnants of sleep evaporated in a burst of dismay as Kilian finally realized what was happening to him. The comfortable little apartment where he had lived for four years under open detention was to be exchanged for a window-less dungeon.

'Does Prior Waringlow know of this – this highly eccentric order?' he protested. 'You know how ill Father Abbas has been. At times he even shows symptoms of dementia. I can't believe he was in his right mind when he issued this order. I've done nothing to provoke such punishment –'

'Abbas Noachil is as rational as you or I,' the Hebdomader said without emotion. 'The command for your close confinement came directly from High King Conrig, via the Royal Alchymist, Lord Stergos. There's no mistake.'

'I see.' He extended his wrists for the fetters, and said not another word as they conveyed him into the bowels of the abbey, down to the third basement, where the drains from the upper floors debouched into an evil-smelling underground watercourse. There were only a handful of dismal cells down there, reserved for the most heinous sinners. Usually, no prisoner remained there long before being handed over to the secular authorities for execution.

Is this to be my fate, he wondered, only hours from the coup that was to have liberated Darasilo's Trove, set me free, and restored my lost powers? What could have happened to make Conrig do such a thing? Had Vitubio, Felmar, and Scarth revealed their intentions through some blunder? Has my nephew Feribor implicated me in his political intrigues? Or – worst thought! – is Beynor responsible for this, playing some treacherous double game in hopes of eliminating me before I can take possession of the trove?

'In here, if you please, my lord.'

They had reached the dungeon. Vra-Ligorn unlocked a cubicle carved from solid rock that was hardly two ells wide and three ells long, and motioned for him to enter. As a wearer of the iron gammadion of shame, stripped of every talent and privilege of the Mystical Order, Kilian was no longer honored with the title of Brother or Vra. But no one could deny his noble Blackhorse blood, and so his gaolers had called him 'my lord' during his period of detention – albeit with an ironic inflection.

The cell door clanged shut behind him. It was iron, with a rotary hopper through which food and other items might be passed and an observation slot covered with metal mesh. Dim light from the corridor illuminated a narrow cot and a heap of blankets, a large covered water-jar, and a tiny table that held a pottery basin with a block of soap and two rough towels. A wooden stool stood beside the table.

'Father Abbas has graciously consented to leave a lighted lantern outside your cell,' Ligorn said, 'so you and your fellow-inmates need not suffer the added privation of utter darkness. Your meals will also be as usual – not bread and water – and you have warm bedding.'

Fellow inmates?

'How long must I remain here?' Kilian asked.

'Until it pleases Father Abbas to release you. If you are well-behaved, you will be given books to read and candles later. There is a latrine beneath the stone lid in the cell's far corner, and a box of green leaves for your comfort. If you urgently require anything else, inform the Brothers who will bring your breakfast.'

The Hebdomader and the others went away then, and Kilian called out softly through the door-slot, 'Who else is here?'

'Niavar.'

'Raldo.'

'Cleaton.'

So the three close associates who had been convicted of treason along with him were also imprisoned. But clever young Vra-Garon Curtling, who had joined Kilian's cause hoping to escape his vow of celibacy, was evidently still free. More importantly, so was Prior Waringlow . . .

'My poor comrades,' he said. 'I fear that King Conrig has roused Father Abbas's suspicions of us. Our mutual friend may find it more difficult to aid our escape, but I'm confident that he'll still find a way to carry out the plan.'

'Master, something must have gone seriously awry down in Cala,' said Niavar. He had been Kilian's principal deputy and Keeper of Arcana. Diminutive stature and an eyeball that wandered grotesquely around in its socket had made him an object of ridicule when they were both novices; but the handsome, imposing Kilian had unaccountably befriended clever little Niavar and thus earned his undying loyalty. 'I warned you not to trust Vra-Vitubio. The man was eager, but too slow-thinking to be reliable. It's possible that his clumsiness has undone us all.'

'We're finished!' Raldo's voice was shrill with terror. He had been the Palace Novicemaster, a stout, deceptively jolly-faced man notorious for savagely punishing the slightest infraction of the Rule. 'Conrig has discovered everything and we're dead men!'

'Nonsense,' said Kilian.

But Raldo persisted. 'Master, you'll only have your head chopped off because you're noble. But we commoners will be hanged, cut down alive, drawn, and quartered. Oh, I can't bear the thought of it. My poor entrails hacked out and held up dripping before my eyes . . . my limbs severed while I'm still conscious!'

'Be silent, you silly bag of guts,' growled Cleaton. He was a burly man with a swarthy, pinched countenance who didn't suffer fools gladly, the former Hebdomader of the Palace

Brethren. 'You only make things worse with your futile imag-
inings. We can't be sure that we've been condemned. Vra-
Ligorn didn't say so. In fact, he sounded almost apologetic
when he locked us up. Why would he be so solicitous of our
comfort if we're going to die? He's hardly known as a font
of kindliness. No – mark my words, there's something odd
going on. Ligorn's caught in the middle, and he wants to
save his arse by obeying old Noachil at the same time that
he preserves Lord Kilian and us from the worst hardships of
this putrid hell-hole.'

Until the downfall of their master, the trio had enjoyed high
positions at Cala Palace, where courtiers, servants, and the
younger Brothers forced to endure their petty tyranny had
dubbed them Squinty, Butterball, and Vinegar-Face. They had
not endured their captivity well. Being stripped of magical
power and authority had turned Niavar sullen and Cleaton
quarrelsome, while Raldo had grown morose and added
another eight stone to his already considerable weight. There
were times when Kilian regretted having included the three of
them in his escape plans. But they were his oldest friends in
the Order, who had served him faithfully for nearly thirty years.

And two of them, at least, might still play useful roles in
the adventure to come.

'I urge you not to lose heart, Raldo,' he said. 'Cleaton is
quite right. We have no solid reason to believe that we're
compromised. If the king had certain knowledge of our
conspiracy, he would have taken much more drastic action
against us.'

'But why else would he suddenly command that we be
shut up in a dungeon?' the fat man asked querulously. 'The
smell of this awful place! I nearly swooned away when we
first arrived.'

Someone gave a snort of derision.

Kilian responded with patience. 'Whatever King Conrig's

reason, it likely has nothing at all to do with our plan of escape. Now listen to me, comrades: at this very moment, our friend Vra-Garon is on his way back to the abbey from Elkhaven, on the great lake. While there on an errand for the abbas, he collected horses and lay clothing for us at Ironside Manor, the home of Lady Sovanna, who is a close friend to my sister, the Queen Mother. What Garon doesn't know is that the lady also holds in safekeeping for me a large sum of money, which will finance our flight to Didion.'

'You told us that Queen Cataldis had balked at sending the gold,' Niavar said. 'What made her change her mind?'

'I sent a secret letter to Duke Feribor, my nephew, who foolishly expects me to help him become High King. He has his own special methods of persuasion.'

'I hear he used them to excess on his late wife,' Cleaton said with heavy sarcasm.

Kilian said, 'The money will be sufficient to pay for everything we need on our journey, with plenty left over to bribe Somarus of Didion, who has agreed to put us under his protection.'

'The rebel prince?' Niavar was hesitant. 'Master, he and his followers are little more than a ragtag gang of brigands!'

'So Conrig and Honigalus would have everyone believe. But things are not always what they seem. Somarus has a wide base of support among the barons of that kingdom's remote hinterlands, who give only lip-service to the Sovereignty and consider King Honigalus a craven traitor for having submitted to vassalage. If Honigalus and his heirs were eliminated, Somarus would inherit Didion's throne. And a person who was in a position to . . . assist the new king in a significant manner would share his power.'

'Do you speak of yourself, Lord Kilian?' Cleaton asked. 'And is the elimination of Didion's royal family mere wishful thinking, or something more?'

Kilian did not reply to the questions. 'After we escape from the abbey, we'll ride directly to Elkhaven. It will be arranged so that no one notices that we're missing for many hours. Vra-Garon has hired a cattle-transport boat and crew to carry us and our horses north to Roaring Gorge, at the head of the great lake. About thirteen leagues up the gorge is a cave that almost no one knows about. There we'll take shelter, and wait for certain companions who'll travel with us over the Sinistral Range. We will follow tracks known only to shepherds – and to Vra-Garon, who spent his boyhood in the border highlands. Eventually we'll come to the Lady Lakes region of the Elderwold, where we'll join Prince Somarus and his men.'

Raldo said, 'Master, I always presumed that Great Pass was the only safe way to cross the Sinistrals.'

'It's the first place Conrig's troops would look for us.'

'Riding through high mountains on backcountry tracks sounds very difficult and dangerous,' Raldo protested. His high-pitched voice trembled with anxiety. 'And the Elderwold is said to be full of fierce creatures and Green Men! Who will cook our food and care for the horses? Where are we to spend the nights? I don't think I could bear sleeping on the ground.'

'Bazekoy's Burning Brisket!' growled Niavar. 'Stay here in the dungeon, then, Butterball, and enjoy the food and warm bed. After a few weeks, you won't even notice the stench.'

'Master, it won't just be soldiers hunting us.' Dour Cleaton was deadly serious. 'You said we'd have magic to shield us from windsearchers. But how –'

'And so we will. The person who will release us from this prison has promised to unlock our iron gammadions as well.'

Niavar and Cleaton uttered oaths. Raldo quavered, 'My talents? I'll have my talents back?'

'Only those we were born with,' Kilian said, 'not the additional powers we gained when we were ordained. The combined magic of the four of us should be sufficient to defend us from ordinary pursuers and all but the most powerful wind adepts. And I have conceived a new cover-spell of peculiar efficacy, which I shall erect over us as soon as my talent recovers from the years of disuse.'

'Who in God's name is this collaborator within the abbey?' Niavar asked. 'And why is he willing to break his vows to Saint Zeth and commit treason against the Sovereignty in order to help us?'

'He helps *me*,' Kilian said, 'because he expects a reward. That's all you need to know.'

'Part of the Cala treasure?' Raldo suggested archly. None of them knew the nature of the Trove of Darasilo, but they all were aware that Kilian had sent agents to the capital months earlier to steal something of consummate value.

'Be silent, fool!' Niavar said. 'Have you forgotten that the master ordered us never to speak of that?'

Ignoring Raldo's mumbled apology, Kilian continued. 'I must try to sleep now, in case there is another dream-message from Beynor of Moss. If you find yourselves unable to close your eyes, I suggest that you spend the time praying for bad weather. While clear skies persist, we cannot escape. We need clouds and rain to conceal our getaway from ordinary human eyesight, since we have no true darkness at this time of year.'

'It's Blossom Moon,' Cleaton pointed out. 'The weather may remain clement for weeks.'

'I think not,' Kilian said. 'I was allowed to work in the herb garden yesterday, and I noted a ring around the sun. This often presages a change. There could be a storm on the way.' He paused, then added softly, 'A very great storm indeed.'

He went to the cot, arranged the ample bedding, and lay atop it fully clothed. But his brain was a beehive of swirling thoughts that he could not repress, no matter how hard he tried, and he remained wakeful until the tolling

of a far distant bell marked the hour of rising in the abbey
above.

To his surprise, Beynor knew about the attack on Cala Palace
as soon as it happened.

Kilian had told him that the assault and theft were scheduled for the quiet hours around seven or eight in the morning
on Solstice Day, but he never anticipated any personal
perception of the event. Cocooned in a sleeping-sack, he lay
in apathetic misery beneath the small boat's canvas dodger,
a kind of half-awning which only gave scant protection from
the flying spray, enduring the slam-bang progress of the craft
over the rough Boreal Sea. The team of monsters towing
him insisted on swimming at top speed, and he would have
been flung overboard by the constant severe jouncing if he
hadn't taken special care to wedge himself between a padded
thwart and the oilskin supply bags crammed in the bow.

Beynor was ordinarily an intrepid sailor; but on this
appalling voyage, withdrawing into the windworld was the
only way he'd been able to avoid mortal seasickness. It was
quiet and tranquil on the black bosom of the wind, except
for the inconsequential mental yammering of the Salka, which
was easy enough to ignore if he didn't try to translate it. He'd
almost managed to drift into uneasy slumber when a mental
shriek pierced his cranium like a red-hot needle.

He gasped, sat up, and made a muzzy attempt to track the
chaotic tangle of voice-threads. It emanated out of the south.
He knew after a few minutes what it must signify.

The silent clamor was perceptible to him, but evidently
not to the dull-witted Salka, who swam on unconcerned.
Wild with curiosity, Beynor tried to scry Cala Palace. But the
distance was too extreme, nor was he able to make any sense
of the wind-shout itself. Nevertheless, he had no doubt that
it was a reaction to the attack by Kilian's agents.

Had they successfully made off with Darasilo's Trove? There was no way for him to find out without bespeaking them, and no way to do that without knowing their individual signatures and the password that Kilian had refused to entrust to him.

Curse the bloody secretive alchymist! Beynor decided to re-invade his dreams and demand the information yet again. Both of them needed to know what was happening.

He concentrated in the usual way, calling Kilian's name over and over, but there was no answer. The bastard was probably awake.

Beynor attempted to envision Zeth Abbey with his windsight and was rewarded with a ghostly mental picture of the fortresslike structure. Built of pure white limestone, it was perched high among the crags of the southern Sinistral Mountains. There were certainly loud strands of windspeech being exchanged between its inhabitants and persons in Cala Palace. Beynor could not understand the messages, but it seemed likely that the Brothers in Cala were bespeaking tidings of the disaster to their fellows at the abbey.

Someone was bound to tell Kilian what had happened. But he, Beynor, would be kept in suspense for hours, until the next time the alchymist went to sleep! He ground his teeth in frustration.

Just then, a disquieting thought sprang into his mind, and with great care he sent another probe winging in a new direction, towards the kingdom of Moss, Fenguard Castle, and the chambers of his sister Ullanoth. Was it possible that she'd also perceived the wind-scream from Cala? Might she be observing the scene with her Subtle Loophole?

The refurbished old stronghold was much closer than Zeth Abbey and clearly visible to his scrying, but Ulla's private rooms were not. Even though she no longer owned a Fortress sigil, a heavy spell of couverture shielded her quarters from his mind's eye. The good news was that no betraying trace of the Great Stone's sorcery shone out through the concealing opacity. Ulla was not using Loophole to oversee Cala Palace or anything else. It was quite likely that she had failed to hear the outcry.

He maintained his watch on Fenguard for another hour or so without detecting any unusual arcane activity. The wind-senses of the Glaumerie Guild members were not as keen as his own, and they remained oblivious. None of them seemed interested in observing Cala, and none of Conrig's windvoices attempted to communicate with the Conjure-Queen. Thus far, the thieves fleeing with the trove would seem to be safe from Loophole's invincible oversight. And if Kilian was right about Conrig's distrust of Ulla, they'd stay that way.

At this minute, the precious books and the sigils were probably being spirited out of the ruins of the palace's cloister wing by the agents. Before long, the trove would be on its way north. By day's end, the well-disguised thieves might be almost halfway to the designated rendezvous in the north country, taking advantage of the initial confusion as Kilian had planned. Beynor himself would be within easy wind-searching range of the fleeing agents before another day went by – not that such a search was practical. Without knowledge of their signatures, or at least their names and physical appearance, he had little chance of scrying them out.

Names and physical appearance . . .

A half-formed idea crept into his mind, and he drew in his breath sharply, hardly able to acknowledge that such a thing might be possible. It seemed almost too fortuitous, too perfect.

If Conrig's officials were efficient in organizing pursuit of the agents, they might unwittingly give Beynor his chance to secure the trove for himself before the thieves could hand it over to Kilian. The alchymist had rightly feared that Beynor might try to waylay his men and seize the sigils and books; but the revised plan that now suggested itself to the deposed young king was far more ingenious than a simple ambush.

All I need do, Beynor thought, is find them with my mind's eye. There was no need to confront the men physically or even have a wind-conversation with them. If they simply listened to a certain irresistible temptation insinuated anonymously into their dreams, and succumbed to it, the trove would be his!

And the temptation *would* be irresistible.

The site of the allurement would have to be chosen with care. It must be a lonely spot, where no one was likely to stumble upon the abandoned books and sigils before he retrieved them.

Kilian was no problem. Even if his windpowers were somehow restored, he'd be unable to scry out the unscriable. No adept could oversee magical moonstones. They were secure from the windsight of every sorcerer save Ullanoth and her Subtle Loophole, and she had no reason to go looking for them because she didn't know they existed.

Such a simple plan . . . He wondered why it hadn't occurred to him before. He'd wait a few hours, until Conrig's officials recovered from the initial shock of the conflagration and organized the pursuit of the fire-raisers. Images of the suspects with their names would surely be transmitted by palace alchymists to every reliable wind adept and wizard in the southern part of the Sovereignty. The magickers would be commanded to draw up reward notices carrying the pictures and post them in all the principal towns of Cathra and Didion.

What Beynor had to do was scry one of those notices – trickier than it might seem – or find some person willing to do the job for him. Unfortunately, he had few loyal friends left, and most of them lived in Moss, too far away to be of use.

It came to him.

There *was* someone he could bespeak, someone who would – by the end of the day, if not before – have obtained a full description of the awful events that had taken place down in Cala. One who would probably also know whether those responsible for the conflagration had been identified, and how the hunt for them was progressing. The man he was minded to bespeak was by no means completely trustworthy, but neither was he a friend to the Sovereign of Blenholme. He'd probably tell the truth, as he knew it, especially if Beynor passed on useful information of his own in exchange.

All I need do is wait, he thought, until matters in the south have stabilized a bit, and Queen Risalla's wizards have transmitted details of the disaster to their colleagues in Holt Mallburn.

The choppy waves had subsided a little, and Beynor finally dozed off in spite of himself. His dream was a familiar one – frightening to begin with, as the small boy found himself trapped on the broad flats of the Darkling River with the oncoming tide racing toward him. The dream turned even more terrifying when the red-eyed monsters appeared, surging up out of a deep-water channel to seize him while he screamed.

Then the dream became amazing and joyous as he realized that the fearsome creatures were *rescuing* him! The reclusive Salka of the Little Fen had for some reason taken pity on the doomed small human. In time they would befriend him, teach him their language, and open his mind to the world of the wind and the potential of the magical moonstones –

Beynor woke with a cry of pain. The speeding boat crashed and smacked over the waves with stunning violence, hurling him against the gunwale and dousing him with icy sea water. The pleasant dream was extinguished, leaving reality.

He began screaming furious curses at the amphibious brutes in the tow-harnesses, not stopping until Ugusawnn, the Supreme Warrior, compelled his companions to slow down.

The two brown-robed Brother Caretakers who brought breakfast to the prisoners could hardly stop talking about the disaster, even though they seemed to know few details aside from the obvious: the entire cloister wing of Cala Palace was burning fiercely, and the Royal Alchymist, Lord Stergos, had been so badly hurt that physicians feared for his life.

'But how could a fire take hold and spread in a place housing so many wind adepts?' Kilian asked. 'Surely their combined powers would have stopped the flames in their tracks.'

'It's said the incendiary agent was tarnblaze.' The older of the caretakers spoke in a tone freighted with dread. 'That stuff can't be quenched by talent, and it gives off great heat. I didn't talk to anyone at the palace myself, of course. My powers are too puny. But the Brother Cellarer was in the kitchen when we fetched your food, and he had windspeech with his opposite number down there, who said there were two great explosions inside the Alchymical Library. It had to be tarnblaze. And not simple firepots, either: steel bombshells!'

'How dreadful,' Kilian said. 'I shall pray for Lord Stergos, of course, but the loss of all those precious books is also devastating.'

'Books!' the second caretaker piped up. 'Nearly forgot, what with all the excitement.' He opened a lidded basket smaller than the ones that had held the food, took out several volumes and some candles, and began passing them through the door-hoppers to the prisoners. When he came to Kilian's cell he said, 'Prior Waringlow selected this book for you special, my lord. He hopes it'll help you pass the time. Just poke the candlewick through the wire mesh on this peep-slot and I'll get it burning for you.' Using a bit of straw, he transferred flame from the wall-lantern to Kilian's candle.

'Please tell Father Prior that I'm grateful for his kindness,' Kilian said. His cronies also murmured thanks as the other caretaker lit their candles.

'Is there aught else you need, my lord?' The older Brother added sheepishly, 'Save liberty, o'course.'

'We have no view of the outer world.' Kilian gave a sad sigh. 'Tell me – is this Solstice Day sunny and bright?'

'A bit overcast. What we countryfolk call buttermilk sky. There might be rain before the midnight chime.'

'Ah. Thank you, Brother.'

'We'll see you again at suppertime. Should be a fine meal. We're roasting six pigs and four fatted calves in honor of the holiday.' He and his companion gathered up the empty baskets and left the dungeon.

'Rain!' Cleaton exclaimed. 'Our prayers are answered.'

'So it would seem,' said Kilian. 'But no more talk. Let's eat our food before it gets any colder.'

The meal was an excellent one – breadrolls with a crock of honey-butter, boiled eggs, a cheese ramekin, and a squat jug of brown ale. But instead of following his own order, Kilian opened the book he had received and leafed through the pages. Almost immediately he found just what he expected.

Drawing the candle closer, he began to read the note from Prior Waringlow. When he finished he burned the bit of parchment, then ate with a hearty appetite.

The next time Beynor woke the sky was grey and the sea undulated with great slow rollers. He crawled out from under the dodger and saw the dark hunched forms of the Salka surging through the water. Eight of them were linked to his boat and ten more functioned as outriders, leading the way toward a distant black peninsula with a tip like a gnarled finger pointing south. Beynor recognized the distinctive silhouette of Gribble Head. Beyond it was the entrance to Didion Bay, and at the bay's end was the mouth of the River Malle, and King Honigalus's capital city of Holt Mallburn.

His animal-skin garments were sodden and slimy, so he took time to shed them and don dry things from one of the sacks. Then he took the makings of a meal from another. Just as he'd been forced to improvise clothing during his stay with the monsters, he had also developed his own food supply. The Salka had plenty of seafood, but they invariably ate it raw. By trial and error, Beynor learned to cook and smoke fish and other marine edibles. He eked out his diet with the starchy tubers of the reedmace, boiled or baked, and small quantities of berries he could glean from the tundra surrounding the citadel. For seasoning he had sea-salt and an onionlike arctic plant with red flowers that the Salka called *cheev*. His only beverages were water and various herbal teas. Beynor's talent now heated up a flask of willow-winter-green tisane, which not only alleviated his chill but also took away the worst of his aches and pains. He ate a slab of smoked salmon and some of the bland roots. Then he settled himself comfortably and prepared to bespeak Fring Bulegosset, the Archwizard of Didion.

First Beynor scried him – a hunched, fleshy man with pallid features, whose dark-lashed blue eyes had a frankly sensuous gleam. He wore an elegant robe of black brocade and a matching skullcap. As Beynor watched he moved about a small alchymical laboratory gathering stoppered phials and small boxes, which he then packed carefully into a compartmented leather traveling bag. No doubt he was getting ready to accompany the royal family on its progress upriver tomorrow.

Fring was Didion's most powerful wind-talent – which wasn't saying much. That barbarian nation's finest adepts were half-baked dabblers compared to the top conjurers of Moss or Tarn. Even Cathra's Brothers of Zeth possessed more innate magical talent. But Fring was reasonably competent, and if rumors from Beynor's confidants in Moss could be believed, the Archwizard was also a political malcontent who secretly favored Somarus, the rebel brother of the Didionite king.

It was high time Beynor and Fring became reacquainted.

'Archwizard! Respond to one who knew you some years ago, and now wishes to share certain valuable information.'

Who's that? Good God – it's the failed boy-king, Beynor of Moss!

'To be sure – but now I'm a man of one-and-twenty, and preparing to mend my somewhat battered fortunes. Do you recall the last time we were in contact? You and Honigalus were aboard the flagship of Didion's warfleet, sailing south to attack Cathra while Conrig crept in through your back door and sacked Holt Mallburn.'

Of course I remember. You were Didion's staunch ally then. Honigalus bade you use your Weathermaker sigil to speed our vessels along to Cala Bay, while delaying the Tarnian mercenaries who were coming to the aid of Cathra. As I recall, you did a fine job of it. So fine that the huge storm you created sank the navies of Cathra and Didion without discrimination – to say nothing of the luckless Tarnians and a flock of Continental corsairs.

'It was my sister Ullanoth who unwittingly caused the storm, not I! And by good fortune, you survived. Less happily, so did Conrig . . . and Honigalus. If either man had perished, both our nations would have been spared vassalage.'

I am the loyal servant of the King of Didion. And of his liege lord, Conrig Wincantor.

'Of course you are. But how much happier we both would be if a stouter-hearted monarch ruled in Holt Mallburn. One who would never have signed the damned Edict of Sovereignty. You know who I mean! The information I wish to share with you concerns him. But if you aren't interested –'

I'm very interested in anything that might pertain to a certain brave prince, who is always in my prayers.

'I thought as much. I've learned something that may redound greatly to his advantage. And that of his good friends! But before I speak of it –

You want something in return.

'A mere trifle. As it happens, I'm curious about the conflagration that took place earlier today at Cala Palace. My windsight is insufficiently powerful to oversee it directly, just as your own is, but I hoped that wizards in Queen Risalla's entourage would have bespoken you concerning what happened. Were many people killed or injured?'

Why do you wish to know?

'I'll be frank with you, Fring. I hate Conrig Wincantor with every fiber of my being. He conspired with my sister to rob me of my throne. If he's suffered a great setback as a result of this disaster, I'll rejoice. What damage was done? Is it known who was responsible?'

Rejoice then. My sister's boy, who is an adept in service to Queen Risalla, told me that the library and the entire cloister wing of the palace were destroyed. The king's brother Stergos and some two dozen Zeth Brethren were injured. Six people were killed – including one man who may have helped start the fire.

'Who was he? Did he act alone?'

He was a Brother of Zeth, one Vitubio Bentland. It seems he and two other alchymical scholars came to the palace together, from Zeth Abbey, some months earlier. No one seems to know much about them yet. The two survivors have disappeared. There's a royal warrant for their arrest and a great hue and cry throughout Cathra and Didion, with a sizable reward for their capture. And here's a fascinating detail: the three used tarnblaze to blast open a secret crypt in the Royal Alchymist's bedroom. By now, half the palace has seen the hole with their own eyes. It's said that some treasure was stolen from there. No one in authority will admit that, but it would explain why the attack occurred in the first place. If someone merely wanted to kill Stergos, they could have found an easier way.

'And no one knows which way the surviving thieves went?'

If they were wise, they hopped on a fast boat and sailed away. Pictures of the pair are being circulated in all parts of Cathra. The roads leading from the capital are blocked, and every traveler is being questioned.

'I don't suppose your informant transmitted images of the fugitives?'

Hah! Now we come to it. He did indeed, and I etched them on vellum with my talent . . . for reasons of my own. If you wish to oversee the portraits, produce the valuable information you said you would share with me.

'Very well: under no circumstances should you accompany Honigalus and his family on the royal barge upriver. Become diplomatically ill. Say you will travel overland to catch them up when you feel better. See that you *don't* feel better until they approach Boarsden Castle, in six days.'

. . . What's going to happen?

'Nothing you would enjoy participating in.'

But – but I should give warning! The royal children –

'The one you should alert is Prince Somarus. Roust him out of his lair in the Elderwold wilderness. Tell him to trim his beard, pare his fingernails, and clean up himself and his drabble-tailed band of followers, so he appears approximately regal when he's unexpectly summoned by Duke Boarsden and the other high lords of Didion to take up the crown.'

Almighty God! How can you know –

'I do know. Now show me the picture of the two thieves, and give me their names.'

Kilian heard the approaching footsteps long after the midnight bell. His three companions had long since surrendered to exhaustion and filled the dungeon with their snores, but he lay sleepless, turning over details of the plan endlessly in his mind, trying to anticipate potential obstacles and working out methods to overcome them.

The dim lantern-shine in the corridor outside his cell brightened. Rising, he waited at the iron door of his cell until a key grated in the lock and it swung wide open. Standing there was the tall figure of Vra-Waringlow, wearing the usual red robes of the Order. But the gammadion pendant hanging at his neck was not gold inlaid with onyx, as befitted the abbey's second-ranking official. It was finely wrought platinum.

'So all went as we hoped!' Kilian said by way of greeting.

Waringlow's impassive face showed the barest flicker of a smile. 'Noachil was a tenacious old man, in spite of his many painful ailments. He entered into eternal peace shortly after a noon collation of shirred eggs with anchovies, one of his favorite dishes. It was an easy death. God grant such to all afflicted souls.'

Kilian nodded piously. 'May I offer my felicitations upon your elevation, Father Abbas?'

'Thank you, my son. And I, in turn, must express my profound gratitude for your having taught me the subtle coercive spell that swayed the vote of the governing council in my favor. I thought it best to use the magic before your departure – not that I doubted the spell's efficacy for a moment.'

'Vra-Garon has returned with the horses?'

'He awaits you in the ravine just outside the postern gate.' The new leader of the Mystic Order of Zeth lifted a tiny key. 'Please turn around.'

Hands manipulated the lowered hood of Kilian's robe. He heard a sharp click and his onerous neck-chain, together with the iron gammadion it held, fell to the floor. He felt his heart leap with a sudden influx of arcane power. Now he was no longer dependent upon the chancy goodwill of

Beynor, who had claimed – perhaps falsely – to know a spell that would free him of the talent-quenching iron.

'It may take a few days for you to regain the fullness of your natural abilities,' the abbas said, 'especially the ability to windspeak and scry over distance. I'll do my utmost to confuse any pursuers until you are once again able to weave a spell of couverture.'

'You've been a staunch and loyal friend, Waringlow. In time, when the tyrant Conrig is overthrown and my own power is consolidated, be assured that I'll reward you further.'

'No further recompense is necessary. Thanks to you, I have what I've always wanted.' He picked up the iron gammadion and handed it to Kilian. 'You'd better dispose of this. It's a pity that the totality of your magical endowment as an ordained Brother of Zeth cannot be restored to you. But as you know, new golden gammadions for you and your companions would render you perceptible to ordained wind-searchers. Still, I have no doubt that you'll find other ways to augment your sorcery.'

If you only knew! Kilian thought. But he simply inclined his head.

Waringlow continued. 'You should know that our Brother, Vitubio Bentland, perished in the Cala disaster. Felmar and Scarth are suspected of starting the fire. Interestingly enough, they are reported to have stolen certain items belonging to the Royal Alchymist, but no description of the things has been circulated. As yet, the authorities seem to have no notion as to the whereabouts of the fugitives. They are presumed to have discarded their own golden gammadions early on.'

After Waringlow opened the other three cells. Kilian roused his associates with sharp commands, then stood by while their iron pendants were also removed. He ordered them to sink the things in the deepest part of Elk Lake when they embarked the next day.

'Vra-Garon will be blamed for engineering your escape,' Waringlow observed. 'If I were you, I wouldn't trust that young fellow overmuch in a tight situation. Loyalty is hardly his strongest virtue.'

Kilian nodded. 'I know the strengths and weaknesses of all my men well enough.'

'It's time to go. Link arms and come up behind me very closely, two by two.'

They did as he bade them. The abbas lifted his hand and pronounced an incantation, and the former prisoners vanished from sight.

'Now follow me as silently as you can, and you'll soon be free. The night's a rather nasty one, I fear, with both wind and heavy rain.'

'Good,' said one of the invisible men.

The new Father Abbas lifted his lantern and headed for the flight of stairs, chuckling.

EIGHT

Ullanoth, Conjure-Queen of Moss, slept for nearly thirty-six hours, paying her enormous pain-debt during slumber, as it had to be paid. When she could endure it no more she broke away and awoke on the morning of the day after Solstice. It was only with difficulty that she forced herself to leave her bed. The latest act of Sending had left her with almost no physical energy.

I should have told Conrig to wait, she thought. There was no good reason why he needed to know the truth about Queen Risalla's unborn babe immediately. He was driven only by impatience and his desire to remain in control of every situation that concerned his Sovereignty.

But he had begged so urgently for her help . . .

She summoned servants to help her dress. An attendant held a mirror up after her pale hair had been combed, and she sighed as she saw her face. She was only twenty-three years of age, but the reflection now seemed to be that of a woman almost ten years older, gaunt and ravaged, with circles like bruises about her abnormally sunken eyes and deep lines furrowing her brow.

She had still been beautiful when she last Sent herself to Conrig; she was beautiful no longer.

The Lights had not done this to her. She had done it to herself, freely, in exchange for the sorcery of her Great Stones – Sender and Weathermaker, and above all Subtle Loophole. A lesser proportion of her debt had accumulated through helping her own people: she had used Weathermaker to generate storms to beat back the clumsy incursions of the Salka, and studied her evil younger brother through Loophole to make certain that Beynor remained securely exiled during the uneasy first years of her reign. But by far the greater component of her devastation was due to her inability to deny Conrig Wincantor when he sought her assistance.

I'm a fool, she told herself, gesturing for the mirror to be taken away. How often has he given himself to me or my Sending since assuming his throne? Less than two dozen times in four years! And each time we bedded, my desire for him strengthened, while he remained the same – professing love, taking me with a fierce passion, yet never opening his soul to warmth, never cherishing my self but only the hurtful magical power that comes through me.

And my people: do *they* love me? Moon Mother have mercy, but I think not . . .

Servants had been bustling about the royal apartment while she was being dressed, but when she dismissed the tirewomen and forced herself to leave her bedchamber she found no food set out for her in the adjacent sitting room, as was usual.

A little old man wearing a green satin tabard emblazoned with the golden swan of the royal arms bowed and smiled.

'Majesty, your breakfast table is laid on the balcony, since the rain has gone away and the day is gloriously clear and mild. But if this is not to your pleasure –'

His name was Wix, and he had been her personal slave

from the time of her girlhood. When she became queen she freed him and created him her Lord of Chamber. He was elderly but strong of body, and he had dedicated his life to her service. No woman had ever been Ullanoth's confidante, but she trusted Wix without reservation, and on occasion shared with him her innermost thoughts.

'I'd enjoy eating outdoors,' she said, returning his smile. 'Thank you for thinking of it. And please have a second chair brought to the table, for I wish to speak with you.'

The other servitors saw them seated, and poured mead before withdrawing and closing the balcony doors.

Ullanoth was silent for some time, sipping her drink, gazing over the broad estuary of the Darkling River, and thinking on the notable achievements of her reign. Wix sat comfortably and nibbled on a bread roll. Across the river, the expansive flats of the Little Fen were brilliantly green with summer growth, their ponds sparkling like mirrors amidst silvery skeins of the narrow waterways. The peat-brown Darkling itself was alive with boats heading to and from the settlements surrounding Moss Lake, west of Fenguard. The docks below the castle bristled with the masts of merchant ships and fishing vessels.

No longer was Moss the poorest nation of High Blenholme, as it had been in her father's day and during the abortive reign of Beynor the Patricide, as she had officially styled her deposed brother. She had made her country prosperous, using Conrig's generous annual guerdon to finance the revival of the amber mines and the seal-fur industry, rebuild neglected by-roads, and promote commerce on the great river and along the seacoast. Through cajolery and magical coercion, she had compelled Moss's self-centered conjure-lords to stop squandering lives and treasure on ancient feuds and let their peasantry live in peace, growing crops and livestock to the advantage of the entire realm. She had founded a brand-new industry by encouraging the marshfolk to gather herbs and simples that were prized by physicians and cooks of the south. She brought in military consultants from Cathra to create a small standing army that now patrolled the Rainy Highroad, Moss's only land-link to the other island nations, and put down the gangs of human bandits that had long infested it and rendered it useless to traders and travelers. From Didion she acquired six fighting frigates and contracted for ten more, so that in future Moss need never again suffer the depredations of the Dawntide Salka. The monsters dwelling in the Great Fen were still unremittingly hostile; but that part of the country had few human inhabitants and little in the way of resources.

'It's hard to believe that only four years have passed,' she said to Wix at last, 'so greatly has our kingdom been transformed. I've worked without stint to improve the lot of our people. And yet I fear that their hearts are not fully with me. Do you agree?'

He nodded slowly but refrained from speech. The sad acknowledgment was sufficient.

She said, 'So many of our leaders and learned ones continue to mistrust my motives. It saddens me that they still believe me to be a tool of Conrig Wincantor rather than a loving monarch who puts the needs of her own folk above all other considerations. The people loved my ancestor Rothbannon, for all his sternness, but I sense that they do not love me. Why is this, my friend? You must speak honestly, even if the truth be hard for me to accept.'

Wix said, 'I'll tell you, Majesty, if you promise to eat. Your body will not recover its strength without food, and if the body is weak, the spirit lacks that resolve necessary to bring about change.'

She sighed, but lifted the silver dish covers and took portions of coddled duck eggs, poached cod, and rush-pollen fritters.

'First,' Wix said, after a hearty pull of mead, 'let's compare the first years of your reign with those of Rothbannon. He was a hard man but highly revered, as you say, even though the foundation of his kingdom came through Coldlight sorcery. He obtained his Seven Stones a century ago by outwitting the Salka of the Dawntide Isles, and in time managed to turn the monsters' own ancient magic against them, to the benefit of his people. He was able to do this because he took the time to study the sigils, and because he only used the Great Stones rarely and for the furtherance of his new realm. Indeed, he never used the Unknown Potency at all, believing it would undermine the magic of the other sigils.'

'I know this.' She spoke petulantly, through a mouthful of fish. 'It's always been my intention to study Rothbannon's writings about the stones when I have sufficient time.'

'But you haven't found the time,' Wix pointed out. 'Neither have you used your stones as the first Conjure-King did – with careful circumspection and only for the good of your nation.'

She did not look up from her plate. 'You're right. Far too often, I used the magic of the sigils for Conrig, whom I love.'

'And who is hated by our proud people, for daring to make Moss his vassal.'

'Most of our progress in the past four years came about because of Conrig's gold! Don't the people understand that? Would they rather live independently and be destitute?'

'They would rather you had not helped Conrig to estab-lish his Sovereignty in the first place. They would rather you had not spent your physical strength so profligately through use of Sender and Loophole – only because this foreign over-lord asked it of you, and you were too spineless to refuse him. Majesty, they believe that you love Conrig more than you love them.'

She started up from her seat, letting her napkin slide to the balcony floor. 'They're wrong! They don't understand modern politics. Being a part of the Sovereignty has made Moss stronger and safer – and God knows we're richer than we've ever been before.'

'You have done your queenly duty well, Majesty. The people know that and are thankful. But you asked me for the truth – why they don't love you. And the only answer to that is your determination to love another – to serve another – ahead of them. And this person is clearly unworthy of your devotion. Conrig Wincantor is ruthlessly ambitious and arrogant. True, he's been generous to Moss – but his treatment of Tarn and Didion has been very harsh. Furthermore, he cast aside his first wife for expediency's sake and entered into a loveless match with the Princess of Didion. He has no true devotion to you, either, my lady, and in your heart I think you know it.'

She slid slowly back into her seat, her face drawn with anguish. 'I once thought to use him as a stepping stone to domination of this island. But I've ended up being used by him. I never intended to love him, either! Yet I can't help it, even though I know what manner of man he is. He may not love me . . . but he needs me.'

'We need you more.'

They sat together quietly. He finished his cup of mead and his bread and sat with folded hands, waiting to be dismissed. It was plain that he had no more to say.

'Thank you for your candor, Wix,' she said finally. 'I'll think about all of this. You may go now. Please tell Grand Master Ridcanndal that I'll attend today's meeting of the Glaumerie Guild. I require the guild's advice on a thaumaturgical matter.'

'Very good, Majesty.' He bowed and withdrew from the balcony.

She could not stomach the greasy fritters, but she forced herself to eat most of the eggs, some fish, and a single roll with butter, thinking furiously all the while.

There was one way sure way to escape Conrig's thrall. It had come to her as the good old man spoke: a solution both drastic and permanent, but one that could only come about if she no longer owned that which the Sovereign needed . . .

Do I dare give them up? Can Moss survive if I render them lifeless and destroy them? Can Conrig?

His downfall was not the only thing she had to fear. Shortly after she assumed her throne, a flash of unwelcome insight had come to her. Was it possible that her own collection of moonstones, which she had found hidden in the fens, was not the gift of her dead mother after all? What if the dream of Queen Taspiroth had been a cruel deception of the Coldlight Army, and the gift of sigils intended to further some scheme of theirs?

Why the Lights might do such a thing was incomprehensible to her. But *someone* had led her to the moonstone cache, presumably for a good reason. She was no longer so naive as to believe in benevolent ghosts – especially the ghost of poor Taspiroth, who had suffered an atrocious death after misusing one of Rothbannon's Great Stones. No mother would risk exposing her daughter to a like fate – a fate that now seemed all too probable if she continued using the sigils . . .

Conjure-Queen Ullanoth. Do you hear? Vra-Sulkorig Casswell bespeaks you on behalf of High King Conrig.

Moon Mother mine! Could *that* be the answer to the why of it? But if she were actually destined to advise and safeguard Conrig, then who besides the Lights could have led her to the gift?

Do you hear me, Conjure-Queen?

'I hear you,' she replied. The matter would have to be

thought through later. 'Why is it that you bespeak me, Sulkorig, rather than the king's brother Stergos?'

So the news hasn't reached you, Majesty? Alas! There's been a terrible fire at Cala Palace, and Lord Stergos was gravely injured.

'I am grieved to hear it. What is the outlook for his recovery?'

The alchymists have high hopes, but he may be much scarred by burns.

'Perhaps my Royal Physician can provide valuable consultation. There is a certain rare plant growing in our fens that Moss's healers have long used to prevent disfigurement by burning. I will have Master Akossanor bespeak you about it immediately. The medicine can be put aboard one of our fastest schooners and will reach Cala in a few days.'

Gracious queen, I'll tell King Conrig of this welcome offer. There is another matter, also concerning the Royal Alchymist, that the High King commands me to put to you. The two malefactors responsible for the attempted murder of Lord Stergos are called Scarth Saltbeck and Felmar Nightcott. They are renegade Brothers of Zeth, who may be expected to use powerful magic to foil those who pursue them. Here are images of their faces . . . His Grace beseeches your help in tracking them down.

'My help?' She felt a mortal chill stab her vitals.

'The High King requests that you use your Subtle Loophole to find the pair, so that they may be brought swiftly to justice. He realizes all too well that using the Great Stone will wreak a lamentable toll of pain upon you in your already weakened state, but he begs that you will agree to the search for the sake of the great love he bears you.

There was silence on the wind.

Your Majesty? What answer shall I give King Conrig? He is here at my side, praying you will help him and his suffering brother.

'Tell – tell the king that I will try. As the compassionate Moon Mother knows, I can only try. But since the effort will endanger my life, I request of my liege lord a twofold promise.'

The High King asks what it might be.

'If my land of Moss should ever be threatened by an enemy either natural or supernatural, he must promise to come to its aid with all the forces at his command. And if I am disabled or expire through performing this service for my liege, he must continue paying Moss its annual guerdon so long as the Sovereignty endures.'

Conrig Wincantor, Sovereign of Blenholme, swears on his Iron Crown that he will fulfill both promises without reservation.

'Thank him for me, Vra-Sulkorig. If I find the fire-raisers, information about them will be spoken to you on the wind by one of my people. I myself will probably be indisposed. Farewell.'

Ridcanndal, Grand Master of the Glaumerie Guild, hovered over her couch, his face grey with apprehension. The Royal Physician and the High Thaumaturge, Lady Zimroth, stood by him.

'For the last time, Majesty, I implore you to reconsider this rash action,' Ridcanndal said. 'Your physical condition is too delicate to endure further pain-debt. And finding those who set the fire in Cala Palace is hardly crucial to the recovery of Lord Stergos.'

Akossanor, the physician, added, 'I've consulted with the doctors who care for him and sent them the proper physick. His life is not in danger – but yours may well be if you undertake this search.'

'Conrig only wants revenge,' said Lady Zimroth. 'Either that, or he hasn't told you the full truth about the conflagration. I've heard a rumor on the wind that the arsonists are also thieves, who stole some important magical items from Stergos. Whatever these things may be, they can hardly be worth jeopardizing your life.'

Thieves? Ullanoth felt her breath catch in her throat.

There was indeed something the fire-raisers might have stolen that was beyond price. She'd known about Darasilo's Trove for four years, yet had never tried to find it with loophole. Whenever the notion occured to her, it always seemed imperative that she must set it aside until later. And so she had.

Why?

'Please don't do this, Majesty. Think of the needs of your kingdom. Of your duty!'

The aged High Thaumaturge had been one of Beynor's closest friends. Lady Zimroth had never fully reconciled herself to his dethronement and exile, even though the Beaconfolk, and not Ullanoth herself, had ultimately brought it about. Nevertheless her probity and loyalty to the throne were beyond reproach.

'I do think of my duty to Moss,' Ullanoth said. 'But this one last time I must help Conrig.'

'Last time?' Zimroth's eyes widened. 'You'd deny him sigil magic in future?'

'I had meant to discuss the matter, together with a certain course of action I'm considering, with the entire Guild today. As it happens, the discussion is now unnecessary, since I've extracted certain promises from Conrig that ensure the survival of our beloved realm, even if this use of Loophole should disable me . . . Ridcanndal, give me the box. I must do this before I lose my courage.'

The Grand Master picked up a small casket of platinum from a table beside the Conjure-Queen's couch. 'But Majesty, what are these promises?'

She shook her head. 'Attend me closely. This effort will require all of my remaining stamina. If I do locate the fugitives, I'll not be able to speak. You will have to extract the result directly from my mind. Later, when you bespeak the Cathran alchymist Vra-Sulkorig with the search results, he will tell you about Conrig's promises. Now open the box for me.'

The head of the Glaumerie Guild bowed his head and obeyed. The velvet-lined box contained her six remaining sigils: Beastbidder, Interpenetrator, Concealer, Weather-maker, Sender, and Subtle Loophole. The latter was a small open triangle with a handle attached, exquisitely carved from translucent moonstone and glowing with arcane energy. Looking through it, one obtained a vision of anything that was requested. But unlike the silent and often murky over-sight vouchsafed by windsight, Loophole showed its objective clearly, with all sounds attending.

Lying in her private sanctum, with the most powerful sorcerers in her realm kneeling at her side, Ullanoth took the sigil and lifted it to her eye.

By noon on the day after Solstice, the Salka had towed Beynor's boat to the entrance to Didion Bay. He directed them to continue on a course well to the north of the main shipping lanes so that his singular method of propulsion would not be detected, and continually scanned the sea for stray fishing smacks and coasters. All went well and no one noticed them.

Round about the ninth hour he ordered the great crea-tures to pull into a deserted marshy inlet about twenty leagues north-east of Holt Mallburn. They came to a halt in a salt-pond, well hidden among the tall grasses and shrubs, and Beynor summoned the Supreme Warrior for a conference.

Ugusawnn's hideous face rose slowly above the gunwale and his great red eyes blinked in the low sunlight. 'Well?' he inquired with an ill-natured sneer.

Beynor responded mildly. 'We'll stop here for the night. It's time for me to step the boat's mast, rig her, and switch to sail. From here on, we must travel more slowly, and any towing by you Salka will have to be done very cautiously, with only a few knots' advantage over the local small craft, so I won't look conspicuous.'

'Knot? What kind of a knot?' The Supreme Warrior's brow wrinkled in a fierce scowl.

'It's a unit of velocity. A way humans have of saying how fast a boat moves over the water . . . Oh, never mind. If your haulers just follow my bespoken instructions, I'll keep us moving along properly. You Salka will have to swim deep as we enter Mallburn Harbor. The sea there will be cloudy from river-mud after the rain, but even so, we don't want to risk some crow's-nest loafer catching a glimpse of you.'

'Mmm.' The monster was thinking. 'It is necessary that I stay close enough to the surface to keep you in sight at all times. And I – not you – will give directions to the Salka haulers.'

Beynor tipped him an ironic salute. 'It's your decision, Eminent Ugu. But once we get into crowded waters, you'll have to look sharp to avoid dangerous mistakes. If I ram another vessel because your warriors ignore my orders, the Harbor Patrol will be on us like stink on a swamp-fitch. They'll arrest me and confiscate the boat to pay for the damage. Do you understand what I'm saying? Once we start up the river, it would be best if you let me sail completely unencumbered –'

Ugusawnn gave a furious growl. 'I think you hope to trick me, human excrement! It will not work. Abandon any thought of escaping my vigilance.'

Beynor gave a shrug. 'I want this scheme to succeed. So should you. I've sailed through busy harbors and up crowded rivers before. I know the kind of problems that can arise.'

An awful smile spread across the countenance of the amphibian. His teeth gleamed like crystal marlinspikes. 'I have a solution. We will disconnect all but one harness. I myself will wear it – pulling you as it becomes necessary, and also keeping you secure.'

'Suit yourself.' While the Salka milled about in the marsh, reorganizing themselves and catching fish for a meal, he set about preparing the boat. It took the better part of two hours, and while he worked he sent his windsight in search of the royal barge.

It had left the capital early and made its first overnight stop at the large town of Twicken, where the king and his family received the homage of prosperous local landowners and merchants at a dinner party held aboard. Beynor found the barge tied up at a riverside jetty splendidly decorated for the occasion. It was a handsome craft with a snow-white hull and abundant gilt trim, adorned with banners, bunting, and swags of flowers, designed to be propelled by forty sweeps that could be augmented by sails if the wind was favorable. Its figure-head was a gigantic black bear, emblem of the barbarian nation.

Honigalus Mallburn and his family were plainly visible to Beynor's windsight, resplendent in full regalia and gathered with their guests at a long table under a white-and-gold striped awning on the poopdeck. The king was a stocky man of medium stature and plain features. His wife Bryse Vandragora, daughter of the greatest of Didion's timberlords, resembled him so closely that they might have been brother and sister. They were a couple devoted to one another and to their three young children. Crown Prince Onestus, who was seven years of age, and his brother Bartus, who was five, perched solemnly on highchairs at the feasting board with their parents and the guests from the town. Their little sister Casabarela, who had celebrated her first birthday only two months earlier, lay asleep in the arms of her nurse, who sat behind the queen.

Beynor could hear nothing on the wind, of course, but the occasion was plainly more sedate than jovial, with the worthies of Twicken showing no particular enthusiasm for the royal visitation.

Good to know the king's still unpopular among the

commons, Beynor thought in satisfaction. Four years was a long time, and he had not entirely trusted the dream-reports periodically given to him by Somarus. It seemed as though the seditious prince had gauged the temperament of the middle class accurately enough, but the nobility might be another kettle of fish. The only important peer who was openly sympathetic to Somarus was Duke Lynus Garal, whose rich tin mines were heavily taxed by King Honigalus. Lynus was a cousin of Somarus's wife Thylla. He had kept her and her two young children under his protection during the years that Somarus ranged about the wilderness with his rebel army, stirring up trouble.

Over time, Beynor had managed to invade the sleep of Lynus Garal, as well as that of most of Didion's other landed peers and timberlords; but lacking their explicit cooperation in the intrusion, he had been able to sift only fragmented information from their minds. It would probably be a good idea to bespeak Fring and attempt to clarify the situation. There was no sign of the archwizard at the royal dinner party, and Beynor presumed he had stayed behind in Holt Mallburn . . .

The musclepower of the Salka helped Beynor to erect the small boat's mast. After he had fastened the shrouds and stays that kept it upright, he rested and called out soundlessly on the wind.

'Fring Bulegosset! Respond to a good friend who wishes you well.'

So it's you. You're a lot closer to the capital than you were yesterday.

'I'm moored in a marsh twenty leagues away from Mallmouth Quay, getting my vessel all shipshape before starting up the river. Are you still at home in Holt Mallburn?'

Yes. I'm supposed to be suffering a severe case of griping bowels after dining on suspect shellfish.

'Regrettable.'

Is it still going to happen?

'Of course. Would you like to watch?'

I believe I would.

'There's a stream called Boar Creek that flows into the Malle just below Boarsden Castle. Be there in late afternoon on the day of the king's scheduled arrival. It would be useful if any number of impartial observers from the castle accompanied you. Perhaps you and the duke and duchess and some others could ride out to watch the royal barge negotiate the rapids and the deep eddy in that section of the river. Always an exciting spectacle – and apt to be especially memorable this year.'

Ah. Yes, of course.

'Were you able to bespeak one of the wizards in Somarus's company and pass on my advice?'

I did so. The prince will be within a day's ride of Boarsden on the day in question . . . in case he should be needed.

'He will be. You have my solemn word on it. Tell me now the mood of Didion's nobility. If Somarus assumed the throne and declared war on the Sovereignty, how would they react?'

War?!

'My dear Fring – do you know so little of your prince's temperament? Of course there'll be war! Which peers will support a call to arms?'

The barons of the outlands will certainly follow Somarus, since they never approved the capitulation of Honigalus to the Sovereignty. Duke Lynus Garal is no friend of the present monarch, as you already know; he might well favor a war of independence. The Duke of Karum on the west coast rules his fief like an independent principality. He'd favor any king who turned a blind eye to the marauding forays his cronies mount against shipping in the Western Ocean. If a war enhanced his opportunities for piracy, he'd rally round. Duke Boarsden was a first cousin to the late Queen Siry, Somarus's mother. He might declare for the new king or he might not. His fief is close to the Cathran border and would be a prime target for attack by the Sovereignty.

'Which lords might balk at accepting Somarus?'

The lords of Riptides and Highcliffe are solidly for Honigalus. The Sovereignty has brought tremendous prosperity to their traders and shipbuilders, even with the higher taxes imposed by Conrig. They'd resist going to war. So also, I think, would Duke Kefalus Vandragora, the most powerful peer in our nation, whose wealth derives from timber sales. With Conrig continuing to augment Cathra's navy and trade fleet, Duke Kefalus can only grow richer. War would be disastrous to his fortunes.

'Unless the war were won quickly – by Didion!'

And how might this miracle take place?

'In the same manner that Conrig Wincantor obtained his victory over your nation: through high sorcery.'

I – I am at a loss for words, Beynor. Am I to understand that you yourself intend to give some sort of magical aid to Didion?

'Yes.'

Forgive me for pointing out the obvious: in the late conflict, your efforts proved wretchedly inadequate. And thanks to your sister Ullanoth, all Blenholme knows that you have been cursed by the Great Lights and denied use of their sigils. So from what will this new font of high sorcery derive?

'I had intended to impart this news to you later, after Somarus was crowned. But perhaps it's for the best that I reveal it now. I have gained access to an entirely new collection of moonstone sigils. Their usefulness no longer depends upon the vagaries of the Beaconfolk, nor do the stones exact a toll of crippling pain as the price of their magic.'

Astounding! If true . . . May I ask how these sigils came into your possession? Did you obtain them from the Dawntide Salka?

'Where they came from is irrelevant. Neither am I prepared to use them until the appropriate time. I told you about the new sigils so that you might help bolster the confidence of Somarus . . . and convince him that I'm a worthy friend to him and Didion. You and the prince may well ask what I require in return for my magical assistance. The answer is simple. Help me destroy the Sovereignty and bring down the two people who deprived me of my own kingdom of Moss: Conrig Wincantor and my sister Ullanoth. All I want is to rule my native land, free of vassalage. I presume Somarus and the Sealords of Tarn have the same ambition.'

Tarn? Oh, I see . . . I see!

'Keep this knowledge secret until the day Somarus becomes king. Then share it with him. Use it, both of you, to convince the lords of Didion to throw off Conrig's yoke. I myself will convince Tarn to join us.'

You'll demonstrate this magical power, I presume.

'When the time is ripe, and only then. I've spent four years planning the downfall of Conrig and my sister, and I won't have my hand forced. Somarus will have to trust me. I'll give him ample reason to do so – in just a few days. And now farewell. I'll be preoccupied with other matters until the royal barge approaches Boarsden, so don't attempt to bespeak me.'

Very well. May all transpire as we would wish!

Beynor took more smoked salmon and reedmace root from the victual sack and went to the boat's cockpit for a brief meal. The pond was almost mirror-calm in the bright evening. Ugusawnn was nowhere in sight, probably lurking underwater, but the other Salka had hauled out on a mudbank to rest after feeding. A casual observer might have mistaken them for giant sea-lions, save for the green-black color of their bodies and the occasional languid movement of a tentacle.

The deposed young king watched the monstrous creatures without emotion. They'd brought him safely to Blenholme, and he had no doubt that they'd follow his orders from here on, albeit grudgingly. No Salka had ventured up the River Malle for nearly a millennium. In such unfamiliar circumstances, surrounded by humanity and its swarming watercraft, even their brutish self-confidence would falter. They'd be unlikely to countermand his decisions or quarrel with him out of sheer bloody-mindedness.

Beynor gave a great sigh and allowed himself to relax for the first time in many days. He'd travel in more comfort once they reached the river. It would be a huge relief to have some personal control of the boat at last, rather than jouncing about like a bale of inanimate cargo. He'd still have to rely on Salkan motive power when the wind was insufficient . . . until the time came when he was ready to escape.

Going into exile, he'd taken a well-filled purse to the Dawntides, not realizing there'd be no way to spend the money. He'd spend it now, no matter how much the Salka might object – not only on decent clothing, but also on food. A loaf of real bread! A spicy meat pie! A beaker of ale! Fresh strawberries . . . Beynor choked back a moan of longing and tore off another leather-tough mouthful of salmon. Soon, he told himself. Soon!

NINE

Snudge and his companions reached the town of Teme very late on the day following the Solstice. Vra-Mattis had bespoken ahead to the mayor's windvoice, informing him of the royal warrant they carried, which obliged all subjects humble or exalted to extend the king's men every possible comfort and assistance.

It had been a hard day's ride from Cala. The armigers and the novice were taken at once to the kitchen of the mansion for a late supper, while the two young knights dined more formally at a table in the breezy parlor, reluctantly vacated on the warm evening by the lady mayoress and her women.

'I wished us to eat alone for a reason,' Snudge said to his friend, while chewing on a roasted pheasant leg. 'I have a confidence to impart and something to show you. I request that you keep these things secret unless grave circumstances dictate otherwise.'

'Say on!' Gavlok heaped a piece of soft manchet bread with thin slices of beef, slathered on mustard, and took a huge bite.

'You would have known about this years ago, had Mero

Elwick not taken your place on the expedition to Mallmouth Bridge, during our invasion of Didion.'

'I remember. The bastard convinced Lord Feribor to remove me from the mission at the last minute.' He rolled his eyes. 'Of course, if I'd gone along, I'd be dead in battle – like Mero and the other two luckless sods who accompanied you. All heroes, to be sure, but I'd as lief be unheroic and abide among the living.'

'The armigers Saundar and Belamil were not killed in battle, as was said at the time. Mero slew them foully after we secured the bridge for Conrig's army.'

'No!' Gavlok lowered the bread and meat from his mouth and quenched the fire of the mustard with a gulp of beer.

'Yes. He committed murder because he coveted this.' Snudge wiped his greasy hands on the tablecloth and opened the front of his shirt, extracting a small square carving of milky stone hung on a golden chain. In the shadowed room, it shone with a greenish inner radiance. 'Do you remember this amulet of mine?'

Gavlok nodded. 'The lucky charm you wore when first you joined the Heart Companion company of armigers. I remember Mero teasing you about it. I don't remember it glowing, though.'

'It wasn't alive then. Now it is – and it's not a lucky charm. It's a powerful magical tool, a moonstone sigil named Concealer, able to render a man invisible. I took it from the body of Beynor's agent Iscannon, the one I killed in Castle Vanguard.'

'Bloody hell! How does it work?'

'All I do is command it. The sigil obeys only me because I'm its rightful owner. I can also use it to hide other persons who stick close to me, and even conceal things such as the horse I'm riding or a small boat that I sit in, if they're within about four ells of me and the stone. On the Mallmouth mission, I made all four of us armigers invisible. This is how we gained access to the drawbridge tower and opened the way for our army.'

'Futter me blind! And you say Mero wanted to steal this sigil from you?'

'Yes, and when it seemed he would fail in the attempt, he tried to smash it with his broadsword, not knowing that a sigil can defend itself from one who would separate it from its bonded owner. My Concealer burnt Mero to ashes and was unharmed by his blow. I told King Conrig that the moonstone was lost during our fight to secure the bridge. I've maintained this fiction ever since – although His Grace suspects the lie.'

'But why deny the sigil's existence? The ability to go invisible would be a priceless asset for . . . one who is a king's man.'

'You mean a spy,' Snudge said without rancor. 'I declined to use Concealer anymore because it draws its power from the Beaconfolk, those terrible entities who masquerade as the Northern Lights.'

Gavlok looked at him askance and quaffed more beer. 'I – I thought they were only a tale told to frighten naughty children.'

'Here in Cathra, where the Brothers of Zeth practice an orderly and scientific form of magic and influence the beliefs of the people, the true nature of the Beaconfolk has been nearly forgotten. But the people of Didion, Tarn, and Moss know full well that the ones they call the Great Lights or the Coldlight Army are very real. The Beaconfolk had a shadowy relationship with the Salka, the spunkies, and other inhuman beings who inhabited this island long before Bazekoy's conquest. Through moonstone sigils like this Concealer, the Lights are capable of exerting a malignant influence on humankind as well.'

Gavlok eyed the thing with apprehension. 'But only if you use its magic, right?'

'Yes. The Great Lights share their power with sigil owners, and extract a price in return. Each time one uses a sigil, one suffers subsequent pain during sleep until the debt is repaid. The suffering is proportional to the type of sorcery produced by the stone.'

'But . . . why should this be so?'

'The Beaconfolk have still another name: they're the Pain-Eaters. Ages ago, they encouraged the Salka and some other inhuman creatures living on our island to make sigils so they could satisfy their diabolical hunger. Much later, a few human beings also used the stones. I was told by Lord Stergos that the Beaconfolk are both irascible and capricious. If they become angered – or sometimes for no good reason that people can fathom – they may abruptly condemn a sigil user to death, or even damn his soul to the Hell of Ice, where he lives and suffers forever.'

'Blessed Zeth, what a horror! I marvel that you're willing to dare such peril by using that thing.'

Snudge replaced the moonstone inside his shirt. 'Concealer is deemed a very minor sigil, and the pain it gives is not so severe, nor is there much danger of insulting the Beaconfolk through its use. But there exist so-called Great Stones, such as those owned by the Conjure-Queen, that inflict a prolonged and debilitating agony upon the owner, and place the person using them in a more precarious position. One sort of Great Stone is called Weathermaker. Both Ullanoth and her brother Beynor used Weathermakers during the war with Didion to create strong winds and storms. Even worse is a sigil called Subtle Loophole, also owned by the Conjure-Queen. This kind of stone is capable of scrying anyone or anything in the world, given proper instruction. Ullanoth has used her Great Stones overmuch in the service of our High

King, out of besotted love for him, and greatly injured her health. I think the woman must be daft . . . but then, I've never been in love myself.'

'So it's true,' Gavlok whispered. 'Conrig gained his Sovereignty through high sorcery, even though he publicly denies it.'

'I believe that our king's own bravery and intelligence played a greater role in his triumph. This is why I remain his faithful servant. But the magic of the Beaconfolk also aided his cause, and so my conscience has been torn between loyalty to my liege lord and certain knowledge that sigils are evil and can't help but ruin the souls of those who use them. Queen Ullanoth may do as she pleases with her own awful stones. But I faced a moral dilemma with my lesser one. I still don't know if I've made the proper choice – but after thinking the matter over, I decided I would use Concealer again if it became absolutely necessary. I do this only because I've judged King Conrig's cause to be worthy.'

'I understand.'

'On the Mallmouth Bridge mission, I didn't tell my companions the true nature of Concealer: its link to the Beaconfolk. They knew only that it was a magical thing I'd taken from a Mosslander wizard. They were unaware that it could kill. They were also unaware that if I had died, its bond to me would have been severed – whereupon some foolish or wicked person might seize the inactive sigil with impunity and perhaps bring it to life again. There is a particular danger of this happening in Tarn, where we're headed, because the shamans of that nation are both powerful and resentful of the Sovereignty. To prevent my sigil from falling into the wrong hands, I ask a boon of you. If I should perish on this mission, take Concealer from my body and smash it to dust. You'll know it's harmless if the pale inner glow disappears. But if I only seem to be dead, or am separated somehow from the sigil and it still glows, then beware. The thing will harm you or even kill you if you touch it. Scoop it up instead with a metal implement and bury it deep where no man will ever find it. Will you do this for me, Gavlok?'

'I will.'

'My friend, I thank you.'

Snudge frowned as an unpleasant notion came to mind. There was small chance that their party would stumble upon the two thieves carrying the Trove of Darasilo. He'd wind-searched for them on the journey from Cala to Teme as the king had commanded him, finding nothing. He thought it probable that the pair were well hidden by some sort of strong magic and traveling nowhere near the Great North Road, which was alive with royal troops and reeves' deputies who stopped and questioned anyone fitting the fugitives' description. Nevertheless, Snudge decided Gavlok had to be warned, in case the unlikely should happen.

'There's something else I must tell you. Concealer isn't the only moonstone sigil in existence. Will you swear to similarly dispose of any others you may happen to find – whether they be alive or dead?'

'Of course I'll swear, Deveron, if you really believe it's necessary.'

'The notion of acquiring the powers of high sorcery doesn't tempt you, then?'

'Great God, no!' The young knight was aghast. 'It scares me stiff.'

Snudge released a long breath and slumped back in his chair. 'You're a fortunate man. Pronounce the solemn oath.'

After Gavlok did so, the two of them ate ravenously. They were finishing jam tarts and the last of the beer when there came a scratching at the chamber door.

'Enter!' said Gavlok.

The apprentice windvoice Vra-Mattis poked his tousled

head in. His face glowed with excitement. 'Sir Deveron, I've been bespoken by Vra-Sulkorig. It's an important message for you from the High King.'

Snudge felt the food in his belly congeal into an indigestible lump. In his fatigue, and his anxiety at confiding in Gavlok, he'd forgotten that Conrig had promised to transmit his decision about seeking help from the Conjure-Queen and her Loophole.

Gavlok climbed to his feet. 'I must visit the jakes anyhow. I hope the news is good.' He pushed past the little Brother and disappeared.

Snudge said, 'Come in, Mat, and close the door. The beer's gone, or I'd offer you some. Have a tart, if you wish. I hope you and the others ate well.'

Mattis shrugged off the irrelevancy. 'The High King wishes to inform you that there is fresh word of Princess Maudrayne.'

'What!'

'A witch of Donorvale in Tarn bespoke a blanket windcall to the Brethren at Cala Palace. This person, whose name is Yavenis, is an unsavory character who peddles nostrums and spells to the lower orders in the Tarnian capital. Nevertheless, she claimed to have important information about the princess, which she said she'd reveal in exchange for a large reward. The king authorized payment through the Sovereignty's ambassador in Donorvale, and Yavenis related the following tale, which she supposedly received from an outlaw shaman of Northkeep called Blind Bozuk.'

He recited an abbreviated version of Maudrayne's escape from the sea-hag, her arrival at Northkeep Castle with her maid 'and the maid's small son,' and her subsequent abduction by Ansel Pikan.

'But this Blind Bozuk has no notion of where Ansel may have taken the princess and the others?' Snudge asked.

'Yavenis says he told her that he didn't know. He may
have lied. Bozuk is apparently a talented spell-weaver who
cannot be controlled by Ansel, hence his designation as an
outlaw. His windsearching ability is exceptionally keen even
if his eyesight is not. He was obliged to use Yavenis to bespeak
his message to Cala Palace, since he lacks the ability to
converse across great distances. Thus the two magickers will
split the reward. Yavenis suspects that Bozuk will hold back
any further information he may have about the princess until
he can be sure of receiving a larger reward that he can keep
all for himself.'

'Hmph.' Snudge nodded with grudging respect. It was the
sensible thing for the rogue to do.

'Yavenis threw in another piece of intelligence for free.
High Sealord Sernin set sail from Donorvale in the wee hours
of this morning, accompanied by a fleet of fifteen swift
warships. He was said to be en route to Northkeep, which
is ruled by Maudrayne's brother. All of the windvoices in the
vicinity of that castle save Bozuk have been bound to silence
by Ansel Pikan. It's possible that the Lord of Northkeep
intends to meet Sernin at sea and discuss his sister's visit
with him. Vra-Sulkorig said you would understand the potentially flammable political repercussions of this.'

Snudge groaned. 'God's Blood! If only we had set out to
Tarn by ship! It'll be more than ten days before we can reach
the Tarnian coast traveling overland. Vra-Sulkorig gave no
order for us to turn back?'

'Nay. As a matter of fact, we are instructed to ride north
with all speed this very night.'

'What's that?' Snudge leaped to his feet, his face suffused
with incredulous anger. 'You silly knave! Why didn't you tell
me this before?'

Mattis was unruffled. 'Because I was ordered to relate the
other information first. Sulkorig said you must assimilate the

news of Princess Maudrayne calmly, before being informed
about Queen Ullanoth . . . and Lord Kilian.'

'Kilian?' Snudge was dumfounded. 'What of *him?*'

'I'm ordered to tell you of the Conjure-Queen's doings
first. At the king's request, she has used her sorcery to locate
the fleeing fire-raisers, Scarth and Felmar. The two Brothers
are traveling up the eastern shore of Elk Lake, probably
having ridden north from Cala through Heathley and the
Beech River valley with many changes of horse. The queen
oversaw them in early evening, approaching a village called
Pikeport. They were then disguised as royal dispatch riders
and were screened by a spell of couverture such as the
Conjure-Queen had never encountered before. Both the
reeve of the lakeshore and Viscount Olvan Elktor sent out
large search parties, but they found nothing. However, if the
villains realized that pursuit was closing in, they'd likely
change their appearance and go to ground.'

'But why hasn't Queen Ullanoth kept them in sight,
guiding the chase?' Snudge demanded.

'Because she is at the point of death. Whatever magic she
used to find the miscreant pair took a frightful toll of her
strength. Indeed, the doctors at Royal Fenguard are fighting
to save her life.'

So Ullanoth had peeped through Subtle Loophole once
too often! 'But surely the Brethren at Zeth Abbey would also
have been enlisted into the search.'

'Vra-Sulkorig said they've had no success using windtalent.
He suspects that the fugitives are shielded by an entirely new
type of cover-spell that defeats scrying. If this is true, and
they have also discarded the golden gammadions of their
Order, it would explain why they've eluded all wind-
searchers save the Conjure-Queen up until now. The High
King says the matter now rests in *your* hands, Sir Deveron.'

The apprentice eyed Snudge with a mixture of puzzlement

and speculation. 'Vra-Sulkorig had no notion what those curious words might mean, nor would King Conrig explain further.'

Snudge did not enlighten him, but instead rose from the table and gazed out of the solar window. It was nearly midnight and the sky had a carmine sunset glow that would linger for hours without fading. There was plenty of owl-light to enable them to press on, much as he shrank at the prospect. He was less sanguine than Conrig, however, about his own ability to windsearch the thieves. He'd exerted his talent heavily on the journey from Cala to Teme, and he was flagging like a foundering horse. And if the fugitives were indeed hiding under an impervious spell of couverture –

He said to Mat, 'Tell me about Kilian Blackhorse.'

'He escaped from Zeth Abbey, either late last night or early in the morning, taking three fellow-traitors and a young alchymist named Vra-Garon Curtling along with him. The Brethren of the abbey have windsearched for them without success. The High King believes that Kilian intends to meet the two fire-raisers for some nefarious purpose.'

Nefarious indeed, Snudge thought. Especially if Kilian had already learned how to activate the Trove of Darasilo.

But if that calamity hadn't happened, Snudge realized there was a small chance that he might yet outwit the bastards, given the fact that they would be unable to wind-watch *him* as he pursued them! He had a few other tricks up his sleeve as well, as Conrig was well aware – although he'd hardly be able to utilize them while dead tired.

And then there was Concealer . . .

Aloud, Snudge said, 'We must do our utmost to forestall a meeting between the thieves and Kilian. Fortunately, he and his fellow-traitors were completely stripped of all talent by the iron gammadion, so we need not fear them using sorcery against us. The thieves and this Vra-Garon are perhaps another matter. What was it you said earlier about discarding golden gammadions to foil windsearchers?'

Mattis held up the silver pendant that hung about his neck. 'I'm only a novice, and my own gammadion is a mere symbol without magical power. But an ordained Brother of Zeth who wears the sacred pendant of gold gains significant arcane abilities in addition to whatever natural talent he was born with. Also, the gold makes him subject to the commands of his superiors in the Mystical Order. Among other things, this means that the superiors can easily scry Brothers who wear gold gammadions. Felmar, Scarth, and this fellow Garon would certainly have got rid of theirs. Keeping them – even for the powerful defensive magic the pendants confer – would have been much too dangerous.'

'So all we have to contend with are the natural talents of those three, plus whatever cover-spell Felmar and Scarth have conjured.'

The novice hesitated. 'I wouldn't want you to think natural talents are negligible, sir. My own are rather meager, except for my ability to windspeak. Yet I'm able to hide myself from ordinary folk without much difficulty. I simply compel them not to notice me! The deception doesn't always succeed – particularly in bright daylight, or when more than two or three people are looking.'

'Hmm.' Snudge pretended to think this over. He himself possessed the selfsame natural ability; but as Mattis had noted, it was a chancy thing – not to be compared to Concealer's powerful and versatile spell of invisibility. 'Well, there are six of us hunters, so we may hope that the quarry won't escape us . . . Now go along and tell the others to prepare to ride out.'

'I've already taken the liberty of doing so, sir. The mayor's lackeys are readying fresh horses.'

'Good. We'll head for Northway Castle and change mounts

again there before cutting west to the lake. Bespeak the local lord's windvoice and tell him we'll need the strongest coursers he has, as well as a remount for each of us. It may be impossible to obtain sufficient numbers of good replacement animals in the villages along the lakeshore.'

'I'll see to it, sir.' The apprentice withdrew and closed the door.

Snudge paced before the parlor window, striving to make sense of the tangled situation. If Kilian had already discovered a way to activate the sigils of the trove, and if Felmar and Scarth managed to reach him and hand over the moonstones, then the peace of the Sovereignty of Blenholme (and perhaps the rest of the known world) would come to an end in a burst of cataclysmic sorcery.

But if Kilian still lacked a vital part of the puzzle – if he and Beynor were still allied, with each one of them perhaps possessed of some essential element the other lacked – then hope remained, at least until the two conspirators linked up with one another.

Where might such a meeting take place? There was no sure way to tell, but it seemed unlikely to occur in the civilized regions of Cathra, where the Sovereignty was strongest and both Kilian and his thieving agents were marked men. The rugged mountains between Cathra and Didion were a far more attractive option – or even the barbarian northern nation itself, where vast tracts of land were little more than a howling wilderness.

Snudge called to mind a map of the Elk Lake area. If he were in the thieves' place, reasonably safe from oversight but actively endangered by pursuers on land who might recognize him with ordinary vision, he'd take to the water. The big lake provided a perfect way to avoid roadblocks and close scrutiny by the law. In addition to the inland manors, which had vast flocks of sheep, there were many small villages along its eastern side, whose people earned a living selling freshwater fish and mussels, livestock, fruits, and vegetables to the large cities of Elktor and Beorbrook to the north. All of those little places were bound to have trade-boats willing to carry passengers. There might even be regular longshore ferry services between the towns, since roads in the area were rather poor. The western side of the lake was more sparsely inhabited, being almost wholly pastoral, but Kilian's party might well have embarked from a village called Elkhaven, which was only thirty leagues from Zeth Abbey.

Was it possible that the two groups of villains planned to meet somewhere at the head of the lake? Elktor was situ-ated up there; but why risk using the city as a rendezvous when there were uninhabited mountains a dozen or so leagues further north, where the Elk River carved a great gorge before spilling into the lake?

Roaring Gorge, famed in Cathran legends as a haunt of demons . . .

Might there be a way over the mountains somewhere in there? Snudge had never heard of such a thing, but that meant nothing. The precipitous range that virtually bisected High Blenholme Island was so hostile and impenetrable that only three widely separated passes were used by ordinary travelers. The fugitives would be obliged to avoid the nearest and most heavily used, Great Pass, at all costs because it was so closely guarded. If they were bound for Didion, they'd have to find another route, one not too far from the lake-head, but so obscure it was unlikely to be on any map. The gorge seemed as likely a prospect as any.

And if the renegade Brothers were heading that way, where ordinary search-parties would be reluctant to follow, then the Royal Intelligencer might well be the only one with a chance of finding them. King Conrig's enigmatic message showed that he realized it, too.

Snudge was too muddle-headed from fatigue and beer to attempt using his wild talent tonight. He'd try tomorrow, when he and the others reached the shore road and they were presumably closer to the fugitives. It seemed strange that Kilian and his talent-stripped cronies had evaded wind-searchers from Zeth Abbey, but perhaps the young alchymist Vra-Garon had learned how to weave the novel cover-spell, just as the thieves had done.

Did Snudge and his men on horseback have any chance of reaching the gorge before boats did? He had no idea, but he had to give it a try. If the weather stayed fair and there were no serious delays, they might get to Elktor in less than two days, with minimal time lost in sleeping. Beyond there, the mountain track would be so bad that horses would do well just to maintain a fast walk. Still, the quarry would probably be riding no faster; they might even be going afoot.

If fortune smiles, Snudge thought, we might bag one lot or the other – Kilian or the thieves. It was a plan with long odds against its success, but all he could think of in his present weary state.

Sheer luck, having nothing to do with magic, was all that saved Felmar Nightcott and Scarth Saltbeck after they were found by Ullanoth's Subtle Loophole.

Their dispatch-rider masquerade had enabled the pair to travel much faster than their pursuers expected, attesting to the excellence of Kilian's advance planning. They commandeered new horses every forty leagues or so with a flourish of their counterfeit royal warrant, and by the eve of the day after Solstice they had reached a sizable village on Elk Lake called Pikeport, situated on a bay above the outflow of the Beech River. There they stopped at an inn to switch mounts once again and have supper.

Fortune favored them in that the local windvoice was a

wretched draftsman, and the posters he drew carrying their alleged likenesses might have depicted half the men in town.

Their royal livery made the clientele at the White Waterlily stand-offish, so they dined alone at a small table in a shadowy corner, while locals sat at the long trestle-board and ate family-style from a kettle of fish stew, bowls of new peas, and plates of salad greens with radishes, vinegar, and bacon grease. More men, and a handful of women, were there to drink, whooping and laughing as the potboy kept stoups of ale and beer coming.

Then a trumpet sounded outside.

Nearly a score of the male patrons groaned and uttered obscenities. One of them said, 'A whole day's work draggin' for mussels, and now the fockity reeve musters us to posse afore we've even et!'

He and the other complainers gobbled what food they could and guzzled the last drops from their beakers before scrambling out the front door. Those left behind were either elderly, less than able-bodied, or not subject to posse-duty that year.

The host emerged hastily from the kitchen, cursing up a storm as he ran after the ones who had decamped. 'Think ye can run off without payin' just 'cause the bugle sounds? I know who ye are!'

One of the remaining diners remarked, 'Poor sods. Wonder what the deputy wants with 'em so late in the day? Any of you lot heard of a kiddie gone missing or other trouble?'

The remaining men gave negative responses. A skinny shabbaroon reached for one of the unfinished bowls of food that had been abandoned and began tucking in.

Felmar caught his companion's eye. 'Outside, if you value your life.'

'You think the alarum's raised for us?' Scarth murmured.

'We knew it'd happen sooner or later. For the love of Zeth, don't look like you're in a hurry.'

They retrieved two leather fardels embossed with the royal
arms from under the table and ambled to the stableyard,
where the new horses that the landlord was compelled to
provide for the royal messengers awaited them. Felmar gave
the old ostler a halfpenny tip, then the two thieves swung
into the saddle without haste and rode slowly back the way
they'd come, activating the magical spell taught them by
Kilian that would make them all but unnoticeable to passers-
by and secure from ordinary windsight. The distant trumpet
was still sounding Assembly. More freemen trudged along
the road toward the center of town, carrying rusty swords,
billhooks, fishgaffs, and staves.

'The hunt for us is well and truly on,' Scarth remarked.
'I wonder how they pinpointed our position?'

'Who knows? Turn off here.' Felmar guided his horse
into a crooked path that led down an embankment toward
the shore. At the bottom of the slope the track turned soggy
and clouds of biting midges rose up to torment them. Like
most arcane practitioners, the runagate Brothers were incapable of performing more than one magical action at a time.
They opted to deactivate the cover-spell and use their talent
to shoo away the bugs. They were now well hidden from
people on the road, and there wasn't much chance of
anyone windwatching them amidst the thick brush. They
picked their way along the strand until they came to a
tumbledown boatshed with a rotting dinghy lying near it
in the mud.

'Perfect,' Felmar said. 'Unsaddle your beast and bring your
things inside. We have a little while before anyone thinks to
look here.'

From the beginning, they'd been prepared to take on new
identities if conditions warranted it. They carried beggar's
rags and peasant clothing, among other things; but the
magnitude of the search presently being organized suggested

that only the most ingenious disguise was going to get them safely out of Pikeport.

Hence Pregnant Goodwife and Worried Woodsman Husband.

Scarth, who was tall and brawny and lantern-jawed, portrayed the male member of the duo. Felmar, being small of stature and fine-featured, was to be the woman. He needed his companion's help to get the bodice laced over his hugely augmented chest and stomach. Then he shaved so closely that his face was nearly scraped raw and arranged his wig and linen cap. All the time this was going on, Scarth suppressed snorts of laughter.

'You'll laugh out of the other side of your face,' Felmar snarled, 'if there's a more competent resident wizard in the next town, and he puts up decent pictures of us.'

'Don't bother your pretty head, Felmie dear,' Scarth chortled. 'No one will recognize us in this get-up.' He began converting his own neat beard into a scruffy stubble, adding smears of grime to his features.

'They damned well better not,' muttered Felmar. If the pair came under the close personal scrutiny of law officers they were bound to be recognized. The cover-spell's eye-clouding aspect was only effective beyond a distance of five feet.

Kilian had given instructions to divide the trove into two portions in case they became separated, so each Brother had carried a fardel holding a single ancient book and a leather pouch with fifty-odd inactive moonstones. Now that they were obliged to go on foot, this arrangement was no longer practical. They wrapped the loot in a few pieces of spare clothing and shoved the bundle inside the foldable wicker cage that swelled Felmar's front. Scarth sorted out food and other supplies and put them into a saddlecloth that he gathered into a pack. This he tied to a thick cudgel that could be carried over his shoulder. In his woodsman disguise, he wore a cased hatchet at his belt, along with a large hunting knife;

but their suspiciously fine swords had to be concealed beneath Felmar's voluminous skirts, where the scabbards knocked against his legs with every step.

After they had weighted the saddles and the rest of the discarded baggage with stones and sunk them in the lake, the two fugitives led their mounts along the shore until they came to another path that was at least half a league distant from the shed. There they stripped off the horses' bridles and turned them loose. The animals began to graze unconcernedly on the lush grass.

'Up to the high road now,' Felmar said, 'and back to the Pikeport jetty, bold as brass. That's the safest course. This village is one of the stops for the ferry that serves shore towns between Beech River and Elktor. The boat'll be here early in the morning. We're lowly folk now, you and me, not high-flown royal dispatch riders, so we don't want to waste silver taking a room for the night. The weather's fine after the early rain. What we do is find a place to snooze at the ferry dock, as is perfectly natural, and stay there till the boat for Elktor comes by tomorrow.'

'Wouldn't it be safer to buy passage on some other vessel with fewer passengers?' Scarth said.

Felmar shook his bewigged head. 'No. The more folk around us, the better. Your name's Hoddo and mine's Juby. Anybody questions us, I'll snivel and bewail my lot like preggie women do. You act short-tempered and distraught, and scold me for wanting to go to my mother at Elktor instead of having the babe in our hut down in the Beech Swamp. Trust me: none of the other ferry riders will want to have anything to do with us. Once we reach the city, we'll buy horses and new clothes and head for Roaring Gorge. If all goes well, we should reach the rendezvous with Lord Kilian in a couple of days.'

*   *   *

The wind on the lake was light and variable after the early morning rainstorm passed, less than ideal for the livestock boat Vra-Garon had hired to take Kilian and his party to the head of the lake. They had left Elkport at dawn, but after several hours under sail, the boat had traveled less than five leagues. The surly crew were disinclined to man the sweeps until Kilian promised to pay an extra fee, but even then the craft made a slow go of it, creeping northward along the rugged western shore of the lake at a relative snail's pace throughout the first part of the day.

Kilian spent most of his time in the cockpit, pumping the skipper for local information. His natural talent had recuperated to the extent that he was capable of distorting his facial features. That and the lay garb he now wore would make him unrecognizable to casual windwatchers. He still lacked the ability to screen the other four members of his party, however, so they were forced to stay inside the boat's deckhouse where they were less likely to be noticed. The cabin was cramped and odorous, even with its door and two tiny portlights open, because the doorway faced astern and the feeble breeze came from the starboard quarter. The only furniture consisted of bench-lockers with torn leather padding that doubled as bunks, a cold cookstove sitting in a tray of sand, a woodrack, and a splintery table.

'It wouldn't be so bad,' Raldo fretted, 'if the boat weren't utterly filthy! The deck outside is so crusted with manure that I can't bear the thought of setting foot on it.'

Garon, a handsome young man with chestnut curls and a cleft chin, whose fondness for female company had undermined his acceptance of a celibate lifestyle, only laughed. 'It's a cattle-transport, Brother Butterball. What d'you expect? Drifts of rose petals?'

'I don't see why we couldn't leave our horses behind and secure new ones at the head of the lake,' the fat man grumbled. 'Then we might have hired a faster and more comfortable boat.'

Cleaton had been sitting in gloomy silence, mending a split seam in his new riding gauntlet. He lifted his saturnine face and gave Raldo a sour look. 'If you'd taken the trouble to study the terrain as the rest of us have done, you'd know that there's no settlement at the place where we intend to disembark – and certainly no seller of decent horseflesh.'

'According to the maps I saw at the abbey, there's *nothing* at the mouth of the gorge,' Niavar said. 'Nothing inside it either, except a skimpy path above the river that seems to peter out well before it reaches the border divide. But it's still the safest route out of Cathra for the likes of us. Right, Garon?'

'Oh, yes,' the young Brother agreed. 'There's a game-trail that goes over the top into Didion. I herded the family sheep up Roaring Gorge in summertime when I was a boy and explored all its nooks and crannies. We may have a few sticky moments in places where we have to ford torrents or cut around landslides or washouts, but at least we don't have to worry that Count Elktor will lead his troops very far in there after us.' He laughed. 'Like most folk of the region, Lord Olvan has a superstitious dread of the deep interior of the gorge. Thinks it's crawling with demons, the simpleton! What a disappointment he must be to his father, Duke Parlian. Members of the Beorbrook family have been Earl Marshals of the Realm forever, but Parlian knows his lummox son lacks the stones to inherit the office. When the old man can no longer serve, the Sovereign is sure to bypass Ollie Elktor and install another clan in Beorbrook Hold.'

'Look!' said Cleaton, who had ignored the dynastic discourse. 'The boat crew have pulled in their oars. I think there's a fair breeze filling the sail again.'

'Well, thanks be to Zeth,' muttered Niavar. 'Maybe we'll reach the lakehead later tonight after all.'

'The very idea of sleeping aboard this floating dungheap turns my stomach,' said Raldo.

A coarse joke at the stout Brother's expense occurred to Garon, but before he could get it out of his mouth, the tall form of Kilian appeared at the deckhouse door.

'Good news, comrades,' he said. 'A breeze is rising now that the sun is lowering behind the mountains. We'll move along a little faster from here on, and enjoy more fresh air as well.'

The others murmured gratefully.

Kilian said, 'I've been exploring the wind-world very cautiously, trying to sharpen my disused talent, and I discovered some interesting things. There's a great to-do going on, with windspeech threads filling the air like spider gossamer. Searchers from Zeth Abbey are raking both shores of the lake.'

'Looking for us?' Niavar inquired grimly.

'It's possible, although Abbas Waringlow promised to deflect the hunt away from vessels on the lake. I rather suspect the surge of magical activity involves Brothers Felmar and Scarth – the two coming up from Cala to meet us.'

'With the treasure?' Raldo blurted.

Kilian stared at him wordlessly for a long minute. 'They carry an important collection of arcana, which I was forced to leave behind in the palace when I was sent to the abbey. It's hardly a treasure, since it has no value to anyone but me. Still, if my property is safely returned, all of us will be immeasurably better off in our new lives at the Didionite court.'

'Ah!' said Garon, his eyes narrowing with interest. 'Will you tell us more about this arcana collection, my lord?'

'Not until it's safely in my hands.'

'Have you bespoken these other Brothers to see how they fare?' Garon persisted.

'That would be the height of foolishness, since my windspeech thread might be backtracked to me by an expert practitioner, revealing my own location.'

'Oh.' Garon was abashed. 'I didn't think of that.'

'A person who was rash enough to attempt to contact those men before we've reached the safety of the mountains – or windsearch for them – would jeopardize all that we've accomplished so far. Is this clearly understood?'

They murmured in unison, 'Yes, Lord Kilian.'

'Good.' He went to the table and unrolled a small map. 'Come close and study this. It was procured for me by my sister, Queen Mother Cataldis, and shows the region between Roaring Gorge and the Lady Lakes of Didion, according to the best of current knowledge. Of course, much of the high-mountain area is still *terra incognita*, but we must trust that our Brother Garon will be able to guide us through it safely.'

'Absolutely, my lord!' Garon bent over the sheet. 'Well, just look here: The good queen's mapmaker is evidently unaware of the cave where we're to rendezvous with our two other companions. That's fortunate. I haven't been there for nearly ten years, and I feared the hole might have been discovered by others. It'd be a nasty surprise, wouldn't it, if we got there and found someone else besides our friends waiting for us.'

The others looked at him, appalled.

'Don't worry, I'll go on ahead and scout it out,' Garon reassured them. 'And Lord Kilian can give the cave a good scry before we venture inside. We wouldn't want to meet a bear!'

'A bear?' Raldo wailed.

'Some Tarnian shamans can windsearch through solid rock,' the alchymist said in a distant voice. 'And certain conjurers of Moss are also said to have that ability. But I do not. So you see, Vra-Garon, our security will rest entirely in your hands.'

'You can depend on me.' The young Brother gave him a confident smile. 'Don't worry about bears. They leave signs of their presence and they're afraid of fire, like all animals. If I find that one is living in our cave, I'll roust him out. We may end up having him for dinner!'

'Zeth forfend,' Kilian snapped. 'Garon, I want you to explain the details of the gorge travel route to our comrades while I go back to the captain. I've decided that it's most important that I understand how this boat is steered.' He set a tall glass bottle that he had been carrying onto the cabin table. 'Here's a treat for all of you to share later – a magnum of vintage Stippenese Moen Valley wine, courtesy of my sister's friend, Lady Sovanna, whose hospitality we enjoyed last night in Elkhaven. I've already given the crew members and the captain a taste, and they were very appreciative of its quality. You may finish it off with your supper before settling down to sleep.'

Warm cries of gratitude.

Raldo asked timidly, 'Master, is there no hope that we might reach our destination tonight?'

'Small chance of that, I fear, even with the lug-sail up. And these gathering clouds are a sure harbinger of more rain. Nevertheless, I suggest you all bed down atop the deck-house, amongst our baggage and horse tack. It's certainly the cleanest place aboard, and you can cover yourselves with squares of canvas from our camping supplies. I doubt you'd enjoy sleeping in this cabin with the crew members not on watch. They're even more aromatic than the boat, and I flicked a flea off myself not long ago. Just take care not to roll off the roof and fall into the lake. Some of the black eels living in these waters weigh more than twelve stone. They don't hesitate to attack full-grown elk wading in the shallows, and you can imagine what they might do to a floundering man.'

He left the deckhouse, laughing softly.

Not long afterward, the Brothers unpacked food for a cold

supper and the wine began its first round. Garon held the
bottle out to Raldo. 'You look a bit pale, Brother. A good
swig of this will perk you up.'

'No, thank you,' the fat man whispered. 'I'm not feeling
at all well, and red wines give me a headache. I think I'll
light a fire in the stove and brew up a pot of mint tea instead.'

'All the more for the rest of us,' Niavar said, seizing the
bottle. 'Cheers!'

'Source! Respond to Ansel.'

I'm here, dear soul.

'How is she – our poor Dobnelu? Is her physical body still
viable?'

*It may take more time for me to ascertain that, but I have high
hopes. The fragile bones and gristle of her throat were not crushed
as she was throttled, nor were the great bloodvessels in her neck
irreparably damaged. She died gently – not that this is a good thing,
for it means that she teetered on the brink even before the boy Vorgo
touched her. It may be possible to coax lifeforce back into this material shell, but whether her soul can safely lodge there is quite another
matter.*

'I see . . . Perhaps you already know that I've recovered
Maudrayne and her son, along with the maidservant.'

*Yes, I oversaw her for a short time. Did the princess confide her
secrets to anyone at Northkeep?*

'I'm not sure. She and the others remain in an enchanted
sleep in the back of my wagon. I may have to keep them
unconscious for some days, at least until we cross Gold River
and reach the land between the volcanos, and there's no
chance of their trying to escape. Liscanor put out to sea in
his frigate and is heading south. It's possible Maude told her
brother everything, but I think it more likely that she didn't.'

Soul, this hope may be a vain one.

'I scried the people in Northkeep Castle and read their lips.

Liscanor's wife and her servants believe that young Dyfrig is the maidservant's child. That's one secret safe – and Maude would hardly reveal Conrig's talent without also revealing his son and heir. I think all we need worry about at the moment is keeping Maude's location unverified. Thanks to my threats to the windvoices in the area, what news there is won't spread from Northkeep for at least ten days. Liscanor himself is another matter. Once he reaches the Tarnian capital, he'll tell the council of sealords that his sister is alive. Whether they believe him is problematical. I'll try to sow doubts in their minds.'

Can you reach a suitable hiding place before too long?

'I'm considering three possibilities. Which one I choose depends upon factors still beyond my control. But be easy, Source. No one save Conjure-Queen Ullanoth has the power to scry me on this journey, and she is mortally ill and unable to use her Great Stone. Even if it becomes generally known that Maude lives, the fact matters little if no one can find her.'

TEN

Waterfowl filled the saltmarsh with their cries, and Beynor found himself unable to sleep, so he spent much of the undark night windsearching. He had no luck finding Kilian, which made him wonder whether the alchymist's lost talent might somehow have been restored. After a few hours he abandoned that effort and turned his attention to the two thieves, methodically scrying the villages along the eastern shore of Elk Lake, since only fools or lunatics would have risked travel on the Great North Road, and Kilian's agents presumably were neither.

In time, he noticed the hue and cry going on in the vicinity of Pikeport and gave the place special scrutiny. Even so, he almost missed his quarry, who were dossed down on the village ferry dock together with a number of other sleeping travelers too frugal to take rooms for the night.

Something about the snoring knot of people seemed odd, yet Beynor felt disinclined to study them more closely – a fact that finally rang alarm bells in his head. He forced himself to intensify his oversight and finally detected the unusual spell of couverture. After some hard work, he unraveled it to his satisfaction.

There they lay, Scarth and Felmar, dressed as a countryman

and his pregnant wife, sleeping like well-fed babes with their
heads pillowed on a pack that might hold Darasilo's Trove.
Felmar looked rather peculiar because his linen coif was
twisted awry – and so was the wig beneath it.

Beynor had to admit that the magic obscuring the scape-
grace Brethren had been most cleverly wrought. There was
none of the fuzziness that often betrayed the presence of
cover-spells, only a subtle hint of distortion that was easy to
miss. It had to be Kilian's work. None of the other Zeth
Abbey alchymists possessed such expertise, which would
have done credit to a member of Moss's Glaumerie Guild.
Cathran adepts were rather good windspeakers; but most of
them were mediocre at best in the arcane arts of visualization and couverture, except for Kilian.

And one other . . .

Beynor very nearly cursed aloud as a long-forgotten name
flashed into his memory: Deveron Austrey! *He* might be able
to locate this well-concealed pair of thieves, just as he'd
managed to track down and slay Beynor's wizard-spy
Iscannon a few years earlier. In addition, King Conrig's wild-
talented intelligencer was as unscriable as the moonstone
sigils themselves. His total spectrum of arcane abilities was
a mystery – apparently even to himself. One might almost
suspect him of having Tarnian blood.

Beynor wondered why Austrey should pop suddenly into
his mind unbidden. Was it a forewarning that the wretch
was about to meddle in his affairs again?

Deveron Austrey had dared to steal Beynor's own
Concealer sigil from Iscannon. He had somehow penetrated
Kilian's inner sanctum while he was still Royal Alchymist
of Cathra and had taken one of the three ancient books
with moonstone disks fixed to their covers. He'd resisted
Beynor's dream-threats and refused to turn over Concealer
and the book to Salka couriers sent to retrieve them. The

book had been taken away by Ansel Piken to some unknown place, but not before the shaman had helped Deveron Austrey use its medallion to empower Concealer – with consequences that had proved disastrous to Beynor's former allies in Didion.

It seemed certain to Beynor that King Conrig would send his intelligencer after the men who had stolen Darasilo's Trove. Deveron could be closing in on Felmar and Scarth even as Beynor oversaw them. Was there some way to alert the pair, to get them out of harm's way?

Reluctantly, Beynor decided that there was nothing useful he could do. Knowing their names and faces, he was now in a position to invade the thieves' dreams, even if he couldn't windspeak them directly without the necessary password. But if he suggested that they alter their chosen route to avoid Deveron Austrey, the Brothers would suspect a trick. Kilian had seen to that.

No, Felmar and Scarth's best chance to evade capture was to get aboard a boat – as they obviously intended to do – and flee over the Sinistral Range into Didion. The mountainous country at the head of Elk Lake was the worst sort of terrain for scrying, which tended to be inhibited by massive barriers of rock. He'd have to keep a close watch on the pair from now on. Once they were well into the highlands, they'd be almost impossible for any windsearcher to find – including Beynor himself.

On the other hand, his plan for injecting a fatal temptation into their sleeping minds remained perfectly feasible. They must already be extremely curious about the nature of their arcane booty, since Kilian would never have dared tell them the truth about the things they'd stolen. They were thus predisposed to yield to his urging. It would be best if he began planting the impulse immediately, making it more imperative each time the fugitives closed their eyes. He'd compel them to *do it* just as soon as they reached a resting place that was suitably remote.

With luck, both of the thieves would succumb to his inducement and perish without a trace, leaving Darasilo's Trove for him to retrieve at his leisure.

Raldo dozed uneasily on the deckhouse roof. His corpulent body was unable to find a comfortable recumbent position on the planks, so he slept sitting up, propped against a heap of saddlebags, a piece of tent-canvas fending off most of the warm drizzle. Kilian's half-jocular warning about rolling off was unnecessary, since the roof had a low railing around it. All the same, Raldo chose a sleeping spot well away from the edge.

So when the first noisy splash woke him, he didn't immediately realize what had happened.

The twilit sky of early morning was covered by low rain-clouds that had swallowed the jagged tops of the mountains. Their looming expanse was black and featureless, seeming to close ominously around the lake like a great wall now that the boat approached the narrowing northern end. Overhead, the much-patched sail was filled by a moderate breeze. Raldo looked about with his befogged vision but saw only the shapes of his companions scattered among the baggage. They were all sleeping deeply, not even snoring.

A soft sound of footsteps came from the main deck below. Horses snorted, whiffled, and stamped their hooves uneasily. Then there was a second splash.

Raldo lifted the canvas away and looked astern, squinting in the half-light. He saw the boat's wake, partially obscured by the bellying sail. In the midst of the foam was a dark object resembling a piece of driftwood with twigs at one end. The object moved, extending itself up from the water before slowly sinking from sight.

Not driftwood. An arm, with fingers.

Another splash, this time on the opposite side of the boat. Raldo waited, and another black shape bobbed in the wake until it was lost to sight.

The fat man felt his skin crawl. His Brethren slept on. He wormed his way further aft so that he could peer down onto the deck where the horses were tied. The cockpit in the stern was empty and the tiller lashed tight with a length of rope to keep the rudder steady.

A noise, directly below him. Someone was emerging from the deckhouse. Raldo held his breath as the indistinct form of a naked man appeared. He was obscured by what was evidently a weak cover-spell, dragging an inert body that had dark-stained clothing. The man heaved his burden over the side, then returned to the deckhouse. Moments later, he reappeared with another limp form and disposed of it, leaving obvious bloodstains on the rail.

God save me, Raldo prayed, he's murdered the crew! There must have been something in the bottle of wine that rendered them senseless. By chance, Raldo was the only one who hadn't drunk any.

What will I do if he comes up here on the deckhouse roof?

Raldo saw the blurry naked man go to the boat's water-butt and pour several full dippers over his besmeared body. After washing himself thoroughly, he used a bucket to slosh more water over certain areas of the deck and the rail. Murky liquid disappeared into the scuppers. Then the man sluiced out the deckhouse as well. When he finished he went to the stern, dried himself with a rag, and donned clothing that lay neatly folded on the stern thwart. Bending over the tiller, he removed the line that had secured it and settled down to correct the boat's course. His identity was still hidden by magic.

But Raldo knew that only one person among them was capable of weaving a cover-spell. Kilian's natural talents had yet to regain their full strength, but they were adequate to cloud his bodily form while he went about his pernicious work.

The fat man shrank back from the edge of the deckhouse roof, too petrified to move further. It seemed that he and the other Brothers were going to live – at least for a while longer – and he thought he knew why. If their pursuers caught up with them during the flight over the mountains, Kilian would require the combined magical abilities of all his companions to defend himself. Later, when the alchymist joined Prince Somarus and his band of warriors in Didion, the Brothers' pitiful portions of talent would no longer be needed . . .

Raldo lay with his face pressed against the wet boards, tasting bile in his throat and feeling tears mingle with the soft rain trickling down his cheeks. His iron gammadion and its chain, which he'd hidden in his jerkin pocket and forgotten to toss overboard, pressed uncomfortably against his hip.

What am I going to do? he asked himself. But he could think of nothing except the giant black eels of Elk Lake, and what they were feeding upon this early morning.

Snudge and his men reached Pikeport at about the seventh hour after midnight, after riding all night. They stopped at the White Waterlily, the only tavern in town, where their perfectly genuine royal warrant and demand for free horse fodder, a meal, and a quiet place to catch a few hours' sleep aroused the suspicions of the short-tempered landlord.

Inexplicably, he decided that the mud-splashed, well-armed strangers purporting to be king's men had to be in league with the masquerading firebugs who had stopped at his establishment on the previous evening, victimized him with a fake warrant, and got him in trouble with the law. A wild commotion ensued, in which breakfasting tavern patrons happily took the aggrieved landlord's part. Snudge's party were forced to draw their swords and make a stand.

Order was restored by the deputy reeve and the town watch only after the local windvoice bespoke Lord Northway's castle and confirmed the legitimacy of those purporting to be the king's men.

While the still-simmering landlord had his people lay out food and see to the needs of the horses, Snudge learned from the deputy that the ferry plying between Beech River and Elktor had called at Pikeport and left over an hour earlier. More than a dozen other commercial sailboats had also embarked round about the same time, fishermen and transports of every sort, heading in all directions for various purposes. No persons bearing the slightest resemblance to Brothers Felmar and Scarth had been discovered yestereen in the vicinity of the village quay or anywhere in the surrounding countryside. The posse was preparing to set out again, but it seemed that the false dispatch riders had vanished without a trace, leaving only their abandoned mounts behind.

Without much hope, Snudge left his men eating a meal of scorched porridge, hard cheese, and flat beer and retired to the grain store behind the stables. This was the only place the disgruntled landlord would let them use as sleeping quarters, but it was at least fairly quiet, while the inn itself was not.

Snudge composed himself and began to windsearch, trying to ignore his throbbing head as he closely scrutinized more than two score small boats sailing, rowing, or drifting about the southern half of Elk Lake. In the end, his debilitated talent was unable to detect anything at all, so he gratefully surrendered to sleep.

Somarus Mallburn, Prince of Didion and one-time general of its armies, soaked in a steaming hot spring in a bosky dell of the Elderwold while birds sang their morning songs, squirrels romped on the moss-hung branches of the venerable trees, and his shieldbearer Kaligaskus knelt by the pool and combed his master's newly trimmed hair with a fine-toothed comb to banish lice and nits.

'Almost done, Highness,' the lad said cheerily. 'Might be a good idea to give it a rinse of turpentine, though, to make sure none of the wee devils slipped past me.'

'No turpentine!' the prince barked. 'You can rub in a dose of delphinium tincture if you think it necessary. At least it doesn't stink so badly.'

'Yes, Highness.' The boy climbed to his feet and trotted back to camp to fetch a phial of the stuff from Tesk the wizard.

Somarus slowly submerged, closing his eyes against the slight sting of minerals in the water, and stayed under until his breath was gone. Then he rose up, inflated his lungs with sweet-smelling forest air, and let himself float. The water was less than three feet deep, but it was marvelous to lie there, warm and supported, gazing up at the leaf-framed sky, thinking about the wonderful things that might – just might – take place within the next few days.

Fring had warned him not to get his hopes too high. Both of them knew that Beynor of Moss was a vainglorious young blowhard, treacherous as a weasel and even more wily. But if there was any chance at all that the deposed Conjure-King could pull off the assassination of Honigalus and his heirs, Somarus would embrace him as his newfound brother – Beaconfolk curse and all.

For as long as it was expedient to do so.

Through Fring, Beynor had suggested that Somarus hold himself in readiness a day's ride from Boarsden Castle. But why not move in closer and actually witness the fateful deed himself? Fring had known none of the details, only that the killing was supposed to take place at the Big Bend of the Malle three days from now, late in the afternoon.

He could ride out with a small party from the Lady Lakes camp, using only the simplest form of disguise, reach

Castlemont Fortress in a couple of days and enjoy the hospitality of his friend Lord Shogadus, complete the journey easily
by traveling the Boar Highroad –

And stand on the south dike of the river, watching the
yellow-bellied traitor die!

True, Somarus wouldn't fulfill his greatest dream. He'd
never know the satisfaction of sinking his blade into the heart
of the half-brother who'd cravenly yielded Didion to Conrig
Wincantor because he'd lacked the courage to die in battle.
But what the hell! All that mattered was that the throne
might come to him at last.

It was another cherished dream of his, one that seemed
even more impossible than the first because Honigalus had
begotten two sons and a daughter, who stood ahead of him
in the line of succession, along with their mother, Bryse
Vandragora, who might only inherit under special and
unlikely circumstances. But if Beynor actually did manage
to wipe out the entire viper's nest, then he, Somarus, would
become King of Didion.

And at that same hour, he vowed, though I must keep it
secret in my heart until the time ripens, will I declare war
on Conrig Wincantor's Sovereignty, and dedicate my life to
its destruction . . .

'Highness?'

He opened his eyes, let his body sink to the bottom of the
pool, and knelt upright in the water. The wizard Tesk stood
there in a dusty black robe, nervously licking his too-red lips
and blinking short-sighted eyes that always watered in
summer. He held out a little corked bottle.

'I brought the tincture myself, Highness, because I've just
received a message on the wind for you, from High Queen
Risalla.'

Yesterday, after first hearing of Beynor's amazing intention, the prince had sent a carefully worded inquiry to his

younger sister in Cala Palace, hoping that she would find a way to side with him if he rebelled against the Sovereignty. The two of them had always been devoted to one another, being the offspring of the valiant Queen Siry Boarsden, second wife of the late King Achardus. Both royal parents had died fighting Conrig in the Battle of Holt Mallburn.

'Tell me quickly what Risalla said!' Somarus demanded.

'Highness, she asked that her response be quoted verbatim: "Dearest Brother, my heart and soul will always be with you in every worthy undertaking. But my duty now lies with my husband and children. For the sake of my conscience, tell me nothing of your plans. Only know that I will always love you."'

'Damn!' said Somarus. 'She was ever a mild-tempered but stubborn lass, even as a girl. Having pledged her loyalty to Conrig at her marriage, she'll remain steadfast to him. Duty is everything to her. Do you recall how she came boldly before Conrig on the day he conquered Holt Mallburn, demanding the bodies of the king and queen for proper burial? Conrig could not withstand her. I suppose I knew how she would reply to my request, even before you gave me her message. But it's a bitter draft to swallow.'

'I believe that those striving for high goals must be prepared to drain such cups rather often,' the wizard said sadly. 'Shall I apply the delphinium tincture now, Highness? You might wish to return quickly to camp. The sentries have captured a Green Man.'

'What?! Great Starry Bear – is the whole world turning upside down? How did the slippery thing let himself be taken alive by a human?'

'Perhaps I should have said Green *Woman*, Highness. As to your question, I suggest you put it to the creature yourself. She's asked to speak to you. Or to be more exact, she asked for an audience with King Somarus of Didion.'

'Well, well! Flattering – if a bit premature. Never mind the tincture, man. Fetch me my clothes.'

A light tunic and trews of fine linen had been laid out for him as undergarments, along with woolen stockings and new boots. The garb he intended to wear on the trip to civilization was still in a coffer in his pavilion. He dried his body with a homespun cloth, then dressed without assistance. Somarus was a man far more impressively built than his older brother the king, lean and hard-muscled as a result of years living in the open since his withdrawal from the court. His beard and brows were red and his long hair was a few shades lighter, like the dark gold of cloudberries. His face was weathered and high-colored, with eyes like blue flint, webbed with fine lines at the corners. He was one-and-thirty years of age.

The camp had been set up in a large forest clearing divided by a brook. The smallest of the three Lady Lakes was partially visible beyond a stand of trees downstream, sparkling in the sun. To the south, the steep rampart of the Sinistral Mountains rose with daunting abruptness from behind wooded hills, the loftiest peaks piercing a cap of white clouds. Northward lay the Elderwold, over five thousand square leagues of desolate heath, boglands, and dense primeval forest, where the ancient and beleaguered race of Green Men had retreated in a final stand against humanity.

The warrior band of Somarus, which was often augmented by men loyal to the outland robber-barons, ventured into the Elderwold only rarely. Most of their raids and skirmishes took place much further to the north-west, where they preyed on caravans of Tarnian and Cathran merchants traveling the Wold Road during the warm months of the year. During winter, they holed up in the castles of the prince's secret sympathizers. Somarus had only lately brought his core group of men into the Lady Lakes country, after one of

Beynor's dream-visitations promised that a climactic event of surpassing importance would likely take place round about the Summer Solstice. The prince had told no one about Fring's hint of the proposed assassination, and so the captive Green Woman's styling of him as 'king' both puzzled and intrigued him.

The force in the camp was small but well-equipped, and included not quite three score mounted warriors, eleven landless knights, four barons who had been outlawed and stripped of their fiefs by King Honigalus for crimes against the Crown, and a flock of servants, shieldbearers, and itinerant wizards. All save the knights and nobles were accommodated in twenty tents, set up in two lines and separated by a wide aisle of trampled ground. The larger pavilions of the prince and his officers had been erected across the brook in an area of scattered trees, while the horses were picketed downstream where abundant grass grew. This early in the morning, a multitude of cook-fires sent up plumes of smoke as breakfast was prepared.

Preceded by Tesk, Prince Somarus went to the pavilion of Baron Cuva, the highest-ranking of his followers, where a murmuring crowd had gathered in a rough circle. At the wizard's cry of 'Make way!' the throng parted, and the prince passed through to find Cuva seated on a folding stool, a quizzical expression on his hawkish face. Three glowering wizards and two huge warriors with drawn swords stood in front of the baron, guarding a small figure.

Cuva rose as Somarus approached, offering his own seat to the prince with a gracious gesture. 'Highness, a most unusual capt – uh – *visitor* has asked to see you. I'm not sure I got her name right. Was it Sithalooy Cray?'

'Call me Cray,' the Green Woman said.

The voice was surprisingly low and resonant for one who stood less than five feet tall. Her aspect was completely human, save for the vivid emerald hue of her somewhat over-large eyes. It was impossible to tell her age. Her unlined face was deeply sun-tanned, and her neatly plaited hair was dull silver, streaked with primrose-yellow. She wore a calf-length moss-green gown with a divided skirt. Her boots were deerskin, and her hooded cloak of mingled shades of grey, brown, and black almost perfectly mimicked treebark. A bulging purse embroidered with colored thread hung from her belt, along with a little gold-hilted dagger in a skin sheath.

As Somarus sat down on the stool and regarded her with what he hoped was appropriate aloofness, she stepped forward a few paces. One of the warriors guarding her lifted a restraining hand, but she gave a negligent wave and the gigantic man froze like a statue. Cries of consternation came from the gathering.

'Let her be,' Somarus said. 'You may come closer, Cray.'

'Are you King Somarus of Didion?'

He said, 'Not yet.'

The little woman gave him a casual bob of her head and smiled. 'You will be king . . . after the drownings.'

More astonished exclamations from the crowd.

'Be silent!' the prince said. Then to Cray: 'Did you come here to tell me that?'

'No. I was sent by the Source, commanded by him to accompany you on your journey to the wide river.'

'Is that so! Well, I've never heard of this Source, so why should I do as he says?'

'Because you want very much to be king.'

'And your Source would forestall me if I declined to obey? Or *you* would?' The questions were asked without heat.

'We have no wish to do so. Only take me with you and all will go well. I'll be no trouble. I eat very little and I can ride pillion behind one of your men if you can't spare me a palfrey. If need be, I'll protect you from your foes' – she shot a sly glance at the still-motionless warrior – 'more adroitly than your pack of hedge-wizards.'

The affronted magickers fixed her with venomous glares.

Somarus threw back his head and roared with laughter. 'I believe you could! What else do you want of me, Mistress Cray?'

'A cup of ale would be lovely,' she said. 'I've come a long way. There was wildfire in the wold and I had to go around it.'

Somarus rose to his feet, still grinning. 'Come and have breakfast. I'd like to talk more with you. Like most human beings, I've never seen one of your race before. I was told you had green skin and pointed ears and leaves instead of hair, and that your women – uh – bewitched luckless fellows who lost their way in the Elderwold.'

'We used to do that in days gone by,' she said demurely, 'but not so much of late. Tastes change.'

Someone sniggered nervously.

Somarus swept his gaze around the hovering group of nobles, warriors, and wizards. 'All of you, get back to your duties! Baron Cuva, I'll ride out this morning for Castlemont with you and a party of ten knights. Light armor and weaponry, surcoats and banners with the Boarsden blazon for disguise, everyone looking spruce and stalwart. Find a suitable mount for Mistress Cray.' He looked down at her. 'Shall we go to my pavilion?'

'In a moment.' She went to the paralyzed man and spoke a word softly. The warrior straightened, sheathed his sword, and walked off dazedly after the others. 'I hope his friends don't tease him too badly,' Cray said.

'He's big enough to take care of himself. Come along now. I'm famished.'

She stood before the prince, staring at his right shoulder with a little frown. 'Oh, my. You missed one.' She reached up and touched a damp lock of his curling hair. There was a sizzling snap and Somarus smelled a whiff of smoke. 'That's taken care of the creeping little whoreson! Now you look much more like a king.'

The ferry put into eleven lakeside towns and villages before reaching the end of the line at the city of Elktor, and at each stop people got off and on, while crewmen unloaded and loaded cargo at tedious length. The clouds had lowered steadily throughout the day; and by late afternoon, when the knoll crowned by Elktor Castle finally came into view of the passengers, rain was falling steadily and the dramatic mountains above the walled lakeside city were wreathed in eerie swags of mist.

Felmar and Scarth had secured inside seats on the boat early on, so they had a fairly comfortable trip, even though the benches were hard and the cabin atmosphere fuggy with the odor of unwashed humanity. Their quarrel-and-snivel act, performed regularly, kept most of the other passengers at bay, although one garrulous old biddy insisted on sharing memories of her own catastrophic pregnancies with the fake mother-to-be.

Most of the time the two fugitives slept. So when they finally disembarked at Elktor Quay they were ready to set out for Roaring Gorge as soon as they could purchase suitable clothing and equipment and secure horses. It was only the fifth hour after noon, but their hopes of a speedy getaway were deflated almost at once when a one-eyed dockside loafer informed them that most of the shops and market stalls had shut down early because of inclement weather and a dearth of customers.

'As for horses,' the fellow continued with lugubrious relish, 'ye won't have an easy time gettin' anything first-rate. Town's all skimble-skamble, with a grand hunt on for a pair of scoundrelly Zeth Brothers who set Cala Palace on fire and like to killed the High King's brother. Word came to Count Ollie late yesterday to beat the bushes for 'em hereabouts, and his captains have commandeered damn near every sound nag in the city to mount search parties. Maybe ye could hire a wagon –'

Felmar uttered a falsetto squall. 'No, no, the track to Mother's croft is too steep for wheels. We need horses to get there. Hoddo, *do* something! We can't keep standing here in the rain!'

Scarth patted his mate's hand and said, 'Now, now, Juby. Calm down, lambykin, or you'll drop that babe of your'n afore its time.'

The idler screwed up his face in an orgy of concentration. 'Lemme think now. There might be one place still with a mount or two left to sell. If I could just recall . . .'

Scarth gave a grunt of disgust and pulled a silver penny from his belt wallet. 'Does this jog your memory?'

The one-eyed man smirked. 'No – but add another and the name's bound to come to mind.'

Without a word, Scarth pressed two coins into the dirty outstretched palm.

'Bo Hern's stable. Follow the Quay Road a quarter-league to the north edge of town, nigh unto the Mountain Gate. Old Bo sells donkeys and mules. Good for ridin' in rough country. And he has saddles and tack, too.' The rascal tugged his forelock. 'Luck to ye, master and mistress.'

'Is there an inn or cookshop near the stable where we might get something to eat?' Scarth asked.

'Bo's wife can fix you up. Otherwise there's the Rusty Gudgeon tavern acrost the way – but some say they use catmeat in their pasties.' The one-eyed man ambled off, ignoring the rain.

'I vote for Bo's place,' Felmar said. 'We can't hang about here any longer.'

Scarth hoisted the bundle to his shoulder and they set off

along the waterfront. 'Mules aren't a bad idea, Fel. They're not fast, but a good one is more reliable on a bad track than a horse. Our map shows that it's fifteen leagues or so to the gorge mouth, and most of the way is twistier than earthworm guts. Then almost an equal distance to the cave, over a miserable sheep-trail. We're in for a rotten time of it if we press on. Maybe we should stop at the stable for the night and start out early tomorrow.'

'No,' said Felmar emphatically. 'We're well-rested. All we need is a meal and some food and drink to take with us. And I've got to shed this wicker birdcage tied to my belly! I'll keep the rest of the woman's garb till we're well away from the city, but there's no way I can ride wearing this futterin' thing.'

'It's raining harder,' Scarth said. 'We could at least wait a few hours to see if it stops.'

'We've got to move on. I don't like the feel of this town. There are alchymists up in Elktor Castle and other windvoices prowling about with the searchers. I can sense them! Thus far, our spell of couverture is holding firm, but something's not right. I almost feel as though we've been overseen. Right through the bloody cover.'

'I won't say you're imagining things,' said Scarth, 'since you've got more talent than I do. But if the Brethren did have a windeye on us, Lord Elktor's guardsmen would have met us at the ferry dock and clapped us in irons.'

'The windwatching – if that's what it was – wasn't done Zeth-style.' Felmar was silent for a few minutes. They splashed on through spreading puddles, paying no attention to the occasional beggar who whined from a doorway. Most of those walking along the quay were seamen, some with giggling doxies on their arms. Half a block ahead, a hanging sign with a lion's head designated a good-sized inn. Unattached sailors were heading toward it like iron filings to a magnet, but the two disguised Brothers tramped on past, steeling themselves against the scent of brown ale and roasting mutton. It was not a place where poor countryfolk, such as they were supposed to be, would be welcomed.

'There's another strange thing,' Felmar said, after a time.

'What?'

'While I was sleeping off and on in the ferry, I had the most unsettling dreams. About the things we took from the Royal Alchymist's crypt. Noises would wake me up, but when I slept again the same dream always returned. This happened three, maybe four times.'

Scarth stopped short with his mouth open in dismay. A single drop of rain hung at the tip of his long nose. 'You know what? I had strange dreams, too. I'd forgotten. I only remember bits and pieces, but I think I dreamt of Lord Kilian. Something about him frightened me, but I can't for the life of me think what.'

Felmar tugged his friend's arm. 'Keep walking . . . I dreamt that when we finally brought these moonstones and books to him, he laughed like a fiend and called us idiots for never suspecting how valuable the things are, for not realizing that we could have used them to become the most powerful sorcerers in the world!'

'I don't remember anything like that. But I think I do recall Lord Kilian laughing at me.'

'Think about it, Scarth. We agreed to risk our lives stealing this mysterious collection of arcana for him. He told us the sigils pre-dated Bazekoy's invasion, that they were ancient magical tools able to conjure the power of the Beaconfolk, and only Beynor of Moss could bring them to life. He said that Beynor had sworn an unbreakable oath, promising to share the activated stones with him and us. Kilian claimed he had a foolproof way to prevent Beynor from playing us false. But what if his talk of the Mossland conjurer was only a red herring, intended to distract us from the truth?'

'What truth?'

'It stands to reason that Kilian *didn't* know how to conjure these moonstones while he lived in Cala Palace and kept them hidden. But what if he's since learned how to do so, perhaps by studying some long-forgotten materials in the abbey? He's had access to the great library throughout his four-year confinement. What if the method for activating the sigils is contained in the two books that were in the cabinet with them? They're written in a strange language, you know.'

'Do you mean that Kilian might have been unable to read the books before – but now he can?'

Felmar shook his head uncertainly. 'My dream seemed to hint at something else. I can't remember what. All I'm really sure of is that we've both been deceived. I'm starting to suspect that if we give these things meekly over to Kilian, he won't bother sharing them with us. In fact, we may be lucky to escape with our lives!'

Scarth's heavy jaw hardened in growing anger. 'Brother, if I hadn't had my own dreams about Kilian, I'd deny your conclusion with my dying breath. He had me completely persuaded. But now . . . I think you may be right about the danger. I feel like a fool.'

'I was taken in, too,' Felmar muttered, 'as well as poor dead Vitubio. Even wearing the iron gammadion, Kilian Blackhorse is a consummate wizard. He converted Prior Waringlow, the greatest intellect in the abbey, to his cause. It's no wonder we were taken in.'

They walked in silence for some time. There were fewer people on the streets as the rain intensified and the air grew more chilly. The small shops, brothels and drinking establishments were thinning out as they neared the great wall at the northern end of the city, giving way to shuttered wool warehouses, empty and deserted at this time of year. When a sheltered alcove presented itself, Felmar discarded his artificial pregnancy, wrapping the arcana that had been concealed inside the basketry in his apron and tucking the bundle securely under his arm.

While the smaller man was rearranging his cloak, Scarth said, 'Have you any notion what we should do now? I'm damned if I'll simply keep heading for that cave in the gorge where Kilian's waiting.'

They began to walk again. Felmar said, 'I'm trying to think. We've got to get up into the mountains quickly, that's for certain. The masses of rock will help foil windsearchers – whoever they may be. North of the city, the road forks. To the left is the steep shepherd's path that we were supposed to follow to Roaring Gorge. To the right is a better track that leads eastward to Beorbrook Hold and the Great North Road. It winds through desolate moors and foothills, but avoids the most rugged part of the mountains.'

'You think we ought go that way?' Scarth was dubious.

'Only for a short distance, until we find a suitable place to go to ground. You and I must do some heavy thinking about our future.'

'Look there.' Scarth pointed ahead. 'It's the wall and the northern city gate. We're almost to Bo Hern's stable. I hope to God the goodwife's willing to feed us. All this scary talk's made me peckish.'

Felmar chuckled. 'If we're going to die tonight, let's hope we can at least do it with full stomachs.'

'You don't think we've much of a chance then?'

'I'm not so sure about that. You know, Scarth, we were so busy fleeing King Conrig's men that we never had a chance to look closely at the things we stole. I think it's high time we did, don't you?'

ELEVEN

The abrupt blast of powerful wind came out of nowhere, just as Kilian was congratulating himself on having successfully guided the cattleboat single-handedly to the mouth of Roaring Gorge. Earlier, the unsuspecting skipper had told him about the tricky route through the gravel-bars at the lakehead, and how important it was to stay in the middle of the channel.

In a light, fair breeze, Kilian had navigated well enough. But the sudden freakish blast turned the boat toward the shallows. The keel grated alarmingly on loose stones, and the five horses began to squeal with fright and pull against their ties.

He tried to correct the course with a quick thrust of the rudder and a tug on the lugsail brace, but he'd misjudged the potential contrariness of the clumsy boat in a strong wind. It yawed, charged toward the opposite side of the channel, struck a submerged rock, and slewed about wildly. The sail flapped like thunder, the deck tilted, and two of the horses were thrown down.

'Futterin' hell!' the alchymist cursed. The damned wind might capsize them unless –

He seized a small axe from a bracket on the side of the cockpit, clambered onto the angled deck, clawed his way toward the mast, and severed the halyard ropes. The lugsail, yard and rigging tumbled down, causing further panic among the horses, but at least the wind no long threatened to push them over and the deck came level again. Avoiding flying hoofs, he made his way to the bow and heaved out both anchors. One of the chains went taut and the boat swung about. With a piercing squawk, the hull came free of the rock and scraped along more gently into gravelly shoals before grounding in about three feet of water. As suddenly as it had risen, the gale fell off.

The horses calmed, and so did the alchymist. Amazingly, none of the animals had been injured by the falling yard. The ones that had lost their footing rose amidst the tangle of canvas and rope and stood trembling and blowing. Several pieces of baggage had tumbled from the cabin roof onto the deck, but the four Brothers sleeping up there appeared to be safe. With groans and a few muttered oaths, they threw off the pieces of tarred cloth that had sheltered them from the elements and stared wide-eyed at Kilian.

'Stop gawking,' he ordered. 'Pull yourselves together, get down here on deck, and give me a hand with this mess. We've arrived.'

'What happened?' Raldo mumbled in bewilderment. The impact had rolled him like a human ball, crushing him against the row of saddles.

'Why are we still so far out in the water?' Niavar wanted to know. 'I thought the skipper was going to bring the boat close to shore.'

'Where *is* the skipper?' Cleaton asked. 'And the rest of the crew?'

Young Garon surveyed the bleak panorama of encompassing cliffs, the whitewater of the Elk River rushing from the gorge mouth, the stony beach, and the weeping grey sky. He knew very well that their vessel had gone aground and was unlikely to move again, and even entertained suspicions about the missing boatmen. Shaking his head, he silently started down the ladder. After a few minutes, the others followed. Raldo came last, after pulling his jerkin closed and buttoning it. He never noticed that the iron gammadion and chain had fallen from his pocket and draped itself inconspicuously around one of the roof stanchions.

'I regret to tell you that our crew deserted us during the night,' Kilian said.

Three of the Brothers reacted with astonishment. 'But why would they do that?' Niavar asked.

Kilian said, 'Late yesterday, the captain attempted to back out of our agreement to land in the vicinity of Roaring Gorge. He claimed it was too hazardous and told me he intended to put in at Elktor Quay instead. Its lights were visible in the mist by then, over on the eastern shore. Naturally I told him it was out of the question. He demanded a huge sum of money to fulfill his part of the bargain. I realize now that he was all but asking me to purchase his boat outright. When he remained adamant, I finally agreed and turned over to him almost all of the gold I received from Queen Cataldis. Then I settled down in the cockpit with him to make certain that he kept his promise. Unfortunately, I fell asleep. When I woke, I discovered that the tiller was lashed and the captain and his men were missing. They seem to have gone away in those two coracles that were fastened on either side of the deckhouse. We were only a league or two away from land.'

Garon regarded the alchymist with frank incredulity. 'And so you just carried on through the night, sailing the boat slick as a whistle all by yourself?'

'No.' Kilian's patrician face was like granite. He stepped close to the young Brother so that their eyes locked, and forced him against the rail. 'I muddled through with considerable incompetence, if you must know. Even though I'd done my best to learn how the boat was driven, I ultimately made a hash of matters and piled us up on a gravel bar. But we're alive, our horses have survived, the boat doesn't seem to be sinking, and all of our equipment is safe. We'll have to wade ashore, but at least we're on the proper side of the Elk River. Your sheep path should be somewhere up that steep slope to the right.'

He stepped back, to Garon's evident relief. 'Yes, I suppose it is. We'll find a way to it somehow. Maybe by backtracking down the shore.'

The alchymist nodded, satisfied that he was once again in control. 'I don't know the hour, but it can't be too late in the day. It looks like the rain will continue, so we may not reach the cave before owl-light. But let's give it our best try. Before we disembark, we'll feed the horses and ourselves. Raldo, will you please build a fire in the deckhouse stove?'

'Certainly, Lord Kilian,' said the fat man. In a half-daze, he shuffled into the cabin, wondering whether the horrifying events he had witnessed earlier might have been some sort of nightmare.

Then he saw rusty spots still staining the damp floor around the wood-rack.

He stood immobile, feeling the pulse pound in his temples, unable to breathe, unable to take his eyes from the telltale stains. They were more brownish than scarlet, and might have been caused by anything. Very probably the other Brothers would never even notice them. If he pointed them out, who would believe his explanation?

Repressing a shudder, he stacked a few bits of kindling in the stove's firebox, struck a light with his talent, and watched while the little flames reluctantly took hold.

Sir Gavlok Whitfell was a man of unusually sensitive temperament, and he was becoming deeply concerned about

Deveron Austrey. The party had just ridden out of the lakeside village of Badgerhead, about fifty leagues south of Elktor,
where the road made a wide detour inland in order to avoid
a great swamp. All of the members of the group were still
tired, having eked out only four hours' sleep; but Deveron
seemed hovering on the brink of collapse.

The second time that his friend nearly fell out of the saddle,
Gavlok took hold of his bridle and slowed both horses, telling
the others to ride on ahead. When they were beyond hearing,
he said, 'Deveron, I know that something's very wrong with
you. You're in much worse shape than the rest of us, for no
reason that I can fathom. Have you taken sick? If so, we'll
turn back and find you a bed in the last village –'

Snudge took a deep breath. He could no longer avoid the
issue. If the two of them were to ride in close company for
weeks, on a quest involving heavy use of his talent, Gavlok
would have to be informed of the toll that even ordinary
magic could take upon the human mind and body.

'All right, I'll confess. Vra-Mattis will have to know, too,
I suppose. I was foolish to think I could keep it hidden.'

'For the love of God, man – what is it?' The young knight's
lean features were drawn with anxiety.

Snudge spoke in a low, hurried monotone. 'The moonstone named Concealer isn't my only dangerous secret. I
have another, known only to the High King, Lord Stergos,
the earl marshal, and a handful of other people. I'm a wild
talent, Gavlok. A secret magicker. This is what makes me so
valuable to King Conrig as an intelligencer. My faculties are
strong, and they're also largely imperceptible to other adepts
such as the Zeth Brethren. This is why they never found me
out and forced me to join their Order. I can perform any
number of useful tricks, but the most important are super-
sensitive windspeech and the ability to scry intently over
extreme distances. Also, I myself am immune from being

scried by other adepts. Only Ullanoth's Subtle Loophole sigil can oversee me.'

Overwhelmed, Gavlok rode in silence, staring at the pommel of his saddle.

Snudge continued. 'The reason I'm so bloody beat is that I've been cudgeling my brains windsearching for Brothers Felmar and Scarth since we left Pikeport. When I'm not scrying about for them, I have a go at Kilian Blackhorse and his henchmen, who escaped from Zeth Abbey and are likely on their way to a meeting with the two thieves. So far, I haven't been able to spot any of them. Finding these men is the most important thing King Conrig has ever asked of me – although he may not realize what a great threat they are to him.'

'But why should this be? Kilian is a vile traitor, and the fire-raisers are guilty of murder and mayhem. But how are they a danger to the High King?'

'When I told you that more moonstone sigils taking magical power from the Beaconfolk exist, I wasn't referring to the ones owned by Ullanoth or Beynor or the Salka monsters. There's another collection of sigils – over a hundred of the damned things, all of them inactive. They were hidden in Cala Palace, and the thieves stole them under cover of the fire. I must try to get them back before they're handed over to Kilian. King Conrig wants the moonstones returned to him, but I intend to do my best to destroy them. No man living should own such terrible weapons – even if they're inactive.'

'It's strange that I've never heard of them before,' Gavlok said. 'When I was Lord Stergos's armiger, I often delved into his books of sorcery. But there was no mention of moonstone sigils and their link to the Beaconfolk.'

'Even most of the Zeth Brethren know nothing of them. The stones were found centuries ago by an early Royal

Alchymist of Cathra named Darasilo. He secretly passed them
on to his successor, and so they were handed down for
centuries until they came to Kilian. None of the alchymists
before him tried to bring the sigils to life – maybe because
they were too afraid of the Beaconfolk. Kilian had other
ideas. The trove also includes some ancient books written in
the Salkan language that probably describe how to activate
the sigils. No modern-day Cathran is able to read those books
– but the Royal Family of Moss can.'

'Beynor,' Gavlok said in a flat voice.

Snudge inclined his head in weary assent. 'It's obvious that
he and Kilian made a devil's pact to share the stones and
the knowledge. They bided their time after the alchymist was
convicted of treason. Then Kilian sent his agents to steal the
trove from its hiding place. What I'm not sure of is whether
or not he might have learned the Salkan language while
imprisoned in the abbey. There are thousands of old tomes
in that place, some dating nearly to the time of Bazekoy.'

'God's Toenails! Then Kilian might not need Beynor –'

'I don't know where that Mossbelly whoreson is or what
he's up to.' Snudge gave a great yawn and rubbed his
reddened eyes. 'He was supposed to have been cursed by the
Great Lights and exiled to the Dawntide Isles, forced to live
with the Salka. This is where Ullanoth thinks he still abides
. . . By the way, she apparently knows nothing of Darasilo's
Trove. Conrig kept its existence secret from her. He was afraid
she'd come after it herself. Ordinarily, moonstones can't be
scried. But Ulla's Loophole sigil . . . can oversee them if given
a direct command to do so . . . We don't . . . think that's
happened . . . yet.'

As he spoke, Snudge's eyes slowly closed and his head
drooped lower and lower onto his breast. He caught himself
with a start and an oath. 'Gavlok – can you lash me to the
saddle again, as you did on Solstice Eve when I was dead

drunk? If you lead my horse I can sleep until we reach Elktor. Maybe . . . be of some damned use when we get close to the mountains and start the *real* search.'

'Of course. Pull up and I'll see to it. If the armigers ask, I'll say you have a slight fever.'

'Good. Tell Vra-Mattis all of this . . . *Don't* tell squires, 'specially Wil Baysdale.'

'What about young Wil?'

But Snudge only whispered, 'Don't trust him.'

Gavlok had climbed down from his horse and was removing the long belt that symbolized his knighthood. After detaching his sword, dagger, and purse, he used the stout strap to tie his friend firmly to the saddle. Even before he finished, Deveron Austrey was lost in oblivion.

Using his own limited-range windsight, Garon finally found the shepherd's path – but only after a tedious search. It was much higher above the river than he remembered, nearly two hundred ells. Getting to it from the lakeside, up a treacherous talus slope in pouring rain, was a daunting ordeal. The horses had to be led, and their hooves dislodged loose stones at almost every step. More than once, an animal faltered and crashed to its knees, barely avoiding a fatal fall back down the trackless incline. Kilian and the Brothers were forced to zigzag back and forth to ease the steep angle of the gradient, more than doubling the distance traveled. And all this before they made a single step in the direction of the cave . . .

On Garon's instructions, each of them – even the alchymist – used his recovering talent to calm the increasingly agitated minds of the horses. By the time they attained their goal, an exiguous ledge along a cliff-face, Raldo was sobbing with fatigue and urging his animal to pull him up. Mercifully, the horse obeyed. The two of them were the last to arrive at the path.

The fugitives sat hunched under their capes without moving for some time, regaining their strength, while their mounts licked trickles of rainwater from the streaming rock wall.

Saying nothing to his companions, Kilian experimented with his formidable new spell of couverture. If he could summon the strength to erect it, it would shield them all. But he was not yet fully recovered and had no success. For the time being, he contented himself with an easier kind of magic that altered his overseen appearance, while his aspect remained unchanged in the eyes of his companions.

Finally, he gave the command to mount and move on, watching in silence as the sweating, crimson-faced fat man, too drained to climb into the saddle on his own, was boosted up by the others. They set off in single file, moving at a slow walk. The track was extremely narrow, with a sheer drop to the river on the left. It climbed higher and higher, but the horses seemed willing to negotiate it without complaint. For over three hours, they traveled without incident. Then they became aware of a deep rumbling sound, which grew louder as they continued on, rising eventually to a tumultuous roar.

'Waterfall,' Garon shouted in explanation.

The source of the noise remained unseen until they came around a sharp corner into an area where the path widened, forming a natural terrace at the opening of a deep vertical cleft carved by a tributary stream. The upper section of the waterfall was deep within this cleft, pouring down from a height hidden within low-hanging grey clouds. Billows of vapor surged around the foot of the falls, where a plunge-pool had been gouged from a relatively flat rock shelf that was a continuation of the terrace where they had halted. This was littered with jagged chunks of stone fallen from above, some of them as large as cottages. Water flowed from the pool across the shelf in a wide, shallow stream until it reached the edge, where it dropped off in a second cascade to the floor of the gorge.

Beyond the submerged rock shelf, the path resumed.

'Merciful God,' Raldo exclaimed. 'How can we possibly get past here?'

Garon gave him a superior smile. 'Now you know why I brought rope from the cattleboat.'

'It looks hopeless to me,' Niavar said. His face had gone white and his vagrant eye had nearly retreated behind his nose. 'The passable section near the lip of the lower cascade is only a few feet wide, and it's at least a dozen ells long.'

'It can be crossed,' Garon insisted. 'I've herded sheep across here – although I must admit I never tried it when the water volume was so great. There must have been heavy snows last winter.'

'Explain what we must do,' Kilian said.

'We blindfold the horses and go one at a time. I'll be first, carrying the rope and paying it out behind me. When I get to the other side, I'll fasten the line to that knobby formation under the overhang. One of you will tie the other end here, to this rock, after pulling it tight. As you ride over the shelf, guide your mount only with your knees. Keep one hand on the reins and the other on the rope. If your beast stumbles and starts to go over the edge, let him fall and hang onto the rope.'

'Bazekoy's Blazing Bunions!' Cleaton groaned. 'I'll need a blindfold myself to get across.'

The alchymist was calm. 'Why don't I go next? When I reach the other side, I'll use all my talent to compel your horses to set their feet safely among the stones and running water.'

They tied rags over the eyes of the mounts. Garon handed Kilian the rope coil, took the free end, and rode his raw-boned, powerful chestnut across the streaming shelf as though it were Cala High Street. When both ends of the rope were fixed in place, Kilian followed suit on his tall sorrel mare, moving much more slowly. He, too, reached the other side with apparent ease.

'I'll go next,' Raldo declared, striving to keep a tremor out of his voice. 'I can't bear the suspense of waiting.'

The fat man's huge bay gelding lost its footing after going only a few ells and gave a heart-stopping lurch; but it recovered its equilibrium and went on successfully to the other side, whereupon Raldo burst into tears of relief.

Cleaton set out with lips clamped tight and his eyes narrowed to slits. In the middle of the shelf, his rather nervous red roan suddenly stopped dead and refused to move. He thumped its sides with his heels, uttered lurid curses, and exerted all of his talent. The animal resumed its hesitant pace and joined the other three on the opposite side. The men there had dismounted, leaving blindfolds on the horses, and stood in the partial shelter of the overhanging cliff.

'Last but not least! I'll be right along, boys!' Niavar called, urging his mount into the shank-deep water. The small black cob squealed at the unexpected sharp cold and tossed its head violently. The knot of the blindfold slipped and an instant later the cloth fell away. Stricken with terror at the sight of the dropoff and the pressure of the flowing stream against its short legs, the beast shied. One of its forefeet came down atop a precariously balanced rock and it collapsed, legs flailing. There was a sickening crack as a bone snapped. The cob screamed, rolled to the lip of the shelf, and fell to its death in the misty depths of the gorge.

Kneeling in rushing water up to his crotch, wiry little Niavar clung to the sagging rope with both hands. He was unable to stand, so he used his arms to haul himself the remaining three ells across. The others grabbed hold of him and pulled him safely up.

'Am I going to have to walk to the bloody cave, then?'
he grumbled.

'You can ride pillion with me,' Garon said. 'My chestnut
is strong and neither of us is heavy.'

The Brothers took Niavar close to the cliff and began to
strip off his soaked clothes. Kilian opened one of his saddlebags and took out a long shirt, wool stockings, and spare
boots; Garon contributed homespun trews that fit well
enough when rolled up seven inches and cinched with a
piece of rope; Cleaton found a short waxed-leather cape with
a hood.

As he dressed, Niavar thanked them all.

Raldo said sheepishly, 'I'm sorry I didn't have anything
that would fit.'

'Just be thankful it wasn't *your* horse that fell,' Kilian said
to him.

They resumed their journey, with the fat man bringing up
the rear and mumbling prayers under his breath, trying
vainly to forget the frightful image that Kilian's words had
evoked, and the pitiless tone of the voice that had spoken
them.

Beynor's voyage up the Malle was not as carefree as he'd
hoped, but at least the Salka swimming around him remained
unnoticed, and no one in authority challenged him as they
passed the teeming wharves and docks of Holt Mallburn. The
strong seabreeze that blew during the hours of hot sunlight
kept his dinghy's sail well-filled throughout the first day on
the river. Assisted by his unseen Eminent hauler, he forged
nimbly upstream past less fortunate boats and reached
Twicken by the time the sun dipped low and the breeze slack-
ened off.

'There are food-stalls and small shops on the waterfront
of this town,' he bespoke Ugusawnn. 'I'm going to put in,

tie up, and buy something to eat. Don't worry, I won't try to leave the boat. Just see that you stay out of sight.'

The only response was a surly growl on the wind.

He lowered the sail and rowed to the public landing-stage, where he tied up, paid the toll, and then began restowing the various bundles in the boat. After a few minutes a stout, pink-cheeked matron in a clean gown came along, carrying a wide basket covered with a cloth. She stopped at each vessel with people aboard, offering cold meat pies, but sold only a few.

'A fine evening, goodwife,' Beynor said, when his turn came. He proffered a silver quarter-mark coin. 'I'll gladly take two of your pies.'

'I don't have the change for this,' she admitted. 'Business has been slow this evening. The big crowd came to the river-side this morn to see off the royal barge – but I couldn't get my baking done in time for selling to them. My old dad came over poorly, and I've had to nurse him most of the day. If you care to trust me, I'll step over to yonder inn and get the change there.'

'You look like an honest woman,' Beynor said. Her easy friendliness might have its uses. He gave a winning smile and opened his purse. 'I'm very sorry for your hard luck. I've had a bit of that myself today, out on the water. Gave my ankle a bad knock, and now I can barely walk. I don't want to go tramping about ashore if I can help it, but I've not much food left in the boat, and no drink at all. If I gave you more money, could you also fetch me some some loaves of good wheat bread from the inn, and maybe some butter and jam, and some boiled eggs in their shells if the kitchen has such things? And ask the potboy to roll over a firkin of ale for me. I'll gladly pay you for your trouble.'

'Oh, you poor lad! Of course I will. Just guard my pies whilst I'm gone. Is there anything else you're needing?'

'Fresh strawberries?' Beynor ventured, 'I live on a island

far up the coast, and earn a good living from sealing. But I haven't had such luscious things for four years, since last I came to visit my people up in Mallthorpe Greenwater.'

'If anyone on the Twicken waterfront has any, I'll bring them to you,' the woman said. 'Imagine! Four whole years without strawberries!'

'I'd also be most grateful if you could send my way any old-clothes vendor who might be out and about this evening. As you can see, my garb is unsuitable for the warm weather you enjoy here, although it served me well in the chill at sea. I'd buy more comfortable things if I could.'

The women was thinking. 'You're a tall, thin one, just like my old father. And he, poor soul, spends much of his time abed these days and has small need of street clothes. After I see to your provisions, I'll slip away home and look in his coffer. There might be something you can use.'

'I'll pay whatever you think is fair,' Beynor said. He gave her another quarter-mark and she bustled off.

After a minute or two, Ugusawnn spoke truculently on the wind.

What did you say to her, groundling?

'I only asked her to fetch more food and some clothes for me. She had some interesting news to report. The royal barge left here this morning. It'll be upriver at Tallhedge by now, and tomorrow it goes to Mallthorpe Castle and stays for two days before going on to Boarsden. We'll have to get ahead of it to set up the ambush. The distance from here to the Big Bend is nearly ninety leagues. You may have to do some night hauling to get us there in time.'

I will do what is necessary.

'Good. You and your warriors can give the barge a good look-see while it's tied up at Mallthorpe, so you'll be clear about what I expect you to do later.'

Ugusawnn gave an ill-tempered grumble.

'The matter has to be handled just right. You must follow my orders exactly, or –'

Or WHAT, you insolent heap of whale-puke?!

'Eminence, I'm not trying to insult your intelligence, or that of your warriors. I'm only anxious that we succeed. Be easy in your mind! When the present King of Didion and his family are dead, we'll have taken the first step in destroying Conrig Wincantor's Sovereignty – and giving the Salka back their ancestral home.'

So you've said . . .

'Believe it,' Beynor assured him, with all the coercive power his great talent could summon. 'Believe it!'

Snudge and his men reached the south gate of Elktor at about the tenth hour after noon. It had been locked for the night an hour earlier; but Vra-Mattis had previously bespoken the Brothers resident at the castle warning of their coming, so they were admitted with alacrity. They paused in the shelter of the guardhouse, and Snudge showed the royal writ to the sergeant of the guard. By then the rain was coming down steadily, but the intelligencer had managed to sleep in the saddle in spite of it and felt much refreshed.

'Sir Deveron,' said the sergeant, handing back the parchment with a salute, 'one of my men will lead you to the castle if this is your wish. Count Olvan is in residence. He'll be eager to tell you of the search for the fire-raisers being conducted in this region, as well as offering his hospitality.'

Snudge thanked him. 'We'll tarry here a moment while my windvoice announces our arrival, then welcome an escort.'

While the novice attended to this, Snudge beckoned the other riders to come close to him. 'If it's true, as I believe, that the fugitives have gone into the mountains at some point above this city, then they must necessarily travel much slower than heretofore. Mat and I will confer with the

Brethren at the castle and make contact with Zeth Abbey as
well. We'll ask that all windsearching now be concentrated
in the area of Roaring Gorge.'

'Will we go after the villains at once if they're overseen,
sir?' asked the armiger Valdos.

'All of you are in need of sleep,' Snudge said. 'We'll likely
wait until morning. Vra-Mattis and I will confer with the
resident wind adepts to see if there are new developments.
But it's likely the fugitives have also stopped to rest – especially if they're mounted. We'll ride out with a force of Lord
Olvan's rangers tomorrow.'

Vra-Mattis pushed the hood of his cloak back from his face
and announced, 'They're awaiting us at the castle.'

One of the guards joined them, having fetched a horse.
'Mortal steep road up the castle knoll,' he said with a grin.
'Those poor beasts of yours look about done in, so I'll take
it nice and easy.'

He set off. Snudge motioned for Mat and the armigers to
follow, while he and Gavlok brought up the rear.

'Do you really think someone will be able to scry out our
quarry?' the lanky knight murmured doubtfully. 'Surely
these local magickers have already combed the area to the
best of their ability.'

'My hope is that I myself might catch an oversight of the
thieves from the high vantage point of the castle, now that
I've recovered my strength somewhat. We can always
pretend that Mattis found them, and he can direct the
searchers with my prompting.'

'Ah.' Gavlok smiled. 'The lad nearly popped the eyeballs
from his skull when I revealed your wild talents to him
earlier. He was very impressed with my tales of your prowess
– defeating Iscannon, taking Redfern Castle, and opening the
Mallmouth Bridge. I had to caution him not to make his
hero-worship of you too obvious.'

Snudge gave a brief bark of mirthless laughter. 'Me, a hero? I think Vra-Mattis – and the High King – will find another name to call me if I have no luck finding those two wretches and the stolen trove!'

TWELVE

Riding on muleback, Felmar and Scarth traveled eastward for about nine leagues along the Beorbrook track from Elktor. They were still without a firm plan of action, and tonight their only wish was to get as far away from Kilian as possible. The rain increased to a near-blinding downpour. Soon it became obvious that they could go no further. Even the sure-footed mules were starting to balk as they sank into deepening mud.

Dropping the cover-spell briefly, both Brothers cast about with their talent for a likely place to take shelter. They had purchased a piece of stout canvas that could be used as a tent in a pinch; but the deserted croft, when they scried it, was a much more attractive option, even though it looked more like an animal lair than human habitation. The hut was situated in a sheltered moorland hollow where stunted junipers grew, backed and hemmed about by outcroppings of bedrock. It was well out of sight of the track and looked reasonably secure from windwatchers as well. A rill of clear water ran nearby and there was even a patch of rain-flattened grass for the mules.

The entrance was an inverted V formed by two slabs of

rotting wood. There were no windows and the interior was dark. Felmar struck a flame at the tip of his finger with his talent and peered inside, alert for wildlife, but the place was empty except for some ancient sheep droppings. The field-stone walls and the turf roof were still sound and the dirt floor almost dry, except in the corner where a smokehole above a simple hearth let rain drip in.

'This is as good as we'll find tonight,' Felmar decided. 'Let's hobble the mules and get our things inside.'

A little later, after Scarth had chopped up dead branches from the small trees with his woodsman's axe and got a fire going, they were reasonably comfortable. The canvas covered most of the dirt floor, and saddles and pads made acceptable beds. Felmar was finally able to remove his hated female disguise. The two of them shared some of the harsh brandywine that Bo Hern's goodwife had sold them at exor-bitant cost, and ate some of her excellent honey-raisin oatcakes.

Then they decided it was time to examine the Trove of Darasilo.

For the next two hours, they pored over the books and the two bags of moonstones they had taken from the crypt in Cala Palace. The fragile volumes contained pictures of countless sigils, along with blocks of indecipherable text. The trove included one hundred and twelve milky translucent carvings of varying shapes, most rather small and some dupli-cates. Many stones were strung on golden chains or decaying leather cords, and all of them were minutely incised with arcane symbols or exquisite tiny pictures that gave tanta-lizing hints of their function.

'This book shows fewer stones,' Felmar noted as he turned crumbling pages, 'but the illustrations are larger and more elaborate than those in the other one, and the descriptions are much longer. I suspect that my book describes the more important sigils. Let's see how many of those we can find in the collection.'

To their vast disappointment, only four of the carvings matched the criterion: a moonstone finger-ring; an oblong sigil that looked just like a tiny door, complete with simulated latch; a thing about the size of a man's little finger that was shaped like a carrot or an icicle; and a short rod or wand with a drilled perforation at one end, incised with the phases of the moon.

'Well,' Felmar said with an ironic smile, 'at least there are two for you and two for me. Shall we draw straws for first pick?'

Scarth gave him a startled look. 'Are you suggesting that we somehow keep back these – these *important* sigils for ourselves?'

Felmar set the stones aside, put more wood on the fire, and sighed. 'I'm only joking.'

He unsheathed his knife, picked up a stick, and began to trim off splinters. 'Here's something we have to consider, Brother. Lord Kilian promised to bespeak us when he was well into the mountains and there was only a small chance of the thread of his windspeech being traced back to him. Very soon – perhaps tomorrow or the next day – we're bound to hear his call. If his talent has sufficiently recovered from the strictures of the iron gammadion, I wouldn't be surprised if he tried to scry us as well.'

'We won't answer him! And if we keep the cover-spell in place, he won't be able to find us.'

Felmar gave an exasperated grunt. 'Kilian devised the spell of couverture we're using. You can be sure he knows how to puncture it – or even turn it off completely. We can only hope that his powers remain weak for a while longer, giving us a chance to put more distance between us. The mountains will help block his windsight if he does obliterate the cover-spell.'

'But eventually, he'll be able to find us, Fel! And if he thinks we're running away from him with the trove, he'll come after us and kill us.'

'True. That's why we can't simply ignore his call on the wind. When it does come, we must answer him, so his suspicions aren't immediately aroused. But what we ought to say . . . as yet, I don't know.'

'What would he do,' Scarth said carefully, 'if we didn't take the trove with us when we fled? What if we hid it in some safe place and told him where to find it?'

Felmar paused in his whittling. His eyes glittered in the firelight. 'Brother, you may have hit on the solution! He'd certainly be furious at us for abandoning the trove – but not to the point of chasing us down. He's a fugitive, too, and his life depends upon getting over the border into Didion as fast as possible.'

'He'd know he could retrieve the things sooner or later,' Scarth said. 'He could even scry them in their hiding place and know we were telling the truth.'

'Yes. Good point! If we spin a plausible yarn, I think Kilian would be satisfied to let us go our own way. When he bespeaks us, why don't we say that we were unable to follow the path to Roaring Gorge. We only escaped a search-party by the skin of our teeth. They're hot on our heels and we don't want the trove to fall into their hands. Our only chance now is to travel cross-country – north into the trackless mountains.'

'That's no lie, either.' Scarth's long face was somber. 'The story sounds good to me. We could leave the trove right here – maybe hide it up in the roof of this hovel.'

Felmar resheathed his knife. He had made four tiny wooden sticks of differing lengths. 'Ready for the magical moonstone drawing?'

Scarth frowned. 'I thought you were just fooling.'

'Come on! Just for the fun of it.' Felmar put his hands behind his back, fumbled, then held out a fist with the stick-ends peeping out. 'Take any two. Longest chooses his important sigil first, then we take turns, on down to the shortest. Each man says what his sigils are capable of. Then we decide who's the greater sorcerer.'

'Oh, hell. Why not?'

Scarth won the first and third choices. He picked the ring and the icicle. Felmar got the miniature doorway and the wand.

'A pity we *can't* take these with us,' Scarth mused. 'I suspect this ring might be a Weathermaker, like the one Conjure-Queen Ullanoth owns. And maybe the moonstone icicle can freeze a person in his tracks! Can you better that?'

Felmar rubbed his fingers over his own treasures. 'This thing of mine looks like a door. It must *be* a door! Conjure it and it opens into a better world – one full of sunlight and good food and friendly, carefree folk who don't have to work for a living.'

'Take me with you when you step through,' Scarth said wistfully, 'and I'll concede you the sorcery contest hands down . . . What do you think that other thing of yours does?'

But Felmar was tiring of the game. 'Who cares? Probably nothing that would be of any help to us. We'd better turn in so we can make an early start tomorrow. Help me get these regular sigils back into their sacks. Let's wrap the four important ones in the linen hood from my goodwife disguise before we tuck them in with the others.'

'You're still thinking about keeping them when we run?'

Felmar shrugged. 'Only thinking. We could probably sell them for a pretty penny to a magicker up in Didion – or better yet, in Moss. Would Kilian even know they were missing when he scried the two bags of sigils? Seems to me it'd be nigh impossible to count the things, all bunched together like that. And he might not be able to fetch them for years.'

They discussed this interesting topic at some length, passing the brandy flask back and forth, speculating on what the four stones might be worth. Why, they might even offer them to the Conjure-Queen herself! She'd know their true value.

'She c'd perteck us from Kilian's revenge, too.' Scarth gave a tipsy giggle. 'Maybe help us join the Glaum'rie Guild! I w-wouldn't mind takin' a job at the Mossback court.'

'Better'n holin' up in the Diddly morass f'rest of our lives.'

Neither of the Brothers had tasted hard liquor since entering the Order, where it was forbidden because of its deleterious effect on talent. But when Bo Hern's wife offered plum brandy in addition to the other provisions, they'd hesitated only a moment. Hard times lay ahead of them. Ardent spirits were medicinal. They banished aches and pains and helped a man sleep when his mind was plagued by fear and worry.

Scarth and Felmar hadn't planned to empty the flask that first night, but somehow it happened anyway. With all their troubles forgotten, they settled into inebriated slumber.

At first, Felmar's dream was much as it had been before. He was a young boy again, no more than ten or eleven years old, sitting under a flowering apple tree in the garden of the family manor house. His kindly grandsire was there beside him, warning him to beware of great danger from the wicked Kilian Blackhorse.

Now Felmar was able to tell Grandad about the newly hatched plan to outwit the alchymist. He described it eagerly, in much detail. But the old man shook his head in disagreement.

No, my lad. There's a much easier way to get the better of Kilian. One of those moonstones you stole can provide a foolproof means of escape for both you and Scarth. I can show you how. You very nearly guessed the secret when you were playing your game.

'What do you mean?'

The sigil resembling a tiny carved door is called Subtle Gateway. It won't take you to paradise, but it can transport you and your friend anywhere in the world in the blink of an eye.

'But the stone is inactive, Grandad! I can't read the conjuring instructions.'

That's not necessary, Felmar. There's a simpler method of bringing sigils to life. Of course, only a very brave man can make use of it! But you're no coward. I'm confident you can do it. Darasilo, the silly fool who first found the stones, never knew anything about this. Neither did his successors – including Kilian Blackhorse. All one need do to activate the sigil is hold it firmly, then touch it to one of the moonstone medallions affixed to the book covers.

'That's . . . all?'

If this is done, the supernatural Guardian of the Moonstones will pronounce a strange phrase three times. A great sense of fear will come over you. There'll be a good deal of pain, too. But if you keep up your courage until the phrase is said for the fourth time, the sigil will come to magical life, glowing with a green inner light. Hang it about your neck. Then all you need do is take hold of your friend's hand – or anything else you want to transport along with you – and speak your destination in a loud voice. Instantly, you'll be there!

'It seems too wonderful to be true.'

Try it! What have you got to lose?

'What about the other stones in the trove? Can they all be activated in the same way?'

Of course.

'I could . . . take all of them for myself?'

If you wanted to.

'Thank you for telling me, Grandad.'

Felmar forced his eyes open and struggled into a sitting position with his back against the saddle. His head spun from the brandy he'd consumed, even though Scarth had taken the lion's share. The dim interior of the croft seemed to ripple like a disturbed reflection in water. He smelled acrid wood-smoke and wet leather, heard the other man's slow snores and the rustle of gentle rain. The fire was still burning wanly.

The dream.

Could it be true?

He pushed aside the blanket covering him and crawled to where the bags of sigils and the books lay. Through bleared eyes he saw milky mineral disks in narrow gold frames fastened to each cover. Mere ornaments, surely.

Or were they?

Try it, a remembered voice inside his head seemed to urge. *What do you have to lose?*

He emptied both bags of moonstones onto the canvas that covered the floor, pawing and scattering the sigils in a frenzy of impatience until he found the tight wad of cloth that held the four important ones. He shook it open, dumped the stones, and selected – what had Grandad called the thing? – Subtle Gateway! The magical door leading to safety and to power. More power than he'd ever imagined.

Felmar grasped the little oblong carving and pressed it against a book disk, then gave a low cry of astonishment.

Both the sigil and the medallion began to shine with a gentle greenish light. He thought he saw a movement within the croft out of the corner of his eye, but before he could turn to look at it a deep voice that had nothing human about it spoke a question inside his head.

CADAY AN RUDAY?

Terror, deeper and more paralyzing than he'd ever known before, seized him like some ravening beast. There was pain as well, as though an ice-cold lance were being driven into his breast.

CADAY AN RUDAY?!

The awful voice was bespeaking him on the wind, more

loudly this time and with angry impatience. The Guardian of the Moonstones, Grandad had said. The swelling pain was atrocious. His ribs were being torn apart and his heart crushed by frigid pincers. If he let go of the sigil, let it fall away from his flesh, the suffering would end. But then he would lose all chance of bringing the Gateway sigil to life –

CADAY AN RUDAY?!!!

He was deafened by the monstrous voice, blinded by hurt, shrieking voicelessly into the wind as the nerves of his body burned in icy flames. But he was brave. He would persevere, hold fast until the fourth time that the Guardian asked his question. He would remain courageous until the end.

The end came, engulfing him in an agony of silent Light.

Beynor withdrew his bedazzled windsight, shaken to the core in spite of himself, and lay trembling in the bottom of the dinghy.

He rested for a long time, then sent his sight soaring once again to the interior of the faraway hut. Felmar Nightcott was gone, his flesh, blood, and bone reduced to a heap of gritty cinders. Although Beynor was unable to scry them, he presumed that the ancient books and the sigils were unharmed. From the conversation of the thieves, he had managed to identify three of the four Great Stones in the trove. The fourth was still a tantalizing enigma.

Perhaps when he entered the dream of the second man, he could coerce him into describing it.

But Beynor discovered very quickly that Scarth Saltbeck lay in a drunken stupor so profound that his mind was in-accessible to any invader. The jug-bitten wretch was incap-able of dreaming! His natural talent was also totally incapacitated, and the protective spell of couverture had dissolved even before he and his companion had fallen asleep.

Beynor gave up trying to penetrate Scarth's sodden brain

after numerous failed attempts. His own head ached abom-
inably from the effort and he cursed his bad luck. There was
no helping it: he'd have to wait until later, when the liquor's
poisonous effects had worn off a little. Meanwhile, he'd keep
windwatch on the surviving thief as best he could, hoping
no one else would scry out the unshielded lummox and come
after him.

He relaxed on the pallet he'd made up in the bottom of
the boat and stared up at the crimson night sky. With sail
furled, oars stowed aboard, and no one at the tiller, the
dinghy glided arrow-straight up the wide River Malle. Only
a handful of people near the docks at Tallhedge noticed its
uncanny passing, and they turned away from the sight in
superstitious fear and told no one.

On Snudge's orders, the guards at Elktor's Mountain Gate
had been questioned about strangers leaving the city late in
the day. The officer who had been on duty clearly recalled
a quarreling married couple mounted on mules – the man
tall and robust, the wife petite and bristly about the chin.
They had passed through shortly before the gate was locked
for the night, even though the guards had urged them to
wait until morning.

Heartened by this first solid evidence that the fugitives were
in the area, Snudge told Count Olvan Elktor that he would
use a map to guide his windvoice, Vra-Mattis, in a fresh search.
The two of them ascended to the top of the castle's lofty north
tower, and from that vantage point Snudge himself had
labored for over three hours, nearly exhausting his limited
store of energy in a futile scan of the land route to Roaring
Gorge. Meanwhile, Mattis dozed peacefully at his master's
feet, wrapped in a frieze cloak against the persistent drizzle.

To Snudge, the shepherd's path leading to Roaring Gorge
had seemed the most logical way for the thieves to go. But

the precipitous rock formations in the area proved a near-insurmountable barrier to his talent. The only living things he scried among the misty crags and ridges were animals.

Finding the boat was an unexpected piece of luck.

He had all but decided not to extend his search all the way to the gorge mouth, since it lay twelve leagues from Elktor, and there had hardly been time for the thieves to travel so far on such a difficult path. But wishing to complete the job he'd begun, he continued scrying the portions of the path most readily visible to his mind's eye, and at length came to the broad stony beach at the outflow of the river. The abandoned livestock boat out in the shallows caught his attention almost at once, and his heart leapt with hope. The presence of horse droppings on the deck at least made it feasible that the vessel had transported Kilian and his party.

Intent on finding something to confirm his judgment, he focused more closely on the craft, even exerting himself to scry through the wooden bulkheads. He saw an empty wine bottle fallen into the scuppers. Its label revealed that it had held a fine Stippenese vintage – a beverage far too dear for the purses of lowly watermen.

A promising sign, but it wasn't proof positive.

He inspected the cockpit, the deck where the horses had been penned, and the interior of the little cabin, finding nothing of interest. A ladder had been positioned so that the roof of the deckhouse could be accessed, and something seemed to be caught on one of the rail stanchions up there, dangling down the opposite side. Again he strained to scry through the wood, and realized he was looking at an iron gammadion on its chain . . .

Snudge withdrew his sight and slumped down onto the parapet, drained by his efforts. Mattis was still asleep. The efficient castle steward had provided them with a covered basket containing a stoppered flask of spiced cider, bread rolls, and smoked goat-cheese. Snudge drank from the bottle and forced himself to chew several mouthfuls of bread. After a few minutes he felt himself recovering from the ordeal.

He now had a solid clue to the whereabouts of Kilian; but if the alchymist and his companions had gone into Roaring Gorge, there was probably no chance he'd be able to oversee them from here. They would have to be hunted by a ground party – and most probably not one including him and his people, unless King Conrig himself gave the order.

He reached out a hand to awaken Vra-Mattis and have him bespeak Cala Palace, then hesitated. A wild notion had popped into his mind. Rising to his feet, he walked across the flat roof of the tower to the opposite side. On his left soared the dark rampart of the Sinistral Range. Rolling moorlands lay at the foot of the mountains and extended eastward, interspersed with isolated masses of upthrust rock similar to the tor on which the castle stood. There was a track down there that wound over the heath toward Beorbrook Hold.

What if the thieves had gone that way? What if something had prevented them from taking the fork in the track that led to the gorge, giving them no choice but to turn in the other direction?

Shutting his eyes and summoning his last reserve of talent, he focused his windsight once again.

Conrig Wincantor brought his fist down with a bang on the table of the Council Chamber, causing Vra-Sulkorig, who was seated on his right, to blink in unspoken disapproval. The other chairs were empty and the table was littered with abandoned sheets of parchment, rolled charts, waxed tablets, and styluses. The candles in their gilt stands burned low.

'What do I care if he's busy helping Vra-Mattis windsearch?' the king bellowed. 'He can take a few minutes off to talk to his liege lord! He should have given me a progress report yesterday. We wouldn't even know that he'd reached Elktor if Ollie's windvoice hadn't had the sense to notify you.'

'Let me bespeak Vra-Alamor again, Your Grace. I'll insist that he interrupt Sir Deveron.' The Keeper of Arcana drew his hood over his face and bowed his head.

Conrig sat back in his chair, fuming. It was well after midnight and he'd dismissed all the Privy Council members except Sulkorig, who was serving as deputy to Stergos, after a long but none too productive conference about the situation in Tarn. The king had felt it necessary to inform his advisors about Maudrayne's possible survival after another windspoken message was relayed to the palace from the outlaw shaman, Blind Bozuk – this time through a different, and presumably less expensive, intermediary.

Bozuk claimed to know where Ansel was taking the princess. He was willing to part with the information in exchange for five thousand gold marks, which the shrewd magicker demanded be kept in escrow for him until Maudrayne's capture. The Sovereignty's Ambassador to Tarn, Lord Grendos Wedmorril, had no such enormous sum at his disposal. It would have to be borrowed – either from bankers in Donorvale, who would demand punitive interest, or from the Tarnian Lord Treasurer, who would hem and haw and perhaps even insist on tax concessions. News of the extraordinary transaction was bound to spread quickly to Cathra via the financial grapevine, and the Lords of the Southern Shore would ask embarrassing public questions of the Crown.

Conrig had put the matter up to his Council: should he respond to Bozuk's offer and obtain the money, or put the shaman off – at least for the time being – until the Royal Intelligencer was on the scene and in possession of all the facts?

The Council had waffled. In the end, Conrig decided to wait.

But he was not willing to wait for a report from Snudge.

How dare the intelligencer remain incommunicado? He was supposed to report to the palace every evening, even if there were no new developments –

Sulkorig straightened and pushed back his hood. 'Your Grace, I've bespoken Vra-Mattis. He says that Sir Deveron has scried out the hiding place of one of the fire-raising thieves, Scarth Saltbeck. He has also located an abandoned boat at the head of Elk Lake, which was very likely used in the escape of Kilian Blackhorse from Zeth Abbey.'

'Thank God!' cried the king, starting up from his chair at the head of the table. 'Tell me more!'

'The man Saltbeck is hiding in a hut on the moors some eight leagues east of Elktor. A party of warriors, led by Deveron, will set out shortly to arrest him. When this is accomplished, Deveron will bespeak me personally with all details of the venture.'

'I trust that the miscreant has Darasilo's Trove with him.'

'There would be no way to determine that, sire, until the thief is taken. Sigils cannot be scried. Neither, I presume, can the two magical books, since they have moonstones on their covers.'

Scowling, Conrig expelled a noisy breath. 'I'd forgotten. God grant that the entire trove be there in the hut, and the intelligencer is able to take it safely in hand! What's this about a boat?'

'Sir Deveron is convinced, from various clues he oversaw on the empty vessel, that it transported Kilian, his fellow-traitors, and their horses to Roaring Gorge at the head of Elk Lake. It's possible that the chasm would provide an escape-route into Didion for the whole gang of conspirators, provided they had an expert guide. When Kilian and his three friends fled the abbey, they took with them a young Brother named Garon Curtling. He belongs to a mountain clan and would likely know the gorge area well. A force led by Lord Olvan

Elktor will pursue Kilian and his companions – although the troops will have a hard time of it because of dangerous terrain and unfavorable weather.'

'I don't give a damn whether Kilian escapes into Didion, so long as he doesn't carry the Trove of Darasilo with him.' Conrig pulled a wry face. 'I won't sleep this night until I know whether Deveron's pursuit is successful. Will you keep watch with me?'

Sulkorig rose. 'Why don't we go to Lord Stergos's chambers, sire? We can wait comfortably in his sitting room without being disturbed. If we receive good news, we can inform the Royal Alchymist at once. Lord Stergos would be greatly comforted. Perhaps he can also advise Sir Deveron how best to ensure the security of the recovered trove – no small matter, you'll agree.'

'No,' Conrig agreed. 'It's not. I'll have to give it careful thought myself.'

They thundered down the steep road from Elktor Castle and galloped apace for the Shore Road and the Mountain Gate: six of the count's most intrepid household knights and four times that number of men-at-arms, heedless of the misty drizzle that enveloped the countryside, intent upon apprehending at least one of the Sovereignty's most wanted criminals. Snudge led the troop, with Vra-Mattis riding at his side. He had deemed the other members of his party too inexperienced to accompany him, and had left them behind in the castle, sound asleep and heedless of the climactic events now unfolding.

Persuading his eager host, Lord Olvan, to lead the hunt for Kilian rather than the more exciting apprehension of Scarth Saltbeck had been a touchy matter. Although the young nobleman was brave, generous, and of a cheerful disposition, Ollie Elktor's character disastrously combined rash impetuosity with a truly monumental fat-headedness. His people loved him in spite of his flaws and were inclined to overlook his errors of judgement; and happily, these had become less egregious since the viscount's redoubtable father, Earl Marshal Parlian Beorbrook, had installed a handpicked steward to manage the castle household and an iron-willed constable to maintain discipline among its knights and warriors.

Lord Olvan yearned with all his heart to go after the notorious villain who had fired Cala Palace; but in the end, even a valiant dullard such as he understood the reasons why Sir Devron Austrey sent him in the opposite direction. Chasing a fugitive over the eastern moorlands presented no special tactical difficulties to a newcomer to the region, provided he had local men riding with him. Roaring Gorge, on the other hand, was hazardous territory where specialized knowledge was vital to survival. Lord Olvan had actually ventured into the dreadful, haunted place a few times, if only for short distances. Sir Deveron knew nothing about the gorge, and confessed to being inexperienced in mountain travel to boot.

So Ollie manfully conceded the point. While Deveron and his men raced off on their lightning foray, the viscount assembled a larger force that was equipped for a long haul, and rode out at a more prudent pace an hour later. By then, Snudge was more than halfway to the croft where Scarth Saltbeck lay in a state of sodden insensibility.

The truth was that the intelligencer had a stronger reason for not wanting Olvan – much less any of his sharper-minded lieutenants – witnessing the arrest of Scarth. He intended that none of the Elktor people should ever know about the Trove of Darasilo, much less what he planned to do with the trove if he found it.

Before leaving the castle, he had begged its master mason to lend him a certain tool, saying vaguely that the thing might help in extracting the criminal from his hiding place.

But if the opportunity arose, Snudge planned an entirely different use for the sledgehammer wrapped in sacking, which was now lashed to the back of his saddle.

Being only human, Beynor dozed off.

His more vigilant inner self – or something – caused him to wake with a cry of dismay and a great start that set the briskly moving dinghy to wallowing.

What is wrong with you, groundling? the Supreme Warrior inquired in a peevish tone, from somewhere under the river. *Did your execrably unappetizing meal disagree with you and bring on an evil dream?*

'Something like that,' Beynor muttered. The monsters had no notion what he'd been up to. His ability to invade dreams was a secret he didn't intend to share.

How long had he been asleep? Long enough for Scarth's binge to have worn off a little? He sent the thread of his oversight aloft on the wind, ranging west-south-west to the desolate highland region between Elktor and the Great North Road, to the tiny hut crouching in its rocky hollow, well out of sight of the only track. The mules stood their patient vigil amidst dripping junipers. Inside the croft, the surviving renegade Brother had shifted his position slightly and started to snore. Behind their closed lids, his eyes were moving just a bit. The spell of couverture was still extinct, but that was to be expected.

Before attempting another dream-invasion, Beynor decided to cast about with his windsight to determine if any search-parties were abroad. It was unlikely. The local lord, famed as he was for happy-go-lucky stupidity, would hardly send his men out scouring the moors in the middle of a rainy night . . .

Beynor bit back a disbelieving curse when he saw the double line of torches moving eastward along the rough track. It couldn't be happening! The heavily armed knights and the warriors wearing Elktor livery had to be riding out for some entirely different reason; perhaps they'd been summoned to reinforce the troops at Beorbrook Hold.

He focused closely on the men at the head of the column. How strange! The apparent leader was a slight figure dressed in a rain-cloak, beneath which were the robes of a Zeth Brother. He rode beside a saddled horse that lacked a rider, and yet the adept turned his head now and again toward the empty saddle, as though someone invisible were there.

Someone who could not be scried . . . such as Deveron Austrey.

In a panic, Beynor wasted no time surveying the troop further. He screamed into Scarth's unconscious mind with all the power he could muster.

He'd only just begun to dream the new dream.

He was in the opulent throne room of the Conjure-Queen, approaching her with a confident stride. He wore the black garb of a high-ranking Didionite wizard, flowing robes of rich silken brocade trimmed with sable, and a matching skullcap. The queen's counselors, clustered about her dais, whispered to each other behind their hands, wondering who this magnificent stranger might be, not knowing he was there by royal invitation!

Warlock-knights of the Royal Guard presented their flaming swords in salute as he went down on one knee before Ullanoth of Moss. Smiling, he lifted the lid of the simple little honey-wood box he carried. 'I've brought the stones, Great Queen,' he said, going straight to the point, 'just as I said I would.'

The courtiers murmured at his temerity, but Queen Ullanoth rose to her feet, her lovely narrow face alight with avid anticipation and her eyes like green stars. She beckoned for him to approach. He did, holding out the open box so she could see its contents for herself.

The young queen reached out a slender hand. On one finger was a moonstone ring, identical to the one he had brought to her except for the glow of power that suffused it. Hanging on thin chains about her neck were two more living sigils – one small and drop-shaped, the other an open triangle an inch or so wide, with a short handle.

'May I examine these stones of yours, wizard?' she asked him with regal courtesy.

'Certainly, Your Majesty.'

She took the icicle-shaped stone from his box, regarded it in silence for a moment, lifted her head to meet his gaze –

And screamed at him: *Scarth! Scarth Saltbeck! Wake up, you fool! They're coming for you – the king's men! You have less than half an hour before they find you.*

He staggered back, dropping the box. 'What are you saying?' he gasped.

Gather up the sigils and the books. Put on your cloak and boots. Hurry! Don't bother with anything else except your sword. Saddle the strongest mule. Go north across open country, to the mountains. And if you value your life, put up the cover-spell before you ride out! . . .

She vanished, along with all of her court.

Scarth was back in the rude moorland hut, lying on the floor, half-covered by a rough blanket. A faint red glow came from the embers of the dying fire, but he could see nothing clearly. His head throbbed with agony and the Conjure-Queen's warning seemed to echo inside his skull like the clanging of Zeth Abbey's gigantic bronze bell.

A dream. It had been another intensely vivid dream.

'Felmar?' he called out, in a voice roughened by phlegm. 'Felmar?'

When there was no answer he crawled to the hearth, tossed on a few sticks, and puffed at the coals until the wood caught and there was enough light to see by. He sat up and called his companion's name again, turning about and squinting into the shadows. But he was alone in the hut. Felmar's saddle, his improvised pallet, and all of his things lay as Scarth remembered them. Moonstone sigils, for some odd reason, were scattered everywhere, and the leather sacks that had held them were tossed aside. Even stranger was the abundant sandlike material strewn over the canvas floor-covering. The two old books were nearly buried in it, as was the cloth packet that had held the four important sigils. What did it mean?

Moving with trancelike slowness, he crept toward the door. Maybe Felmar had gone outside to answer a call of nature and got lost. Stupid idiot. But what did it matter, when he himself felt so tired and ill? The mystery of his companion's disappearance seemed unimportant, as did the curious mess on the floor. To hell with Felmar. Sleep was all that mattered. Sleep, and his dream of the lovely Queen of Moss –

Scarth! Scarth Saltbeck! Wake up, you fool! They're coming for you – the king's men! You have less than half an hour before they find you.

Shocked into wakefulness again, he found himself on his hands and knees before the croft's open doorway, straining to see what might be outside.

'Felmar!' he yelled. 'Where are you?' The only reply was a soft grumble from one of the mules. He turned about, picked up a pinch of the stuff on the floor and rubbed it between his fingers. Ashes. They felt nothing like the residue of burnt wood but were grainy and foul-smelling, like sea-coal cinders. Mixed with the ash were sharper fragments that almost resembled charred bone . . .

Terror smote him like a blow to the gut. Somehow, he knew what had happened – if not why. Vomit rose in his gullet and he was barely able to crawl out the door into the grey drizzle before he spewed the contents of his stomach.

He moaned his friend's name one last time, knowing that there would be no answer. Then he wiped his mouth on his sleeve, staggered to his feet, and re-entered the croft to gather the things Queen Ullanoth had commanded him to take. His hands trembled violently, his vision was still impaired, and he was half-crazed with fear. The need to flee this awful place without delay overwhelmed every other thought in his pain-wracked brain.

All those sigils scattered about . . .

Let them be! Take only the four important ones!

Where were they? He found the ring, the rod, the stone icicle – but the tiny stone carving of a door wasn't there. He scooped up the three and put them in his jerkin pocket.

Why take both books? Only one is needed. Hurry!

He stuffed the tome pertaining to the Great Stones inside his shirt and next to his skin, where it would stay dry, then buckled on his sword with fumbling fingers and fastened his cloak.

Hurry!

The rain had almost stopped by the time he clumsily saddled the mule, and the sky was brighter in the east. He put a foot into the stirrup, swung up after three ineffectual tries, then drew a deep breath and pronounced the incantation for the spell of couverture. To his surprise, it worked.

Hurry, damn you! To the mountains!

'To the mountains,' he mumbled. They weren't far away, and there were other large rock formations even closer, where he might be able to find a good hiding place.

He turned the mule's head, kicked its ribs, and set off.

THIRTEEN

Snudge had been windwatching the sleeping thief inter-mittently since he and the warriors rode out from the castle, even though his talent was greatly fatigued. The empty brandy flask lying on the floor of the hut showed plainly enough why the heretofore impenetrable cover-spell had failed in its protection. But the two empty wash-leather bags on the floor – plus the even more ominous presence of the missing Brother's gear and mule – filled him with foreboding.

Then Scarth awoke. The man's inexplicable terror, nausea, and frantic preparations to ride out caused Snudge to bark out an oath of vexation.

'What's wrong, sir?' Mattis shouted over the noise of pounding hoofbeats.

'Use windspeech,' Snudge bespoke him. 'Our thief is preparing to flee. Scry him out yourself, if you can. He's frightened out of his mind for some reason, but not saying much, so I can't read his lips and find out what's going on . . . Damn it to hell! He's put up the cover-spell again.'

'I don't see him, sir,' Mattis admitted. 'There's only the stone hut and a mule.'

'There were two mules a moment ago,' Snudge said tightly. 'Look carefully at the ground around the place. Let's see if either of us can scry a trail of hoof-marks in the mud.'

Close scrutiny was all but impossible while jouncing along on horseback. As the troop came closer to the croft, Snudge was finally able to determine that there were no fresh prints ahead of them, on the track to Beorbrook. So their prey had taken off cross-country, probably in the direction of the mountains.

'We won't be able to track him over the open moors until we reach the hut,' Snudge said. 'The ground's too stony and cluttered with heather and brush for close scrying. On the other hand, he's not going to be able to go very fast. Do exactly as I say when we arrive at the hut. Don't forget that *you* are the only windvoice in our company.'

'I understand, sir.'

They reached the faint side-path leading to the croft in another quarter-hour. Snudge held his hand high as a signal for the troop to stop, then pointed out the new direction. The men followed single-file over the rougher ground, at a cautious walk. When they rode into the hollow and caught sight of the tiny dwelling in the murk, Snudge once again called for a halt and motioned for the six knights to come close for a conference.

'Gentlemen, my windvoice and I are going to ride forward and call on Scarth Saltbeck to surrender. Fan out your warriors and follow us. Keep back about ten ells and be alert if he tries to run. Remember: we want this man alive.'

One of the knights said, 'Is he likely to attack us with sorcery?'

'It's not likely. Mattis is very weary from having performed an arduous windsearch earlier, and he's temporarily unable to scry through the stone wall of the hut. But when he oversaw our villain half an hour ago, he was lying dead drunk inside. Inebriation quenches talent completely. Ready? Here we go . . .'

They closed in on the empty hovel. Snudge dismounted, drew his sword, and made the surrender demand. When there was no response, he ducked inside the croft, swiftly surveyed the interior, and gave a sigh of relief as he saw the sigils strewn on the floor and one of the books partially buried in some kind of sand or ash.

He emerged, looking crestfallen, and called out, 'Bad news, lads! Our bird has flown.'

There were disappointed groans and curses from the entire troop.

'All right, here's what we do. I'm going to search this hut. He's left a lot of stuff behind that might provide valuable clues. Meanwhile, Vra-Mattis will scry the ground round about here until he finds the bastard's tracks. He'll lead the new pursuit. Follow him and keep your eyes well peeled. I have to warn you that our villain may be hiding beneath a cover-spell. This kind of magic doesn't really make a person invisible to the naked eye – but it *does* try to fool you into not noticing the one who's covered. If you think you might've glimpsed a man on a mule and your mind tells you it was only fancy, don't believe it! Point him out to your mates and ride straight at him. If you can get within five feet, he'll become clearly visible.'

'Swive me,' one of the men-at-arms muttered. 'Tricky business, running down magickers. Gimme plain old sheep-stealers and bandits any day.'

Mattis had been sitting his saddle with eyes squeezed shut while Snudge addressed the troop, casting about with his windsight. 'Here they are!' the novice cried. 'Tracks made by the fugitive!' He urged his horse up the far side of the hollow and the rest of the warriors streamed after, shouting eagerly.

Snudge waited until the last one had disappeared before

sheathing his sword and tying his horse to a juniper branch. He retrieved the sledgehammer and searched until he found a flattish rock the size of a cottage loaf. Leaving them just outside the croft, he entered the low door. Two men had certainly been here. One had ridden away while the other had disappeared, leaving all his gear, his saddle, a fine sword, and his mount behind. Carefully, he shook out the blankets and other equipment and piled them in a far corner, away from the canvas groundcloth where the sigils and ashes were scattered. The two wash-leather bags had obviously held the moonstones. He squatted and began collecting them, shaking off the clinging grit as best he could.

What *was* that filthy stuff? It had a faint noisome odor that was somehow familiar. He filled both bags with sigils, dusted off the book, and sat back on his heels, pondering. He'd seen ash like this before.

It came to him. The dank lower chamber of Mallmouth Bridge's bascule machinery. The treacherous armiger Mero Elwick in a rage of frustration, knowing he could never use Concealer himself and vowing that Snudge wouldn't have it, either. A tremendous blow with a broadsword that left the sigil unharmed, while Mero himself was incinerated in a flash of defensive sorcery.

Something like that had happened to the missing thief.

'Yes,' said a low-pitched voice from the hut's doorway.

'Who's there?' Snudge cried. Drawing his sword, he crouched back against the opposite wall. A small cloaked person was standing there, visible only in silhouette.

'Come out, sir knight,' he said, 'and bring the sigils and the book with you.'

'Aroint thee, whoreson!' Snudge cried, reaching with his left hand to touch Concealer and turn himself invisible –

He froze stock still, paralyzed in every muscle save those of his face. He spat out a curse.

'Be silent, Deveron Austrey. Or may I call you Snudge?'
The figure stepped back and became discernible in the
dawnlight, a little man whose head would have come barely
to Snudge's shoulder, dressed in a suit of well-cured skin
and wearing a cloak of mingled dark colors in a pattern
that mimicked tree-bark. His skin was sun-browned and his
large eyes were a startling green. 'Be calm. I mean no harm
– not to you, especially, since you're of the blood. I
command you to put away your sword and come out. Bring
the Trove of Darasilo.'

Compelled to obey, Snudge emerged in furious silence,
placed the bags and the book on the ground, and glared at
the stranger.

'My name is Odall,' he said, 'and I've been sent by the
Source. Do you remember Red Ansel's Source? The one he
spoke of when you and he sat in a small boat on Cala Bay,
and you summoned the Light and quickened the Concealer
sigil you wear next to your heart?'

Snudge felt his scalp prickle and his throat grow tight.

'Do you remember?'

'Yes,' Snudge whispered. He began to inch toward Odall.

'The Source has decided that you're needed in the New
Conflict. Ansel himself doesn't know, and we Green Men aren't
allowed to tell him about you for a while yet. Don't *you*
mention this meeting of ours to him or anyone else, either.'

'You're . . . a Green Man?'

'Yes. There's more of us about than you'd think. In the
Elderwold, we sometimes rob caravans! But mostly we stick
to the wild places where humans seldom go. If we're taken
unawares by one of you giants, we haven't much of a chance.'

Snudge tried to keep his voice steady. 'What do you want
with me?'

'I came to stop you from smashing the sigils in the trove.'

'The things are evil! They destroy people's souls and bodies.

I know that for a fact.' He continued to edge almost imperceptibly toward the little man.

Odall grinned. 'Nevertheless, you're willing to use your Concealer sigil in what you think is a good cause. You'd use it to help your master, Conrig Wincantor – and oddly enough, that's as it should be. Conrig will never know it, but he's been enlisted to help in the New Conflict, too.'

'I don't know what you're talking about,' Snudge said sullenly.

'It's not necessary that you should.' The cheerful demeanor of the Green Man vanished like a snuffed candleflame, and Snudge realized that he was once again quite incapable of movement. 'Do you recall the words you used to bring Concealer to life?'

'Yes,' Snudge said through his teeth. 'Why do you ask?'

Odall didn't answer. He went into the croft, and after a few minutes came out with the saddle and harness that had belonged to the missing thief. The things should have been too heavy for one of his slight build to carry, but he flung pad and saddle onto the back of the mule as though they were weightless, expertly tightened the cinch, and shortened the stirrup leathers. 'How splendid that I can go home in style! I've had a long foot-slog.'

When the mount was ready he picked up the ancient book, and as Snudge watched in fascinated horror, he tore off the cover with its moonstone disk and set it carefully on the rock Snudge had selected earlier as an anvil for his hammer. Then he opened one of the sigil sacks and took out a small oblong moonstone.

'See this? It's name is Subtle Gateway, and it's one of the Great Stones. Hold it tight, close your eyes, and say EMCHAY MO. Then tell it where you want to go. It will carry you anywhere in the world. If you should desire to take up to ten other persons with you, or three horses, or a boat up to four ells long, or a heap of goods equivalent to the weight of three horses, say EMCHAY ASINN. Clear enough?'

'No, it's not, damn your eyes!' Snudge strove without success to overcome the paralysis. His feet seemed rooted to the ground. 'I don't want to use a Great Stone that'll put me in deep thrall to the Lights!'

'Well, that's as may be, and you do have a point. But the Source thinks you'll need Subtle Gateway in order to carry out your bounden duty, so you're obliged to take it. With luck, you may only have to use it a few times and the pain-debt will be not too onerous. When your duty's fulfilled, we'll show you how to drain the stone's life, then get rid of it for you.'

'It should be destroyed now, and so should the rest of Darasilo's Trove! For God's sake, Odall, why are you preventing me from ridding the world of these terrible things?'

'Easy, lad. Have no fear. These bags of sigils and the cover-less book I'm taking will be destroyed, all right. But not just smashed to bits, as you planned to do. They'll be disposed of in a manner that serves the Source and hastens the down-fall of the Evil Lights.'

Odall placed the sigil named Subtle Gateway on the book cover and vaulted onto the back of the mule. 'Don't forget now: EMCHAY MO and EMCHAY ASINN are the words that conjure its power. The words of activation are the same as those you used for Concealer. And be very sure to name yourself Snudge to the Light, rather than Deveron Austrey, just as you did before. As Ansel told you, Snudge is your name, and yet it's not. And so you're not as beholden to the Lights when using their sigils as are certain other persons I could mention.'

'But you haven't explained –'

The Green Man flicked the reins and turned the mule in the direction that Mattis and the warrior troop had taken.

Speaking over his shoulder, he said, 'See that you move along to Tarn as soon as possible. Your duty lies there.' Odall and the mule vanished into thin air, and Snudge's body came back under his control.

'Wait! Who is this Source? What's he up to? How did he know how to find the sigils? They can't be scried!'

True. But since sigils are a channel to the power of the Great Lights, the Lights may decide who shall oversee them. These were known about from long ages past, but were inaccessible until the two thieves removed them from Cala Palace. And of course we had to keep them safe from the Conjure-Queen as well.

The soft voice seemed to emanate from no particular direction, and was weighted with a profound sadness.

Snudge eyed Subtle Gateway and the torn book cover with loathing. 'Curse you, Odall!' he shouted at the unseen speaker. 'I'll be no one's cat's-paw!'

Someone laughed, a melancholy sound. *If you believe that, then see that you fulfill your duty to King Conrig – not blindly and without question, but only as best you can.*

'I wasn't talking about the king.' Snudge looked about in bewilderment.

When you've finished activating the Gateway, crush the moonstone medallion and the book cover. Tell Lord Stergos – no one else – what happened here today. He, not you, is the proper one to pass on news of the trove's destruction to his brother Conrig.

Snudge felt his anger fade, leaving a mounting fear. 'You're not the Green Man. Who are you?'

I am the One Denied the Sky, the lowliest of the Likeminded, but despite that, designated to lead the New Conflict. Someday I hope I may tell you my tale. But that cannot happen until there is an ending.

'An . . . ending?'

Bespeak your young friend, Vra-Mattis. Have him inform the warriors that he has lost the trail of Scarth Saltbeck. They must all return to Elktor with you now.

'Do you intend to let Scarth escape? What happened to the other thief, Felmar, and the second book?'

Both wretched men had roles in the New Conflict. Felmar is dead and Scarth will not live much longer. You may also tell this to Lord Stergos. The second book need not concern you. Eventually, it will also be destroyed.

'What about Kilian Blackhorse? Is he also a participant in your Conflict?'

Yes. And so is Beynor ash Linndal of Moss, who has returned to this island to commit heinous sins. But ask me no more questions. Do the things I've requested of you, Snudge. You must, if it's all to come right in the end. Otherwise the Pain-Eaters will triumph. Farewell.

He took off his gauntlet and pressed the carving of the tiny door to the disk with his bare hand. As before, the irascible inhuman voice boomed on the wind, asking what he wanted.

CADAY AN RUDAY?

'GO TUGA LUVKRO AN AY COMASH DOM.' May the Cold Light grant me power.

The pain was tentative as the terrible being asked who he was. *KO AN SO?*

He told the truth that was not the truth, praying that Ansel and the Source were right. 'SNUDGE.'

An icy spear plunged into his breast, but stopped short of his heart. He endured, suffered, waited while the Great Light pondered his request to share power and pay the price. They were fickle beings, fond of deadly jests, as likely to slay a supplicant as to bestow their awful gifts. But once again, Snudge was one of the fortunate.

THASHIN AH GAV. We accept.

'MO TENGALAH SHERUV.' Thank you.

He was struck down then, as before, only to come to his senses later with the memory of horror causing hot tears to pour from his eyes. The agony had been much more severe than that he experienced during the activation of Concealer. Giving thanks for his survival, he lay there until his face dried and the sound of hoofbeats vibrating in the ground under his ear warned him that the others were returning.

He sat up. It was bright dawn, with the dark clouds all fled to the east. The small oblong carving glowed faintly green when he opened his clenched fist. The sigil was perforated, like Concealer, and fit easily on the same golden neck chain. He tucked the two stones away, feeling them warm and alive against the flesh of his chest. Then he got to his feet, took up the sledgehammer, and smote the book cover and its moonstone disk again and again, until they were so pulverized that no man could ever tell what they had been.

When Garon deemed the evening light too faint for safe travel, he called for the men behind him to halt. It was perhaps two hours until midnight. The clouds, tinctured faintly with crimson and violet, had lifted and the rain was over.

Kilian's party had attained a flattish triangle of land covered with grass and alpine herbs, several acres in extent, that jutted out over the depths of the gorge like the prow of a rockbound ship. On two sides the drop-off was almost sheer; the third abutted the shoulder of a hulking mountain. Shrubs and a few gnarled pine trees had taken root among the large rocks closest to the path, and a ring of fire-blackened stones revealed that someone had previously used the place as a campsite.

'We'll stop here,' the young Brother told the alchymist, after he and his pillion-rider, Niavar, had dismounted. 'Later on, it may get windier than we'd like, but now that the rain has let up it shouldn't be too uncomfortable. I grazed sheep in this little meadow betimes. With my dog keeping guard, I never lost one over the precipice, but it won't be safe for the horses to graze free. We'll tie them up by the trees and cut grass for them.'

Raldo, who had suffered some bad bumps earlier when his mount wrong-footed and he tumbled off, was appointed cook so he would not have to move about too much. Cleaton took charge of the horses, and Niavar was sent to a nearby cascade with a canvas bucket and leathern bottles for water. Garon and Kilian prowled the flower-dotted open area, cutting grass with their keen-bladed hunting knives and gathering whatever dead plant material might be coaxed into burning.

'If you look beyond this south-facing cliff,' Garon remarked to the alchymist, 'you can see part of the way we've come. The lake is at the horizon. Double Waterfall is visible if you follow the course of the river back to the great rock-cleft. The eroded section of trail where Raldo fell lies beyond that ridge of very dark rock.'

Kilian approached the edge of the precipice and scanned the striking panorama. 'We've climbed very high today, but not traveled as far from the lake as I hoped. What do you estimate – seven or eight leagues?'

Garon shrugged. 'Closer to five as the raven flies, I fear. The two near-disasters slowed us considerably. It's a miracle that Raldo's bay didn't slide down into the ravine when he mis-stepped. We'll have to poultice the beast's right front fetlock, but he'll be fine. I wish I could say the same about Brother Butterball. The man must be a mass of bruises. By tomorrow, he'll hardly be able to move.'

'It could be a problem,' Kilian said.

'We won't have an easy time of it crossing into Didion. In some spots, we'll have to climb on hands and knees, hoping the horses can follow along after us. A disabled man will find the going hard. If the track turns truly foul, we may have to leave our mounts behind altogether.'

'Mmm. Will we be able to find food?'

'I have a shortbow and arrows to take hares and marmot-squirrels. There are also plenty of snowcocks, although their flesh is sometimes unpalatable. Beyond the divide, where the climate is wetter and there are alpine bogs, there'll be elk and red deer. We won't starve.'

'What about creatures who would eat *us?*' The chiseled features of the alchymist wore an expression of academic curiosity.

'The great brown bear is all we have to fear, my lord. Tundra-lions don't live in the eastern Sinistrals, and the lynxes and wildcats are too shy to bother humans.' Garon paused, smiling dismissively. 'Some say that small enclaves of Green Men make their homes in the mountains further to the west, and they may be the demons who give Roaring Gorge its fearful reputation. But I've never seen a trace of the little devils myself, nor has any member of my clan.'

'Well, I'll give our route a careful scry as we proceed. And since we have attained an admirable vantage here, I believe I'll attempt a cautious windsearch right now, seeing what lies ahead of us – and behind as well. The two Brothers coming from Cala to join us may already have set out along the gorge path.'

'I'll take the grass you've cut to the horses,' Garon said. 'It'll be a while before Raldo gets supper ready. After I've gathered fuel for the fire, I'll give him a hand.' He added Kilian's sheaf to his own and meandered back to the camp.

The alchymist seated himself among a heap of lichen-scabbed rocks at the cliff-edge, pulled the hood of his cloak over his head, and sent out the slenderest possible thread of wind-sight. It swept those portions of the gorge path ahead that were not obstructed by thick rock. The track continued to climb toward the jagged northern skyline. About two leagues beyond the camp was a vast tumble of slabs that they would have to negotiate in the morning. In one part of the rockfall, the way seemed totally impassable, but that might have been an illusion of perspective. Kilian devoutly hoped so.

When he could no longer scry the forward route, he turned his attention to the way they'd come. The sections visible to his mind's eye were empty of both human and inhuman beings. Finally, he scrutinized the portion of the shepherd's track they had not traversed, which skirted the lakehead and led to the Mountain Gate of Elktor.

Rain still fell on the city and the region east of it. No search parties were abroad outside the walls, and there was no unusual activity apparent within. The cottages and huts scattered among the nearby hills were shuttered and locked against the short summer night, their domestic animals safe in folds or byres.

Kilian extended his windsight further to the east, along a moorland track where mist obscured the countryside, and in time discovered a dilapidated hovel with a tiny plume of smoke coming from its roof-opening. Two sleek mules were tethered outside of it. The stone walls made scrying the interior difficult, but he was able to discern two covered human forms lying asleep on the floor.

He frowned. They had to be benighted travelers, taking refuge from the rain. It was impossible for him to see their faces, but one of the bodies was much larger than the other . . . Surely they weren't Felmar and Scarth! Why would they have taken the track leading away from the gorge? No, the sleepers had to be other men. Still, it might be wise to scry them out more closely early tomorrow morning and make sure.

Kilian rose and stretched his aching muscles. It had been several years since he'd ridden, and his legs would have to readjust to the saddle. A pity the waterborne part of their

journey to Didion had been so brief! Idly, he scried the
grounded cattle-transport. It was as they had left it, bound
to be discovered sooner or later, but with nothing left aboard
that could point conclusively to them. By the time that the
boatmen were missed and their connection to the abandoned
vessel established, he and his men would be so deep in the
mountains that pursuit was impossible.

Tomorrow, he'd try to bespeak Felmar and Scarth. He'd
have to make a stab at contacting Beynor, too, unless the
young Mosslander invaded his dreams tonight. The ambush
of Honigalus was scheduled to take place only a few days
hence, and Kilian was keen to know how matters were
progressing with his co-conspirator and the Salka.

Interesting times lay ahead.

'Supper!' Raldo croaked. The tantalizing scent of grilled
sausages wafted through the dusk. Kilian smiled and trudged
over the meadow to where the others were gathered around
the fire.

He slept well that night, even though the ground was hard
and rocky, and his dreams were inconsequential rehashings
of his days as a Privy Council member under King Olmigon,
uninterrupted by Beynor. When he awoke, he sat up with
a start of alarm, not remembering where he was, thinking
he'd heard Zeth Abbey's rising bell. But the only sounds were
the snores and wheezes of his companions, quiet movement
among the horses, a distant rushing noise from the torrent
in the gorge below, and the thin sweet song of some alpine
bird. Pink and gold beams of dawnlight glorified the east
where clouds still lingered. The sky above Roaring Gorge was
almost clear and duck-egg green. The crisp, chilly air would
likely warm quickly once the sun came up.

Kilian threw off his blanket and rose. Like the others, he'd
slept fully dressed. Thinking to perform another windsearch,

he crossed the dew-spangled meadow to the southern edge
of the projecting precipice. Before attempting the more difficult task of scrying the path, he let his sight range to the
moor beyond Elktor. The travelers who'd sheltered in
the stone hut had roused his curiosity. The distance between
Elktor and Beorbrook Hold over that track was only thirty
leagues – less than a day's journey on horseback. So why
had the men spent the night in an abandoned croft, rather
than organizing their trip more prudently? Could they be
brigands?

To his surprise, he found no mules tethered there. A well-
caparisoned knight's courser had inexplicably taken their
place, and stood munching the trampled grass. The hut itself
was empty except for a few odds and ends of equipment.
Outside its front door, a sledgehammer lay beside a medium-
sized rock.

The track was empty for leagues in both directions, so
Kilian turned his talent to the area between the dwelling
and the mountains. Immediately, he scried a troop of more
than two score mounted men, milling about a small hooded
rider who sat a horse much too large for him. They were
knights and men-at-arms, and the central figure wore the
robes of a Brother of Zeth. As Kilian watched in consternation, the adept gave a hand signal and the entire troop set
out at a fast trot in the direction of the hut.

Great God! Who had they been pursuing over the open
moors?

He searched further, among the great rock formations that
reared up from the heath closer to the looming bulk of the
mountains, but found no one. No one who could be perceived
by scrying . . .

Kilian cut the thread of windsight and stood irresolute at
the edge of the cliff. If Felmar and Scarth had been in that
hut, and if they'd fled pursuit under the spell of couverture

he'd taught them, the hoof-prints of their mounts might have been followed by the troop of warriors. And now the hunters had given up the chase, perhaps because they'd lost the trail in increasingly rocky ground.

I could extinguish the Brothers' cover-spell now without putting them in danger, Kilian thought, and confirm that they've gone wildly astray, carrying the Trove of Darasilo with them.

But that was a drastic step and one he was loath to perform. He'd have to use a generalized incantation that would lift the spell *wherever Felmar and Scarth might be.* What if they weren't on the moorland after all, and stood in a vulnerable position elsewhere? Once he broke the spell, he could not re-establish it; that would have to be done by the two agents themselves. But would they realize what had happened? From within, a cover-spell was manifested to its wearer only by the most subtle alteration of one's surroundings. The Brothers might not realize they'd been exposed until it was too late to save themselves from capture. No, Kilian decided. It wasn't worth the risk.

If the moorland commotion did indeed have nothing to do with Felmar and Scarth, the two men might be on their way up the gorge path at this very minute. It was preferable to let things be so long as there was a chance they might still be heading for the cave.

He settled himself again, pulled down his hood, and began windsearching for them along the gorge route, beginning at the fork in the track outside the city wall. He didn't find them – but in time he did discover the mounted force of Count Olvan Elktor, halted in a rough bivouac on the near side of Double Waterfall. It was obvious that they had set out from the city during the murky night hours. They'd made the dangerous crossing and then paused to rest, but they were certain to move on before long.

Grimly, he counted at least forty men wearing the livery
of the castle garrison, a dozen household knights in bright-
colored surcoats, three Brothers of Zeth, and numbers of
servants on ponies leading sumpter mules loaded with
supplies. The presence of such a large force could only mean
that the authorities were fairly certain that either Felmar and
Scarth or Kilian and his party had come into the gorge.

White-faced, the alchymist withdrew his sight and hurried
to waken his companions. Garon, Niavar, and Cleaton heard
him out in bleak silence, while Raldo made incoherent
sounds of distress, too stiff and aching even to rise from his
pallet.

'It took us three hours to get here from the waterfall,'
Garon said, rolling up his blankets with swift economy. His
brow was creased by concern. 'We were tired and didn't
travel very fast. The pursuers will come on much faster.'

'But can we outrun them?' asked Kilian. 'Or perhaps go
another way?'

'There is no other way. As to outrunning them – it would
be better to prevent pursuit altogether. By blocking the track.'

Niavar and Cleaton brightened at this and began to ask
eager questions. Raldo stood by, apparently apathetic, but his
eyes were alert. Garon bade all keep silent and continued
addressing Kilian. 'My lord, when we planned this journey,
you spoke of combining our talents to produce defensive
magic. Is it not possible for the same type of joint effort to
block a section of the trail behind us, so that no one would
be able to follow? Perhaps we could amplify the landslide
where Raldo took his fall.'

The alchymist said, 'To make an effective blockade, we'd
need to find a spot where rocks above the path were already
unstable and a modest bolt of magic might bring them down.
The place where Raldo's horse slipped is hazardous with
loose surface stones, but not susceptible to rockfalls. The

mountainside itself is virtually solid there. Without golden
gammadions, our group lacks the strength to burst apart
living rock.'

Garon nodded in understanding. 'I think I know the perfect
spot for our purposes. A short distance beyond this camp,
we come to a hanging valley between two tall peaks. A side-
path leads to extensive grassy pockets, dead ends all, where
I used to pasture my sheep for weeks at a time. I never took
the flock beyond there because forage becomes scanty at
higher altitudes, but I did explore the ongoing route for my
own amusement. If one continues along the gorge track for
another hour or so, one arrives at a broad slope composed
of great cracked slabs, where some cataclysm caused half the
mountainside to break away and fall into the chasm.'

'I know about this area,' Kilian put in. 'I scried it last night
and thought it looked uncommonly perilous.'

'Normally, the slabs can be crossed with care by a man on
foot,' Garon said. 'I believe our horses could negotiate them
if they were led. Having overseen the place, my lord, do you
think we'd be able to bring down more rock and render it
totally impassable?'

Kilian said, 'Wait,' and left them, going out into the
meadow where the scrying angle was better. After a few
minutes he returned with a wolfish smile on his face. 'We
may not be able to render the slope impassable. But if the
column of pursuers were strung out all across it and we *then*
caused a rockfall . . .'

Garon, Niavar, and Cleaton stared at him in comprehen-
sion. Raldo only hung his head.

'Let us move on as quickly as we can, then,' said the
alchymist. 'We'll have to break our fast as we ride.'

Garon, Niavar, and Cleaton packed their gear with alacrity,
while Raldo hobbled about, tumbling the unwashed cups and
bowls and spoons from last night's supper into a sack, scraping

bits of cold porridge from the pot with a spoon, and wiping
the greasy wire grill with a handful of grass. His sunken eyes,
pursed lips, and trembling hands betrayed his misery.

'How do you fare?' Kilian asked blandly.

'I'm doing the best I can, my lord. I'll scour the cooking
things well at the end of the day.'

The alchymist grunted and said to Garon, 'Saddle his horse,
lash his bags in place, and help him to mount.'

They set out at a quick pace, most of them feeling more
confident riding the narrow path than they had been on the
previous day. The sun shone brilliantly and the air was crystalline, with every detail of the landscape sharply visible. The
hanging valley, when they reached it, was a concave emerald
corridor between peaks layered with brick-red, ochre, and
black rock strata, sublimely beautiful against an azure sky.
But by that time none of them was in a mood to appreciate
it – especially Raldo.

He sat in his saddle as inert as a sack of grain, his head
lolling and his hands hardly keeping hold of the reins. One
foot had slipped from its stirrup. His big bay was an intelligent beast, and it sensed that its rider sat unsteadily. Rather
than take advantage of the situation and toss Raldo off, as
the animal had done yesterday, it moved more and more
slowly and delicately, almost as though it felt compassion for
the wretched man on its back. Raldo brought up the rear of
the group, and lagged ever farther behind the others.

Finally he seemed to rouse from his stupor and shouted
in desperation, 'Wait! Please wait for me!'

Kilian pulled up and said to Garon, 'Go back and see if
anything can be done for him.'

The young Brother dismounted and picked his way
through the others along the narrow path, then continued
to the place where Raldo had stopped. The two men spoke
for some minutes. Garon replaced the fat man's foot in its

stirrup and wrapped the reins about one hand before returning to Kilian, shaking his head.

'I'm at a loss, my lord. Brother Raldo insists he can ride on. But he seems very ill. I wonder if he might have suffered some internal hurt in the fall? At any rate there seems little we can do, save hope he will regain his energy. I think it would be unwise to attempt to lead his horse. The animal is enormous, and if it should fall it would pull down the horse and rider leading it as well.'

The small Brother with the squint said, 'Old Butterball's a goner, then? We just leave him?'

'He said he intends to press on,' Garon said. 'He may be lucky enough to reach the slide before the troops are upon him.'

'We must continue,' said Kilian, 'as fast as is safe.' He clicked his tongue and urged his mount forward. After a moment, the others followed suit, not looking back.

Raldo cried, 'I'll follow! I'm coming!' But his horse stood still, receiving no signal to move from its rider. After a time, the others were lost to his sight around a bend in the trail.

Raldo shut his eyes and exerted his negligible windsight. They weren't scrying him – at least they hadn't lowered their hoods. To be safe, he waited a while longer, then dismounted with more agility than might have been expected. He led the big bay horse to a place where there was shade and a trickle of water. His bruises ached and he was unable to walk without a limp. But there was a small smile on his face as he took bread and smoked meat from his saddlebag, lowered his ample fundament to a flat rock, and began to eat his delayed breakfast.

Around noon, Kilian and his three remaining companions came to the slide. It was a formidable thing, in places resembling a giant staircase with tilted treads, nearly a hundred ells

wide and frightfully steep and rugged. The waý across that
Garon remembered from his youth was now obstructed by
slabs and boulders that had shifted position during the intervening years, so he spent another hour scouting a new path,
after which they all made their way slowly to the other side.

They tethered their mounts further on, well out of sight
of those who were coming after them, and concealed themselves among rocks where they would not be easily scried or
endangered by falling rock. Kilian led them in thaumaturgical exercises to refresh their minds in the technique of
melding talent. Then they essayed a practice bolt, aiming at
a small slab balanced far up the opposite side of the slope. A
flash jolted the target, and an instant later there came a loud
crack and a rumble as the rock bounced a few ells downhill.

'Not very impressive,' Kilian admitted, and the others gave
nervous laughs. 'But then, we didn't put our hearts into it.'

Garon eyed him askance. 'Do you think we have a chance
of pulling this off, master? I've never been one for overt
magic myself.'

'Needs must when the devil drives,' muttered Niavar. 'If
you can save your skin no other way, you'll find your overt
talent sharpening along with your resolve.'

'Can you scry them coming, Lord Kilian?' Cleaton asked.

The alchymist pulled his hood down and concentrated. 'It
won't be long.'

They waited. The air was still and hot. They loosened their
jerkins and eventually shed them, drinking ale from the
leather bottles they'd tied to their belts. They'd left their
swords hanging on their saddles. Physical weapons would do
them no good.

'How far is the cave?' Niavar asked, breaking a long silence.

'Another two hours' slow ride,' Garon said. It's off to the
side and up a ravine, not on the main path.'

Somewhere, a raven gave a raucous bark.

Cleaton said, 'My lord, what of Brothers Felmar and Scarth?'

'And the treasure?' Garon appended softly.

'I tried windsearching for them back at the campsite yesterday,' Kilian admitted, 'and made another attempt while were were riding here. They don't appear to be anywhere on the gorge trail as yet, but if they're using the spell of couverture I wouldn't be able to scry them unless I obliterated it – and that's too dangerous. I've held off attempting to bespeak them because puncturing a heavy cover-spell requires a very 'loud' windvoice. As I said before, I don't want to risk some adept tracking the thread back to me. But perhaps that doesn't matter any more. The hunters seem to know we're here.'

'Then why not give the two lads a shout?' Niavar suggested. 'It'd ease my mind, for one, to know that Felmar was in good fettle. We were mates back in the abbey. Runts sticking together.'

'We'll wait,' Kilian said, 'until this situation is resolved. 'Here comes the vanguard of the troops, rounding that tall crag.'

They exerted their windsight for a closer view. 'Codders!' Garon said. 'It's Ollie Elktor himself leading the pack. Who'd have thought it?'

The count and his knights spurred their horses to the edge of the rockfall but made no attempt to enter it. 'They'll send scouts ahead to find the route,' Garon murmured, 'just as I did for us.'

But nothing of the sort happened. Lord Elktor and his knights dismounted and so did the warriors. For the next half hour they waited. At last a man-at-arms rode up through the stationary column from the rear, leading a huge bay horse carrying a bulky figure directly to the viscount's side. The two men spoke. The fat man pointed to the upper section of the rockslide and made a sweeping gesture.

'Raldo!' Cleaton exclaimed.

'He's told them of our plan,' Kilian said in a voice gone flat. 'They're not going to cross en masse. We've lost our chance to panic them.'

The others groaned. Niavar said, 'Damn that Butterball! He must have been gulling us, acting more sick than he really was.'

'He was in very bad shape,' Garon protested. 'I examined him before we slept. He had bruises and scrapes almost from head to toe. He kept me awake with his groans of pain.'

'I think our Brother despaired of being able to make this difficult journey,' Kilian murmured, 'and conceived of a plan to ingratiate himself with our pursuers and thus gain lenient treatment when he surrendered.'

'Let's smite him with a bolt!' Cleaton's swarthy face was merciless. 'That'll show the lard-arse weasel!'

'No,' the alchymist decided. 'We won't waste our talent in petty revenge. We'll need every bit of it in making our escape.'

'But it's a stalemate, master,' Niavar said. 'They won't cross while we're waiting to bring the rocks down. But if we run, they'll be after us like wolves. You can be sure those local Brothers riding with them are adept at scrying. They've probably got a mind's eye on us right this minute.'

Kilian said, 'They won't scry us if we're under a cover-spell.'

'You said you couldn't cover us all!' Garon said.

'I propose weaving a new kind of spell, incorporating all our talents. I'm stronger now, and we're no longer encumbered with Raldo. I'm afraid we must leave our horses behind, but that would strengthen the illusion that we were still lurking here. All we need is an hour or so head start. A man can move nearly as fast as a horse on this wretched track. And even though Lord Elktor has a reputation for rashness, I think we can trust him to wait at least that long before daring the rockslide.'

'Will we be safe once we're inside the cave?' Niavar asked.

Kilian glanced at Garon. 'You said its entrance was hard to see from the path. I'll be able to disguise it with my talent as well.'

'And so we *walk* to Didion?' Garon said.

'Would that be impossible?'

'No, but –'

'Other opportunities will present themselves,' the alchymist said with serene confidence. 'No doubt we'll have to stay in the cave for a few days until the searchers lose heart and return to Elktor, but that will give Felmar and Scarth time to catch us up.'

He retrieved his jerkin and gestured for the others to do the same. 'No time to waste. Come close to me, one behind the other with a hand on the shoulder of the man ahead.' He described to them how they should blend their talent with his to reinforce the extended blanket of couverture. 'There's still a long chance we might be spotted by the naked eye. We'll duck-walk to the horses to lessen the possibility. Ready?'

They murmured assent. He took a few moments weaving the spell, than laid it over the four of them. The bright sunlight turned fractionally dimmer. The others augmented the enchantment as they'd been told to.

'Now,' Kilian said. They crouched and moved off to safety while the Brothers who accompanied Lord Elktor exerted their windsearching faculties in vain.

FOURTEEN

It was not until late morning that Beynor was able to finish dealing with Scarth.

Much earlier, an hour or so after the small troop of knights and warriors from Elktor had abandoned their pursuit of the fleeing thief, Beynor had tracked him into a region of broken cliffs at the southern edge of the mountains. There the density of the rock formations, combined with the cover-spell, defeated even his powerful windsight. From Scarth's ravaged appearance, it seemed likely that he would soon need to rest. Once he was asleep and susceptible to dream-invasion, his fate would be sealed.

With the advent of strong daylight, Beynor had been obliged to hoist the dinghy's sail and be content with slower progress upriver. The assistance of the submerged Salka Eminence was now all but imperceptible to human observers. Beynor spent the boring hours on the Malle scrying the barge of the royal family, watching Prince Somarus's party as it emerged from the wilderness and set out along the road to Castlemont, and scrutinizing events taking place at Elktor, where Sir Gavlok, the youthful windvoice called Mattis, who had led the chase after Scarth, three other squires, and presumably the unscriable Deveron Austrey, seemed to be making preparations to leave the castle. The large force that had gone after Kilian was only sporadically viewable as it continued to search high in the mountains near the head of the gorge. Of the alchymist himself there was no sign.

A bell in a village on shore tolled the eleventh hour of morning, and Beynor decided to try Scarth again. His wind-search once more proved fruitless, so he attempted a dream-invasion. He found the thief not only asleep, but also suffering a horrendous nightmare – the best possible framework for mental manipulation. Beynor waited while the awful scenario played out in the dreamer's mind, so that he himself might fully understand its portent and make use of it. Then he artfully banished all remnants of Scarth's fear, leaving the man's unconscious open to coercion.

Nothing was moving inside the dark fissure in the cliff-face. It was probably sleeping off its meal, the lucky brute, while *he* felt his empty belly knocking against his backbone, tormenting him with spasms of hunger.

Scarth was well concealed behind a large rock, not badly wounded after all, carving collops of meat from one of the haunches of the mule's partially devoured body and stringing them on a stick for roasting over the little fire he'd started with his talent.

A noise! Someone was coming up the slope. The sound of footsteps crunching over broken rock was steady and undoubtedly human, perhaps a local hunter or trapper who could render aid. He decided to risk a cautious hail.

'Psst! Over here! And for God's sake, if you value your life, tread softly and keep your voice down.'

A familiar small figure came into view. It was Felmar! Scarth almost whooped for joy, but restrained himself as his friend crept to his side and clasped him in an enthusiastic embrace.

Scarth, Scarth, I thought I'd never catch up with you. But look at you, Brother, all banged and bloody! And what in hell's happened to your poor mule?

'I thought you were dead, Fel. Thought the moonstones had burnt you to ashes.'

No, but it was a narrow squeak. Did you get away with the book and the sigils?

Scarth slapped the pouch hanging at his belt. 'Three of the important stones are safe. The fourth was lost in the confusion of my escape. I've still got the book stuffed in my shirt. But tell me how you found me here!'

No, you go first. My escape was pretty ordinary, but I can see you've had a rare old time of it.

'Well, yes. I was chased across the moors by troops from Elktor, but I gave 'em the slip under my cover-spell . . . But how were you able to find me? I've still got the spell in place.'

This is a dream, friend. Everything's possible in a dream! What happened next, after you evaded pursuit?

'Things went well enough until I reached this place and started looking about for a path into the mountains, or at least a place to rest where scryers wouldn't spot my mule when I dismounted. There's a deep cleft yonder where the rock-face rises up. It looked ideal, so I lit a faggot and started inside to look it over. Then I caught a whiff of this vile stench, and saw the bones. But by then it was after me, roaring and slavering. Whether it smelled me or just saw through the spell, I don't know. I thought I was a dead man for sure, but it stopped to savage the mule I'd left hobbled. I got away down the slope, slipping and sliding and blubbering like a baby. I fell and smashed my head and bled from the scalp like a stuck pig, but the wounds aren't serious. I hid for a while, then came out to take a bit of meat from the mule's carcass. By then I was starving.'

Booger me! What a tale. You've had rotten luck, Brother. But

*thanks be to God and Saint Zeth you're all right . . . Which sigils
did you take with you from the hut?*

'Three of the four important ones we played the game
with. They were all I had time to gather up. The doorway
sigil must have been buried by the strange ash that lay all
over the floor.'

Felmar smote his own forehead, and his face was twisted
in an expression of frustration. *You know, I can't remember
what the other three stones look like! My mind's gone blank from
all the travails I've suffered. Will you just describe the things?*

Scarth fumbled with his belt wallet. 'I'll show you —'

No, don't go to the bother. Just tell me what they look like.

Scarth frowned. 'Well, there's the ring I thought might be
a Weathermaker, and the icicle or carrot or whatever it is.'

Yes, its name is Ice-Master. And the third?

'A little wand with phases of the moon carved on it.'

Felmar's eyes went wide with shock and he gave a loud
gasp. *Just a simple rod, with a hole at one end? And phases of the
moon, you say?*

'Yes . . . Look, let me take them out. You can see for yourself.' He opened his pouch and proffered the sigils in the
palm of his hand.

But Felmar had closed his eyes, as if in ecstatic contem-
plation.

*A Destroyer! That's what it is. One of the greatest of the Great
Stones. The Lights slew my poor mother for using it contrary to their
wishes. But if it were neutralized by the Potency, there'd be no
danger at all to the user.*

'Fel, I don't know what you're saying. What's a Destroyer?'

*We'll have to keep the sigils safe until I can come for them. I
don't suppose the book matters anymore, since I don't need it for
the activation, but we might as well include that, too. Take one of
the empty saddlebags from the dead mule, old friend. Put the book
and the stones inside, strap it up tightly, and follow me.*

It was only a dream, so Scarth obeyed without argument. He was curious to see what would happen next. Felmar beckoned him to follow, circled around the little fire and the dead animal, then set out uphill, straight for the tall opening in the rock. He peered into the fissure, then put a finger to his lips.

Come on. But be very, very quiet! There's a nice dry ledge, head-high on the right and only a couple of ells from the entrance. Put the saddlebag there.

Scarth held back. 'Be careful! What if it wakes up and smells us? It's a monstrous thing! Nearly six feet tall at the shoulder!'

Listen. I've found a fine place for us to hide out. Good food and drink, comfortable beds for as long as we want them, and no one can scry us there. You'll love it. But we don't dare bring the sigils and book. We've got to put them in a safe place and pick them up later, when the hue and cry has died down. Understand?

'All right.'

Scarth could smell decaying flesh inside the den even before he entered. The bones underfoot and the rough rocky floor had smears of fresh blood. Alert for the slightest sound from the inky depths, he pushed past Felmar and set the leather bag on the high ledge. Felmar was right: this was a perfect place to hide it. No one who looked casually inside the hole would catch sight of the bag, and it was surely safe from scrying.

'That's that.' He turned about, ready to leave – and saw that Felmar was gone. Quickly, he strode toward the fissure's mouth and looked outside, but there was no trace of his friend.

Wake up. Both of you.

'Fel?' He opened his eyes, felt his knees buckling, caught his breath in stark terror at the strange hooting snuffle that came from the darkness behind him. Something stepped on a dry bone and crushed it. He heard a low growl, risked a fearful glance, and saw beady black eyes and lips drawn back in a snarl from enormous ivory teeth.

'It's a dream!' Scarth Saltbeck screamed at the top of his lungs. But he had been sleepwalking . . .

He stumbled down the slope, but the giant brown bear caught him easily before he reached the shelter of the tall rocks, and dragged him back to its den.

The exhausted men-at-arms, the knights, the windvoices, and their dauntless leader Lord Olvan straggled back down the mountain path even before daylight had begun to fade, intending to make a safe camp on the far side of the great rockfall, where they'd left their mounts and supplies before pursuing their quarry on foot.

Kilian and his companions watched the retreat through the spell of couverture disguising the entrance to their cave. When the last of the hunters had disappeared, he extinguished the magic.

'They'll be back tomorrow,' Garon said. 'There are game trails up there going in different directions. The wind-searchers can't have explored them all. Do you want to move on? The weather's fine, there'll be a nearly full moon tonight, and we've had a good rest. We might almost reach the divide by dawn tomorrow. I don't think they'd dare follow us much further than that. These are castle garrison troops, not crack mountaineers like the ones on duty at Beorbrook Hold. A lot of them are looking over their shoulders, afraid that demons might be stalking them.'

Kilian thought about it. 'I must try to windspeak Felmar and Scarth again. There's a useful high point on the ridge above the cave. I can reach it if I go up this ravine. Let me try to scry our friends from there. Should I fail in that, I'll extinguish their cover-spell and bespeak them. If I still have no luck, we'll move on without them.'

Garon inclined his head. 'As you wish, my lord. However, for your own safety, I insist on accompanying you on the climb up to the ridge.'

'Very well.'

The two of them left the cave together. Niavar and Cleaton came out to stretch their legs and relieve themselves.

'Wicked hike it was, getting here,' Niavar observed. 'Maybe not so tiring for you, with your long legs, but I'm not keen to press on, I can tell you.'

'We'll make young Garon carry you pickaback,' Cleaton said with an evil grin. 'Give him less breath to talk down to us, the conceited gowk. Just because he's highland-born, he thinks the sun shines from his bum.'

Niavar shrugged. 'The lad knows we'd be helpless up here without him – and he's right. Possess your soul in patience, Clete. When we've safely reached Somarus's camp, it'll be different. Lord Kilian won't let a jumped-up highlander lord it over two experienced administrators like you and me.'

They sat without speaking for a time. Then Cleaton said, 'I think we made a great mistake not blasting Butterball to smuts back at the rockslide.'

'How so?'

'He won't be content telling the king's men about our failed ambush. Mark my words, Var, he'll spill his guts of everything he knows. Felmar and Scarth and the treasure. Waringlow's complicity. Even Kilian's intention to ally with Beynor and Somarus.'

'Well, how bad can that be for us? Who cares if the new Father Abbas gets the chop? And the sigils and books were only a kind of bribe for Beynor, weren't they? I mean, it'd be a fine thing for Kilian and the Mosslander to have a few active moonstone sigils at their command – but if the things are lost, our master won't give up on his great scheme. He'll change tactics, that's all. He implied that Beynor has a plan to put Somarus on the throne of Didion sooner rather than later. All kinds of interesting opportunities might present themselves to clever magickers if a hothead king reigns in the barbarous northland.'

Cleaton gave a gloomy grunt. *'Interesting.* A nice word. I suppose we're talking war with the Sovereignty.'

'Wars provide interesting opportunities, too,' said Niavar.

They fell silent again, then by mutual consent unrolled the blankets of their bedrolls, intending to catch a few winks of sleep before Kilian and Garon returned.

'So you think both Felmar and Scarth are dead, my lord?' Garon asked. 'And the treasure's gone?'

Kilian wiped perspiration from his brow. He sat on the summit of a crag, waiting for his heart to slow after the strenuous effort needed for the generalized call on the wind. His windsearch of the desolate border region where the moor met the mountains had eventually revealed the mutilated body of a mule and a bloody trail leading to an animal den. A man's boot and a dead campfire with uncooked pieces of meat on a stick were the only other clues.

There had been no need for him to obliterate the cover-spell shielding Felmar and Scarth. It no longer existed anywhere within the range of his windtalent. His attempt to bespeak the Brothers using their private password had failed. So had the only remaining option, an open windcall that might have been perceived by anyone. All he had done was call the men's names. The timbre of his windspeech was sufficient to convey the urgency of his cry.

But there had been no answer.

'Yes, I believe they are dead,' Kilian replied. 'And what you have so blithely referred to as "the treasure" is lost to us. It's a severe disappointment. but by no means an insurmountable disaster. Other magical resources are available to me – and to those who are loyal to me – in Didion.'

'I'm happy to hear it, my lord. Shall we go back to the others? If we're to set out again tonight, we won't want to waste time.'

Going down the steep ridge was harder than the ascent. But even as Kilian concentrated on placing his hands and feet as Garon directed, a part of his mind was occupied by more urgent thoughts. He'd spoken confidently to the young Brother, minimizing the effect of the trove's loss on their future. But the reality of the situation was more ominous – especially as it pertained to Kilian's alliance with Beynor. The Mossland sorcerer cared only about the Trove of Darasilo. Once he learned that the large cache of moonstones had been lost, he was bound to view Kilian as an ally of questionable value.

It was even possible that Beynor already knew about the fate of Felmar, Scarth, and the trove. Why else would he have held off bespeaking Kilian in his dreams? Beynor's tremendous natural talent might have been able to pierce the new cover-spell, in which case he had probably wind-watched the lot of them ever since he arrived on High Blenholme Island.

I may be in serious trouble, the alchymist thought. However, there was a small ray of hope . . . or perhaps even two rays!

Firstly, Beynor still lay under the Lights' curse, which prevented him from utilizing sigil magic. Nevertheless he coveted his sister's stones and might also have designs on stones possessed by the Salka. Perhaps he might be foolish enough to think he could use Kilian as a sigil-wielding deputy, as he had once used the wizard-assassin Iscannon.

The second hopeful possibility lay in the other principal player in their Didionite adventure. Prince Somarus Mallburn was a mature warrior who was justifiably wary of Beynor.

He had been present at the young Conjure-King's unforget-
tably calamitous coronation, where Ullanoth had made her
brother the laughing-stock of the entire island. The prince
would also remember Beynor's magical failures that had
culminated in Conrig's victory over Didion at sea. So wouldn't
the new King of Didion welcome an advisor who was inti-
mately acquainted with the minds of both Beynor and
Conrig? The gold intended as a bribe for Somarus was gone,
alas, left behind with his horse – except for the small amount
Kilian had been able to secrete about his person. But he still
had his wits and his talent. They'd have to serve.

I must get to Somarus before Beynor does! Kilian said to
himself. He wondered where the prince was, right at this
very minute. Beynor must have told him to be ready to come
out of hiding immediately upon the assassination of his
brother. Would Somarus be rash enough to lurk about the
vicinity of Boarsden, hoping to observe the deed? And if he
were hiding there with an entourage, might not one of his
men be a windvoice who'd respond to a general hail?

'Watch your foot, my lord!' Garon exclaimed. 'That rock's
unstable. Use the one to the right instead. Please pay closer
attention to my instructions. A fall from here could result in
serious injury.'

Kilian hastened to obey. 'I'm sorry, my boy. My mind was
wandering. I won't let it happen again.'

When the discouraging news came from Lord Elktor's adepts
that evening, and it seemed likely that Kilian had made good
his escape into the high country, Snudge knew he could no
longer postpone his long-delayed personal report to the king.
He bespoke Vra-Sulkorig, asking if Lord Stergos was strong
enough to receive and transmit wind-messages.

The Keeper of Arcana replied with understandable coolness.
The Royal Alchymist may be able to hear you, Sir Deveron, but

it would still tax him to bespeak you over such a long distance. I
fear you'll have to make do with my own humble talents.

'Oh, come off it, man.' Snudge was too downhearted to
be bothered with hurt feelings. 'I need his advice on a
personal matter, that's all. It can wait . . . Is His Grace there
with you?'

Yes. We've been waiting to hear from you for a night and a day,
here in the sitting room of the Royal Alchymist's new apartment.
The High King believed you would wish to consult immediately with
Lord Stergos concerning the safeguarding of the recovered trove, so
he wished to stay close to his brother. He's been conducting all his
business from here. Please wait while he finishes issuing instruc-
tions to the Lord Treasurer.

'Feribor Blackhorse?' Snudge was taken aback. 'Well, well!
Nothing to do with my mission, I trust.'

His Grace will discuss the matter with you if he sees fit. Please
wait.

Snudge relaxed in the padded chair that sat before the
cold fireplace in the chamber he shared with Gavlok. The
other knight was elsewhere in Elktor Castle, making arrangements for their departure on the morrow, should the High
King approve it. Gavlok had forgiven Snudge for not taking
him on the hunt for Scarth, but the squires Valdos and
Wiltorig were still nursing their wounded pride.

Sir Deveron? If you please, I shall now relay the High King's
words to you. His first remarks are full of colorful language
expressing his resentment at your lack of courtesy. I leave them to
your imagination. From here on, I give you his words verbatim:
Have you recovered the Trove of Darasilo?

'Tell His Grace that its fate is still uncertain. However, both
of the thieves are dead. Of this I am sure. Within another
day or two, I hope to learn more about the trove. It certainly
has not fallen into the hands of Kilian Blackhorse or any
other evil person.'

*The king is gratified to learn that, but justifiably impatient to
know where the trove is, and why you're unable to get your hands
on it. He regrets that the thieves were not taken alive so that they
could be questioned and then given their just desserts. How fares
the hunt for Kilian?'*

'Ollie Elktor's forces chased him far up Roaring Gorge.
They narrowly avoided a deadly trap the alchymist had
planned. Their escape was due to the fortuitous capture of
one of Kilian's henchmen, a certain Raldo – the former Palace
Novicemaster who was called Butterball by some of the
Brethren. This man was injured and his companions rather
foolishly left him behind . . . and alive. He traded some very
useful intelligence in return for clemency, which Count
Elktor was glad to grant.'

*His Grace says that Ollie has a futtering great nerve pardoning
an enemy of the Crown, but under the circumstances he'll not object.
What did the fellow have to say?*

'First, Kilian and his cohorts escaped Zeth Abbey through
the good offices of Abbas Waringlow. This worthy hastened
the demise of his predecessor so that he could coordinate the
abbey's windsearch efforts, and ensure that Kilian and the
two thieves were not found by any of the resident Brethren.'

*The king's reply is lamentably obscene. What was Waringlow's
motive for committing treason?*

'The oldest in the world: power. Kilian taught his friend
a spell that subtly coerced the ruling council of the abbey so
that they'd elect Waringlow as successor to old Noachil.'

*His Grace notes that the new abbas will have a brief tenure. What
other information did this Raldo convey?*

'Kilian and Beynor of Moss are in league with Prince
Somarus of Didion. Beynor is on High Blenholme, but I'm
not certain where. He and Kilian are plotting to assassinate
Honigalus and put Somarus on the throne in his place.
Unfortunately, Kilian didn't disclose details of the scheme to

underlings such as Raldo. It may be proper to warn King Honigalus of the danger.'

The High King will take that under advisement. Anything further?

'Kilian and his cronies had their iron gammadions removed by Waringlow. I myself saw one of the discarded pendants on the boat they used in their escape. I'll leave it to you to explain the ramifications of this to His Grace. The most crucial thing is, Kilian now has the potential ability to activate moonstone sigils and use them – while Beynor, who is under a curse, cannot.'

His Grace asks your opinion about the odds of capturing Kilian.

'I don't think Ollie has a hoot in hell of pulling it off. I might be able to track Kilian myself if I go into the mountains. But that could take weeks, and he has an excellent guide – a young Brother from the abbey who knows the country. Tell His Grace in the strongest terms that I would prefer to carry on with my mission to Tarn. Leave the search for Kilian in the hands of Lord Olvan.'

. . . After consideration, King Conrig agrees. He commands you to proceed to Beorbrook Hold early on the morrow. There you will be joined by two highly experienced Mountain Swordsmen, members of Earl Marshal Parlian's elite force, who will assist your incursion into Tarn. You will not spend the night at Beorbrook, but instead go on directly to the principal fort at Great Pass. After resting there, continue along the Wold Road with all speed. Enter Tarn by whatever route you think best.

'I understand. Is there further news of Princess Maudrayne? It's very important that I know which area of Tarn to concentrate my search upon.'

A renegade local shaman claims to know where the princess is being hidden. He may be lying. We're looking into the situation. If his information is plausible, we'll inform you without delay. Do you have more to say to his Grace?

'Not at this time. Apologize for my tardy report. So much

was happening, and I wished to convey as complete a picture of events here as possible.'

The king graciously forgives you, and bids you rest well.

'Tell him the same from me, Sulkorig. But for God's sake let me know immediately when Lord Stergos is able to speak on the wind.'

I will. Good luck to you, Sir Deveron.

'Thanks,' Snudge replied tersely. He cut the wind-thread and sat back in his chair to recuperate. 'Rest well,' he muttered. 'Not bloody likely.'

Then he bespoke the head windvoice at Beorbrook Hold, and told him to collect the men who had been assigned to help him. They would have to confer on the wind at some length, organizing the mission to Tarn.

Conrig took his wife Risalla to his bed that night, and after they had enjoyed the consolation of their bodies, he did not sleep but instead rose up, put on a light robe, and invited her to join him on the balcony.

'It would be my pleasure, husband,' she said.

Barefoot and wearing only a shift of delicate lawn, she took two goblets and a ewer of mead, then came out and sat with him at the wicker table where they sometimes ate breakfast in high summer. The night was clear and warm, with a great silver moon. Mercifully, a breeze from the west spared them the lingering odor of the burnt cloister wing.

Conrig sipped mead for a few minutes before speaking. 'I had communication with my intelligencer, Sir Deveron, earlier this evening. The pursuit of the fire-raisers has ended with their deaths. He was able to question neither man, but we've learned that they're connected to a conspiracy headed by my former Royal Alchymist, Kilian Blackhorse. He was confined to Zeth Abbey but has recently escaped. He's presumed to be fleeing into Didion.'

'Ah.' The queen waited for him to continue.

'I've not spoken to you about this man before, Risalla, but
I suppose you've learned something of Kilian's unsavory
history from the court ladies. He and the former Conjure-King
of Moss, Beynor, were closely linked in a plot to kill me.'

'I had heard,' she said evenly, 'that they also tried without
success to thwart your invasion of Didion. And Beynor, at
least, attempted to assist the fleet of Honigalus when he
fought against your Cathran navy.'

'True,' he admitted, not meeting her gaze. He drank deeply
from the cup and poured more mead. 'You have been a loyal
and dutiful wife and a loving mother to our children. But
you're not a woman made of stone. I know that deep sorrow
and resentment must remain in your heart because of my
own role in the death of your mother and father, as well as
Didion's submission to the Sovereignty.'

'I pray for King Achardus and Queen Siry each night. But
nothing can bring my parents back to life. I take what consolation I can from the knowledge that they died with honor,
fighting for our country. My older brother Honigalus surrendered to the Sovereignty and accepted you as his liege lord.
So did I, because he asked it of me. I have pledged you not
only my bodily fidelity but also my political allegiance. Never
would I do anything to harm you or the union of nations
you have forged. And may God strike me dead if I lie.'

She put down her goblet and extended both her hands to
him. He clasped them, and she could see his dark eyes glint
in the moonlight.

'I believe you,' he said. 'And I trust you. So you must know
what else I learned from Sir Deveron tonight. An informant
he believes to be truthful claims that your brother Somarus
has conspired with Kilian and Beynor to assassinate Honigalus,
with a view to putting Somarus on the throne.'

She cried out, drawing away from him. 'I don't believe it!

I know Somarus is bitter about our brother's surrender, for if Hon had died in battle, our nation would still be free. Or thus Somarus believes, as do many others who sympathize with him. He foments rebellion against your overlordship and attacks Cathran caravans traveling to Tarn, but he's not a fool. If he was known to have engineered the death of Honigalus, all Didion would turn against him in revulsion. Our people are fierce and contentious, but they're also unshakably devoted to tradition. A regicide can never occupy our throne. The great dukes and barons will not allow it.'

'But if murder could not be proven?'

'Didion and Cathra are no longer at war. In wartime, the succession devolves to the claimant most likely to lead the nation to victory. But in peacetime, the dead king's progeny succeed him – male and female without discrimination. If Honigalus were to die, his oldest son Onestus would inherit the crown and Queen Bryse would be named regent until his majority. Next in line are Prince Bartus and his sister Casabarela. Furthermore, if it were approved by the great lords, Queen Bryse herself might be named queen regnant. She would then have the option of marrying and declaring her husband co-monarch. This is the ancient law of our country.'

'What if not only Honigalus, but also his wife and three children were to be slain? And Somarus was left the only surviving heir?'

'Impossible!' Risalla exclaimed. 'My brother would never sanction such an infamous crime.'

'Are you certain? I think no crime is too heinous for Kilian and Beynor to perpetrate if it would serve their own ends. And I wonder if Somarus might not give tacit consent to the deeds of villains, if those deeds opened to him a clear path to Didion's throne.'

'I know Somarus,' she insisted. 'He would never stoop to such dishonor.'

Conrig sighed and rose to his feet, the moonlight giving luster to his fair hair and beard. 'Wife, your sisterly loyalty does you credit. Nevertheless, I beg you to have your wizards bespeak Honigalus as soon as possible, warning him of the potential danger to him and his family. And if you have any influence over Somarus, beseech him to abandon this horrendous scheme forthwith and sever any alliance he might have made with Kilian and Beynor.'

She looked away. 'I – I had intimations that Somarus would soon rebel against the Sovereignty and Honigalus in some manner. He sounded me out, sent a message asking if I would side with him secretly. I refused. I told him I'd always love him, but said I would never go back on my pledge of fealty to you. I also ordered him not to tell me anything more of his plans. So – so that my conscience would not compel me to reveal them to you.'

'I wish you had told me of his message,' Conrig said evenly. 'But I understand why you did not, and I can't hold it against you. Love will not be gainsaid.'

'If I'd known he was contemplating murder . . .' She trailed off, her voice full of woe. 'But perhaps he isn't, after all. Kilian and Beynor may have kept him in the dark, and I pray this is so. Still, I don't doubt he'd take advantage of the death of the royal family without a second thought. Somarus is a firebrand, Conrig – once set burning, he must flame on until his consummation. Whatever that may be.'

'Will you at least warn him that Kilian and Beynor don't have Didion's best interests at heart? Somarus means nothing to them, except as a potential weapon to use against me. Both of them are sorcerers who wouldn't hesitate to ally themselves with the Beaconfolk. Beynor is half mad, like his father before him. He seeks revenge against his sister Ullanoth and is convinced that she cost him his throne. The truth is, he affronted the Beaconfolk and they laid a curse on him.'

Risalla's face went blank, as though her flesh suddenly shuttered her soul. She whispered, 'There are those who say that *you* are in league with the Great Lights.'

'I know about the rumors. But they lie. I formed a pact with Ullanoth, that's true enough. She promised to use her magic to assist the cause of the Sovereignty. But never was any unholy bargain made with the Beaconfolk to assure my success.'

'Other rumors say she is your lover, who can deny you nothing – not even at the cost of her own life! Oh – don't look on me that way. I'm not jealous. You said it yourself: love will not be gainsaid! But I do pity her, poor soul, since it seems that her great sacrifice on your behalf was all in vain. Is it not true that she's dying after exerting her sorcery overmuch hunting for the fire-raisers?'

He turned away from her, arms crossed, and stared over the balcony rail at the moonlit palace gardens. 'So her close advisors say. If it gives you satisfaction, know that I never had a heartfelt love for her. I was infatuated for a time, but that passed away, leaving only – only respect and appreciation for all she had vouchsafed to me. You're right to pity her, Risalla . . . And any other woman who loves without being loved in return.'

Risalla rose on tiptoe and kissed his unyielding lips. 'I'll go back to my own chambers now. Good night, my lord husband. It may give *you* satisfaction to know that some women are content with other things besides love.'

He said nothing, but only stood looking down at the silvered trees and flowerbeds until a deep-throated double hoot rang over the palace grounds. The huge winged form of an eagle-owl glided above the curtainwall like a wraith and disappeared behind a clump of weeping willows in the garden. Something screamed. The giant bird lofted up again, carrying its prey, and flew off toward the parklands along the River Blen.

Snudge! the king thought. His self-chosen heraldic device was an owl, the stealthy hunter.

'Hunt her down, lad,' he whispered. 'For Maude will never be content as needy Ullanoth and wise Risalla are. Lacking my love, *her* only satisfaction will be in my destruction.'

FIFTEEN

'Induna!' the old man cried testily. 'Are you wasting time picking wild strawberries again, you idle chit? Attend me at once!'

When there was no response he repeated his demand on the wind, and this time the saucy young minx condescended to reply. *It won't do you any good to yell and call me names. I'm coming as fast as I can. And if you don't treat me with the respect I deserve, I'll just go back to Barking Sands – see if I don't! – and you can bully someone else into doing your longspeaking and scut-work.*

He ground his few remaining teeth in fury, but held back the stinging rebuke she deserved. She was only seventeen, and the young boys and girls out berry-picking along the river were better company than a cranky old blind man on a fine sunny day. She'd make a good shaman in time, once she got the girlish giddiness out of her system. He should have thought of her before, rather than using that greedy old witch, Yavenis, to relay his overtures to the Cathran king. And now his need for a trustworthy confederate had become even more crucial.

He picked up his staff and moved painfully to the door of

his cottage. His oversight picked her out, coming up the path with a basket in one hand, a wee slip of a thing in a blue kirtle, with hair as brightly golden-red as rowan fruit. When she came to the stout gate in the fieldstone wall surrounding his steading she flicked open the latch with her talent and walked through the herb gardens without haste, humming a tune.

'Hurry!' he growled. 'I need you to bespeak Cala Palace for me immediately.'

'Then I suppose you've no time to share my strawberries,' she said with a sly smile. 'I picked enough for two, Eldpapa, but if you're going to be grumpy and hateful . . . well, never mind.'

The notion that she'd do him that small kindness shamed him out of his ill humor. 'I'm sorry, Induna. I'm impatient. And I'm worried that King Conrig thinks I'm only a charlatan trying to dupe him out of a bucket of gold. He should have replied to my proposal by now, even if the answer was No.'

'You asked for too much,' the girl said. 'If he wants to bargain, don't slam the door in his face.' She took two bowls from the cupboard of the neat, well-appointed kitchen, then sat down at the table and began to hull the tiny sweet berries.

'It's what I need to retire to Andradh in style,' he mumbled resentfully. 'Young people don't understand these things. If you settle in a foreign land, they only respect you if you've got money.'

'You already have a nice cottage, with Tigluk and Wollu to take care of you. I don't know why you want to go to Andradh. They're all wicked pirates.'

He started for his sanctum. 'It's none of your business why I want to go there. Come along with me. Let those berries be till after we bespeak the Cathran king, and I'll have Wollu bring clotted cream from the ice-house for us to eat with them.'

The girl sighed. 'Oh, very well, Eldpapa.' She wiped her reddened fingers on her apron and followed.

Blind Bozuk's sanctum was in the loft of the cottage. There were dormer windows of real glass in gablets on all four sides so he could scry in any direction without material hindrance. The walls were lined with shelves full of jars, crocks, and boxes containing the magical ingredients that he used to concoct his wonderful spells and potions. None of the containers had labels; he knew where every item was. Cobwebs dripped from the rafters, and all the surfaces were filthy with dust because he never allowed the housekeeper upstairs to clean. Induna planned to do something about that before too much longer. She had good eyes, even if her grandfather didn't, and she wasn't going to work and study in a pigsty. If he wanted to be her teacher, he'd have to change his slovenly ways. Otherwise she'd go back to her own home at Barking Sands and carry on as Mother's apprentice.

'Sit down, girl,' Bozuk growled. He plumped himself into a heavy old armchair with tattered cushions.

She wiped off a stool with her apron. 'I'm ready, Eldpapa. Shall I bespeak the Cathran wizard Vra-Sulkorig, as before?'

'Yes. Tell him I have important new information for King Conrig, which I'll pass on to him gratis. It concerns a rendezvous between Tarnian ships that took place early today off Kolm Head. The High Sealord, Sernin Donorvale, met and conferred with Liscanor Northkeep, the brother of Princess Maudrayne. I read their lips. They talked about a boy who should by rights be sitting on the throne of Cathra. They said that the boy's father is ineligible to reign, because he secretly possesses arcane talent. Ask if King Conrig would like to have the conversation between Sernin and Liscanor repeated to him, word-for-word. At no charge, of course.'

Induna sat with her head bowed for some minutes. Then she opened her eyes and grinned.

The blind old man snapped, 'Well? Well? What does the Cathran king say?'

'He's very eager to hear what the two sealords said, Eldpapa. And he says it gives him great pleasure to agree to your fee of five thousand gold marks for information on the whereabouts of Princess Maudrayne and her son.'

The old man let out a gusty sigh of relief. He recited the conversation between Liscanor and Sernin, and prompted Induna as she relayed it to Conrig. When the girl finally cut the thread of windspeech and would have left the sanctum, he held up a hand and said to her, 'Wait. There's more.'

'Another message to be sent?'

He shook his head, 'No, Granddaughter, a more difficult thing by far. Please be seated again while I tell you.'

Rolling her eyes impatiently, she resumed her place on the stool.

'Ansel Pikan has taken Princess Maudrayne and her son into the far east, beyond the volcanos. At such a distance, with such massive rock bastions hindering even my mind's eye, it becomes increasingly difficult to track him and his captives. Thus far, Ansel has used a cover-spell that has proved no hindrance to my oversight. I am fairly certain of his ultimate destination, and when the Cathran king's messenger arrives with the gold I shall know where to direct his men in their preliminary search.'

Her shrewd little face had tightened with premonition. 'Eldpapa, what has all this to do with me?'

'Be patient! When the Cathran manhunters set out after Maudrayne, Ansel will know it. He'll shift her to another hiding place. And this time, he'll erect a more formidable magical cover – one that I'll be hard put to pierce because of the great distance that now separates us from the fugitive princess and her son. And so, my dear, I desire that you should leave here at once, and travel to the region where the precious pair are secreted, and be my agent on the spot to direct Conrig's hunters. I'm not so foolish as to believe you to be too frail and vulnerable to undertake such a mission. You're tough as a sealhide boot – and a formidable magicker already, in spite of your tender years. There will be perils on the journey, Induna, but none, I think, that would overwhelm you. You need not endanger yourself by approaching the princess's hiding place. You need only oversee her from a safe distance and report to me if Ansel Pikan attempts to spirit her away elsewhere.'

'Where am I to go, then,' she asked in a level voice. 'If I accept this charge? And what will be my payment?'

He burst into delighted laughter. 'A wench after my own heart! Your fee, little love, will be one-third of what I wring from Conrig. And the place you must go is the uttermost eastern coast of Tarn, north of that Fort Ramis which is held by a kinsman of Ansel. Of course I shall find stout companions to accompany you –'

'No,' she said.

'No?' The blind eyes widened in dismay. 'But all could be lost to me otherwise, for Conrig will never pay what he owes until he has the woman and her son in hand!'

'Silly Eldpapa! I didn't mean that I would not go, only that I wish no clumsy guardians hindering my freedom.' She rose from her stool and took his bony hands in hers. 'I rejoice at the opportunity to have a real adventure. Have no fear that I might behave rashly: I value my own skin too much to risk it as a foolhardy boy might do. Even less would I risk losing such a fine reward for my services.' She unhanded him and stepped back. 'We must plan everything with care. Come back downstairs, and we'll do it while we eat the sweet berries.'

They were two hours out of Elktor, riding at a fast pace over the moorlands toward Beorbrook, when Sulkorig sent out the brief hail.

Snudge let his mount fall behind the others, after making

the excuse of an urgent call of nature, then halted beside a peat-stained stream where graylings leapt from the water in pursuit of clouds of gauze-winged insects. The place was also alive with voracious midges, but at least Snudge was able to sit on firm ground while windspeaking.

'I'm ready. You said there was both good news and bad.'

The good is that the Tarnian shaman Blind Bozuk has agreed to tell us where Ansel has taken Maude. For reasons of state, the High King has decided to send the shaman's considerable payment to him by ship, guarded by the Lord Treasurer, and so we will not have Bozuk's information immediately.

'Feribor Blackhorse! I wish to God it were anyone but him going to Tarn. He might insert himself into this affair whether King Conrig wills it or not, and the results could be disastrous. The man's a villain, Vra-Sulkorig, but the king will hear no bad word spoken against him.'

He's embarking around noon on the high tide, taking the fastest naval frigate available. With luck, he may reach Northkeep, where this rascal Bozuk resides, in five days. The agreement is, we hand over half of the sum, and he tells us Maudrayne's hiding place. It's somewhere in the deep interior of Tarn. Lord Feribor wanted to set out after the princess himself with an armed company, but the king has strictly forbidden it and commanded him to wait in Northkeep with the balance of the payment. His Grace has no mistrust of the Lord Treasurer, but rather fears that Ansel Piken would easily discover what Feribor was about and move the princess elsewhere. The king believes you will have better luck outwitting the High Shaman and capturing her than any military force, since you come from an unexpected direction and have unexpected tactical advantages.

'Well, at least I'll have a solid lead to follow by the time I reach Tarn myself. Now tell me the bad news.'

The princess seems to have told her brother all of her secrets. And Liscanor has spilled the beans to the High Sealord. They met earlier

*this morning at sea and are returning to Donorvale, where Lord
Sernin plans to call a secret meeting of his high council.*

'My God! All of Maude's secrets? Not just the fact of her
son being Conrig's legitimate heir? Do you mean she actually told her brother of the High King's . . . personal problem?'

*Yes. You needn't dissemble. I'm aware now that His Grace
possesses a small portion of talent – although Zeth knows I would
rather be in ignorance. The princess feared that something might
happen to her and the boy, Dyfrig, before she could confide in Sernin
Donorvale. She was determined that Conrig's secret should be
revealed to the world. Or at least to the sealords of her homeland,
so they might use it and Prince Dyfrig as a lever to free themselves
from the yoke of the Sovereignty.*

'How has His Grace reacted? Is he there with you'

*He has closeted himself in his private apartments to consider his
options. The salient fact, of course, is that the Tarnians will have to
present incontrovertible proof of both their allegations. This is not
as easy as it may seem, especially since they don't have custody of
the princess and her son, so they probably won't act in haste.*

'Are there any new instructions for me from His Grace?'

*No. Nor are there likely to be, until the Sealords make their first
move.*

'Then I request that any new messages to me be relayed
via Vra-Mattis. Our armigers still remain ignorant of my
talent, and I hope also to keep the knowledge from the two
Mountain Swordsmen who will join our party later today.'

Very well.

'The only exception will be news of Lord Stergos. It's crucial
that I bespeak him as soon as possible – but on no account
should you say anything of this to the king. There are
uncanny forces actively at work on our island, Sulkorig, and
not all of them are human. Beynor could not have left the
Dawntide Isles without the consent and active assistance of
the Salka. I fear that he may intend to use the monsters in

an attack against Moss and Queen Ullanoth, now that she is unable to defend herself. And the Salka may not be the only inhuman beings involved in Beynor's mischief-making.

Surely you don't refer to the Beaconfolk!

'Tell Lord Stergos what I've said. Beseech him to wind-speak me soon. The fate of all High Blenholme may depend on it.'

Ullanoth's torment was oceanic, ebbing and flowing, some-times a wild tempest of agony and at other times a flat melan-choly devoid of all hope and ambition. She would plunge into the abyss, believing that the end was sure, only to be buoyed up through sweet transparency where the pain was absent. But the sure knowledge that suffering would soon return haunted her like the mocking laughter of a torturer. During the brief respites she was aware of her surroundings, although incapable of movement or speech, and remembered why she had come to this terrible pass.

For his sake. Because he had seemed in desperate need of her help.

In hindsight, she realized that his request that she use Loophole must have been motivated by something more than vengeance upon the two fugitive villains. He had certainly been robbed of Darasilo's Trove. But his desperation had been real. He had been convinced that she was the only one who could find the pair, and she could not help but respond.

And now she would die and spend eternity in the Hell of Ice because of her foolish, unrequited love.

'O Mother,' she prayed, 'why was I compelled to do as Conrig asked? Knowing!'

It is one of love's mysteries.

'And your leading me to find those terrible stones – was that, too, a perverse act of love?'

No, dear soul. It was an act of necessity.

Suspended in the clear void, resigned to the renewal of pain, she did not realize at first that the voice had a Source other than her fevered imagination.

'Mother? Queen Taspiroth? Is it you?'

I am not your mother. But I am the one who took on her form and bespoke you in a dream long years ago. I led you to the hidden cache in the fens so that you would not be crushed by the power of your brother Beynor. So that you would become Conjure-Queen, and bend the destiny of Conrig Wincantor. Both of you are part of the New Conflict that pits the Pain-Eaters against their enemies.

'Pain-Eaters?' Her mind was fogged and weary unto death, but the words cut to her mind's core and kindled a blaze of understanding. 'The Great Lights feed on my pain, and the pain of all who use their sorcery. This came about . . . how?'

Through the Old Conflict, when the Lights were first divided. One who was very wise and very foolish played a game – as his kind have done from time immemorial – thinking it would bring no great harm to the slow-witted game-pieces. But the game's awful potential was seized upon by others. The Source of the game lost control of it, sought help from Likeminded ones who tried to stem the burgeoning calamity, and failed. Vanquished, the Source was degraded and enchained, while the Pain-Eaters ate their fill.

'You are the one called the Source. Someone spoke of you to me once, long ago. Was it my mother?'

Queen Taspiroth was a brilliant sorceress who delved, perhaps too eagerly, into many mysteries. But she was consumed before we could enlist her in our just cause.

'You speak of a just cause . . . but you still play your game!'

War is a game. A contest between two sides. We Likeminded are vastly outnumbered, but we still must fight. I created the channel between the Sky and the Ground through which the pain flows. I am the One Denied the Sky and only I can lead the Likeminded to close off the channel. You will help me either willingly or not, as others of your race have done, beginning with Emperor Bazekoy.

'I have no choice?'

I offer you respite from agony. A temporary oblivion in which you live but have no sentience. Others who have helped us, but come perilously close to the Hell of Ice in the end as you have done, we have snatched to safety in the same manner. You will not die, but your new existence is not true life. Your consolation – and you will remain aware of it, comforted by it – is that the hoped-for victory will restore you again to the world you renounced. And that world will no longer be subject to the thrall of the evil Lights.

'Why me? You let my poor mother fall into hell.'

She clung to the power! You took the first steps in renouncing it. And sadly, her life did not have the potential to bring about change, as yours does.

'I don't understand . . . and I feel them returning to feed.'

Yes. I must tell you that there is a small chance you may survive their present devouring. You might recover your physical strength, as you did many times before, and re-enter the world of groundlings. So the choice you must make now is a real one. Will you join in the New Conflict, or trust that the capricious Great Lights will preserve your life once again rather than destroy you?

'If I let you take me, what will become of my people?'

Some will die, but not in the appalling manner that the Lights kill. War is coming, dear soul, which you cannot prevent. It will be fought in the Sky and on the Ground. If you come to me, the Conflict may be shortened and a good outcome is more likely.

'But not certain?'

No.

'When I put myself in peril at my lover's behest, I extracted a promise from him: that if anything happened to me, he'd defend Moss. I think he's able to do this more effectively than I, since I'm so weakened. Therefore, I agree to join your side of the Conflict . . . What must I do?'

Look upon me.

'Oh, Moon Mother! You're a Salka!'

No. I'm the One Denied the Sky. One of those you call the Great Lights. But since my essence is incorporeal, it cannot suffer. After the Old Conflict was lost, the victorious Pain-Eaters would have destroyed all the Likeminded if I had not agreed to this base transformation. It's right that I suffer in a Salka body, since in my heedless pride I used them, more than all the other entities, as pieces in my game.

'Source, I begin to understand. But don't tell me any more. I can't bear it. Just take me.'

It seemed to swim through the lucent transparency toward her, an apparition as dark as the spaces between the stars, lacking eyes and mouth, both of its coiling limbs cuffed and chained in dull-glowing sapphire links. She extended her hand and touched it.

Immediately she was gone, and the tiny green sphere began to fall. It splashed into the ocean of pain and drifted down toward the abyss of ice, until a black tentacle caught it up and bore it to safety.

Maudrayne came to her senses after Rusgann and Dyfrig woke, so her first awareness was of familiar voices, the boy asking bewildered questions and the serving woman doing her best to reassure him. She opened her eyes and saw a canvas roof overhead, held up by a curved framework. Heard clopping hooves. Smelled straw and equine sweat and musty wool. Felt movement.

Rusgann was saying, 'We're riding in a covered cart all laced up tight so we can't peek outside. But there's nothing to be afraid of, Dyfi. Your mother and I won't let anything happen to you.'

'The bumps make my stomach feel queer,' the boy fretted. 'I need to pee, too.'

A man's deep voice said, 'We'll stop in a few minutes.'

'Who's that?' the child said. His eyes were wide with fear.

'I think it's our old friend, Red Ansel,' Rusgann said drily.

She raised her voice. 'Master shaman! Did you hear what
the lad said? Stop this wagon at once!'

Maudrayne pulled herself up to a sitting position, but
almost at once was knocked down again as the wagon gave
a sudden lurch and began to bounce more violently. She
groaned, and Dyfrig cried out, 'You're hurting my mama!'

'Hang on,' Ansel called out. 'We're almost to a smoother
place.'

They jounced along for a few more minutes, then came
to a stop. Those inside the covered wagon heard high-pitched
whinnying and the stamping of hooves. Crunching footsteps
came around to the rear of the wagon and someone began
to undo the fastenings. A moment later, the canvas flaps
were pulled aside and Ansel's ruddy face greeted them with
its usual broad smile. He held out a hand to Dyfrig.

'You'd better come first, lad, and we'll see to your needs.
Put your shoes on. The ground has sharp bits of glassy stuff
here and there. Ladies, take your time alighting.'

The boy clambered out and he and the shaman promptly
disappeared from sight, leaving the princess and her maid
crouching amidst a tangled nest of blankets and bundles,
staring in astonishment at the strange landscape. Most of the
surface of the ground was tumbled, pitted rock – cindery
scoria and solidified dark lava. The irregular areas were interspersed with broad drifts of windblown, glittering black sand,
unmarked save for the fresh ruts of their wagon wheels and
the dimpled impressions of small hooves. Here and there,
pockets of lighter-colored soil supported wiry shrubs and wildflowers. Two enormous volcanos dominated the far horizon
behind the wagon, emitting thin white plumes of vapor.

Maudrayne murmured, 'Mornash and Mount Donor?
Great God of the Heights and Depths! Could we have come
so far east? How long have we slept?' She climbed out of
the wagon-bed, followed by Rusgann.

'Madam, have you any idea where we are?' the maid whispered. An uncanny silence surrounded them.

Maudrayne turned slowly about. The wagon, which she had remembered being drawn by two mules at the Northkeep waterfront, was now hitched to a team of four rough-coated ponies that drooped in their traces. A league or so onward the black wasteland came to an abrupt end in a row of hills, their lower slopes clothed in green and their summits nearly bare. The tallest, toward which the wagon seemed to be heading, was a nearly perfect dome of pale grey rock.

'I've never been here,' Maudrayne said, 'but I believe we've nearly crossed Tarn from west to east. Behind us are the volcanos and goldfields of my nation's interior. This black desert is part of the Lavalands, a desolate wilderness where nothing human can survive. Beyond those strange-looking hills lies the sea, the Icebear Channel that separates High Blenholme from the Barren Lands.'

Rusgann was shading her eyes from the hazy sun, studying the hills. 'There's something man-made on that highest bald-top. Like a little castle.'

Ansel's voice said, 'It's Skullbone Peel, our destination. It takes its name from the rounded shape of the hill.'

The two women turned about to find him and Dyfrig returning to the wagon from behind an upthrust monolith of reddish rock. 'Why?' the princess asked in a harsh tone. 'Why in God's name have you brought us here, to one of the most isolated and untenanted parts of Tarn?'

'For your safe keeping,' the shaman said to her. He lifted the little prince into the wagon, saying, 'Wait inside for a few minutes, and then I'll show you something interesting.'

'But I'm hungry!' Dyfrig protested, thrusting his head from between the canvas curtains. He would have climbed out again, but Ansel laid his hand atop his tawny curls.

'Rest, child, until I summon you.' The boy's eyes went blank and he withdrew without another sound.

Maudrayne addressed the shaman in a low, furious voice. 'And will you force Rusgann and me to rest again as well? Why not keep all of us sunk permanently in magical sleep? It would be so much more convenient for your purposes.'

'But not good for your health,' he said without heat. 'Your well-being is very important to me, dear Maudie.'

'Drop your pretense of solicitude for our welfare, Ansel Pikan! That was never your true motive for hiding my son and me. For if that were so, you would have no good reason to prevent us from taking refuge with my brother Liscanor or with my dear uncle, the High Sealord Sernin.'

Ansel said, 'If Conrig found you and Dyfrig, he would have you killed. And that is the truth.'

'But not the entire truth!' she raged. 'My son overheard you and the sea-hag talking one day, and even though he was unable to understand, he remembered your words well enough to repeat them to me: "We must make certain he remains king. He's the only one strong enough to hold them back. Without him, we have no hope of liberating the Source."'

'I'm sorry you learned of this. The matter is complicated and –'

'And you believe me too simple-minded to understand? I think not! You've kept me and my son prisoners for Conrig's sake, not ours. You seek to protect *him* from *me*!'

'My love for you dictated my actions. I would not have the king harm you, but I couldn't allow you to endanger his Sovereignty, either.'

'Your precious Source – whoever or whatever it is – commands your first loyalty. Protecting this Source is your paramount concern. You believe that Conrig Ironcrown is the only one strong enough to defeat the Source's enemies in battle, so you shield him from my righteous retribution. Admit it!'

He inclined his head without a word.

'Who is the Source?' she demanded.

'A force for good. That's all I may tell you now.'

'Who are its enemies?'

'There are two, who threaten both my master and all of humankind who dwell upon this island. Neither enemy is human. The one is incorporeal and can only be influenced indirectly by the might of High King Conrig. The second enemy is all too material, and Conrig is the only sure bulwark against it. I speak of the Salka.'

Maudrayne was incredulous. 'Those miserable amphibian monsters? They were vanquished and decimated by Emperor Bazekoy over a thousand years ago! The few that survive hide in the fens of Moss and in distant islands of the eastern sea. They are no threat –'

'They *were* not, so long as they remained disspirited and bereft of hope. But their mental outlook has changed. Someone has offered them a powerful new weapon that bids fair to restore their ascendance. And their numbers are not few. Over the centuries their population has grown until once again they represent a formidable menace. As yet, only the Salka of the Dawntide Isles have been roused from their ancient lethargy. But if their more numerous Moss-dwelling kin were inspired by the battle-success of the Dawntiders . . .'

Rusgann had been listening intently, and now with her usual forthrightness she did not hesitate to interrupt the shaman. 'You talked about two inhuman forces. Who's the second?'

'You call them the Beaconfolk,' Ansel replied. 'And because you are a native of Cathra, you've long since forgotten their power and their malignant nature, relegating them to legend. But the Great Lights are real, and their evil threatens all parts of the world where the aurora shines regularly in the sky.'

Rusgann gave a guffaw of disbelief, but the princess silenced her and addressed the shaman. 'I am no Cathran. I'm a daughter of Tarn, and perhaps willing to concede that you may be telling the truth. I say *perhaps,* because your word on this weighty matter is no longer enough to sway my conscience. I was greatly wronged by Conrig Wincantor. My son's injury is greater, since he is being denied his royal birthright. If I'm to postpone my demand for justice, you must convince me that there is good reason.'

'I can but try. There are other calls on my time, but from time to time I can visit you in your new residence –'

'Prison!'

'– in your new place of confinement and explain this very complex matter at greater length. I was probably remiss not to have explained it to you earlier. My excuse is that the Source has not fully confided in me, either, and the threat to humanity from the Salka hordes became obvious only a few months ago.' He came closer to her and laid a hand on her shoulder. 'Maudie, you are as dear to me as a daughter. To cage you and your little son tears the heart from my body, and I would that it were possible to set you free. But at present, I cannot. Not while you still threaten Conrig . . . and he threatens you. But the situation is not without hope. The Source has assured me of that.'

She pulled herself away in a sharp motion and stepped back, eyes flashing. 'How gratifying for both of you! Meanwhile, Dyfrig and I must languish in a wilderness, deprived of human companionship and all the things that make living worth while.'

'This place where I'm taking you is far more agreeable than Dobnelu's steading.' The shaman almost seemed to be pleading with her. 'You won't be so closely guarded. You can ride and hunt and fish, and even take short voyages on a

small sailboat. You'll have more congenial people around you
– even young playmates for Dyfrig. I've provided an extensive library for your pleasure. There are musical instruments
and art supplies for your use and for the education of your
son. If you have need of anything, your custodians will do
their utmost to supply it.'

'Really?' Almost as quickly as it had flared, the fire went
out of her and she seemed diminished and subdued. The
high color faded from her face and even her vivid auburn
hair seemed to dull. The sunlight was waning as the overcast thickened. To the west, the tall volcanos on the horizon
were turning to opaque grey shadows.

He drew a silver tube from inside his tunic and held it out
to her. 'It was to be a gift for young Dyfrig – the "something
interesting" I promised to show him. Spy through it at the
summit of the tallest hill, and you'll see where we're bound:
Skullbone Peel, the fortified summer residence of Ontel
Pikan, my cousin, and his family.'

With reluctance, she lifted the cylinder to her eye. It was
far from being a conventional spyglass, and she saw the
distant structure enormously magnified, a small but massive
square keep, built of shining white stone and topped by
battlements. A gable-roofed wing extended from its south
side, at the end of which rose a narrow round turret topped
with an odd construct that looked like a windmill.

She lowered the glass. 'It looks impregnable.'

'No one will harm you while you dwell there. The view
from the watertower is said to be stupendous. On a clear
day you can see for sixty leagues in all directions. There are
broad steps hewn from the living rock descending the
seaward side, and at their base is a sheltered cove where
whalers and other boats that ply the Desolation Coast may
put in during storms. Skullbone Peel is an outpost of Fort
Ramis, which lies forty leagues to the south. The fort is also

held by my cousin Ontel, who is a skilled shaman famed for accurate predictions of the weather. He is much respected by the seamen of the area.'

'A weather-wizard.' She sighed. 'I hope he's better company than the crabby old sea-hag.'

'We'd better be moving on,' Ansel said. 'It'll be two more hours before we reach the hill. Please take your ease while I check the team. There's food and drink in a basket inside the wagon. Dyfrig will wake if you touch his forehead.' He went to examine the ponies' harness.

Silently, Maudrayne handed the spyglass to Rusgann, who peered eagerly at their new home. 'I see someone on the battlements. A woman!'

'My cousin's wife, Tallu,' Ansel said. 'She's a remarkable person, Maudie. You may get on well with her.'

'Another magicker?' the princess asked, turning away with a conspicuous lack of interest.

'Oh, no,' said the shaman. 'Tallu is a noted sea-warrior of the Desolation Coast. She'll take very good care of all of you.'

The conferring of honors and the great feast were finally over. Duke Berkus Mallthorpe was resting his gouty foot and listening to a string quartet. Duchess Kenna had taken Queen Bryse to her private quarters for quiet conversation, and nursemaids were putting the royal children to bed in the guest chambers. Left to his own devices – a rare enough thing on the closely orchestrated royal progress – King Honigalus strolled the parapet atop the wall of Mallthorpe Castle with Galbus Peel, Fleet Captain of the Realm, who was also his closest friend and most trusted adviser.

The King of Didion was a stocky man whose thoughtful features were almost homely, and not even the most sumptuous attire was capable of making him an imposing figure. Once he had joked to Peel that the royal regalia made him look like an honest packhorse tricked out in the gaudy caparison of a tournament destrier. He was happiest at sea, and before the death of his father Achardus, he had commanded the Fleet with reasonable efficiency, acknowledging his continuing debt to the naval prowess of Galbus Peel.

On the throne he had been less of a success. He came to the kingship bearing the onus of defeat. But even if he had not surrendered to Conrig, he was perhaps too civilized to reign over a land barely lifted from barbarism. He utterly lacked the fighting panache and animal vitality that had made his hulking father respected even by the marcher lords who regularly rebelled against him. Honigalus Mallburn had accomplished near-miracles restoring his vanquished, starving nation to prosperity, but many of the great merchants and lords seemed unwilling to grant him credit for his efforts, while the common people had never forgiven his capitulation to the Sovereignty.

Honigalus knew all this, and accepted it stolidly. What happiness he gleaned from life came from Queen Bryse's unconditional devotion, the gratification of having sired three handsome, intelligent children who loved him with all their hearts, and the support of a handful of staunch friends such as Galbus Peel, who were not afraid to speak to him as though he were a man, rather than a monarch.

'Look at that moon,' the Fleet Captain murmured. 'Red as blood! They say forest fires are burning in the Elderwold. The smoke in the air no doubt causes the baleful color.'

'It may be a portent as well, Galbus,' the king said quietly. He rested his elbows on the hewn stone of the battlement and stared at the carmine orb rising downriver.

Peel shot him a look of concern. 'Of what, sire – if I may ask?'

'Before we sat down to feast, my wizard was bespoken by a high-ranking Brother who is a senior servant to King Conrig.

It seems that the Cathrans have uncovered a far-ranging conspiracy. The conflagration at Cala Palace was a sort of opening salvo in a series of other inauspicious events designed to undermine our Sovereign's rule. The good Brother was careful not to go into specifics – which leads me to suspect that the happenstances must be very dire indeed. Conrig warns me that there might also be dirty work afoot in Didion.'

'What kind of dirty work?'

'Conrig's people have heard rumors that Somarus may be plotting against my life.'

'Anything specific that we can look into?' Peel was pragmatic.

'Not much. My sister Risa had a message from Somarus, asking if she'd support him if he challenged the Sovereignty. She refused, God love her.'

'Prince Somar's been trumpeting insurrection for years, sire, and doing precious little else but spouting hot air. What reason have we for taking him seriously now?'

'The tip about an assassination scheme came from an unusual source,' the king said. 'Old King Olmigon had a Royal Alchymist who exerted an unhealthy influence in the Cathran Privy Council. The man's name is Kilian, and he and Conrig were at daggers drawn from the time the Prince Heritor earned his belt and began to take an active role in affairs of state. Kilian was convicted of high treason and imprisoned. He recently escaped, and seems to have instigated the big fire in Cala Palace – among other high crimes. One of Kilian's cronies turned his coat and exposed details of a grand conspiracy the alchymist had hatched. Part of it involves killing me and all my family so that Somarus can assume the throne.'

'Great Starry Dragon! I've heard of this Kilian, sire. He was supposed to be working with Beynor of Moss at one point.'

Honigalus nodded. 'And may still be, according to Conrig's

windspeaker. Kilian has lost a lot of his magical power, but he's still a force to reckon with. What's more, he's apparently making his way into Didion – presumably to link up with Somar in the Elderwold.'

Galbus Peel blew out a relieved breath. 'Well, then! If the bastard is nowhere near here, we need have no immediate fears for your safety. We can obtain a sketch and a description of him and spread the alarum throughout the kingdom. Archwizard Fring can cope with sorcerous threats.'

'Fring!' The king's fingers drummed on the stone and he frowned. 'He still hasn't joined the progress. Let's make certain he does so before we leave Boarsden. He's the best windsearcher we have. We can put him to work ferreting out this traitorous Cathran magicker.'

'Sire, you may have to look closer into your brother's activities as well. I know you've been loath to take him seriously, but that may have been unwise. He needs to be put under constant wind surveillance, if our bumbling wizards can manage it. And we should try again to insert normal-minded secret agents into his mob of followers – naval types rather than adepts beholden to Fring. I'm not sure how trustworthy the Archwizard is.'

The king sighed. 'How I wish we could stay here in Mallthorpe another day! Duke Berkus is a kindly old stick without a conspiratorial bone in his body, and my wife adores the duchess. Things are likely to be much less pleasant at Boarsden Castle tomorrow. My late stepmother's people are obliged to extend their hospitality, but I'll likely have to turn a blind eye to all manner of petty affronts.'

'If that's all that disquiets your visit, sire, you may count yourself lucky. I wouldn't put it past Prince Somarus to pop in on his uncle and auntie just to pay his respects.'

'He wouldn't dare!' Honigalus exclaimed. 'He's banished from court.'

'Duke Ranwing is a quirky sod. It might just tickle his fancy to encourage a surprise encounter between you and Somarus.'

'I'll have Ran's guts for garters if he does,' the king growled. But both of them knew the sad truth: Lord Boarsden was too important a peer to antagonize. If Somarus turned up, Honigalus would have to grin and bear it.

The king and his friend stood side by side for a few minutes more, watching the moonrise, then decided to go to bed early. The royal party was scheduled to embark before dawn because the voyage between Mallthorpe and Boarsden was a long one. The rapids in that section of the river and the eddy off Boar Creek would test the mettle of the oarsmen and the nerves of the barge's more timid passengers.

'It'll be a lively ride tomorrow,' the king observed. 'Gorgeous scenery, and the thrill of breasting the whitewater. Queen Bryse and the older children always enjoy the excitement. And knowing what I might have to face later on in Boarsden, I'm looking forward to a little fun myself.'

SIXTEEN

Royal Fenguard Castle was thrown into an uproar when Ullanoth vanished from her bed of pain, for her counselors knew she was too weak to walk, and no servant would admit to having assisted her in leaving her private apartment.

Wix, the queen's elderly Lord of Chamber, the only one she had entrusted with keys to every room in her tower, was the one who finally found her. Reluctantly, he dared to enter her inner sanctum, where she had been accustomed to perform her most delicate magical operations. He burst into tears when he saw her, cold and unbreathing and without a heartbeat, lying on the peculiar tilting couch that she sometimes used while Sending. Still weeping, he summoned Grand Master Ridcanndal, the High Thaumaturge Zimroth, and Akossanor the Royal Physician. They were the ones whose official duty it was to confirm that the Conjure-Queen was dead.

The doctor studied her ruined young face, all bony angles and transparent, tight-stretched skin. He lifted one of her eyelids. The pupil was wide and black, indicative of lifelessness. A mirror held to her nostrils remained unclouded. She had no pulse, and her lips were tinged with blue. Rigor seemed to have passed already from her body, but it was cold as ice and nearly as unyielding to the touch.

'Our poor queen is gone from this world,' Akossanor announced in a somber voice. 'Summon her tirewomen. Let her corpse be washed and dressed in full royal regalia, so that she may sit upon her throne according to our custom and receive the homage of the people one final time.'

'Wait,' Lady Zimroth said. 'Stand aside, physician.' The elderly Thaumaturge, dressed all in grey samite, lifted Ullanoth's right hand, which had been partially covered by her gown. The moonstone ring on the queen's index finger glowed faintly green. 'Look there. That stone is alive!' Cautiously, Zimroth pulled up two thin chains that hung about the queen's neck and drew from the bosom of her night-shift two more Great Stones. Subtle Loophole and Sender also retained their inner luminosity. 'Her lesser sigils! Fetch the container, Wix!'

The loyal old man's grief had vanished in an instant. Eagerly, he took a key from the ring at his belt and unlocked the cabinet where the sigils were kept when not in use. He removed a platinum casket and lifted its lid. 'They're glowing!' he cried. 'Beastbidder, Concealer, and Interpenetrator are alive!'

'And therefore Queen Ullanoth also lives,' Zimroth declared, 'but not, I think, within this poor physical shell.'

'Where is she then?' Wix implored her.

Zimroth and the Grand Master of the Glaumerie Guild exchanged glances. He shook his head and said, 'Only the sorcery of the Great Lights could have done this to her. I know not how it was done, or to what purpose. The matter will have to be studied.'

'But is she still suffering?' Wix asked anxiously. 'Oh, tell me that her soul is safe somewhere and not in pain!'

'I have no answers,' Ridcanndal said. 'Never have I heard

of such a thing as this happening before. She certainly has not been cast into the Hell of Ice as her mother was, since her flesh is unfrozen and her features tranquil for all their ravaged appearance.'

'I believe Ullanoth may be in a kind of limbo state,' Zimroth said. 'Neither alive nor dead. We must take special care of these remains. There must be no evisceration, no packing with spices, no enshrouding, no interment in an airless crypt. Her body must be kept ready to receive her soul if it should suddenly return from its uncanny exile.' She looked away, thinking. 'We require a room, totally secure, where no enemy may intrude. Let her be dressed well, and her hair arranged. Lay her out on a couch as a woman sleeping. Every day, someone must look upon her in case there is a change . . . for better or worse.'

'So you think she may yet die?' Akossanor asked quietly.

'If the body falls into corruption, it cannot be reanimated and we shall have to consign it to the usual funeral pyre. But I believe it will not decay so long as she remains in this peculiar state, and the possibility remains that she may return.'

Wix drew himself up with pride. 'I take it upon myself to prepare a suitable place of repose for my beloved mistress. With your permission, I'll put her in the uppermost chamber of this tower, where tall crystal windows give a broad view of our land of Moss. There I will guard her until she wakes – or until my own death supervenes.' He looked uncertainly at Zimroth and Ridcanndal. 'Will she keep her sigils with her?'

'I think not. Even though they are still active and bonded to her, there are certain complex spells written down in the Book of Rothbannon able to annul the bonding and transfer ownership of the stones to someone else. We must not let this happen.'

Zimroth went to a nearby workbench and took up a pair of golden tongs. Using these, she teased the Weathermaker ring from Ullanoth's skeletal finger. Cutting pliers severed the delicate neck chains and let the two pendants fall free. With the tongs, the Thaumaturgist placed the three Great Stones in their velvet nests within the platinum box. This she handed to the Grand Master. 'The stones must be secured in the traditional place for ownerless sigils – Rothbannon's tomb, where his ashes lie along with his most arcane writings. See to it, Ridcanndal.' She turned to Wix and the physician. 'You two must take care of her body. And I . . .' She grimaced. 'I shall announce to our people that Conjure-Queen Ullanoth lies enchanted, and until she is restored, the government of the kingdom devolves upon the Glaumerie Guild's officers. After that, I intend to bespeak Conrig Wincantor's windvoice with this melancholy news. I will ask the Sovereign how he intends to fulfill the solemn promise he made to our queen, before she agreed to perform what was to be her final service for him.'

PRINCE, RESPOND!

The generalized hail on the wind contained but two words. It was launched from the crest of the Sinistral Mountains, as Kilian and his weary party paused to rest at the top of the secret pass before beginning their descent from the divide. The alchymist hoped to minimize the possibility of being overheard – although he knew there was scant hope of shutting out Beynor if he was minded to eavesdrop – so he projected the call northward, in the direction of the Lady Lakes, where he believed the intended recipient of his message to be. In that he was mistaken; and he received no reply. His next attempt was even more powerful, directed more to the east.

This time, Tesk the wizard and the Green Woman Cray, riding along the Boar Highroad behind Prince Somarus, heard Kilian's hail clearly. So did another adept, who was surprised to recognize a once-familiar signature unheard on the wind for many years. This listener found the subsequent exchange both revealing and worrisome.

PRINCE, RESPOND!

Tesk was red-eyed and runny-nosed from summer rheum, so shocked by the vehemence of the mental shout that he reacted with a great sneeze that nearly flung him from the saddle of his stocky cob. Cray, who sat astride a dapple-grey pony next to the wizard, merely cocked her head and said quietly, 'Did you hear it, too?'

'Aye. But which prince is its intended recipient?'

'Foolish man! A very powerful adept uttered that hail. Do you really imagine he wants to speak to King Honigalus's infant sons?'

Somarus looked over his shoulder, frowning. 'What's all this, wizard?' The prince, like the others of his cavalcade save Tesk, was disguised as a simple household knight of Duke Ranwing Boarsden.

'I believe I heard windspeech intended for you, Highness. It would be best if we drew aside and stopped for a few minutes.' He shot a glance at Cray. 'The Green Woman heard it, too.'

Somarus spoke a word to Baron Cuva, riding beside him, who in turn commanded the ten knights of the prince's escort to pull up. They had spent the previous night under the friendly roof of Castlemont Fortress and set out very early so as to reach Boarsden and the River Malle by afternoon. It was now about the third hour and the air was hot and muggy, with a faint scent of smoke. This section of the Boar Road crossed a treeless marshland, and the company was sweaty, midge-bitten, and short-tempered, the knights not hesitating to express their unhappiness at being made to pause where there was no shade.

Somarus, Tesk, and Cray drew apart from the others but remained mounted.

Cray said, 'King-in-Waiting, will you be guided by me in responding to this call? I sense overtones of peril on the wind. Answer this person only in general terms and with great circumspection.'

'Indeed! Perhaps I shouldn't answer at all.' Somarus scowled. 'But what if it's Beynor of Moss, wanting to tell us that something's gone awry with his scheme? We'd better know what's happening.'

Cray said to Tesk, 'Did you determine the direction of the hail?'

'Hard to tell with a blanket shout, but I believe it emanated from the mountains, to the south-west.'

'Not Beynor, then,' Cray said to Somarus.

'My curiosity's roused,' the prince said. 'Give an answer, Tesk. Find out what he wants, but don't name me to him.' The wizard covered his eyes with his hand, since it was too hot to wear a hooded cloak. 'An adept servant of a certain nobleman responds to you,' he spoke on the wind. 'My name is Tesk. Identify yourself and state your business.'

Kilian Blackhorse here! My felicitations to His Lordship and to you, Master Tesk. I am the former Royal Alchymist of Cathra and a one-time member of King Olmigon's Privy Council. I now have the honor to be a mortal enemy of the Sovereign of Blenholme, and recently escaped from the dungeon at Zeth Abbey after instigating a notable conflagration at Cala Palace. It's my intention to offer my services as sorcerer and political adviser to the new King of Didion. I believe I can be of good use, assisting his nation to throw off Conrig Wincantor's detestable yoke.

Tesk repeated the communication word for word.

'Well, well,' said Somarus. 'Not Beynor, but rather his shadowy crony! Ask Kilian why he speaks of a "new King of Didion" when everyone knows that Honigalus sits the throne.'

Tesk transmitted the terse message and gave its reply.

After today, there will be a new king. I've been assured of this

by one who is not quite a friend, but not yet an enemy . . . to both
His Lordship and myself.

'Mysteriously spoken.' Somarus said with a cynical smile.
'Tell Kilian I'd already intended to keep a sharp eye on this
not-quite-friend. I don't need sly warnings popping out of
thin air. I probably don't need Kilian! Let him prove he can
be of value to me – and do it at once. Otherwise this exchange
of ambiguities is over.'

Poor Tesk was a simple man, but he did his best to translate the message diplomatically.

As a sample of my usefulness, suppose I reveal to His Lordship
how the transfer of royal power is to be accomplished without casting
suspicion upon the obvious person?

Somarus nodded. 'All right. I wondered about that myself.'

Of course you did. Even those who might otherwise welcome a
new monarch would reject him if he took the throne through foul
and dastardly means. After much thought, I found a sure way to
preserve the royal person's integrity. I myself conceived this plan, not
the one who has doubtless taken credit for it! That one – that not-
quite-friend – had neither the wit nor the subtlety to consider all
aspects of this pivotal situation. I did.

'Tell me how it's going to be done, then,' Somarus
demanded. 'Prove you're as clever as you say you are. All
I've heard of the affair from my own informant is a hint
about a calamity on the water. I assumed some hired villains
were planning a surprise attack – although I must say the
idea doesn't seem especially practicable. The – er – objects
of the action are very well guarded. And how could the
attackers be certain of getting clean away? If even one of
them were taken and tortured into confessing, the scheme
would unravel. To my detriment!'

The ambush on the water will be perpetrated by Salka.

'The hell you say!' exclaimed the prince. Tesk passed along
the essence of the ejaculation.

Unimpeachable eye-witnesses on shore will see the deed done by the monsters. No human guards could possibly capture such enormous creatures, and if any are killed, it matters little. Who would ever believe that the King-in-Waiting could have coerced Salka into acting to his advantage? No, he will be held blameless, accepted as legitimate by Didion . . . and by Tarn as well.

'How did you talk the slimy brutes into cooperating?'

I didn't. This, I freely concede, was done by our friend, who has a certain influence over them because of his nationality.

'I only have your word that you're the great scheme's author.'

I have other proposals for the new king's advancement, equally valuable. Perhaps we might discuss them face to face.

'Or perhaps all three of us can talk things over! You, me, and our not-quite-friend. Then I can pick and choose.'

As you wish. But he may balk at a personal meeting. He much prefers dream-invasion.

'So you know about that, do you?'

He's done it to me, as well as you. But since I know how dangerous the invasion can be to the dreamer, I always take special precautions. Otherwise, the invader may plant evil seeds in the mind of the sleeping person, compelling him to act against his will or reveal secrets. I earnestly hope you have been spared such outrages, Your Lordship.

'Great God of the Starry Roads! I never realized . . . These precautions: can you teach them to me?'

I spent a good part of my earlier life as teacher to a king. Until His Grace's son, out of jealousy and spite, named me a traitor and cast me down. This is why I now seek a new position with a more congenial liege lord, whom I will gladly instruct as he bids me.

'How soon can you reach Boarsden Castle?'

It may take as long as four days. I travel afoot through rugged mountains, with a few trusted companions. But our not-quite-friend is capable of reaching you much sooner. He may already be in the vicinity of the castle, waiting upon developments.

'Then I'll keep him waiting a little longer! Come and talk to me, Kilian Blackhorse, and we'll see whether congeniality prevails. Now, I bid you farewell.'

Tesk lifted his head and opened his eyes. 'The alchymist responds: *Until our meeting.*'

'What did you think of him?' the prince asked. 'Well-spoken sort of fellow, wasn't he?'

'I'm sure he could serve you better than I,' the little wizard said humbly. 'If he really was Royal Alchymist to the Cathran king, he must be a very powerful sorcerer indeed.'

Somarus grinned and clapped Tesk on the shoulder. 'But is he trustworthy? That's the real question. I know I can trust you, old friend.'

'Thank you, Your Highness.'

Somarus turned to the Green Woman, who had been listening with a grave expression on her face. 'Mistress Cray, will you tell me what you thought of this Kilian's proposal – and the man himself?'

'Why should my opinion matter to you?'

The prince persisted. His tone was light and bantering, but nonetheless fraught with intensity. 'You've insisted on attaching yourself to my entourage. Only God knows why – or maybe your Source! You warned me to be cautious while bespeaking this man, and you seem like a person of great good sense. Please do me this small courtesy. Tell me what you think of Kilian Blackhorse.'

'He will never be any man's friend,' she said, not meeting the prince's eye. 'There is no true loyalty in him, only expediency. He would serve you well in time of war, but not in peace. More I cannot tell you.'

'So Kilian would serve me well in time of war, eh?' The prince urged his horse forward with a body movement. 'That sounds good enough . . . Baron Cuva! We'll ride on now.'

*   *   *

Well-concealed in a green cave of dense, overhanging branches
at the river's edge, Beynor crouched in his boat and called
down silent imprecations on his wily confederate. So Kilian
had regained his talent! He'd managed to rid himself of the
iron gammadion without the help Beynor had promised him.
And now the perfidious alchymist made bold to foment doubt
in the mind of Somarus concerning Beynor's integrity, apparently unconcerned about his windspeech being overheard.

That Kilian would act against him so blatantly – and so
soon! – was ominously significant. It seemed plain that the
alchymist felt himself in real danger of being denied a position of power in Somarus's new regime, and knew he had
to act swiftly. He was attempting to bolster his prospects at
Beynor's expense because he had precious little else to
bargain with.

No trove.

Beynor realized that Kilian must have found out that most
of the sigils and both magical books had been unaccountably lost by Felmar and Scarth. He'd know that both thieves
were dead, because they would have failed to respond to his
windspeech. But had he been able to oversee Scarth on his
final journey? Did he know that the lesser sigils and one of
the books had vanished into thin air, but that three Great
Stones and the other magical book were hidden in a bear's
cave on the wrong side of the mountains?

Neither Kilian nor Beynor would be able to go after the
things now. The alchymist would not dare to re-enter Cathra
while he was being actively hunted, even if he had some
notion of the place Scarth had hidden them. It was imperative that Kilian respond immediately to Somarus's rather
half-hearted invitation if he hoped to obtain a place in the
new king's court. He'd worm himself into a position of influence, too; Beynor had no doubt of that.

As for me, the young sorcerer thought, I have more urgent

business to look after! Earlier, Lady Zimroth had bespoken him the welcome news of Ullanoth's enchantment and the secreting of the queen's own collection of active sigils in Rothbannon's tomb. Beynor had been hard-put to damp the elation in his windspeech as he responded to the news. It could not have fallen out more perfectly, had he planned it so! Moss was left vulnerable to a massive invasion by the Salka, and his sister's stones lay in a place that he alone might easily access.

The remnant of Darasilo's Trove was still vitally important to him because it contained the Destroyer sigil, the key to ultimate power. But one step at a time – the Great Stone would keep. All he need do was make certain that Kilian never tried to approach it . . .

He spent some time observing the slow progress of the royal barge up the river. Its enormous square sail was furled because there was little wind; the boat's motive power through the strengthening current was supplied by the forty laboring oarsmen.

He called out quietly on the wind. 'Eminence, are your warriors arrayed in position yet?'

The reply came from under his boat. *My people are in readiness. Are you aware that a party of well-dressed groundlings has ridden out from the castle and now travels slowly eastward along the dike path?*

He wasn't. He'd been absorbed in thought and had noticed nothing. Without acknowledging the fact to Ugusawnn, he scried across the water. On the southern shore, a league or so upstream, Boarsden Castle's gilded gatehouse ornamentation, window frames, and tower finials gleamed in the afternoon sunlight. It was an impressive pile, more lavishly furbished than any other Didionite ducal fortress to reflect the wealth and political importance of its lord. In honor of the royal visit, its battlements and the balustrade rail along the riverbank esplanade were decorated with colorful banners and swags of bunting. Boarsden's urban precincts lay further upriver, where the Malle made its Big Bend to the north. Behind and below the castle, an extensive marshy area threaded by Boar Creek provided a natural water defense. The Boar Highroad from Castlemont crossed the morass on a broad causeway before coming to a Y junction. The left branch went north to Boarsden Town. The right, now called Malle Highroad, continued east to the Firedrake Bridge and the large valley towns before ending at Holt Mallburn.

The party coming out from the castle did not take the high road, but instead followed a lesser track along an earthen dike much closer to the river. As Beynor scrutinized the nearly two dozen richly dressed riders and their entourage, he was gratified to discover that they included Duke Ranwing, Duchess Piery, and the Archwizard of Didion himself, Fring Bulegosset, seeming to be completely recovered from his diplomatic illness. Trailing the nobles was a gaggle of liveried servants on mules, bearing hampers of food and drink, folding stools and tables, and poles and bundles of gaily painted canvas that would soon be converted into awnings sheltering the privileged picknickers from the glaring sun. The destination of the procession was obvious: a few hundred ells above a stout timber bridge at Boar Creek, where the river rapids were at their most dramatic and a great eddy added to the navigation challenge, the dike widened and formed a perfect observation platform where those on shore could view boats struggling upstream through the surging whitewater.

The witnesses were gathering.

At the age of seven summers, Crown Prince Onestus of Didion was still too young to appreciate the richness of the countryside through which the royal barge now traveled, nor could he understand how such wealth made the great landholders prickly and independent-minded in their relations toward the Crown. In this region west of Mallthorpe were ripening fields of barley and oats, orchards that would produce pears, plums, and apples, and lush meadows where large herds of shaggy long-horned cattle grazed and fattened. As the barge passed each prosperous shore village, the prince and his royal father and mother stood together on the boat's ornate sterncastle, beneath a suncover brave with colored pennants, and waved to the yeomen and villeins who had gathered to watch their passage. Some of the villagers cheered and called out blessings, as the citizens of the large cities had done earlier in the progress; but most were silent, only holding high the white banners with Didion's heraldic Black Bear as they had been commanded to do by the overlords of their districts.

The single exception to the tepid welcome vouchsafed the royals by the countryfolk of the upper Malle came late in the afternoon, as the barge passed beneath the high-arched Firedrake Bridge that lay about ten leagues downstream from Boarsden. Several hundred spectators crowded the decorated span, waving banners of the timberlords of the north and shouting, 'Long live Queen Bryse Vandragora!' Bouquets of roses were tossed down onto the maindeck, and Onestus was kept busy retrieving the flowers and heaping them into the arms of his mother. Each time she inclined her head in a gesture of thanks to those on the bridge, they responded with a roar of applause.

The prince said in a low voice to his parents, 'I wish people at the other places had been so friendly.'

'These are free northern folk loyal to my family,' the queen told him, 'who have come a long way of their own will to show their love – unlike the others, who were compelled to show homage.'

'I see,' the boy said somberly.

'Take the roses down to the cabin and ask the ladies to

put them in water,' the king said. 'Soon we'll come to the
lively section of the river. Your little brother is already on
the foredeck where the view is best. Why not join him? I'll
be there shortly myself.'

The boy bowed. 'Yes, sire.'

When he was gone, Honigalus and Bryse watched the crew
raise the great sail again. The oarsmen would need all the
help they could get as they strove against the force of the
swift-flowing water.

The queen said, 'Nesti is beginning to understand the
reality of our situation, poor lad, for he's wise beyond his
years. Yet how I wish his childhood could be as carefree as
mine was – and yours.'

Honigalus sighed. 'It was a simpler age. All we can do is
pray that by the time he wears the crown, the old enmities
will be forgotten and he will have won the love of his subjects.'

'You have long years ahead of you to accomplish the same
thing,' Bryse said gently. 'Your reign has only just begun.'

In spite of the day's warmth, the king felt a sudden chill,
but shrugged away the portent with a defiant smile and rose
to his feet. 'Ah! Look down there on deck – Captain Peel
has come to supervise the helm as we breast the rapids. I
think I'll have a word with him. Shall I summon a few of
your ladies to keep you company here?'

'Nay,' said the queen. 'I'll join them and our daughter in
the grand saloon. My presence will have a calming effect on
the fainter of heart. It would be a pity if dear little Casya
should be frightened by the hysterics of a few silly women.
She's a brave girl, but some of my younger ladies are as timid
as sheep – and you know how infectious fear can be – even
when there's no good reason for it.'

Prince Bartus knew enough to stay out of the way of the
boatmen while they attended to their duties, so he had climbed

into the pulpit just behind the bowsprit, where he amused himself by tossing leftover bits of bread roll into the water, pretending they were men overboard and seeing how long it took them to drown or be devoured by some hungry fish.

Then the big thing had come swimming along and finished off the last victim, and he'd pointed it out excitedly to the men and asked what it might be.

'A water-kelpie, I reckon,' said the sailor named Zedvinus, winking at his mate, while the two of them checked the headstay. 'My great-great-grandad got dragged off the deck of his lugger by one when he was fishing by Tallhedge. Terrible monsters, they be – ain't that right, Dagio? Bite a man clean in half.'

'Oh, aye,' muttered the other man, not bothering to glance over the side. 'Fearsome critters, water-kelpies. You want to be careful when they're about, Prince Bart.'

'Really?' The five-year-old prince's eyes were wide with interest, but the sailors had failed in their attempt to frighten him.

'All deckhands to the mainsheet!' cried an authoritative voice. 'Double-man the sweeps! Coxswain, beat to cadence! Secure the waist-ports and stow all loose gear!'

The two sailors started aft. As Zedvinus passed the Crown Prince, who was just coming onto the foredeck, he said, 'Keep a weather eye on your little brother as we go into the whitewater, Prince Nesti. Best if you crowd into the pulpit with him and lash the pair of you to the rail so you don't bounce around.'

The prince said, 'Thank you for your advice.' The small enclosed platform would provide cramped accommodation for two full-grown men, but there was room to spare for a couple of small boys.

'I don't want to be tied in like a baby,' Bartus growled, as his brother joined him. 'I'm not afraid. And I'll hang on tight.' He brightened. 'I saw a water-kelpie out there in the water. It's been swimming right beside the barge ever since we went under the big bridge.'

'Kelpies are fairy tale creatures,' Onestus scoffed.

'Zedvinus and Dagio say they're real,' the little boy insisted. 'And I saw it myself. It was huge.'

'It's probably just an old tiger salmon,' Prince Onestus said. 'They can weigh seven stone.'

Bartus pointed. 'Here it comes again. Look!'

At first the older boy saw nothing because of the reflection of light on the river's surface. Then, to his surprise, he caught sight of a great dark shadow, only a couple of ells away from the barge's cutwater and swimming a parallel course. The thing was shaped something like a bull sea-lion, but appeared to be nearly three times the size of the marine mammals common in Didion Bay. Its head was broader and more rounded, too, and while the body was indistinct, Onestus thought he saw some sort of paddle-like appendages or elongated flukes at its hind end that propelled it along at a smart pace.

'Codders!' the Crown Prince breathed, awestruck. 'I see it, too! But that's no kelpie. Maybe it's a young whale. Sometimes they come up rivers by mistake. The fresh water's bad for them and they can't find the right food, so they get sick and die.'

'That one doesn't look sick,' Bartus said. 'And it doesn't look like a whale. I think it wants to race.'

'No, he's gone under the barge.' Onestus was disappointed. 'Crumbs! I wish I could've got a better look at him.'

'Look at what?' asked an interested male voice behind the boys.

They turned and saw their father the king standing on the foredeck. 'Papa!' Bartus exclaimed. 'A water-kelpie was right beside us!'

'Probably a whale, sire,' Onestus said loftily. 'Something large.'

Honigalus glanced over the side. 'Nothing there now. Was it white or grey? Did it have a long horn at its snout like a sea-unicorn?'

'It was greeny-black,' Onestus said. 'More than three ells long. Almost like a monster sea-lion, but without the pointed nose.'

The king's brow furrowed in puzzlement. 'Whales and sea-lions aren't green. Very few large sea-creatures are.' Except one, he thought. But that was impossible. None of them had been seen in the rivers of Didion since the country was first settled, some nine hundred years ago . . . 'It was probably a whale, just as you thought. And the greenish color was just a trick of the light, reflecting off weeds in the water.'

Onestus was gazing at the shore. 'The other boats going upriver are tying up at the jetties. We must be getting close to the rapids.'

'Will we tie up, too, Papa?' Bartus asked.

'No,' the king said. 'Ordinarily, only a few boats are allowed to breast the rapids at a time. For safety's sake, they take turns. But our royal barge has precedence. That means we can go on without waiting.'

Honigalus climbed into the pulpit with his sons. Since it was Bartus's first time up, after having spent the previous voyages in the cabin with the women, the king planted himself firmly behind the little boy, leaving Onestus well-braced at his side with one arm locked nonchalantly about a stanchion.

'I see Boarsden Castle on its hill,' the Crown Prince said. 'And here come the rapids!'

One of the royal trumpeters sounded three long warning notes. The coxswain began to beat his drum, so that the sweep of the oars might be perfectly coordinated, and the lookouts assumed their positions fore and aft.

'Whitewater ho!' cried the first mate, and a moment later the barge carrying the royal family of Didion began its cautious ascent of the foaming, rock-choked waters.

Cray the Green Woman showed Somarus the near-invisible path that led from the high road, along the reedy eastern bank of Boar Creek, to the dike track.

'But there's a better place to watch boats in the rapids further upstream,' Somarus protested. 'We used to go there often as children, when my mother visited her relatives at the castle.'

'Other persons have got there ahead of you,' Cray said. 'And the backcurrents in that place don't suit my purposes.'

'Your purposes?' The prince reined up and turned to regard her. 'The time has come to tell me just what those purposes are.'

'No,' she said simply.

'Damn you!' roared the prince. 'I'll know sooner or later.'

'Let it be later,' the small woman said. 'And I advise you to ride on without delay, lest both of us come too late to view the dire event we've traveled so far to see.'

So they continued as swiftly as they could, and now and then a horse bogged down and had to be pulled to firm ground, but none came to serious harm. By now, all of the prince's party had a good idea what was about to happen. The knights murmured among themselves and made coarse jokes to cover their nervousness and rising excitement, while Somarus and Baron Cuva rode on in preoccupied silence. A dirty brownish haze thickened in the western sky, turning the sun orange and casting odd-colored shadows over the stands of reedmace, bulrush, and spikegrass that lined the creek. Some small birds began to sing, as though dusk were falling or a storm were on the way. Far away, three horn notes sounded.

'The barge enters the rapids,' Cray said to Tesk, speaking so low that none other could hear. 'It has begun.'

The wizard bobbed his head, licked his overlarge lips, wiped his leaking eyes on his sleeve, and said. 'Strange-looking sky.'

'There are wildfires in the Elderwold, below the Lake of Shadows,' Cray said. 'They were not extensive when I came to your camp, but they'll spread until a hard rain beats them out.'

'So you came from Lake of Shadows?' Tesk asked her. 'Do your people dwell there? Oh, I hope they're not imperiled by the flames!'

'Thank you for your concern,' she said, smiling, 'but my home lies elsewhere, and glad I'll be to return to it. I'm not a body who travels gladly. As the saying goes, "East, west, home's best."'

Her eyes were like emeralds, Tesk realized, and her hair gleamed like white gold. No wonder her kind had bewitched men in days gone by! 'When will you able to go back?'

Cray looked straight ahead. 'Soon, when I have that which I came for.'

'Mistress Cray,' the wizard said eagerly, 'if there is aught I can do to help you, please ask.'

She tilted her head and pursed her lips, but her frown was not unkind. 'And why should a human – and a magicker attending a future king at that – wish to assist one such as I?'

The plain-faced little wizard flushed. 'I – I admire your courage, coming so far to fulfill a duty laid upon you by another. And you are very beautiful.'

She gave a soft peal of laughter, reached out, and touched his sleeve. 'Beware, Tesk! Many a human male has fallen into the thrall of Green Women, to his doom.'

'You make fun of me. Yet some eldsire of mine must have indeed loved one of you, to have engendered a wizard like me. I ask nothing of you, mistress. But if your appointed task is hard, I stand ready to give you aid.'

'Can you swim?' she asked him, bringing her mount closer. 'Running water is inimical to my people. Indeed, some of us are loath even to cross a stream on a bridge, although I am not quite so constrained. This thing I must do could take me into the river, and I confess to dreading it. If a friend were to stand by me –'

'I will,' he declared. 'And I swim like a fish.'

'Then stay close, for in a little while I'll disappear from the sight of this company, and if you would help me, you must vanish as well.'

'Ahead of us!' Baron Cuva called out. 'The dike – and the bridge across Boar Creek.' He urged his mount forward, with the prince following, and the knights who rode behind Cray and Tesk were so eager to stay with their masters that they splashed into the creek shallows so they could pass by the Green Woman and the wizard.

The two of them straggled up to the dike track at last, where the others were already dismounted and scanning the turbulent river downstream in search of the approaching barge, the knights shouting to one another in order to be heard above the loud noise of the water. The Malle was almost a quarter of a league wide in this place, and made a slight bend below the creek, where willow and alder thickets obscured the view. Finally a tall red-and-gold striped sail hove into sight from behind the trees. Then they saw the royal barge with its flashing oars, fighting against the current, constantly altering course to avoid the perilous places where great dark rocks thrust up from the white pother.

Prince Somarus had pulled a little spyglass from his belt pouch and used it to search the boat and the waters surrounding it. 'By the Great Starry Goblet – Honigalus and his two sons are perched right above the boat's prow!' He thrust the slender brass tube at the baron. 'Have a look, Cuva.'

'I see them,' the dour nobleman said. 'Nothing unusual out on the water yet. But perhaps the ambushers will wait to spring the trap until the barge is above the eddy. If I were running the show, that's what I'd do.' He lowered the instrument and handed it back to Somarus. 'Do the most damage with the least effort expended. Classic tactics.'

Somarus lifted the glass again. 'Then we've got a bit longer to wait. The eddy's rather hard to see from here. It lies a bit to our left, just upstream from the worst of the rocks. The river deepens suddenly at that point, and it's skipper beware! Just when you think you're free and clear of the rapids, the whorl takes hold and flings you about like a berry-basket in a riptide. Of course, experienced river-pilots skirt the thing easily enough. It mostly takes small craft coming downstream who happen on it unexpectedly.'

He swung the glass away from the boat and searched the river's opposite shore.

'What are you looking for, Highness?' Cuva asked.

'A certain sorcerer,' the prince replied grimly, 'on whom all my hopes ride. I'm certain he's out there somewhere, but I don't think I'll find him.'

SEVENTEEN

As the three notes of the trumpet sounded the alert for approaching whitewater, Queen Bryse took the drowsy baby girl from her breast and handed her over to the nursemaid. 'Casya should be quiet enough now. Go sit with her in the forward part of the saloon, where you can get fair warning of bumps and bounces. And hold her in your arms as we go through the rapids, rather than putting her in her cradle. I want her to feel comforting arms about her in case my ladies become affrighted and start a commotion.'

'Yes, Your Majesty.' The maid Dala wore a superior smile. She herself was afraid of very few things now that horrible old King Achardus was dead, and no longer able to threaten her with skinning alive and boiling in oil if she should shirk her duties toward the royal offspring. She took Princess Casabarela from the queen, wiped the baby's tiny mouth, and patted her back to raise a bit of wind. 'That's a good little madam! Now let's find a cozy place up front.'

The saloon was a very large cabin, gorgeously appointed with gilded woodwork, damask draperies, and the finest Incayo carpets, raised above the maindeck and situated just behind the stout mast of the barge. Used variously as a sitting, dining, and presence chamber during the progress, it had glazed casement windows all around to provide the best possible view of the passing scene. These were now firmly shut in anticipation of water being shipped aboard, and the external galleries on either side, which allowed the passengers to stand in the fresh air and watch the laboring oarsmen below, were deserted.

Most of the queen's high-born attendants had gathered in the stern of the saloon, where heavy curtains had been drawn to shield delicate eyes from the sight of the tempestuous river. Shrill exclamations and giggles attested to the ladies' strained nerves, and pages were kept busy passing out scented pomanders, handkerchiefs, and flagons of witch-hazel rosewater to those who already felt faint. A few of the women sipped wine or spirits from lidded drinking vessels. A stack of silver basins stood ready in a corner to accommodate the queasy.

Dala settled herself and baby Casya in a big cushioned chair facing forward, where she could see not only the expanse of rapids but also King Honigalus and his two sons, perched bravely above the bowsprit in their small railed platform. Behind her, the court musicians begin to play, but after a few minutes the soothing melody was almost drowned out by the growing roar and hiss of the water. To relieve the tension, Queen Bryse commanded all the ladies to sing with her, leading them in a clear soprano through the many long verses of *The Blossom Moon Song*.

> *Rosebud, spring rosebud, tight and green,*
> *No soft, fragrant rose petals e'er to be seen;*
> *When will you open wide to me?*
> *When shall I my true love see?*
> *In Blossom Moon, in Blossom Moon, it will surely be.*

Dala hummed along, rocking Casya gently, and the baby slept
even as the barge began to rear and plunge like a rampaging
living thing. The noise of rushing water swelled to thunder.
Some of the women's voices faltered, but none of them dared
to wail or weep so long as the queen kept singing; and this
she did, keeping her back turned resolutely away from the
tumult outside. The barge surged on, expertly steered by its
skipper and powered by the muscles of the valiant oarsmen,
evading boulders and monstrous standing waves, skirting
each rocky patch and climbing the foaming chutes like a
huge homing salmon.

As the last verse of the song began, with only Queen Bryse
and two of the bravest ladies still singing, a faint huzza came
from the men on deck outside. Dala saw that the whitewater
was ending. Only the eddy, a broad, swift-spinning gyre of
foam and floating debris some twenty ells in diameter, now
blocked their way. The skipper steered far toward the heavily
wooded right bank to take them safely around it, then guided
the barge proudly up the deceptively glassy looking center
of the Malle, where the current ran swift and the waters
were dark and deep.

The queen's song ended and the relieved women clapped
and cried out for joy. The cheering of the deckhands intensified and was augmented by glad shouts from male courtiers
swarming out of the sterncastle and racing forward to call
out congratulations to King Honigalus and the two princes
for having held steadfast throughout the passage.

'Well,' said Duke Ranwing Boarsden to the Archwizard Fring,
'that was mildly exhilarating to watch, but hardly the
momentous spectacle you hinted at when you convinced us
to ride out here. Just what did you think was going to happen,
wizard?'

Fring's brow was spangled with sweat and his jaws

clenched tightly together. His gaze was fixed not on the barge but on the smooth expanse of river just ahead of it, where his talent perceived something moving just beneath the water. In the bow pulpit, little Prince Bartus seemed to see something as well. He pointed at it and gave a high-pitched scream as loud and penetrating as the cry of an eagle.

Fring said quietly, 'There. Half a dozen ells in front of the boat. They look something like smooth rocks just breaking the surface of the water. But they're not rocks.'

'Nothing!' Prince Somarus raged. 'Nothing at all happened to Honigalus and his barge! Where are the damned Salka hiding? What are they waiting for? Tesk! Tesk! Curse that sneaky wee magicker – where's he got to, now that I really need him to scry out what's going on?'

Baron Cuva cast a swift glance around the shore near the Boar Creek bridge where the prince's party stood watching the river, but the little black-robed adept was nowhere to be seen. 'Not a sign of him, Highness. And the Green Woman's gone missing as well. I wonder –'

'Shite!' whispered Somarus. His sturdy form went rigid as he stared out onto the river, aghast. 'Father Sun and Mother Moon – will you look at that?'

The barge's skipper set the helm over, steering toward the left bank, and signaled for a last great pull of the sweeps to bring the barge out of the mainstream current and into the backwaters above the landing stage at Boarsden Castle.

The dark heads of the Salka rose from the water.

Carbuncle-red eyes blazing, spiky crests uplifted, maws agape, and crystal teeth flashing in the low sun, the monsters came rocketing downstream toward the barge in a broad inverted-V formation before a single person aboard could give warning. The creatures on the flanks closed in on the sweeps. Their powerful tentacles ripped the oars from their housings with sharp cracks, rending the stout timbers of the hull. Some of the Salka began to pluck howling rowers from their benches, flinging them overboard to other monsters who waited with open jaws. The barge slewed violently as its motive power was lost, and began to drift downstream toward the eddy. Some of the shore observers gave cries of horror as they discerned huge shapes massed at the sides and stern of the vessel, beginning to clamber aboard. A explosive noise signaled that the rudder had been ripped away by main force. A few valiant souls on the boat, having armed themselves with swords and pikes, tried to beat off the inhuman attackers, but the Salka on deck hurled screaming boatmen and courtiers aside as though they were dolls. Black tentacles tipped with clawed digits lashed the air like flexible tree-trunks, making a shambles of the standing rigging and toppling the mast with its square sail.

Then the broken barge reached the rim of the eddy and slowly began its death spin. Terrified men jumped from the fast-settling stern, which the Salka had abandoned in favor of a concerted attack on the glass windows of the saloon cabin. The openings were too small to admit the enormous bodies of the amphibians, so they groped inside with their tentacles in search of prey. Those on shore gasped at the sight of King Honigalus, menaced by three bellowing monsters on the foredeck, taking a small son under each arm and leaping off the bow pulpit into the whirling water. The barge circled faster and faster until it was sucked beneath the surface of the water and disappeared from view.

'Futter me!' Somarus exclaimed. His ruddy features had turned the color of chalk. 'That was grim. At the end, the great brutes were going after the women. I could hear them screaming.'

Baron Cuva only shook his head, speechless. The knights stood in small groups, cursing or dazedly silent, staring upstream at the place where the great boat had vanished.

Then one man pointed to the rapids below the eddy. 'I see floating wreckage coming down toward us. The whirlpool has spat it out! Could it be that some have survived the disaster?'

'You think so?' another said somberly. 'Look – the cursèd fiends are cavorting out there among the rocks, tossing things to one another in some hideous game! Those who drown will be the fortunate ones.'

The others uttered cries of abhorrence and pity.

'It happened as Beynor promised,' Somarus whispered, his eyes glittering. 'As the renegade Royal Alchymist Kilian planned it, so that no man could lay the deed at my doorstep.'

'No, Highness.' Baron Cuva's voice was steady. 'The tragedy cannot be ascribed to you. But the former Conjure-King and Kilian Blackhorse are perhaps not so easily exonerated. It would be wise to keep that fact in mind.'

Somarus was silent.

'What will you have us do now?' the baron asked, after some minutes had passed.

'It'll be awhile before those at Castle Boarsden dare to send search parties out on the water,' the prince decided, 'although land patrols may begin combing the banks for survivors rather sooner. It won't do for anyone to discover us loitering here. We'll have to return to the highway as quickly as we can, then ride back the way we came to the road leading to Boarsden Town. It should be safe to wait there in some handy alehouse until word of the disaster is cried about the city streets.'

'You might be recognized,' Cuva warned.

'What does it matter? This is my tale: I came out of the Elderwold intending to present my respects to King Honigalus as he held court at Boarsden Castle. If I had actually conceived such a saucy notion, dear Cousin Ranwing would not have turned me away, loving a good row as he does . . . So I'm properly appalled at the awful news, and I vow vengeance against the devils responsible, and wait with the duke and his people to see whether any of the royal family has survived.'

'What if one or more of them did?' Cuva asked softly.

'Then Beynor and Kilian Blackhorse will have their work cut out for them. But I don't think we need worry over-much. I'll deplore this lamentable tragedy, while at the same time *you* will make a great show of thanking Providence that the Crown of Didion passes not to a weakling child, as it would have done if Honigalus alone had perished, but rather to a mature warrior ready and able to lead our nation in these difficult times.'

Cuva inclined his head. 'Highness.' His smile was sardonic. 'You must forgive me if I postpone styling you Majesty until the time is ripe. I'm not as audacious as the Green Woman Cray in such matters.'

Somarus scowled and began looking about again, muttering low-voiced oaths. 'Where is she? And that rascal Tesk?'

One of the younger knights smirked. 'Earlier, I saw the wizard making sheep's eyes at the Green Woman. Unlikely as it might seem for two such creatures to be smitten by love's thunderbolt here in a muddy morass, we can't discount the notion.'

'Then let them swive amongst the frogs and midges and be damned,' Somarus said, 'for I won't wait another minute for them.' He turned about, squelched up the creekside path to where they had left the horses, and swung into the saddle.

The nursemaid Dala got up from her chair, holding drowsy little Princess Casabarela tightly against her breast, and watched in frozen disbelief from one of the saloon windows as the nightmarish dark creatures rose from the river. *What were they?* Not seals, not giant squid or octopods, not any kind of animal she had ever seen before. They roared with demonic jubilation as they attacked, and she knew that the frightful things were worse than dumb beasts: they were thinking beings bent on slaughter. The royal barge was their target, and the people aboard were their intended prey.

She was . . . and the baby girl entrusted to her.

Sleek and greenish-black, red saucer-eyes glowing and enormous mouths wide open, the monsters snatched the sweeps away from the oarsmen and began pulling the helpless men overboard to their doom. The barge lost momentum and began to swing broadside to the current. Dala saw King Honigalus and his sons clinging to the rails of the bow pulpit. She felt the vessel shudder, then lurch. A terrible rending sound filled the air, as though the stout wooden frame of the great barge were being torn apart.

She lost her balance and crumpled to the carpeted deck with the baby still in her arms. Unhurt but frightened by the fall and the jolt, the year-old girl began to cry. Without thinking, Dala snatched up a long knitted shawl that had earlier served to cover the baby and swathed the small body completely, head and all, in soft wool. Then she crammed herself and her precious burden into the small space between the heavy padded chair and the bulkhead and began to pray.

At the other end of the long cabin, the court ladies were screaming at the top of their lungs. Someone shouted, 'We're sinking! God have mercy, we're sinking!'

Because of the drawn draperies at the windows round about them, few of those in the stern of the saloon had any real idea of what was happening on the deck outside, nor did the queen seem to understand the atrocious nature of the peril that threatened them. She shouted vainly for all to remain calm, while the boat wallowed and heaved and furniture tumbled and women ensnared in long skirts fell about weeping and moaning.

'Dala!' Bryse shouted desperately. 'Is my little Casya safe?'

'I have her with me, Majesty,' the maid called out from her hiding place, which was nearly ten ells away from the queen, and out of her eyeshot. 'I can swim. I'll do my best to save her.'

'Bless you –' Bryse began to say.

Her words were lost in a great crash as several of the casement windows shattered simultaneously. Boneless dark limbs, dripping blood and water, thrust through the billowing drapes and began ripping the thick fabric away with sharp talons. In moments all those within the saloon knew what was outside, trying to get in.

Dala, at least, had seen them from a distance. Most of the women caught unawares by the sight of the invading Salka fainted dead away from the shock. A few braver souls, including Queen Bryse, tried to escape by opening the doors leading onto the external gallery; but by then the barge was foundering, and a great gout of discolored, debris-laden river water flooded into the saloon, washing them back inside.

A rumbling noise now swelled amidst the human cries and the almost continuous roaring of the triumphant Salka. The barge vibrated like the sounding box of a titanic lute as the eddy currents strummed and whirled it in a narrowing spiral. Then came a crackling fusillade deep within the hull, loud as tarnblaze explosions, as the unbearable pressure of the water began to snap the dying vessel's beams and planking.

Dala was too terrified to move, cringing away from the tangle of writhing tentacles flailing about in search of victims. A glistening black arm encircled the waist of Queen Bryse Vandragora and dragged her out through a broken window frame. With dreadful precision, the monstrous questing limbs sought out and found the noblewomen, the pages, the musicians, and the servants, those who lay senseless and those who frantically tried to escape, and hauled them all away.

The nursemaid no longer heard the human screams or the booming Salka howls. She was conscious only of the rising water now, and the fact that the barge was being engulfed stern-first as it sank into the maelstrom. The forward section of the saloon where she and the baby hid still had most of its windows intact. Equally important, the massive chair had become wedged in a clutter of other furniture. It continued to shelter her, but no longer slid toward the sumberged area where the Salka and the last of the victims continued their struggles. Even when the rising waters finally forced her to stand, Dala was able to conceal herself and the baby behind the sodden folds of the undrawn draperies near her. The child's muffled wails could hardly be heard above the tumultuous racket made by the breaking hull.

Finally, the obscene snarl of probing tentacles withdrew from the saloon. She risked looking out through the window. The landscape spun like a demented carousel, shore and water combined in a dizzying blur. On the tilted foredeck above her, Dala saw King Honigalus leap from the bow pulpit with his sons in his arms. A pack of Salka dived after him. Only three monsters still clung to the hulk of the barge, and as she watched they rolled easily into the water and were gone.

Working quickly, Dala unwound the long shawl from around the baby and used it to bind the small body tightly to her chest, making sure that the child's head was above her shoulder. She studied the latch of the nearest casement. It was a simple thing, and when she turned it the window easily opened inward, letting water pour in. She waited, crooning *The Blossom Moon Song* to the baby. The water rose swiftly and she climbed onto the chair seat and then onto the back, clutching at the drapes, keeping their heads in the air until the last possible moment.

Then she took a deep breath, ducked under, and pushed out through the open casement.

Almost immediately, a powerful current took hold of her. She could see nothing, for the waters of the eddy were not only murky with sediment but also streaked and splotched by bizarre areas of moving light. She kicked and pumped her arms to no effect: swimming was impossible. She would have to let the river take her where it would.

But it was taking her down, down, tumbling her head over heels. The light was dimming and her lungs burned and dearest God what must be happening to the poor baby . . . ?

She struck something, felt a sharp pain in her upper leg, another as her elbow smashed into an unyielding surface. Rocks! The whirlpool was floored with rocks. Panic dug its claws into her pounding heart and she folded her arms protectively about Casya's fragile head.

Then her own skull was struck a glancing blow. White light flared in her brain. The hoarded air burst from her lungs and she sucked in water almost with a sense of relief.

I tried, she thought, drifting into quiet darkness, feeling the motionless tiny body still bound tightly to her. I tried.

The cry of a whooping swan, far away, and the rustle of wind in the reeds. A magenta sky. Softness beneath her aching head. More pain in legs and arms and a lingering rawness in her throat and chest. She was covered to the chin by a blanket.

'She's awake,' a soft voice said. Two faces appeared, smiling down at her: a handsome little blonde woman with brilliant green eyes, and a very ordinary-looking man who sniffled a little and wiped his nose on his sleeve.

'Baby,' she managed to whisper. 'Baby!' Her voice broke and she began to cough.

'Right here beside you,' the man said, 'lying in a nest of dry grass and wrapped in her fine shawl, sleeping soundly.'

'Drink this,' said the green-eyed woman, lifting her head and holding a cup to her lips. She sipped a few drops of warm herb tea, sweetened with honey, then drank deeply and eagerly until the woman said, 'Enough for now,' and let her lie down again.

'Little Casabarela is quite well,' the woman said, 'sleeping off her ordeal as you were. I fed her a bit of mushy bread and cheese curd. But she'll wake betimes and need milk, so we'll have to move along and find a farmstead with a cow or goat. Parties from the castle will be searching the river-bank for survivors, too. And even though they won't be able to see us, we don't want to leave too many traces of our presence to arouse suspicion.'

They were in a dense grove of small trees. River waters gleamed through the leaves and the pungent smell of marsh-land mingled with woodsmoke in the air. Two small horses grazed nearby. A campfire burned briskly in a ring of stones. Hung up to dry beside it on an improvised frame of sticks was a black robe and a set of raggedy trews, evidently the outer clothing of the man, who was clad only in a long undershirt. A second drying-frame held pieces of female clothing: her own! She realized that she was naked beneath the blanket.

'You saved our lives,' she said to the man, overcome with amazement and gratitude. 'You pulled us from the water even though it was alive with ravening monsters!'

He ducked his head modestly. 'You drifted quite a way downstream from the rapids before the counter-currents brought you close to the bank and I was able to swim out and grab hold of you. The monsters are still lurking in the waters near Boarsden Castle. I was never in any danger from them.'

'All the same, I owe you profound thanks – most especially for saving the dear child I had sworn to protect with
my own life. May I know your name, messire?'

'I'm Tesk, an itinerant wizard by profession, and this is my
friend Cray, who is also adept in magic.'

'I'm Dalaryse Plover, called Dala. I am – I was – the chief
nursemaid to the Royal Family of Didion.' She was suddenly
stricken at the thought of them. 'But you don't know, do
you? Something terrible has happened to the king and queen,
and the two little princes!'

'We know,' Cray said. 'The barge was sunk by the Salka
monsters, and all aboard save you and Princess Casabarela
have died abominable deaths.'

'All?' Dala wailed.

'Every one. And I admit that I never expected to find that
you had survived along with the baby.'

'You expected –' Dala felt her senses begin to reel. 'You're
a magicker? You knew this terrible thing was going to happen
and gave no warning?'

'Yes,' Cray admitted freely. 'It was not my duty to issue
warnings, nor would anyone have taken me seriously if I'd
tried. I was sent here from a faraway place by another who
is wiser than I, expressly to rescue Casabarela Mallburn.'

'If the others of the royal family have perished,' Dala said
slowly, 'then the poor orphaned babe is the Queen of Didion.'

'Some day she will be,' Cray said. 'But not now. There are
dire things happening in your country and in other parts of
High Blenholme Island. If it became known that little Casya
were alive, scheming men would try to murder her. The
monsters did not attack the royal barge by chance. They were
incited by sorcerers who intend for Prince Somarus to take
up Didion's crown.'

Dala's eyes widened. 'But how –'

'We'll explain it to you later,' Cray said. 'You have a right to know everything, since it seems obvious that you were fated to be saved along with your tiny mistress – although the Source neglected to mention the fact to me. And glad I am that you're here, Dala! For I know much of magic but very little of child-rearing, and I admit my heart sank to my boots when the Source laid this strange charge upon me. But, there – it'll work out splendidly now, with you and dear Tesk to share the burden.'

The man nodded and smiled and went to the fire to feel the cloth of his robe. 'Just about dry. I'll leave you ladies for a few minutes so Dala can get dressed. Then we must be off. We've a long way to travel.' He took his garments and disappeared into the bushes.

'Where are we going?' Dala asked. 'Can any place in Didion be safe from men so evil that they would kill an entire royal family, innocent children and all, in order to steal a throne?'

'No one will follow us into the Elderwold wilderness,' Cray said. 'That's where we'll go.'

The nursemaid's face crumpled with dismay. 'But the terrible Green Men live there! Have Casya and I escaped one set of inhuman monsters, only to fall into the hands of others?'

'We'll risk it,' Cray said rather tartly. 'Sit up now, and I'll help you get your clothes on.'

EIGHTEEN

As soon as the Salka began their attack, Beynor put his own escape plan into action.

He crouched low in the dismasted sailboat and sent his windsight underwater to find the Supreme Warrior. Ugusawnn was still harnessed to the boat; but he was well out from the riverbank, at least five ells away and slightly downstream, resting on the mud bottom. His great body was poised in a tense attitude that seemed to indicate he was in mental contact with his company of warriors, directing them in their initial sprint toward the unsuspecting people on the royal barge.

Beynor's great Sword of State, which he had brought with him from the Dawntide Citadel, had a double edge keener than the sharpest razor. He removed it now from the oilskin bag where he'd kept it out of sight, buckled on the ornate scabbard, and drew the blade. Then he cut the boat's stern line, which had been tied to one of the trees.

He held his breath, his heart thudding in his breast. The Eminent monster was so absorbed in the events taking place out on the water that he had paid no attention to what Beynor was doing.

Moving cautiously, with the sword still in hand, he went to the bow and checked to make sure that the little craft had not drifted into an unfavorable position within the over-hanging brush and small trees that screened it. All was well. The boat's anchor was not out. Instead, a bow-line tied to a branch kept its stem pointed upstream.

Beynor waited until the Salka warriors attacked the barge's oarsmen, and death-screams began to punctuate the wind. Then he leaned over the side and sliced through the mooring line and the leather harness traces attached to the gunwales, setting the sailboat free. Sheathing the blade, he scrambled to the stern, heedless of the noise he made, seized the tiller, and exerted all of his magical strength to propel the small boat out of its hiding place and into the open river. It was a simple trick, known to almost every talented child in Moss but rarely employed by mature sorcerers, and he counted on it now to save his life.

He gave a mighty shout on the wind: 'Ugusawnn, take care! Press the attack! Fighting men are coming at us from the castle in boats and I must intercept them. Stay here and don't try to follow me. I'll beat them back!'

What?! The distracted Salka still didn't realize that the traces had been cut. *What are you saying?*

With the centerboard up and the small craft drawing less than a foot of water, Beynor raced away upstream through the shallows along the northern shore, praying that Ugusawnn would fall for the ruse and remain with his warriors.

A bellow of rage split the air behind him. *Stop! Where are you going?*

'Do your job!' Beynor retorted on the wind, 'Make certain that no human escapes the ambush alive – else you and your people will never regain this island home that was stolen from you!'

The humans on the barge will be slaughtered and eaten – and

*so will you, when I catch you! Scheming traitor! No one is coming
at us from the castle. You're trying to escape.*

Beynor made the boat go faster, zigzagging and swerving
among the rocks with no thought of the danger. He dared
not pause to scry out possible pursuit, but no monstrous tenta-
cled limb had yet laid hold of his boat, and he was already
opposite Boarsden Castle, where the banners and decorations
still hung out to welcome a king who would never arrive.

Stop! Come back!

'Sink the barge! Kill the people! Do what you came to do
and I'll carry out my own part of the bargain!'

The ground along the right bank was rising now, changing
rapidly from fertile pasture and field into upthrust bedrock
dotted by thin stands of pine. A few minutes later the boat
turned right and charged along the base of the towering
palisade that forced the Malle into its Big Bend. Across the
broad elbow of water lay Boarsden Town with its crowded
jetties and docks and the warehouses of the wool-merchants
and northern timberlords. Clogging the shallowing river
nearly to midstream were anchored rafts of logs sent down
from the forests of interior Didion, waiting for the rains of
autumn to raise the water and give them swift passage to
the mills and shipyards of Holt Mallburn.

Beynor steered for the opposite shore and the town,
crossing the open channel and darting in among the rafts,
agile as a minnow fleeing from a pike. The log platforms
were anchored with multiple iron chains. Swimming underwater among them at speed would be a perilous business,
even for a Salka. If Ugusawnn was still in pursuit, he would
have to move more slowly, perhaps even put his head into
the air to see which way the boat was going. But no tentacles took hold of the brash young sorcerer, nor did the
Supreme Warrior bespeak him with fresh threats. Had the
crafty monster swum on ahead? Was he waiting for his prey

to arrive at the dock before putting a heartbreaking end to the escape attempt?

The wind-world had become a howling chaos of dying minds that Beynor paid no more heed to, feeling no compassion or other emotion at the loss of so many lives, but only a sense of stark and necessary fulfillment. The first difficult step in his rebirth to glory had been taken. If he could only evade Ugusawnn's wrath for a few more minutes, the next step would follow quickly – and be so much easier.

His boat skimmed the water like a leaf blown before a gale, drawing the attention of river boatmen who called out to him with indignant shouts. He ignored them, continuing on his wildly erratic course through larger vessels moored offshore, heading toward the public landing stage. The racing boat's wake made the small craft tied up at the slips wallow and scrape their fenders. Sailors and dockside hangers-on cursed and yelled at him as he reined in his talent, then forced his boat to halt abruptly in a welter of foam just as it was about to crash into the quayside.

He'd arrived.

'A madman!' somebody yelled. Another cried, 'A wizard!'

'Stand clear!' Beynor shouted at the gathering crowd. 'I'm coming ashore.'

He seized the oilskin bag holding his money and personal effects, crouched, and made a great talent-assisted bound high into the air. He flew over the heads of the people on the dock's edge like an acrobat and landed on his feet six ells away from the water. No enraged Salka monster surged up after him. He was safe. He'd won the gamble.

'Here now!' cried the dockmaster, a stout, red-faced functionary who came rushing up with a pair of armed toll-collectors. 'Here now! You can't come roaring in here like this, sirrah! Who do you think –'

Beynor opened his purse and sent a gold mark coin spinning

straight into the master's admonishing hand. The man stopped dead in his tracks, eyes bulging, and finished his sentence lamely.

'– you are?'

The tall, pale-haired young man with the darkly compelling eyes drew himself up proudly. He wore modest garments and had a seaman's duffel slung over one shoulder, but girded about his loins was a sword and scabbard more magnificent than any Didionite prince could hope to wear.

'I am a visiting wizard,' Beynor said politely. 'My name is Lund.'

The angry murmurs of the crowd were stilled and the people shuffled their feet and looked uneasy. It didn't do to offend a wizard, even one who had no notion of how to behave on the water.

Beynor produced another gold coin and proffered it to the incredulous dockmaster. 'If I have trespassed upon your laws or customs by my informal arrival, I beg your pardon. I trust that the gratuity I've vouchsafed to you will be adequate to ensure my temporary welcome here.'

The dockmaster was all smiles now. 'Certainly, my lord! How may we assist you? Do you require accommodation for the night?' The common people began to drift away, along with the two sullen-faced toll-collectors, who were well aware that there'd be no chance of extorting special fees from this well-feathered bird of passage while the lucky dock-master had him in tow.

'Much as I would like to enjoy the hospitality of Boarsden Town,' Beynor said, 'I regret that urgent business summons me elsewhere. I wish to purchase two blood horses, a fine saddle and harness, and a few other pieces of travelling gear. Perhaps you can direct me to a suitable stable.'

'I myself will take you to the best purveyor of horseflesh in all of central Didion! But what of your small boat?'

'I leave it in your good hands, since I have no further need of it. Just give me a moment to collect my thoughts, and then we'll be off.'

'Certainly, my lord.'

Beynor turned away, sending his windsight soaring downstream, and drew in a sharp breath as he saw the royal barge being sucked down into the eddy. There was no time to waste. He must be well away from here before the magnitude of the disaster became generally known. He cut off the dreadful oversight and bespoke Ugusawnn silently.

'Eminent One, it seems you and your warriors have done the job. I congratulate you. May I also commend your good sense in not pursuing me.'

I was sorely tempted to seize you and rip you limb from limb for daring to escape me. But I thought the better of it.

'And well you did. If you'd followed your instincts, you'd have to explain to the other three Eminences why the Known Potency would never be activated. The fact is, I'm still quite willing to bring the sigil to life for you, and lead you to my sister's collection of stones. But I intend to do it in my own way and under my own terms. I'm tired of your bullying and your stupid threats.'

Stupid? You dare to call me stupid?

Resentment and frustration flared in Beynor like a tarnstick igniting waxed tinder, but the tone of his mental speech was glacial. 'Ugusawnn, I've no doubt that you're a brave battle-leader. But when it comes to matters of high policy you're naught but a blubber-brained fool. You have no notion of how to accomplish important deeds save by brute force – no way of seeking other beings' cooperation save through violent coercion. Back in the Dawntides, I tried to deal with you like a civilized being while making my proposal. Your three colleagues treated me with respect – but not you, Supreme Warrior! All you've done from the start is bluster

and try to intimidate me. Well, Eminent Ugu, that's all over
now.'

What do you mean, groundling?

'You won't carry me back to the Dawntides as your prisoner, nor will I immediately bring the Known Potency to life
for you.

You promised –

'I don't trust you to fulfill your part of the bargain. I believe
you've intended from the beginning to kill me just as soon
as I activated the Potency. If you deny it, you lie. Therefore,
the rules of our agreement have changed.'

How?

'I intended to travel directly to Moss by land. You and
your warriors go down the River Malle as quickly as you
can. Return to the Dawntide Isles. Assemble your invading
army, proceed to the Darkling River below Royal Fenguard,
and meet me there in six days. You can do it easily. Bring
the Known Potency with you.'

And then?

'Help me kill my sister Ullanoth. When she's well and truly
dead – and only then – I'll bring the Potency to life, in a manner
that doesn't endanger me. You can use it to activate the
Conjure-Queen's remaining sigils without the usual pain. In a
short time, with the help of the stones, the entire nation of
Moss will belong to you and your people. If you use Moss as
a base of operations, you can conquer all of High Blenholme.'

How do I know you're telling the truth?

'Bespeak your colleagues,' Beynor said wearily. 'Ask their
advice, and for God's sake follow it, for they are far wiser
than you. I'll be at Royal Fenguard myself within six days.
Either join me there, or forget that you ever knew me. And
throw the Known Potency into the depths of the Boreal Sea,
for it will never be more to you than a useless bit of rock.'

*   *   *

It was late afternoon when the remount Sir Gavlok Whitfell had acquired at the Great Pass garrison pulled up lame. By that time, Snudge's party had almost reached the Didionite fortress of Castlemont. Ordinarily, even though the barbarian nation was now a loyal vassal of the Sovereignty, the king's men would have passed the place by and continued on twenty leagues further up the Wold Road to the walled way station of Rockyford, long operated by Cathra for the benefit of royal dispatch riders and important commercial travelers. Gavlok was all for pressing on, insisting he'd be content to ride pillion with one of the two burly Mountain Swordsmen who had joined them at Beorbrook Hold. But Snudge had doubts.

'There's a brown haze spreading over the sky from the west,' he pointed out, 'and a smell of smoke. I'm not one to believe in omens, but I do know that beyond Castlemont we ride into lonely country where outlaws loyal to Prince Somarus prey on caravans and well-found travelers with hardly a blink of disapproval from the local lords. What if villains have fired the Elderwold in places, so as to slow down those on the road and have easy pickings? If there's trouble brewing, it would be folly for us to head straight into it with one of our party lacking a sound mount.'

'There was no hint of bandit activity in the area reported at Great Pass, Sir Deveron,' rumbled one of the Mountain Swordsmen, who was named Radd Falcontop. 'Still, I confess to feeling a prickling of my own thumbs. Have you noted how few people we've met riding south today?'

'It might only be the lull in traffic normal around Solstice time,' said the second Swordsman, Hulo Roundbank. 'But what if it isn't? I believe you're right to stop at Castlemont, messire. We can rest, feed ourselves and our beasts, and pay the castle stable's outrageous price for a fresh horse for Sir Gavlok. Meanwhile, Radd and I can try to pick up some useful gossip. After so many years in the earl marshal's service, we've managed to make a few friends in this part of Didion.'

Falcontop and Roundbank were men of Beorbrook Hold, veterans of border skirmishes and fights along the Wold Road, the only reliable land route connecting Cathra and Tarn. They were of an age with Earl Marshal Parlian, having served him since he was newly knighted six-and-thirty years earlier. The two Swordsmen were long widowed and had only grown children, but although they bore the scars of many battles they were still hardy as badgers. They had volunteered for this strange mission knowing that it involved high sorcery and dangerous state secrets; and if they were surprised at the youthfulness of the expedition's leader, they'd concealed their thoughts well.

Falcontop was the shorter of the pair, stocky, with broad shoulders and arms so powerful they could wrestle down and foot-lash a stag. His hair, thinning on top but ample below and worn in leather-bound plaits, had once been brick-red; but it and his bushy beard and brows were now so diluted with white as to be nearly pink. His dark eyes were hooded and his habitual expression was one of calm forbearance. He had killed twenty-two men in battle.

Hulo Roundbank was two heads taller than his fellow-warrior, not nearly as massive, but giving an impression of indefatigable strength and endurance. His long face was split by a thrusting beak of a nose topped by a single long brow of tangled silver. The rest of his skull was shaven to stubble, save for the area just before his ears, where he had spared two dangling white tresses threaded with bright blue beads that had plainly been chosen to match his eyes.

Both men wore chausses and vests of well-tanned deer-skin, stained blackish brown by long usage, lightweight linen shirts of the same anonymous hue, heavy boots, and oddly folded caps with projecting bills in front. Their impressive array of personal weaponry left no doubt as to their occupation, but for this mission they wore no man's badge.

With Gavlok up behind Hulo and his limping horse on a lead-rein, they traveled the last few leagues to Castlemont. The fortress crowned a rugged crag and guarded the important intersection of the Great North Road, the Wold Road, and Boar Road. At the foot of Castlemont Crag was a high-walled enclosure built of rock, where carts or pack animals carrying valuable cargo could be secured for the night. It had a tall guardtower, a bare-bones inn that offered shelter from the elements and little else, rows of hitching posts, a well, and a store of fodder supervised by a sleepy-looking ostler. The place was empty except for a Didionite mule-train carrying slabs of choice wood, being off-loaded so that the animals might rest well before making the steep ascent to Great Pass and the Cathran border on the morrow.

'No stable down here, no horses for sale or hire,' Gavlok noted. 'We'd best take ourselves up to the fort.'

To reach the stronghold, it was necessary to climb a track with many switchbacks, reminiscent of the approach to Elktor Castle. The gate to the track was barred. At the guardpost, Snudge presented a document identifying him as the son of a Cathran merchant-peer, traveling to Tarn on family business.

The watch-captain's eyes gleamed as he studied the parchment, then let his gaze wander over the collection of dusty but well-dressed young men and the two hardbitten warriors who shepherded them.

'Not a wise thing these days, traveling by land to Tarn,' the officer observed, re-rolling the parchment and giving it back to Snudge. 'Our local breed of lawless men well know what to do with a letter of credit – should you just happen to be carrying one of those! They roast the bearer's feet till he signs it over. My lord, take my advice and hire more

guards when you reach Rockyford Station.' He nodded at
Vra-Mattis. 'Your good Brother there can bespeak the old
windvoice who lives at the place and arrange it all for you
in advance. But first, enjoy the good cheer of Castlemont
Fortress. We're always happy to welcome guests who know
the value of top-notch service.'

'Stay and spend money,' muttered Gavlok's saucy highland squire, Hanan, as they started up the hill.

'Odds on, Sir Deveron, that captain thinks you're going to
Tarn to purchase gold for your daddy.' Radd Falcontop
grinned. 'He's got you pegged: a young spark and his good
mate and your squires and bodyguards, off to do a little business and have a fine adventure in the wild north country.
Then you'll sail comfortably home from Donorvale City, and
brag to your friends back in Cala Blenholme that you dared
the big, bad Wold Road.'

Hulo chuckled. 'The captain might not bother to sell us
out to the nearest robber-band if we tip him well on the way
out of here.'

'We could stay the night,' Gavlok suggested. 'It's the last
civilized place we'll find short of Castle Direwold near the
Tarnian frontier. We'll live rough from here on.'

'I'll consider it,' Snudge said. 'Let's see which way the
wind blows after we've taken our ease and bought you a
new horse.'

The wind blew from Cala Palace, and the voice precariously
riding on it was that of Lord Stergos, the convalescent Royal
Alchymist.

His words came only to Snudge's brain, and were perceived
there very faintly, as he and his companions ate an early
supper together at a trestle table in an open porch near the
fort's kitchen, accompanied by a few other wayfarers. In the
outposts of Didion, there was little regard for the niceties

due to rank; if a noble was too fastidious to sup at the common board, he was invited to take his meal in one of the tiny sleeping cubicles in the dormitorium provided for paying guests.

The intelligencer gave no sign that he'd heard words on the wind, only silently bespoke the novice, Vra-Mattis, who sat on the opposite side of the table. 'Give a low cry – then tell me quietly that you have a wind-message for me.'

The apprentice played his rôle to perfection, so none of the outsiders at the table heard what he said to his master. Gavlok and the armigers exchanged knowing smiles and Radd and Hulo pretended indifference.

Snudge rose. 'Sir Gavlok, explain to our new companions why we must suffer arcane interruptions in our mundane activities from time to time.'

He and Mat strode off to the curtainwall, and after receiving permission from the sergeant of the watch, climbed to the southern parapet with the excuse of viewing the mountain panorama, but in actuality wishing to ease Lord Stergos's bespeaking over distance. None of the fort's men-at-arms approached or questioned them after Vra-Mattis cast a light spell to discourage curiosity. They settled into a broad embrasure between the merlons of the battlement, and then Snudge covered his eyes and responded to Stergos.

'I'm here, my lord, Deveron Austrey in Castlemont Fortress in Didion. I'm in a secure place. There are no expert wind-talents round about here able to eavesdrop upon us, only Vra-Mattis, who cannot overhear unless I permit it – which I won't. Are you in better health?'

I'm mending, thanks to a potion that came some days ago from the Conjure-Queen, sent before she sank into a profound trance.

'Sulkorig told me of her strange fate. What's become of her sigils?'

For safekeeping, they're being stored in the traditional place –

the tomb of the first Conjure-King, Rothbannon – where they will remain inaccessible to anyone save members of the reigning family of Moss: Ullanoth herself, of course, should she be restored to her body, and Beynor also. When I remonstrated with Lady Zimroth and warned her of the potential danger from him, she remained unmoved. Mossland tradition, it seems, may not be flouted! And Beynor is accursed, so even if the stones were inactive he could not touch them without perishing. At least this is what she and the rest of the Glaumerie Guild believe . . . And now please tell me why you are so eager to bespeak me, Deveron, rather than relay messages through Vra-Sulkorig. The effort to speak on the wind is very taxing.

'Lord Stergos, bear with me. Since you were so badly injured, much has happened to me – and some of it may pertain to the situation in Moss. I have secrets to impart. Some must be withheld from His Grace the High King, while others he must hear only from your own lips. This is why I needed to bespeak you so urgently.'

Tell me.

Haltingly at first, then in a torrent of detailed windspeech, Snudge described his meeting with the Green Man Odall at the croft east of Castle Elktor. He said nothing of the unwelcome gift of the sigil Subtle Gateway, but he did tell of his amazing encounter with the One Denied the Sky.

The Source – Ansel's mysterious Source – you say HE is this One Denied the Sky? And you believe him to be one of the Beaconfolk?

'I do, my lord. He said little but implied much during our strange conversation. We of Cathra have long believed that all of the Great Lights are evil. But the Source's talk of a New Conflict betokens that an Old Conflict once took place – and that it must have involved a dispute between good and evil entities of the sky realm over the morality of moonstone magic and pain-eating.'

And the evil Lights won this ancient battle?

'Almost certainly, for the sigils still belong to them. As I understand it, the New Conflict has the aim of severing this pernicious linkage between sky and ground beings. The Source spoke of how I had been *enlisted* in this New Conflict. And I wasn't the only one: the Source spoke of King Conrig, the thieving Brothers, and even Beynor of Moss in this way. Some of the enlistees, like me, were given free choice to join the Conflict or refuse. Others, like His Grace, seem to serve the purposes of this Source all unawares. In my opinion, Queen Ullanoth has also been drawn into the Conflict – or perhaps taken out of it until the Source reinstates her. Even Princess Maudrayne and her little son appear to be part of this supernatural war, since the Source ordered me to continue on to Tarn without delay and fulfill my duty there.'

This is incredible! Do you mean to tell me that the entity called the Source uses human beings as agents or weapons in this battle between factions of Lights?

'So it would seem, my lord.'

Deveron, I – I am at a loss. I know not what to say to you. What you've told me has a terrible plausibility, and yet my soul shrinks from the idea that a merciful God might permit his human creatures to be manipulated in such a cavalier manner by supernatural beings!

'I'm no great thinker, my lord. But even I know that the lesser people of our world are routinely used by the greater for their own purposes. Children are ruled by parents; wives are ruled by husbands; men are ruled by overlords . . . It's the way things are. At least the Source seems to be motivated solely by good intentions.'

My royal brother would find this notion of being used by the Lights to be insupportable. His pride would never accept it as truth, and so I will not tell him about it, lest he doubt the rest of your explanation for failing to retrieve the Trove of Darasilo.

'I agree that would be the wisest course, my lord.'

I myself, on the other hand, am inclined to believe in this One Denied the Sky and his laudable goal. If the opportunity arises, tell him I would cooperate willingly in the New Conflict.

'I'll gladly tell him, my lord, if I can.'

Now I must pass on other important information to you that's only recently come to us at the palace. The shaman Blind Bozuk has told us that Maudrayne and her son are no longer sequestered on Tarn's west coast, but have been carried off by Ansel Pikan to a place far to the north-east, beyond the great volcanos. The region is nearly inaccessible to foreigners, and she's supposedly guarded now by magic more powerful than before. I fear that this will make your own mission impossible to accomplish.

'Not at all, my lord. There's still hope.'

Then tell me of it, for I'm very close to despondency. My poor brain is on fire with pain from the effort of bespeaking you and from my own fruitless efforts to unravel this wretched knot of plots and counterplots. And we still don't know what manner of evil scheme Beynor of Moss and Kilian are cooking up! But to hell with them and their devilry. If you have any consolation for me, lad, be quick to offer it. I won't be able to bespeak you much longer.

'Listen, my lord, and take heart! The Source himself gave me a . . . clue as to the whereabouts of Princess Maudrayne. And after my talk with him, I conceived an idea that may enable us to neutralize the threat she poses to King Conrig – and do it without any dishonorable actions. As yet, my idea is a seed lacking soil to sprout in or water and sunlight to help it grow. But it could work, and it has the potential to save the Sovereignty. I envision a certain compromise, whereby His Grace and the Princess Maude each gain while yielding in part to the other, with the result that the most dangerous of His Grace's secrets will remain hidden, and the consequences of the other secret will be postponed for many long years. With two such prideful and stubborn royal persons involved, getting them to agree to the compromise will not be easy. But there are other things besides sweet persuasion that might compel their acceptance.'

Tell me more.

'Soon, my lord, when I have it straight in my own mind. The Source would of necessity be a party to it.'

Bazekoy's Bones! You'd think of pressuring such a being? Deveron, are you mad?

'No, my lord, I'm a snudge: a sneaking, devious, crafty spy. You'd think the Source would have better sense than to enlist me in his unearthly Conflict! Since he didn't, let's hope he's not surprised at the consequences. He said that he needed me. Well, I also need him, and he'll help whether he wants to or not.'

I can't bear to hear any more. Bespeak Sulkorig when you can tell me your plan in full, and I'll listen. Farewell, Deveron. May you succeed – or at least do more good than harm.

Snudge opened his eyes slowly and found himself lying flat on the fortress parapet, with a throbbing skull and every other bone aching as if from a fierce beating. Ofttimes strenuous bouts of windspeech still afflicted him sorely, although he suffered less than he had when he was younger.

He groaned, rolled over, and pulled himself up on his elbows. And gave a cry of dismay as he saw Vra-Mattis.

The apprentice windvoice was sitting with his back against the battlement, clutching his knees with white-knuckled hands. Tears ran down his face, soaking the front of his robe, and his mouth was an open square of misery, although he uttered not a single sound.

'Good God, Mat! What's wrong?'

The young man's voice was scarcely audible. 'Listen, master! Listen to the wind. So many souls, dying so horribly! I tried to scry out the cause, but the flood of pain and desolation overwhelmed my talent.' He lifted a trembling hand

and pointed eastward. 'In that direction, toward Boarsden.'

Snudge overheard it himself now. But it was many minutes before he recovered his strength enough to survey the scene on the River Malle with his oversight. He saw the Salka sporting in the water, but did not fully understand what had happened until he read the lips of Duke Ranwing Boarsden, the Archwizard Fring, and the other noble witnesses who stood transfixed at the riverside, watching the monsters feast.

NINETEEN

Grand Master Ridcanndal, head of Moss's Glaumerie Guild, finished drafting the appeal to High King Conrig, sanded the ink, and perused what he had written, wondering whether his language had conveyed the urgency of the situation:

> . . . *The terrible tragedy that took place this day in Didion serves to confirm what we have long suspected: that the Salka monsters have for some reason shaken off their age-old torpor and reclusiveness. Emboldened and aggressive, they once again threaten the safety of all human life on High Blenholme. And with Conjure-Queen Ullanoth sunk in a helpless trance, the kingdom of Moss, your loyal vassal, now lies particularly vulnerable to their attacks.*
>
> *While it is true that scriers of our Glaumerie Guild have not been able to detect any evidence of overt hostile activity among the monsters of the Dawntide Isles, it seems reasonable to believe that they were responsible for the heinous attack on Didion's Royal family, which would have required careful planning and a level of leadership lacking in other populations of these ferocious creatures.*
>
> *However, the normally shy Salka resident in the Little Fen*

*have lately been seen in broad daylight, cruising boldly about the
environs of Fenguard Castle and the Royal Naval Yards. Rumors
also have it that the Great Fen Salka are migrating southward
toward parts of Moss occupied by humanity, an unprecedented
event that the Guild and our Grand Council of Lords view with
grave concern.*

   *In light of these ominous circumstances, the Guild and Council
members, acting with full royal authority while our queen is incapacitated, respectfully request that the Sovereign fulfill his solemn
commitment to defend Moss from enemies human and inhuman.
We ask that a squadron of Sovereignty warships be dispatched at
once, to patrol the waters between the Darkling Channel and the
Dawntide Isles in a show of strength and solidarity . . .*

   Ridcanndal nibbled on the feather tip of his pen, wondering
whether he should have written *demand* instead of *request*.
Ullanoth, in her mortal illness, had not hesitated to speak
bluntly to the Sovereign, forcing him to reiterate his obligation to defend the smallest and least prosperous nation of his
Sovereignty before she would agree to help him. But with
her voice now silenced, and the Salka menace apparently
turned toward the much more important nation of Didion –

   Someone knocked sharply at the outer door of the Grand
Master's tower chambers, breaking his thread of thought. He
rose from his desk in the sanctum, grumbling, and shuffled
out into the sitting room. It was early evening, but the sky
outside had gone dark as a storm rolled down from the north.
Rain pelted the windows and the fire was burning low. He
felt a chill rake the flesh between his shoulder-blades. The
knocking came again, louder than before.

   'I'm coming!' He flung open the door and cried out in
astonishment, 'You!'

   'None other.'

   The tall woman of ample figure was dressed in robes of

dark-blue silk, with a silver girdle and silver bands about the sleeves and neckline. Her hair was also silver, worn in a coronet of braids, and her face was amiable and serene, except for a certain sadness clouding her jade-green eyes. On either side of her stood warlock-knights of the Royal Guard, impassive as marble images in their handsome gilt armor and swan-blazoned surcoats, She lifted her hand in a dismissive gesture. 'You men may leave us now.'

'Yes, my lady.' They turned on their heels and marched away.

'Will you invite me in, Ridcanndal?' Thalassa Dru inquired in a gentle voice. 'Or would you prefer that I state my business here in the corridor?'

He backed away from her, bowing slightly. 'Please enter, Conjure-Princess. Forgive my surprise and confusion. It's been – how long?'

'Four-and-twenty years since my late brother Linndal banished me for opposing his marriage to Taspiroth sha Elial. But the Conjure-King and I were reconciled in his final year of life, as you doubtless know, and so I come here to my birthplace a member in good standing of the royal family of Moss, for the purpose of averting a terrible catastrophe.'

Ridcanndal felt the muscles of his upper body stiffen with dread at the formality of her pronouncement. Surely she would not dare –

'Take me to Rothbannon's tomb,' she continued. 'Immediately.'

'Lady, what do you intend to do?' He had to force the words from his lips. 'You are a royal princess of Moss and have the right to enter the tomb, but I cannot believe that you would meddle with the sigils that are the bonded possessions of our stricken queen. Not while our nation stands in such peril, and may have need of them!'

Thalassa Dru came close to him, lifting her plump warm

hands to his jowly cheeks as though she were comforting a terrified child. 'Why are you so worried about what I might do with the sigils? Ullanoth is incapable of using them, or even giving permission for their abolition and re-bonding. Such permission can only be granted by another member of the royal family. Since you did not welcome me and urge me to perform this important service for Moss, I must assume you are expecting another to do so. Are you waiting for Beynor? Tell me the truth.'

He gave a guilty start and withdrew from her touch, knowing that his colleague Zimroth, the Royal Thaumaturge, who loved the deposed young king as a son, entertained just such an intention and had already proposed it to the Guild and the Grand Council.

'I pray with all my heart and soul that Queen Ullanoth will recover and reclaim her sigils,' he said. 'Yet it seemed prudent to some senior royal advisers to consider what might happen if she should never awaken. Prince Beynor is her only suitable successor. In these dire times, the crown of Moss cannot possibly be offered to the boy Habenor, who was placed in the line of succession by our late monarch Linndal. Even though Beynor is debarred from using the stones himself, he can legally give permission for a surrogate to pronounce the spells separating them from our helpless queen and binding them to another person who nevertheless remains subject to the crown's authority. Thus we would retain the magical defensive properties of the sigils, while having a suitable ruler for our country.'

'The scheme might have worked,' Thalassa Dru said, 'if Beynor had not already made a pact with the Salka, agreeing to assist them in an invasion and takeover of Moss.'

'No! He would never do such a thing – any more than he would have slain his royal father.'

'Ullanoth named him patricide and regicide.'

'In this belief, the Conjure-Queen was mistaken!'

'She spoke the simple truth, Ridcanndal – and so do I. Beynor's heart is so warped by bitterness and hatred that he has vowed to admit the monsters to this very castle. While Salka destroy the body of his sister, he intends seize her sigils for his own perverted uses. I have been commanded to prevent the last two calamities.'

'Who commanded you?'

'The Source of the Old Conflict gave the order – he who is called the One Denied the Sky.'

'He's . . . only a myth.' But a spark of doubt flickered in the old sorcerer's eyes.

'No more so than the Great Lights themselves, as the oldest of our histories affirm. The Source is alive and determined to repair the damage he inadvertently caused. I am only one of his servants. Queen Ullanoth, in her last minutes of conscious volition, became another.'

'Unbelievable . . .'

'The New Conflict is upon us, Grand Master, and you'd better think long and hard about which side you choose to support. Beynor is too self-centered to serve the evil Lights of his own free will, but I believe that they have nevertheless made him their puppet. As you are well aware, it's difficult for them to interact directly with our material world, except through the subtle fluxes of power and pain. They need groundling agents – just as my benevolent Source does – and Beynor is their perfect choice. Have you forgotten that he carried away the Unknown Potency when he sought refuge in the Dawntide Isles? All of his other sigils were taken from him – save that one, which the Lights unaccountably permitted him to keep.'

'Thalassa Dru, what are you saying?' Ridcanndal looked at her askance. 'Has Beynor activated the Potency to use against us?'

'It's quite possible that he has – perhaps with the connivance

of the Lights themselves, if they see him as a useful adjunct
to their capricious schemes. Now take me to the tomb!'

It was impossible to deny her. The right of access was hers
by law. But what did she intend to do? Ridcanndal sighed,
took up a tall oil lamp, and ignited a flame that burned within
its crystal chimney. 'Has the Source also sent you to stave
off the incursion of Salka into our lands? Will you take up
the Crown of Moss yourself?'

'Alas, I have no such mandate. Conrig Wincantor is the
only one who can defend you from invading monsters.'

'I was finishing the draft of an appeal to him when you
came to my door. The Conjure-Queen assured us that the
Sovereign of Blenholme would come to our aid if we were
attacked. But what if his help comes too late? In the Salka's
last assault upon us, it was only the queen's use of her Great
Stone Weathermaker that beat the brutes away from our
shores. The warships sent by Conrig served only to harry
and punish them once they had already withdrawn.'

'Thanks to Ullanoth, Moss now has its own small navy
and a force of trained fighting warriors. Use them. But make
plans also against the blackest contingency. This is the only
advice I can give you. Now take me to the tomb with no
further ado.'

He could only obey, knowing that no magic of his could
stop her. He led her from his tower into the main keep of
the castle, and from there down seemingly endless winding
staircases of black, dripping rock into a labyrinth of tunnels
and disused chambers, where walled-off sections masked
ancient secrets or led to places long forgotten.

The tomb of the first Conjure-King was less than a century
old, although Fenguard Castle itself predated Rothbannon by
nearly five hundred years, having long been the home of
renegade Didionite wizards. Some legends hinted that the
deepest shafts and burrows were the work of the Salka, and

humankind had raised the castle on foundations built in primordial times by the amphibian monsters.

'My brother Linndal, when he was a reckless young boy, explored these ancient subterranean portions of Fenguard,' Thalassa Dru remarked as they traveled the maze of dark corridors. 'I'd not be surprised if Beynor did also. Have you considered that some of these passages might lead outside the castle walls, below the Darkling River and into the waters of the Little Fen itself? They might provide a way for Salka to penetrate the defenses of Fenguard Castle – provided they had a guide.'

'I never thought of such a thing,' Ridcanndal admitted. 'We'll take what precautions we can against such an intrusion.' He was becoming increasingly rattled – not only by the way this woman had compelled him to obey her, but also by the confident portentousness of her remarks. How in the world was he going to explain all this to Zimroth and the Glaumerie Guild? At the very least, he should have found a way to alert them to the arrival of the late king's mysterious sister. But bewilderment and chagrin (or was it her sorcery?) had distracted him, and now it was too late.

They had come at last to the sealed entrance to Rothbannon's tomb, which lay at the end of a dry tunnel that looked almost freshly hewn. 'Unbind the defensive spells blocking the door,' Thalassa Dru told him.

Meekly, Ridcanndal pronounced the lengthy incantation that protected the tomb against ordinary intruders. Then the sorceress laid her own hand upon the solid stone door-panel. It was incised with the swan insignia and an inscription:

ROTHBANNON ASH BAJOR
C.Y. 911–1052
FIRST CONJURE-KING OF MOSS AND LIBERATOR OF THE
SEVEN STONES
'PUISSANCE AND PRUDENCE'

'What a pity,' she murmured, 'that he was the only one of his blood to follow that wise motto! Recite the rest of the spell, Grand Master.'

He hesitated only for a moment, then spoke the words, concluding in a loud voice, 'Open to a true descendant of Rothbannon!'

With a harsh grating rumble, the stone door rolled away. She admonished Ridcanndal to wait outside and entered. The sepulchre itself was a polished black marble cube that measured less than an ell on each side, containing the cremated remains of the great sorcerer. Resting on its lid in a carved depression that fitted it perfectly was the small casket of solid platinum that had been made to hold the original Seven Stones Rothbannon had taken from the Salka.

Thalassa Dru lifted the lid, saw the gleam of the six living sigils and the empty place where the Conjure-Queen's lost Fortress stone had once rested. Reverently, she closed the container and carried it out of the tomb.

Ridcanndal stared at her apprehensively, still having no idea what she intended to do. 'And now, my lady?'

'Lead me to the room where my niece's body lies. And then I pray you to secure for me a small drum.'

Dear soul, you've been successful!

The subtle form of Thalassa Dru opened the golden box and emptied the sigils onto the frost-encrusted floor of the Source's prison. Her aura was a triumphant blaze of rainbow colors. 'As you see, my master. The cursèd things are still alive and bonded to her, but that should make their abolition all the more precious to our cause.'

The dead-black shape shackled in sapphire uttered a deep sigh of satisfaction. One of the gemlike manacles confining him now glowed so faintly that it was nearly as transparent as the iceflows streaking the cavern walls. *Shield your eyes, then, while I unite with the Likeminded to deal with these abomi-nations. I think – I hope – But let's see what happens this time, now that the obliteration of Darasilo's Trove has already brought me so much closer to atonement.*

The flash of dissolution was more intense than she had ever experienced before. When Thalassa Dru opened her eyes, long moments passed before she could focus her vision. Then she saw what had happened, and tears of joy sprang to her dazzled eyes.

'One of your arms is free!' she breathed. The pale manacle and its chain lay on the cavern floor, shattered like glass.

I am still held fast by the other limb. But we progress, Thalassa Dru. We progress.

He reached out with the unshackled tentacle and gently pressed one talon into the wall of ice, extracting a small object which he held out to the sorceress. It was a sphere no larger than a pea that shone like an emerald star.

Here is her essence, liberated from their evil thrall and from all pain. You and Dobnelu know how to reunite it to her body. But she must remain with you in your mountain sanctuary until the last remnants of power-hunger are cleansed from her soul. You two will be her guides and teachers. Ansel Piken, unfortunately, can no longer be trusted to act without prejudice.

She tucked the green gem into her bodice. 'What are we to do about him, master? It seems plain that his sentimental attachment to Maudrayne Northkeep has clouded his judg-ment and perhaps even diminished his commitment to the Conflict. Without consulting us, he's hidden the woman and her son in a place where Conrig Wincantor's men are unlikely to find them. I think he still hopes to solve the problem of the princess and her son peacefully.'

As I would also hope to do! I've put into play certain factors that may yet bring about such a fortunate resolution. But ultimately, Maudrayne's fate rests in her own hands. The doleful truth is that

Conrig's Sovereignty cannot be allowed to fall because of her thirst
for revenge. Ansel must be made to understand this. If he balks,
then we must remedy the situation as best we can. I'll bespeak you
if the necessity for action arises. And now farewell, dear soul.

Thalassa Dru awoke in the castle chamber where Ullanoth's
body had lain in state. Two candles burned low on either
side of the Conjure-Queen's bier. The samite-draped platform was empty. She uttered a deep sigh.

'My lady?' A tentative voice came from behind the cushioned chair where the sorceress had sat while performing
the drum ritual. Wix, the little old man who was Ullanoth's
most devoted friend, came to stand in front of her with both
hands clasped humbly over his heart. 'Did it go well? Oh,
please tell me that my dear queen will live again!'

'What did you see when the drumming stopped?' she
asked him.

'You went into a trance. The platinum casket in your lap
melted away like smoke, and then so did her poor lifeless
husk – only before it vanished utterly it seemed transformed,
so that she was once again as young and beautiful as she had
been before the terrible stones consumed her with pain . . .'

'Ah.' Thalassa Dru smiled, then took the spherical emerald
from the bodice of her gown and showed it to him. 'Her
body has been transported through subtle means to my own
dwelling place far away in the mountains of Tarn. But her
living essence resides here. The unnatural link between her
and the Coldlight Army has been severed. I shall carry this
soul receptacle safely home with me now, and after a time
Ullanoth sha Linndal will indeed live again.'

Wix bent closer to look at the shining gem, his face suffused
with wonder. 'I've served the dear lass for all her natural
life. Will you allow me to continue? Will you take me with
you?'

'The journey will be long and we'll sometimes travel in strange ways, but if you wish, you may come along.'

'I'm ready now,' he said simply.

Thalassa Dru restored the emerald to its hiding place, went to the chamber door, and opened it. In the corridor outside were Ridcanndal, Lady Zimroth, and a group of other Glaumerie Guild members, looking both fearful and angry. She swung the door wide, and with a wordless gesture invited them to enter.

'Gone!' Ridcanndal exclaimed. 'The sigils are gone – and you've taken our queen away as well!'

'She was already far from here.' The sorceress's gentle face grew stern. 'And while she reigned, you withheld your love and trust from her. So now prepare to receive a different sort of ruler.'

'Who?' Lady Zimroth demanded. 'Who will take Ullanoth's place? Will it be Beynor?'

But Thalassa Dru walked past her without another word, followed by Wix. The Guild members would have come after them and remonstrated further, but they were overcome by a strange lethargy that slowed their steps, and by the time they recovered, both the sorceress and the old man had vanished.

Snudge bespoke news of the royal assassinations to Vra-Sulkorig at Cala Palace, making it plain to the Keeper of Arcana that he, not Snudge himself, was the appropriate one to gather further information from official Didionite sources before informing the High King.

'And if His Grace shows signs of wanting to send *me* to Boarsden Castle,' Snudge added, 'you must do your utmost to dissuade him. The place is in a wild state of uproar, Brother Keeper. I read a few lips as I briefly scried it and learned that Prince Somarus has sprung up out of nowhere. He's expected to arrive at the castle within the hour, to supervise the search for survivors of the disaster – not that there are any! – and give notice to the world that he's the new King of Didion. You know what Somarus thinks of the Sovereignty. He'll declare war on it as soon as he thinks he has a chance of winning. And he'd probably throw the lot of us into a dungeon if he caught us snooping around. The lads and I intend to hotfoot it out of Didion as soon as we can. Our job is to find Princess Maudrayne, and I'm confident that we can do it. Tell Lord Stergos I might have important news for him soon.'

Bespeak me each day without fail, Sir Deveron. The High King insists that you keep him informed of your whereabouts.

'I'll do my best. Farewell, Brother Keeper.'

Snudge cut the wind-thread and sat quietly on the floor of the parapet for a few minutes to recover his strength. Overcome by shock, Vra-Mattis hadn't budged from the place where Snudge had left him, while spending some two hours overseeing the River Malle and Boarsden Castle. The young Brother's tears had dried, but his eyes were flat and staring and he seemed only half-conscious.

Snudge gently shook his shoulder. 'Mat. Time to go back to the others. Up you get.'

'They were eaten,' he said in a listless voice. 'Eaten.'

Snudge pulled the unresisting novice to his feet. 'It was a terrible thing, I agree. Perhaps you can say prayers for the victims later, when you're feeling better.'

The two of them negotiated the curtainwall stairway with some difficulty, then returned to the trestle table outside the castle kitchen. The other guests had retired to their rooms, leaving only Snudge's men dawdling over mugs of ale in the thickening twilight. The sky had become overcast. Torches flickered in a rising wind and a sound of clanking pots, sloshing water, and vulgar banter came from the adjacent scullery.

'We thought you'd fallen asleep somewhere, Deveron,' Sir Gavlok joked. Then he noticed his friend's grim face. 'What is it, man? You look like death.'

'Death's what we have to deal with,' Snudge said. He beckoned to his younger armiger, Wil Baysdale. 'Vra-Mattis has been overcome by exhaustion after a difficult windspeaking session. See him off to bed and sit with him for an hour or so, to be sure he rests comfortably.'

Will sprang up, a solicitous expression on his face, and led the faltering novice away.

When the two were gone, and Snudge had been served with ale by Valdos, his other squire, Gavlok said, 'What's this about death?'

'Salka monsters have attacked the barge carrying the royal family of Didion on its progress along the Malle River. The king and queen and their children have perished, along with all of their retainers and servants. So far, no one has any explanation why the monsters should have done such an incredible thing. They haven't penetrated into Didion for nine hundred years. Prince Somarus is on his way to Boarsden Castle, which is a stronghold of his mother's people, to seize the advantage. He'll proclaim himself king, and I wouldn't put it past him to do something rash – if not immediately, then perhaps within the next few days. All hell's broken loose in Tarn as well. Princess Maudrayne has told her brother Liscanor that she's the mother of King Conrig's eldest son and heir. Liscanor has passed the information on to the High Sealord Sernin. Unless I'm much mistaken, it won't be long before he and Somarus begin exchanging seditious messages on the wind.'

While Gavlok and the squires sat in silence, stupefied by the enormity of the disaster, the Mountain Swordsman Radd Falcontop spoke up. 'Sir Deveron, I must make bold to give you some advice. With conditions now so unsettled, and likely to get worse, it will be highly dangerous for a small

party such as ours to continue along the Wold Road and into
Tarn. The situation was dicey enough before – but the lawless
partisans of Somarus will run rampant now that they need
not fear retribution from King Honigalus. No travelers from
Cathra will be safe. If you are determined to go on, I beg
you to bespeak Earl Marshal Parlian and request that a
heavily armed company of troops be sent from Great Pass
garrison to escort us.'

'I agree with Radd,' Hulo Roundbank said.

'But then we must forgo our disguise as simple young
merchant-lords,' Gavlok protested. 'Our entire mission was
predicated upon going stealthily, but it will be obvious that
we're on the king's business if we travel with a mob of warriors.'

'We risk being killed from ambush if we continue in our
present state.' Hulo said. 'At best, we'd be taken prisoner
and held for ransom by one of the robber-barons. All of
western Didion favors Somarus for having denounced his
late brother's submission to the Sovereignty.'

Gavlok made a helpless gesture. 'Perhaps we can adopt a
different disguise. Or retrace our steps, go over to the Westley
coast, and take ship from one of the ports there –'

Snudge said, 'All of you be silent. There is another course
of action open to us – one that I had fervently hoped to postpone until we were inside Tarn and close to the hiding place
of the princess.'

They stared at him. His face was pale as he opened his
shirt and drew out the golden chain with its two glowing
moonstones. Gavlok uttered a gasp of astonishment at the
sight, for he had no idea that his friend had acquired a second
sigil. The others were only puzzled.

'My friends,' Snudge said, 'all of you were told when you
agreed to accompany me that this adventure had much to
do with sorcery. Princess Maude and her son are guarded by
the High Shaman of Tarn, one of the great magickers of the

northland. Earlier, although you were not told of this, the two fire-raising villains were also involved in a matter of high sorcery. They used the fire to cover their theft of a valuable collection of magical amulets from the Royal Alchymist . . . amulets such as these.'

He lifted the stones for their inspection. When Radd reached out a curious hand and would have taken hold of them, Snudge exclaimed, 'Beware! Anyone who touches these things without first gaining the permission of the owner risks being severely burnt or even killed. They are called sigils and are tools of the Beaconfolk, capable of formidable magic. I must also tell you that this magic exacts a price from the one who wields it, according to the difficulty of the action performed. A price of pain.'

'Then you are a sorcerer?' Hulo seemed dumfounded.

'No, only the Royal Intelligencer – King Conrig's trusted snudge. I use the magic of the Beaconfolk only rarely and with great reluctance, and only in the service of the King's Grace. How I obtained these stones is a story I may not share with you. I will only say that I wish I had never laid eyes on the damned things, for they put my very soul in peril . . . Nevertheless, since I *do* have them, I will use them as I must.'

'How do they work?' Radd asked. His face wore no expression of awe, as did those of his companion Swordsman and the two squires. His was a coldly practical interest.

'This sigil is called Concealer. Using it, I can go invisible. And not only I myself, but also a few companions who stay close to me. You may have heard of the way the Mallmouth Bridge was opened to our invading army. Four fellow-armigers and I used Concealer to do the trick.'

'Could we use it to travel unseen to Tarn?' Radd asked eagerly.

'Alas, I fear not. It hides those within four arm's-lengths of me only. All of us and our mounts would not fit within its compass, and we could not go on foot.' He sighed and took up the second moonstone. 'This other sigil, which I acquired only very recently, is the one that will, I think, enable us to fulfill our mission despite the difficulties facing us. Its name is Subtle Gateway. It is capable of transporting me to the destination of my choice, instantly. It will also carry the lot of you along with me, if I ask it to.'

'Great God, Deveron!' Gavlok exclaimed. 'Where did you find such a treasure?'

'I didn't,' Snudge said bleakly. 'The Subtle Gateway sigil was given to me, although I tried to refuse it, because a certain person wishes me to find Princess Maude and her son.'

'Who?' Gavlok demanded. 'The Conjure-Queen? Lord Stergos?'

Snudge gave a hollow laugh, but only shook his head. 'You must not ask me about him. All you need know is that using this magical transport is not a trivial matter. It will cause me to suffer agony while the magic is accomplished and afterward as well, while I sleep. I suspect that the greater the distance traveled, the greater the pain must be, and the longer I must endure it.'

They stared at him, horrified. The squire Valdos said softly, 'So that's why you hoped to hold off using it until we were closer to the hiding place of Princess Maudrayne.'

Snudge inclined his head in agreement. 'If I ask Gateway to transport us for hundreds of leagues, the consequences will likely incapacitate me for several days. You, of course, would feel nothing.'

Someone gave an exhalation of relief.

'Practically speaking,' Snudge continued, 'we'll have to go to ground and hide out in some secure bolt-hole until I recover. Then I'll use the other sigil, Concealer, to get the princess and her son away from her captors –'

'Wouldn't Concealer's magic afflict you sorely all over again?' Radd asked.

'No. Concealer is a so-called minor sigil. Its pain-debt is rather small, so long as one doesn't go invisible for a considerable time. But Subtle Gateway is one of those deemed a Great Stone. If you use it, you pay a great price.'

'Oh.' The rugged old warrior was nonplussed, as though realizing for the first time the terrible import of what Snudge had been saying.

'What happens when we have Princess Maude?' Gavlok asked. 'Do we take her and the boy back to His Grace in Cala?'

Snudge lowered his eyes. 'That part of it remains to be seen. I have a certain proposal to put to the lady. Lord Stergos and I both pray she will accept it, since it would solve His Grace's dilemma concerning her and the lad.'

The lanky knight's gaze flickered and he said no more, not wanting to talk of what might happen if Maudrayne refused.

The two Mountain Swordsmen also exchanged knowing glances. Hulo gave a tiny shrug, then said, 'Sir Deveron, when would you undertake this magical journey?'

'Tomorrow will be soon enough. We need time to prepare. We'll ride out of here at dawn, then disappear on a lonely section of the Wold Road, leaving our horses behind. It would be useful if you'd think about the supplies and equipment we'll require for a mission that might take as long as a sennight. Princess Maudrayne is being kept in a wild and remote part of Tarn. All that we need, we'll have to carry with us on our backs. I'll leave you for a time now, since I must bespeak . . . someone and obtain his approval and certain important information.'

The others nodded and murmured, thinking he meant to use Vra-Mattis to consult the High King on the wind. Radd and Hulo began to put forth useful suggestions concerning food and weaponry.

'One further thing I must tell you.' Snudge spoke in a low voice. 'We'll not be taking my armiger Wil Baysdale along with us. I have good reason to believe he's not reliable, which is why I sent him off to care for Mattis before telling you about all of this.'

The other armigers were thunderstruck, but Gavlok merely said, 'A good idea. We should have done something about him before this. I had meant to speak of something odd that happened last night at Great Pass garrison, but the day's excitement drove it out of my mind.'

'What is it?' Snudge said grimly.

'I saw Wil and Vra-Mattis whispering together before we retired. Wil was speaking with great urgency, as though pleading for some favor. Finally the windvoice drew his hood over his head for a few brief minutes, then uncovered. Young Wil then seemed relieved in his mind and went off.'

Snudge muttered a curse. 'I wish you'd told me earlier. But no harm done. I'll deal with this later.'

He tucked the glowing sigils back into his shirt, rose from the table, and walked off toward the guesthouse. But he turned aside once he was out of the others' sight, touched Concealer and murmured the words that made him invisible, then returned to the curtainwall parapet to bespeak the Source.

Wiltorig Baysdale, cousin to Duke Feribor Blackhorse, was well aware that he'd been excluded from the group conference because Sir Deveron didn't trust him. The Royal Intelligencer had never accused him of disloyalty: he was too clever for that. But all too often he'd found errands for Wil to perform, sending him out of hearing while certain others were taken into his confidence – with the result that Wil had not yet been able to pass on a single bit of really useful information to the duke.

Tonight, the squire vowed, that wouldn't happen. Something vitally important was about to be discussed, and he didn't intend to miss out on it.

When Duke Feribor had first insinuated his clever young relative into the service of the Royal Intelligencer, there was no hint of the grave matter that would eventually cause the king to order a clandestine expedition into the north country. The newly dubbed young knight commander required two armigers, so Feribor put forth his cousin as a suitable candidate – simply because he enjoyed the irony of having a spy of his own to spy on the wretch who'd come so close to disclosing Feribor's rôle in the irregular handling of the Royal Treasury funds.

Later, when Deveron was sent off on his supposedly secret mission, having Wil Baysdale available to keep tabs on the search for Princess Maudrayne was a fortuitous stroke of luck for Feribor. He'd heard the same rumors of her survival that had worried Earl Marshal Parlian, but hadn't known what to make of them. Why would Conrig be so desperate to track down his former wife? Why should the High King care if Maudrayne Northkeep was alive and hiding in Tarn? At first, the questions seemed unanswerable.

Until Feribor deduced the obvious solution, and an elegant scheme was born in his mind. Then later, the extrordinary demands of the venal wizard Bozuk played perfectly into Feribor's hands, almost as though fate had decreed it . . .

Wil Baysdale led Vra-Mattis to his pallet in the fortress dormitorium. But instead of caring for the ailing novice's needs, he merely tossed a blanket over him, then crept away through a back passageway to the kitchenhouse. Two silver pennies handed over to the crew of sniggering scullion-lads convinced them to let him eavesdrop on Deveron and the others from behind the partly open door of the scullery.

With mounting excitement and apprehension, he overheard

information more crucial than he might have hoped for in his wildest dreams.

Wil knew that Feribor had taken ship to Tarn with the shaman's bribe. Not appreciating the depths of Feribor's villainy, the squire also believed that the duke meant to go off after Princess Maudrayne himself, after Bozuk revealed her hiding place, simply in order to ingratiate himself with the king.

But if Deveron found the princess first –

The treacherous armiger had nipped off back to the guest-house and Vra-Mattis the moment Snudge mentioned the necessity of bespeaking someone. Being absent when Gavlok voiced his grave suspicions of him, Wil still had expectations of continuing his spying after they all made their magical leap to Tarn.

He began hauling off the novice's boots and clothing, services he'd earlier neglected, intending to look innocent when Sir Deveron arrived. Vra-Mattis was already half-asleep and hardly noticed what was being done for him, muttering vague words of thanks as Wil tucked a pillow beneath his head and offered him water.

Nervously, Wil waited for his master to appear; but no one came. After nearly ten minutes had passed, he went outside to see what had happened. The others were still sitting at the trestle table with their heads together, probably planning the new expedition. But there was no sign of Sir Deveron anywhere in the inner ward.

Where had he gone? Wil was certain he'd heard Deveron say he was going off to bespeak someone about an important matter. But he hadn't approached Mattis, and surely he wouldn't seek out some Didionite wizard to send his wind-message –

Then Wil froze, remembering what Cousin Feribor had said during their final hurried conversation in Cala Palace:

'*Be very careful not to underestimate Deveron Austrey. My disgraced uncle, Kilian Blackhorse, once told me that the bastard is a wild talent – a secret magicker. And after what he did at Redfern Castle and Mallmouth Bridge, I'm inclined to believe it.*'

What if Sir Deveron was away somewhere doing the bespeaking *himself*?

Will had entertained small hope of getting off his own wind-message until the middle of the night or even tomorrow morning, since Mattis seemed so weak and sick – but perhaps he wasn't as bad as he seemed.

'Mat! Wake up! I need your help.' Wil slapped the youth's face and shook him by the shoulders.

Mattis opened his eyes and moaned, 'What? What's wrong?'

Wil knelt next to the pallet, pulled the windvoice upright, and spoke with every evidence of concerned dismay. 'Oh, Mat – I don't know how to tell you. Sir Deveron is so worried about your fragile state of mind that he's decided to send you back to Beorbrook Hold with one of the Swordsmen. The rest of us are going to continue on to Tarn after picking up another windvoice at Rockyford Way Station.'

Tears sprang into Mat's eyes. 'I'm – I'm not surprised. What a disappointment I must be to the master, falling to pieces like some cringing little wench.'

'It's not your fault that your talent makes you overly sensitive to terrible events,' Wil averred. 'We're all made differently. You're a good friend. I'll always be grateful that you were willing to bespeak my family's windvoice back in Blackhorse Duchy, letting me converse with my poor sick mother. I've been so worried about her, Mat! And now I'll have no more word of her at all. I'd never dare ask this other Brother who's joining us for such favors as you were kind enough to grant me.'

'I'm sorry, Wil. I wish there was something I could do.'

'Well . . . there is, only I hesitated to ask. But if you could send Mother one last message – if you feel strong enough—'

Mat ventured a tremulous smile. 'I'll try. Just give me a minute.' Lying back on the pillow, he covered his eyes with his hands. His lips moved without making a sound. Then he spoke aloud. 'Your family windvoice hears me, Wil. What would you like to tell your mother?'

'Say I'm about to ride into great danger, but all will be well because Sir Deveron has just been given two magical amulets to protect us. One is named Concealer, and it can make all of us invisible. The second is called Subtle Gateway, and it will transport us directly to the place where Princess Maudrayne is hidden. Tell Mother not to worry, even if I can't have you bespeak my messages anymore. We'll all be home safe in Cala in less than a tennight. Sir Deveron has promised it.'

Vra-Mattis opened his eyes wide. 'Wil! Is it true?'

The armiger's gaze shifted to the door. 'Yes, of course it is. I wasn't supposed to tell you about that – but what difference can it make? Mother will be so glad to hear we'll all be home soon, with our mission successfully accomplished. Bespeak the message, Mat. Please!'

The novice smiled feebly and closed his eyes once more. 'Of course I will. What wonderful news!' He began to wind-speak soundlessly at some length. Wil rose to his feet and darted to the doorway. No one was coming. There'd be time to do what had now become necessary.

'Wil?' The young Brother's voice was very weak. 'I – I've done it. It took all my strength, but I've done it.'

'Thank you!' Wil Baysdale's gratitude was sincere, over-flowing with relief. He crouched beside the exhausted windvoice. 'You'll never know how much this means to me. Now rest well. Let me just fluff up your pillow for you.'

He lifted Vra-Mattis's head, drew out the cushion, and pressed it with all his strength over the novice's face. His struggles did not last long. When they ended Wil replaced the pillow, closed the dead eyes, and smoothed the features into a semblance of peaceful sleep.

Then he went off to tell the others the dreadful thing that had happened.

TWENTY

Late in the evening, Maudrayne climbed the spiral staircase of the tall turret that bore the peel's windmill and freshwater reservoir. The rain had stopped for the moment, but the wind keened like a lost child and a muffled boom of heavy surf came from the little cove far below. She'd invited Dyfrig to accompany her on her first exploration of the odd structure, but the boy had refused in favor of a game of chess with Rusgann in front of the parlor fire.

The two days of steady downpour that had kept him indoors since their arrival had turned Dyfrig apathetic and withdrawn. He was also disappointed that the sons of Shaman Ontel and Sealady Tallu were taciturn lads of nine and eleven – much too old to be willing playmates to a four-year-old, even one who was bright and mature for his age. After a few initial hours of kindly attention to their young guest, the Tarnian boys had abandoned him to follow their usual pursuits, while Dyfrig was left with only Rusgann and his mother to entertain him. There were no domestic chores for him to perform here, as he'd done so eagerly at Dobnelu's steading; silent, glum-faced servants took care of everything. Lessons would not begin until

Ontel's family and the prisoners moved to the winter residence at Fort Ramis, at the start of Harvest Moon. Soon,
Maudrayne knew, the boy would grow bored and fretful.

And so would she, for Skullbone Peel was hardly living
up to Ansel's glowing description.

The keep was much larger and more elaborately
appointed than the sea-hag's farmhouse, but it was also
charmless – especially on overcast days of summer rain.
The floors and walls were of stone, only sparsely softened
by rugs and hangings, and the rooms were chill and only
dimly lit by narrow windows having panes of yellowish
translucent seal-bladder. There was a library, as promised,
but aside from a small shelf of crudely inscribed storybooks
that had probably been copied out by the boys as school-
room exercises, the volumes were mostly ponderous tomes
without pictures that dealt with Tarnian history and
shamanistic practices – no doubt fascinating to Master
Ontel, but of no interest to a young child.

Ansel himself was still in residence, although he had
informed her at their noontide dinner that he would soon
be departing. Maudrayne's sharp temper had been provoked
by disappointment in the new place of confinement, and she
had rebuffed all of his attempts at friendly conversation.
Eventually he gave up trying to cheer her and went off to
confer with his cousin Ontel, probably organizing her secure
detention.

She was in a foul mood as she reached the top of the
turret, and her heart sank even lower as she surveyed the
domain where she and her son were to be imprisoned. It
was a part of Tarn that she had never visited, proverbial
among the livelier folk of the west for its bleak solitude and
comparative poverty.

The windows up here were thick glass, probably because
the turret also served as a watchtower – although heaven

only knew what kind of sea-raiders would be foolish
enough to attack the tiny local settlements. Visibility was
fairly good after the rain, revealing a vista of savage rugged-
ness. Skullbone Peel lay at the northern end of Tarn's
Plateau of Desolation, a nearly roadless expanse of tundra
and bog that was almost completely uninhabited. The
Desolation Coast, pummeled throughout much of the year
by arctic winds and ferocious seas, comprised two hundred
and sixty leagues of eroded limestone and basalt cliffs, reefs
and stacks, and a myriad of rocky islets softened by sparse
vegetation where only seals, birds, foxes, and lemmings
lived. To the north lay a sterile black-rock peninsula called
the Lavalands. Born of extinct volcanos and ridden with
shoalwater, it was a menacing barrier to coastal shipping
even in summer, when the pack-ice receded. South of the
peel were whaling stations and fishing hamlets, and a single
isolated castle, Fort Ramis, around which huddled the only
town of any size in all of northeastern Tarn. The family of
Shaman Ontel and Sealady Tallu dwelt there during the
long arctic winter, and so, Maudrayne had been told, would
she and Dyfrig and Rusgann.

We'll never escape from here, she said to herself. They'd
capture us easily if we tried to flee inland over that black
desert, and to get away by water is virtually impossible. Small
wonder Ansel had said she'd be allowed to use a sailboat!
There was nowhere to go. After consulting a chart in the
library, she'd discovered that the only sizable ports she could
hope to reach, where sealords dwelt who might sympathize
with her plight and defend her from pursuers, were Ice Haven
on Havoc Bay or Cold Harbor up north on the Icebear
Channel. Both places were over three hundred and fifty
leagues away, and neither had road access to the rest of the
country.

So we're trapped here, she thought, at least for now. But

it can't last forever, not if my brother Liscanor has done what he should . . .

The windmill on top of the small tower must have been well-greased, for the only sound it made as it spun in the gale was a lugubrious low-pitched moan, like some enormous animal softly humming. The noise was insufficient to mask the approaching footsteps of someone climbing the turret stairs. Maudrayne seated herself on the circular bench that surrounded the shaft housing of the windmill and waited for her visitor to arrive.

Ansel Pikan's fiery red hair and beard popped up through the opening in the floor. His face was grave rather than friendly. 'May I join you?'

'As you wish.' She gazed out over the grey sea, white-scalloped with lines of advancing surf.

'I've been bespoken by one of my principal colleagues in the capital. He had some unsettling news. High Sealord Sernin has called for an emergency meeting of the Company of Equals in Donorvale six days from now. Lady Tallu and I will be leaving immediately to attend.'

A small smile curled the ends of Maudrayne's lips. She said nothing.

'Oh, Maudie! What have you done?' Ansel's voice was full of reproach. 'How much did you tell your brother Liscanor?'

'Ask him, when you get to Donorvale,' she retorted.

'If it was only the truth about Dyfrig, then there's a chance Conrig's Sovereignty may survive. But if you revealed the High King's secret talent, then all of Blenholme might be in deadly danger. Do you know that the Salka have attacked Didion for the first time in almost a millennium? It happened late yesterday.'

She shrugged in disdain. 'What is that to me? Let Honigalus and Conrig send their navies after the brutes. Let the Conjure-Queen thrash them with her Weathermaker. The monsters will flee, as they did when they raided Moss a while ago, and that'll be an end to it.'

'The Salka swam up the River Malle and slaughtered Honigalus and all of his family. Somarus is now King of Didion, and there are ugly rumors abroad in Cathra that he might have conspired with Beynor of Moss to bring on the attack. If this is true, then the monsters are his allies. He won't go to war against them.'

Maudrayne was shocked in spite of herself. 'Well, then, it falls to Ullanoth and Conrig to –'

'Ullanoth is dead . . . or as close to it as a human being may be. She fell into a mortal trance as a result of sorcery gone awry. Her magical moonstones can be used by no other person. And the wizards of Royal Fenguard are in a panic, fearing that Beynor will urge the Salka to attack Moss next.'

She flashed him a look of poisoned triumph. 'And so Conrig Wincantor is the one great champion left to defend our island against these inhuman brutes? And *I* am obliged to withdraw my accusations against him and deny my son's birthright in order to preserve his Sovereignty? *Never!* He's an unworthy king – an illegitimate king, by the law of his own land.'

'The Salka will attack Moss in force,' Ansel said. 'My Source has solemnly assured me of this. And they won't stop there. Neither Beynor nor Somarus will be able to control them.'

'And Conrig is the only one who can stop their advance? Nonsense! The Salka have no ships, no weapons except a few puny moonstones. They're stupid, clumsy on land, and there aren't enough of them to be a serious threat to humanity.'

'Uncounted thousands of them dwell in the Dawntide Isles. Even more have lived quietly in the fens of Moss up until now. But the fenland Salka are suddenly on the move, approaching areas inhabited by humans. Some of them are slow-witted, but by no means all. The Dawntide Salka are the elite members of their race, the ones who retained their ancient culture and magical science. The Source believes that they were the ones who attacked Didion's royal family. And thanks to Beynor, who is either criminally insane or else acting as a tool of the Beaconfolk, the Salka leaders will soon obtain new moonstone sigils – powerful weapons of sorcery that haven't been seen since Emperor Bazekoy's day.'

'You're lying,' she said in a voice of ice. 'You and your Source would say anything to protect Conrig. God only knows why! But you don't frighten me with your tales of invading monsters, and you won't shut my mouth. Once the Company of Equals hears all that Liscanor has to say, they'll compel you to deliver me and Dyfrig and Rusgann over to them so we can bear witness to the truth of my accusations. You won't dare defy them.'

He stared at her, unspeaking.

And her eyes widened in speculation. 'Or would you? There's one sure way to make certain that I never endanger Conrig. Are you ready to undertake it?'

When he was well away from Boarsden Castle, after taking supper at a little village below Firedrake Water, Beynor bespoke the Conservator of Wisdom in the Dawntide Citadel, requesting a conference with him, the First Judge, the Master Shaman, and the Supreme Warrior. There was a brief delay while the three Eminences summoned Ugusawnn on the wind, since he was at that time leading his warriors down the River Malle at speed, but soon all was in readiness.

We Four are now prepared to hear you, Beynor, the Conservator said. *But before you speak, know that all of us are mightily displeased with your behavior. The Supreme Warrior has told us how you fled from him.*

'It was Ugusawnn's fault,' Beynor snapped. 'He treated me as a despised servant, not an honored ally, during our journey into Didion. However, in spite of his rude behavior and blatant expressions of mistrust, I still intend to fulfill my promises to the Salka. The King of Didion and all of his family were slain, just as I requested, so I'll activate the Known Potency for you, and I'll also give you the sigils of my sister, Conjure-Queen Ullanoth . . . provided that you first repair the insult to my esteem by vouchsafing another favor.'

You want us to kill the Conjure-Queen, the Master Shaman said. *Ugusawnn has already informed us of this demand. But are you not aware that she lies in an enchanted sleep? She is totally helpless. You can easily destroy her yourself.*

'No! You Salka must be seen to do it, just as you were seen to be responsible for the deaths of Didion's royal family. I'm already unjustly accused of killing my father Linndal. This is a vicious lie – but it would be given credence if people learned that I personally slew Ullanoth. As I told you, I wish to make a new life for myself on the Continent. In order to do this with my honor intact, there must be no proof that I colluded in your conquest of Moss, or had anything to do with the death of the Conjure-Queen.'

I see no reason to deny him, said the First Judge.

He's not to be trusted! the Supreme Warrior roared. *Once the queen is dead, there's nothing to prevent him from rallying the Mosslanders against us and posing as a hero to his former subjects. He could refuse to empower the Potency and deny us Ullanoth's sigils! They lie in Rothbannon's tomb, where only a descendant of his can reach them. Let me remind the other Eminences of another fact: once the queen is dead, her moonstones are dead as well. Beynor could easily instruct a loyal confederate how to re-activate the sigils. Even though he is unable to make use of the six stones himself, his crony could use them against us at his bidding.*

The difficulty can be circumvented, said Kalawnn, the Master Shaman. *Let Beynor come to Dawntide Citadel! After our forces kill the queen, Beynor will activate the Potency, bonding it to me, rather than to the Supreme Warrior. Then Beynor can go in peace, while we open Rothbannon's tomb by means of the Potency.*

Would that work? the First Judge wondered.

In my opinion, Kalawnn replied, *the Greatest Stone should be able to transcend all lesser forms of sorcery.*

'With respect!' Beynor exclaimed, feeling the situation showed signs of getting out of hand. 'This alternative isn't acceptable to me. I won't be satisfied unless I *see* Ullanoth's body destroyed. Not by means of scrying, for clever magic is able to deceive windsight, but rather see the remains with my own two eyes. Only then will I activate the Potency and bond it to one of you. I also refuse to return to the citadel. Within its walls, I am reduced to my former powerless state, dependent not only upon the goodwill of you three Eminences who now reside there, but also upon that of Ugusawnn, the Supreme Warrior, who has forfeited my trust.'

We seem to have come to an impasse, the First Judge said, sighing.

The problem was caused by Ugusawnn, said the Conservator. *He is the bravest and strongest of us all, but nevertheless he has antagonized our would-be benefactor and otherwise shown a lack of wisdom. I must suggest that we reconsider bonding the Potency to him. This problem can be readily solved if our esteemed Master Shaman, Kalawnn, agrees to be bonded to the Potency in Ugusawnn's stead. He can carry the Greatest Stone to Moss, in the company of our army and the Supreme Warrior. Once there, he will stand aside from the fighting, well guarded, so there will be no danger to him or the sigil. Beynor must agree to join him. When the queen is dead, and Beynor confirms this with his own eyes, then let him activate the Potency and bond it to Kalawnn.*

What do you say to that, Supreme Warrior? the First Judge demanded.

I . . . submit to the will of my Eminent colleagues. Under protest!

The judge said, *And you, Beynor of Moss?*

'Let my dear old friend Master Kalawnn carry the Potency to the vicinity of the Darkling River. Let him and his protectors stand safely aside with me while the valiant Ugusawnn takes the castle and destroys my sister. Then I solemnly swear by my human God that I will bring the Known Potency to life and open Rothbannon's tomb.'

Then we are finally agreed? said the Conservator of Wisdom. His ancient mental voice betrayed a profound fatigue.

YES.

All of them voiced affirmation – Beynor declaring it with a fervency greater than that of the Salka, for he had held back from them the vital fact that the Potency bonded to no single person, but might be utilized by anyone once it was conjured alive. And while he was not absolutely certain that the sigil would neutralize the curse of the Beaconfolk, he was willing to wager his life on it. He would find a way to snatch the Potency away from Kalawnn just as soon as it was activated, then escape from the monsters. With both Potency and Ullanoth's sigils in hand, he would turn his attention to securing the Destroyer sigil; and when he owned that last necessary stone, he'd be ready to found his empire . . .

There is one final thing, the Master Shaman said. *A last precaution against misadventure which I would like you all to witness. Beynor, Ugusawnn – please transfer your talent to oversight mode so you may scry what I am about to do. I intend to guard this treasured sigil in the best way I know.*

Puzzled, Beynor complied. He saw Kalawnn slither from his kelp-padded couch in the dank audience chamber of the citadel, take the small carving from its golden tripod, and hold it up delicately between his taloned fingers for all to see.

Then Kalawnn opened his enormous, hideously fanged mouth, put the moonstone on his purple tongue, and swallowed – sending the Known Potency into the secure coffer of his gizzard.

Snudge stood again on the fortress parapet, wondering if he was doing the right thing. Earlier, Lord Stergos had been aghast at the notion of his trying to pressure the Source. But what other course was open to him? Even with a general knowledge of where Princess Maudrayne was confined, he had no way of getting to her. There was only the Gateway. And to use it, he needed to state a specific destination . . . didn't he? And only the Source could tell him exactly where to go.

Or would the Great Stone transport him and his men if he simply commanded it to put them down in a safe place half a league away from Maudrayne's prison?

No. That wouldn't work. Such an irregular request might even antagonize the Lights and have disastrous results.

'Source! You can read my thoughts?' Snudge was horrified at the notion.

Only when you unconsciously aim them at me, dear soul. Have no fear. The contents of your mind are your sole possession. No one can violate them.

'Do you already know the question I planned to ask you?'

I know the impudent plan you confessed to Stergos. But there's no need to threaten me or demand tit for tat. I'll willingly tell you: Maudrayne is in a place called Skullbone Peel, a small keep on the north-eastern Tarnian coast. Command the sigil to carry you and your people to a ravine two thousand paces south of it. There you'll find a sheltered spot beneath an overhanging ledge – not quite a cave, but deep enough to keep you out of the elements while you recover from the pain-price, and shield you from casual oversight.

Snudge hesitated. 'Was – was I correct in thinking that my suffering will be more severe, the farther I travel?'

Unfortunately, yes. And the number of people carried with you also affects your debt. Keep this in mind as you make further excursions.

'Further? I don't understand. What am I to do after I make my proposal of compromise to the princess? Surely you're not suggesting that I use Gateway to carry her and the child back to His Grace at Cala Palace!'

You must do as you think best – for her and her child, for Conrig, and for the Final Conflict in which all of you participate.

'What *I* think best? Damn you, Source, I'm only a poor devil of a spy! How can I make such fateful decisions by myself? What if I make a stupid mistake and get nabbed by the guards at the Tarnian keep? What if the princess won't agree to my compromise – or His Grace declines it? What if Ansel Piken finds out what I'm up to and uses his sorcery to – to stop me?'

Ansel won't stop you. I've already seen to that. As to the other matters, I can't say. Now go and do what you must do.

'You're not being fair, Source! You've got to give me more explicit instructions. I'll abandon the whole thing if you don't! Source? Answer me! Source . . .'

He howled the Light's name on the wind, furious and frightened, but there was no response. Finally he severed the thread of speech, waited until he stopped shivering in the tepid evening air, and asked himself whether he'd really give up the mission now that it seemed so close to being accomplished.

He answered his own question, then sat in numb misery on the parapet floor wondering whether to bespeak Stergos and ask *him* for advice.

'Futter that!' he growled, on due consideration. 'I'll do it my way, just as the Source told me to.'

Feeling dead tired, but at the same time strangely exhilarated, he climbed to his feet and descended to the ward to see what progress his men had made on the preparations for the trip.

They showed Snudge the body of Vra-Mattis Temebrook, which lay as if peacefully sleeping. No one had touched him except Radd Falcontop, who had pronounced him dead. Not a one among the party seemed to have any doubt that the sensitive novice had died of a brainstorm, brought about by his visualization of the unspeakable atrocities committed by the Salka.

'This is still another crime to be laid at the monsters' door,' Sir Gavlok said, knuckling away unashamed tears. 'Poor Mat is their victim as much as the luckless Didionites. I only pray that some day we may be able to avenge him.'

The three squires murmured agreement. Radd and Hulo were silent, their weathered features immobile.

'What will you have us do now, Deveron?' Gavlok asked.

'Without our windvoice, sir, do we dare proceed?' Wil asked ingenuously.

'Oh, yes, we'll go on as planned. That is – all except you, young Wil.' Snudge showed the dismayed squire a sad smile. 'It falls to you, as my junior armiger, to convey the body of our fallen comrade back to Cala Palace. Go at once and find the headman of the mule train that's spending the night here. Arrange to accompany it over Great Pass in safety tomorrow. Proceed directly to Beorbrook Hold with the body, where the resident Brothers of Zeth will perform the necessary mortuary offices for poor Mattis and provide a lead-lined coffin for your journey south. The captain of the Hold garrison will assign you an escort.'

Wil Baysdale hung his head, cursing inwardly. 'Yes, messire.' Surely Sir Deveron could not suspect what he'd done! But Wil nevertheless was well aware that he'd do no more spying for Duke Feribor on this mission.

He consoled himself with the thought that there would surely be others.

Rain began during the small hours, and continued persistently as the king's men quit Castlemont and started north on the Wold Road at the sixth hour of morning. The pack train had departed earlier, but not before Snudge had a quiet word with the grizzled leader of the muleteers. After learning the man's name and his home village, Snudge took his hand and pressed a gold mark into it.

'Swive me!' the fellow muttered, at the sight of the extravagant boon. 'Not that I ain't grateful, my lord, but –'

'I thank you for allowing my squire and his somber burden to go along with you into Cathra,' Snudge said. 'However, my young friend is a headstrong boy, and was keenly disappointed not to continue on with us. There's a chance he may approach you and request that you convey the corpse to Beorbrook, while he himself turns back and foolishly attempts to rejoin our group. I ask that you prevent him from doing so – by force, if nothing else suffices. I won't suffer disobedience or a frivolous disregard for the dead.'

The muleteer's shaggy brows knit as he digested the import of Snudge's words. 'How much force?' he asked quietly.

'Don't damage him any more than necessary. But see that he stays with you for at least half the day. After that, he'll know it's too late to follow us.'

Now, as he and Gavlok rode out side by side, bringing up the rear of their small cavalcade, Snudge told his friend what he'd done. The other knight nodded in approval and said, 'I lay awake all last night in the little guesthouse cubicle we shared, with my sword unsheathed at my side, just in case Wil Baysdale decided to pay us a visit.'

'You think he might actually have done us violence?' Snudge said.

'Not only that. I believe he murdered Vra-Mattis.'

'Good God! Have you any evidence to support your accusation?'

'Just before I retired – you were already asleep – I went to Mat's cubicle to collect his writing materials from his scrip, thinking we might have need of them. I glanced at his face and saw that one of his eyes had come open, as sometimes happens. In the end, I had to put a farthing on the lid to keep it decently shut. But before that . . . I've had little experience with dead bodies, but my grandsire was a great storyteller who oft entertained us children with tales of murder and mayhem. One curious fact he told us is that the whites of a smothered man's eyes will sometimes show small specks of blood. Mat's open eye did indeed have such a sign.'

'Codders! Then the whoreson slew him!' Snudge frowned fiercely in thought. 'Wil must have listened in on our talk of the sigils. As Duke Feribor's creature, he would have thought it imperative to send a message to his master about the magical moonstones. He'd use Mat's windvoice, as he must have already done on other occasions. I don't believe Mat realized who the earlier messages were intended for. They could have contained nothing important, anyway. But this final one, with its news of me having the ability to use high sorcery, might have troubled him when he recovered his wits. Mat might have confessed to me what he'd done, and Wil Baysdale couldn't allow that to happen. Now Feribor knows we have the means to go invisible, as well as a quick way of reaching Maudrayne.'

'We'll surely get to the princess before he does,' Gavlok said. 'How long has he been at sea? Three days? I've lost count.'

'Perhaps a little less than that. But with fair winds, a fast frigate could easily get him to Northkeep and the shaman Bozuk late tomorrow. Feribor is under orders not to search for Maudrayne, but I'm certain he'll disregard them. The temptation would be irresistible. He might offer the shaman an additional bribe to serve as his guide to her hiding place. The old magicker is blind, but there's nothing wrong with his scrying ability. He could do the job.'

'But you said we'll shortly be on her doorstep! I realize we can't do anything until you're fit again, but surely you'll have recovered long before Feribor can get to her.' He broke off, staring at his friend with sudden concern. 'Won't you? I mean, you said you'd just be unwell for a few days.'

'The fact is,' Snudge said, 'I don't know how long I'll be afflicted. Perhaps, since this will be my first use of the Great Stone, the consequences won't be too severe.'

But even as he spoke, he didn't believe it.

After a brisk two-hour ride, during which they encountered no other travelers, the king's men came to a section of the Wold Road that traversed a stretch of open ground. Beyond it on their left rose thickly wooded low mountains and a rough little track that led toward the Lady Lakes. It was possible to see for nearly a league in all directions, and the soggy landscape was empty of other human beings.

'This place will do as well as any for our embarcation,' Snudge said, reining in. 'Valdos, Hanan – gallop your horses up and down that side track a ways, then churn up the mud around here. We want to make it look as though we were set upon by a gang of kidnappers. Word of our supposed abduction will reach Rockyford soon enough.'

And from there, the news would fly on the wind to Cala. Snudge had debated with himself whether to tell Lord Stergos the details of his plan. But in the end he'd held off, fearing that the Royal Alchymist would consider himself duty-bound to inform the High King about Concealer and Subtle Gateway. Every instinct warned him not to risk letting this happen. Let Conrig think what he would of their abrupt disappearance. With luck, Stergos would counsel his brother to have patience.

Snudge dismounted and began to unstrap his pack. Gavlok, Radd, and Hulo followed suit. The two Mountain Swordsmen tied big bundles to each other's backs. They carried most of their food. The pair had also acquired a pair of stout staves back at the fortress, and extra arrows for their shortbows.

'I wish we could take the horses with us.' Gavlok looked at his fine tall chestnut with regret. The mounts would be abandoned here, with all of their tack.

'They'll do us no good where we're going.' Snudge was curt. 'We can only hope that local villains will come across them soon and take them off into the wilderness.'

Finally the excited squires finished their trampling and the mounts were shooed away down the Lady Lakes track, although they did not go far. All members of the party had shouldered their burdens save Snudge, who would simply rest his pack between his feet so as to keep his body unencumbered. He called everyone to draw close to him. His face had gone very pale.

'Friends, let me be frank. I know not what will happen when I make use of this Beaconfolk sorcery. The creatures that some call Great Lights and others deem the Coldlight Army are obscure and terrible. Even the Mosslanders, who are most familiar with them, know little of their true nature. The Lights savor pain. They torture with whimsical cruelty, as wicked boys sometimes torment hapless bugs or animals for the fun of it. If they fancy themselves offended, they may cast the person who insulted them into the Hell of Ice for all eternity, as we would consign a worn boot or a broken pot to a midden-heap. I myself am willing to risk such a fate out of duty. But here and now I give each of you the opportunity to withdraw from this mission – to decline to accompany me, with no stigma attaching to the act. To any man who would leave, I will give a signed note of quittance, and never think less of his courage.'

They stared at him in silence, while the rain streamed over their leather cloaks. Finally, Gavlok's squire Hanan Caprock spoke up with cheeky bravado. 'The horses are gone, and it'd be a devil of a job catching them. So I figure we're all bound to go with you, Sir Deveron, even though we're scared stiff. Let's just get on with it! Maybe it won't be so futterin' wet on the other side of your magic Gateway.'

When the explosion of laughter faded, Snudge said, 'When we arrive, I'll probably be prostrate and useless. Gavlok is your new commander until I recover, but I appoint Hulo and Radd to organize the camp in the ravine as they think best for the security and comfort of the group. You squires are forbidden to wander off on your own. All of you, remember there are magickers inside Skullbone Peel. To avoid being overseen by them, be as silent and wary as an animal. Use rocks and vegetation to screen your movements so no lookout spots you with his ordinary vision. Windwatchers ordinarily don't keep constant vigil; it's too taxing. But they'll be on you like hounds if they suspect intruders are prowling about – and the highly talented ones can scry you in darkness as well as in daylight.'

He drew from his shirt the chain with the sigils and grasped the door-shaped moonstone carving tightly. 'Well, it's time to go. Crowd close to me now. Make no noise, no matter what happens, and don't move a muscle until we arrive and are safe.'

Their damp bodies pressed against him, and he heard only the sounds of their breathing, the creak of their harness and packs, and the anonymous rumble of someone's stomach. Gavlok said, 'Shhh!'

Snudge closed his eyes and intoned 'EMCHAY ASINN,' and told the sigil where to take them.

He was alone, seeming to drift in a cold night sky with no land or sea perceptible beneath him. The uncountable stars were hard and brilliant as gems, at first unwinking against a background of utter blackness, then growing dim as other Lights, many-colored and strangely shaped, began to burgeon and overwhelm them with swelling radiance.

None of the Lights resembled the familiar auroral formations of the Boreal winter sky; there were no flickering beacons or curtains moved by cosmic winds or luminous arcs or glowing clouds. These shining insubstantialities writhed and danced with hectic, intelligent purpose. Some of them showed eyes or evanescent limbs. All of them had what appeared to be mouths that seemed to form words of the Salka language. They asked questions, and he replied.

CADAY AN RUDAY? . . . What do you want?

EMCHAY ASINN . . . Transport all of us.

KO AN SO? . . . Who are you?

SNUDGE.

He braced for the onslaught of pain but it held off. Instead, a wild cacophony of hisses, crackles, and shrill whistles assailed his ears, almost as though millions of small birds were trapped in a confined space, clamoring in fury. The throng of Lights whirled about him at vertiginous speed and their noise resolved into the speech of many individuals, fully understandable for all that the words were churned together.

His name his name we need his name! Snudge? SNUDGE?!
 It is. It's not. It's a trick!
  Snudge? A snudge is a JOB not a name.
His name his name we need his name we must have it to bind him!
 We need his name to own him. This one is trying to cheat us.
  But he is Snudge! He was accepted twice over by us!
   He was given power and gave pain. As Snudge.
For a Great Stone for the Great Link it's not enough.
 His name his name we need his own true name!
  He is Snudge. We accepted it and him. Snudge.
He cheats he holds back he slips away!
 He pays the price whatever his name. Let be.
  Rage rage against the rule-twister!
Hurt him kill him damn him to the Hell of Ice!
 His name is Snudge but it is not. Let be.
  Indifference. Eat his pain. He wins.
Laughter. The jest is on us. FOR NOW.

The chaos of colored Light flared in blinding brilliance as the laughter became thunder.

Then they were gone, leaving him wrapped wholly in pain.

He moaned aloud, felt himself lose balance and start to fall. Down through the jet-black starless void he plunged, down and down and down.

Strong arms took hold of him. 'Easy, sir,' Hulo Roundbank's voice said. There was firm earth beneath his feet, a smell of wet leaves and the sea.

He forced open his eyes and gave a gasp of agony. Daylight made the suffering all the worse. But he had to know whether the Gateway had opened to the right place, whether all of them had passed through safely.

He saw the eroded stone walls of a steep ravine, an overhanging ledge, thick brush growing round about that gleamed wetly with leftover rain. Gavlok and Hulo were on either side of him, holding him up. Hanan was on his knees a few ells away, shorn of all his cocky courage, losing his breakfast while Valdos patiently held his head. Only Radd Falcontop seemed to be missing.

But then the stocky Mountain Swordsman stepped out from the tangled vegetation as silently as a ghost.

'I climbed to the rim of the ravine, Sir Deveron. Saw a little keep on a baldtop hill maybe half a league away. It's Skullbone Peel, sure as dammit. Don't worry. No one saw me. There's plenty of cover up there, and naught about but a few birds.'

Snudge gave vent to a great sigh, unclenched his fist, and let Subtle Gateway drop away on its chain. 'We've done it,' he said aloud.

His eyes closed, and he fell into a dark pit of fire, surrendering completely to the pain.

TWENTY-ONE

Duke Feribor Blackhorse, Lord Treasurer of the Realm, had been confident he could bamboozle the Tarnian magicker and compel him to cooperate. Blind Bozuk wanted money – enormous amounts of it. By agreeing to pay the shaman's original outrageous fee without dickering, King Conrig had undoubtedly suggested to the old rascal that even more gold might be forthcoming, given a bit of crafty maneuvering. Feribor intended to beat him at his own game.

But not for the Sovereign's benefit . . .

The shaman and the duke were now face to face across a table covered with a fine red damask cloth, in the commodore's cabin of the crack frigate *Peregrine Royal,* the swiftest warship in the Cathran Navy, presently docked at the deepwater quay of Northkeep Castle. The duke had politely declined the hospitality of its chatelaine, Lady Freda – Sealord Liscanor was was regrettably away from home – and arranged to receive Bozuk on shipboard. After regaling the ancient shaman with a splendid meal and ample amounts of fine wine, Feribor got down to business. He dismissed the ship's officers, had the table cleared – except for the wine ewer and goblets – and commanded the first of the money-chests to be brought in and opened.

Then he and the blind man were left alone, and the game commenced.

The evening was now well advanced. Rain beat dismally against the stern windows and it was quite dark outside. The luxurious cabin was lit with gilded lanterns, and their mellow light glittered on the gold coins that Bozuk had piled in neat stacks. His eyes were shuttered pits but his manner was that of a sighted man, and Feribor was quite convinced that his guest scried everything.

'Two thousand and five hundred gold marks,' Bozuk said, fingering the last of the coins. 'Half of the amount pledged. I suppose you intend to hold back the rest until you get your hands on Maudrayne and the child.'

'This is what my Sovereign has commanded. You are to tell me where the Princess Dowager resides. My windvoice, Brother Colan, will bespeak the information to Cala Palace, and from there it will fly on the wind to the Royal Intelligencer, one Deveren Austrey, who is already on his way to your country. Austrey will conduct the apprehension. When the High King is satisfied that Maudrayne and the child are alive and in custody, I shall pay you the remaining half of the reward.'

The shaman tilted his nearly hairless head and offered a gap-toothed grin. 'And meanwhile, you cool your heels here in Northkeep, keeping me and my money hostage on your great ship.'

Feribor was suave. 'You will be entertained in the most lavish style for the length of your visit.'

'And yet, I have a feeling that you hold something back, lord duke! I sense another proposition lurking in your clever mind, one you would have got 'round to after plying me with more drink. Well, I shan't refuse another beaker of your wine. But why don't we cut right to the chase? You'd prefer to nab the woman yourself, rather than waiting upon this Austrey fellow. And once you had her, you'd use her to bring down Conrig Wincantor and claim the throne of Cathra and the Sovereignty of Blenholme for yourself.'

Feribor threw back his head and roared with laughter. 'You sly old rapscallion! And to think I once thought I'd find myself dealing with no more than a greedy bumpkin!'

'I am both,' said Bozuk with cool offhandedness, 'and much more. Have I fathomed your scheme correctly, then?'

'You've hit on it, I don't deny. The lady and the boy are the keys to Conrig Wincantor's ruin, and there will be many other great lords in Cathra besides myself who'll rejoice to see him cast down. The Sovereignty is a political millstone about Cathra's neck, as is Conrig himself, with his insane ambition to emulate Bazekoy the Great. My plan was to force him to recognize Maudrayne's son as his legal heir. In time – perhaps a very short time, now that Somarus sits on the throne of Didion – Conrig would perish in some ill-advised battle. Without him, Blenholme would soon become as it was before – four states who trade and squabble as the spirit moves them. While I –'

'While you,' Bozuk said softly, 'dispose of the boy-king and his half-brothers and take the throne to which you have a legitimate claim, through your mother Jalmaire, who was old King Olmigon's only surviving sibling.'

'You've studied up on Cathran genealogy.'

Bozuk cackled with laughter. 'But there's something I know and you don't know, that would make a second deplorable massacre of royal children unnecessary. And give you the throne even before Conrig was dead.'

'What?' Feribor inquired with arch skepticism.

'First,' the old man said blithely, 'the other half of the money. Now! And then the other five thousand marks in gold . . . with which you intended to bribe me to guide you to Maudrayne.'

Feribor went white. 'You can't have known about that! *How did you know?'*

'You and I are fox-kits of the same dam, Feribor, brothers beneath the skin, guileful and wicked and having goals we would kill for, if need be! I want a secure old age in a warm country. You want a throne. Bring in the money and we'll both win this game of wits.'

Without another word, Feribor strode to the cabin door and barked out an order. Then he returned to his seat at the table and sat in stony silence, flexing and unflexing his strong hands into fists, as though crushing something invisible.

Bozuk sipped wine while his sightless eyes seemed focused on the columns of golden disks lined up before him. After a while, the ship's captain ushered in the bo'sun and his mate, carrying naked swords, and a file of seamen bearing money-chests.

'Is there anything else, my lord duke?' the captain inquired, when the open boxes rested upon the table and the men had withdrawn to the corridor.

'There is,' Blind Bozuk declared in a firm voice. 'Outside on the quay, near the foot of your gangplank, you will find my servant Tigluk. He is a man of middle age, strongly built and having a notable black beard. Tell him this: "The master orders you to bring the banker Pakkor Kyle, a dozen of his well-armed lackeys, and the armored cart to this ship."'

The captain looked to Feribor for confirmation. 'My lord?'

'It must happen this way,' Bozuk addressed the duke without heat. 'Either we do this thing together, forced to trust one another by circumstances, or we will not do it at all. You cannot coerce or harm me.' Again he smiled – mostly toothless, cheeks furrowed and white-bristled, balding head dotted with age-spots like the egg of some enormous bird. Bozuk looked incapable of swatting a fly, but behind that unprepossessing, empty-eyed face Feribor Blackhorse somehow saw the shadow of a snarling wolf's-head.

'Do as he says,' the duke told the captain, who saluted and left the cabin.

'And now you wish to know the other secret.' Bozuk opened one of the three newly arrived chests and again began to stack coins. 'It's one that Maudrayne Northkeep has already shared with her brother Liscanor, when she also told him about her son. Liscanor, in turn, informed High Sealord Sernin of it, and before long all of the other sealords of the Company of Equals will know it, too.' He paused. 'They'll know it, but be unable to prove it. Yet.'

Feribor scowled. 'Bazekoy's Ballocks! Get on with it, old man!'

Unfazed, the shaman continued in a leisurely fashion. 'When I learned of the secret myself, lip-reading as I scried the Tarnian leaders discussing it, I freely gave the information to King Conrig, since he hesitated to pay my reward and I feared he'd slough me off as a backcountry crank. But he sooned learned better. Oh, how distressed – how stricken with fear! – Conrig must have been to hear his windvoice repeat my dire words. But he agreed at once to pay all that I asked.'

'Tell me the secret, damn you!'

'Oh, very well. The second secret is this: Conrig Wincantor possesses a small portion of talent.'

'What! That's ridiculous.'

'His arcane abilities are imperceptible to members of the Zeth Brotherhood, but Princess Maudrayne learned of them through the Conjure-Queen of Moss. The king's brother Stergos also knows, but is sworn to secrecy. However, if the king were to be accused before a Royal Tribunal, and Stergos made to testify under oath, he would not perjure himself or dishonor his vows to Saint Zeth. He would affirm the truth.'

'Great God,' Feribor breathed. 'And you say that some of the Tarnian leadership knows of this already?'

Bozuk nodded. 'There is no way Conrig can stop them from accusing him and demanding an official inquiry. It would be up to your cronies, the Lords of the Southern Shore, to make sure that the inquiry proceeds.' He continued making neat piles of gold. 'It would also suit your purposes, while the king's brother Stergos is under oath, to ask him whether Conrig's two younger sons by Risalla Mallburn carry the same taint as their father. It may be that they do not. I think it likely that they do possess talent, as does their older brother! Whatever the case, Stergos would feel obligated to tell the truth.'

Feribor sat back in his chair, his face aglow with ferocious triumph. 'If all this is as you say, then my enemy is delivered into my hands.'

'Maudrayne would willingly act as principal witness to the king's talent, especially if she thinks her son will inherit the throne. But later, if you should challenge the boy's birthright – who can prove for certain who his father is? Your Cathran laws declare that one such as he may inherit the throne *only* if there is no reasonable doubt that the divorced queen never lay with another man while married to the king.'

'Witnesses will surely attest to her fidelity,' the duke said, 'but it would hardly be difficult to ensure that opposing witnesses also came forth.'

Bozuk nodded. 'As I understand it, Conrig was often away from Maudrayne, and she reproached him openly for his neglect.'

The duke was staring at the rows and rows of gold coins. Ten thousand marks, a prince's ransom, half of it the fruit of his own raid on the royal revenues. So, in delicious irony, Conrig would pay entirely for the loss of his crown.

'I agree to pay what you ask!' Feribor said suddenly. He jumped to his feet. Going to a set of cabinets, he opened them and pulled out a rolled parchment. 'Where is the Princess Dowager? Show me her precise location on this map, and instruct me on the difficulties that we might encounter gaining access to her. You will be my guide, of course, as you anticipated. You must also agree to hold me and my men unharmed by the sorcery of the Grand Shaman Ansel Pikan, who is Maude's guardian.'

Bozuk repressed a sudden pang of doubt. Would he be able to do that, even with the wench Induna to help him? But he spoke with full confidence, continuing to count the money. 'Unroll your map and find a place called Fort Ramis on Tarn's eastern coast. The woman is imprisoned near there. In a moment, when I finish here, I will use my windsight to confirm absolutely that she and the boy are still in the place where Ansel Pikan put them.'

Feribor uttered an impatient growl, but contented himself with studying the region in question. It was dismayingly remote, with very few settlements, and would be a formidable ride overland from Northkeep. A single track led from Fort Ramis to a mining center called Gold Creek, that marked the head of navigation on the Upper Donor River. To Feribor's surprise, Donorvale City was only 130 leagues downriver from Gold Creek. But of course the Tarnians would have made certain that their greatest national asset might be easily transported to the capital . . .

'There!' Bozuk heaved a sigh of contentment. 'Ten thousand, as you said, and every coin true gold. Now do me the favor of leaving me alone for a time while I perform the scrying. It's a ticklish business, because of the bulky volcanos lying between here and our goal, so I require perfect silence while I concentrate. Return to me when the banker arrives.' Again, the snaggly grin. 'And you might have your own windvoice bespeak King Conrig, and inform him that Princess Maudrayne and her son are to be found in the stronghold of Cold Harbor, on Tarn's northern coast. That should put his Royal Intelligencer nicely off on a false scent.'

'Well thought,' Feribor conceded grudgingly. 'Do what you must do. But remember that you will travel with me every step of the way, and woe betide you if you think to trick me!'

'Don't talk like an idiot,' the old shaman snapped. 'Either trust me, or take back your damned gold. But I will not stand for insults.'

Feribor stared at the old man with clenched teeth, a muscle in his jaw working. Then he bowed. 'I apologize. And I'll return soon.' He left the cabin and closed the door.

When Bozuk's oversight perceived the duke take up a rain-cloak and head for the main deck, he bespoke his grand-daughter Induna. It was a few minutes before she responded.

I was being shown to my bedroom in the cottage loft by my hostess, she said. *I arrived on the Desolation Coast only today, and have found lodging in a whaling station called Lucky Cove. My hosts think I'm a western herbalist in search of rare plants – which, of course, I am! I've already found some interesting things around here – although a more wretched spot than this never existed on God's green earth. The oil-rendering works is only a few hundred ells downshore from this cottage, and the stink from the blubber-trying pots fair turns my stomach. I'm going to have little but whale-meat to eat here, as well. I've a mind to demand an extra share of your loot, Eldpapa.*

'Never mind that, you silly chit! When I die, everything I own will be yours. Now tell me: where's the princess? Did Ansel lock her up in Fort Ramis, as I thought he'd do?'

No. She's in a small square keep called Skullbone Peel, on the coast five or six leagues north of this hamlet. It's the summer residence of the Shaman-Lord Ontel and his family, who have their principal residence in Fort Ramis. I scried Maudrayne and her son very clearly. There's a rough path that goes along the cliffs from here to there, but nothing my horse can travel. This part of the coast is all cut up with ravines. But I can probably get to the peel's vicinity on foot if need be.

'You're not sure? Why aren't you sure?'

Eldpapa, I only just got here! Don't be so difficult and crabby. I scried the path hindered by intervening rocks, just as I scried the prisoners – and them right through solid stone walls, if you please! Which explains why I couldn't find them earlier. Princess Maudrayne and her son Dyfrig and maid Rusgann are held by Ansel Pikan's cousin. This Ontel isn't much of a wizard himself – except for being a good predictor of weather.

'I know of him.'

But he does have three retainers who are fairly decent wind-talents, and a pack of armed guards. His wife, Sealady Tallu, is a famed Wave-Harrier who'd fight tooth and nail to protect the prisoners, but she went away yesterday to a meeting of her peers in Donorvale. And she took Ansel Pikan with her! As the Grand Shaman of Tarn, he's obliged to attend the meeting of the Company of Equals, along with all the Sealords and Sealadies. She and Ansel went off over the cinder desert to Mornash Town, intending to ride south from there and pick up a riverboat at Gold Creek.

'Oh, bless you, Granddaughter! That's such wonderful news. I was so afraid you and I would have to trade thunderbolts with Ansel!'

You . . . and I? Eldpapa, what are you up to?

'King Conrig's emissary is here in Northkeep. A thoroughgoing rogue named Duke Feribor, who has some distant claim to the crown of Cathra. He wants to seize Princess Maudrayne for reasons of his own, and he insists that I guide him to her hiding place. I agreed. For full payment of the reward, delivered immediately – and an extra five thousand gold marks on top of that! Banker Pakkor is on his way to pick up the coin right this very minute. Once it's in his vaults, not even the High Sealord will be able to winkle it out.'

Ohhh. Eldpapa, you fool! Even if this scoundrel pays you, how can you hope to ride all this way? It's a horrible journey, even for an able-bodied young person. I daresay this Feribor won't want to

*be encumbered with anything so slow as a wagon – but it'll kill
you to ride horseback so far, at the pace the duke will likely set.*

'Don't fuss. We won't be riding.'

What then?

'Duke Feribor came in a fine tall ship, the swiftest in
Cathra. If I lend magical winds of my own to its great spread
of sail, two or three days is all it will take to reach Skullbone
Peel by way of Icebear Channel. And the ship is armed with
tarnblaze cannons, my dear! That chymical is immune from
magical defenses, as you well know. If Duke Feribor threatens
to blast the peel to gravel, don't you think Ontel Pikan will
be happy to be rid of Princess Maude and her brat?'

Brilliant, Eldpapa. Quite brilliant. Your plan will certainly work.

'Well, I had some doubts. If Red Ansel were there, along
with Sealady Tallu, he'd probably find a way to stop us. Take
the prisoners somewhere else, out of reach of the ship's guns.
But I know Ontel Pikan's manner of thinking. He's slow and
steady, not given to quick action. By the time he decides
what to do, the duke and I and the royal prisoners will
already be well on our way to Lucky Cove, to pick you up
and sail home to Northkeep.'

'Deveron Austrey is *what?*'

Conrig shouted so loudly that his spirited white stallion
shied, and it was necessary for the king to hold off questioning Vra-Sulkorig more closely until the beast was brought
back under control.

On this beautiful summer morning, with so much bad
news already sticking in his craw, Conrig had decided to
escape the palace and ride out boar-hunting in the great oak
forest preserve across the River Brent. He took with him
certain old friends and several members of his Privy Council,
as well as the Keeper of Arcana, who still served as Acting
Royal Alchymist and was a keen huntsman. Indeed, it had

been Vra-Sulkorig who scried out the first boar, rightly assigning the quarry to High King Conrig because it was such a huge animal, almost of trophy size. But the ground where the creature stood at bay was boggy, and the king's horse misstepped in the muck, so that his lance failed to pass between the boar's ribs but struck a bone and glanced off. The great beast crashed away bleeding into an adjacent marsh where the hunters could not follow.

Conrig seemed to shrug off the loss, but in his heart he blamed Sulkorig for not having chivvied the boar toward firmer ground before announcing its presence. Such use of overt talent would have been deemed unsportsmanlike, had there been proof of it. But with no other Zeth Brethren on the hunt, who would have known? Unfortunately, Sulkorig, like Conrig's brother Stergos, was a model of righteousness.

And therein lay the difficulty.

Ever since the shaman Bozuk had bespoken them the news of Maude's sensational revelations to her brother, Conrig had been afire with anxiety. Not so much because the Sealords of Tarn had been told that he was talented (lacking proof, they'd debate the matter long and hard before bringing it into the open), but because there was now one more person in a position to take the perilous allegation seriously, whether he had proof or not.

Before now there had been only five who knew for certain: Snudge, Ullanoth, Stergos, Ansel, and Maude, with only the latter posing a danger to Conrig's crown. Now Bozuk also knew, and the Tarnians, but they were not the ones who most worried Conrig.

The problem was Vra-Sulkorig Casswell, the austere former soldier whose own strong talent had only tardily manifested itself, making him all the more zealous to defend the Zeth Codex.

After relaying Bozuk's message to the king, the Keeper of

Arcana had seemed to accept Conrig's assertion that Maude
had been lying. But a few days earlier, the king had learned
from Stergos that Sulkorig was in an agony of conscience
over the matter. The Keeper had asked Stergos's advice,
wondering whether he was obliged to report the allegation
to the Council of Brethren or the Lords Judicial of the Royal
Tribunal. Stergos had counseled silence, since Maude's state-
ment was plainly inspired by spite and revenge and was
apparently backed by no proof. The Royal Alchymist assured
his brother the king that Sulkorig would obey. There was no
need to worry.

But Conrig worried.

The Sovereignty that had seemed so secure at the start of
Blossom Moon now was under assault from every direction,
as was he himself; and Sulkorig's qualms were the last thing
Conrig needed to top his other troubles. Thanks to Maude,
the bloody-minded Tarnians must now think they possessed
leverage to defy his edicts. The advisers of poor entranced
Ullanoth ranted hysterically of an impending Salka invasion
and demanded that he defend them with his navy. Honigalus
of Didion and his family were slain, astoundingly enough,
by the same monsters, leaving the hellraising Somarus as
unchallenged ruler of that unstable nation. Cathra's ambassador to Didion had reported that none other than Kilian
Blackhorse had been welcomed at the new king's court and
now had the royal ear. According to Earl Marshal Parlian,
war-clouds were gathering. It was only a matter of time.

And Snudge, in whom Conrig had placed such high hopes,
Snudge –

What was the Keeper of Arcana trying to tell him about
Deveron Austrey? . . .

'Your Grace,' Vra-Sulkorig said in a low voice, as the king
finally calmed his fractious steed and the two of them drew
apart from the other hunters, 'I beg you to keep your voice

down. A terrible message has just come to me on the wind, concerning the Royal Intelligencer. He and all of his party have vanished near Castlemont Fortress in Didion. They are believed to be either kidnapped or killed.'

'Who says so?' Conrig hissed.

'Several well-harnessed mounts were found running loose along the Wold Road, south of our own Rockyford Way Station. A caravan of honest merchants came upon the animals and brought them to the station garrison. The saddle of one horse bore the owl blazon of Sir Deveron. Another saddle had Sir Gavlok Whitfell's pierced cinquefoil insignia. The station captain directed his windvoice to consult with Beorbrook Hold, and it was from there that he learned the identity of the horses' probable owners – and the fact that they were king's men traveling on the king's business. The mounts were found near the junction of the Wold Road and a track leading to the Lady Lakes, the notorious haunt of Somarus's band of erstwhile outlaws.'

Conrig groaned. 'And to think I cursed Snudge last night when he failed to bespeak me as ordered!'

'The windvoice at Rockyford informs us that a troop of Mountain Swordsmen from Beorbrook will begin searching at once, as will men from the station itself.'

'Commend them,' Conrig said in a dull tone. 'Order the windvoice to keep Cala Palace informed of any progress.'

Vra-Sulkorig drew the hood of his capuchon over his face and spoke on the wind. When he had finished, he said, 'Shall we rejoin the others, Your Grace? There may be another boar less than a league away, near Cadlow Brook. I had just scried it out as the wind-message came.'

'Stay with me a moment, Brother Keeper. There's an important thing I would ask you.'

'Certainly, sire.' The sturdy Brother in the well-cut hunting habit spurred his mount closer.

'Vra-Sulkorig,' said the king, 'let me ask you one question, which I adjure you to answer in all honesty: Is your conscience troubled by the assertion of the Princess Dowager that I possess secret talent?'

Sulkorig reacted to the query almost with relief. 'So it is, Zeth help me! The notion bedevils me to the point where I can scarce think of anything else. Why should it not, since if it were true, then you must forfeit your crown, and our kingdom and the Sovereignty must be turned over to an infant. And with so many perils assailing us! But right is right in so grave a matter, as I told your lord brother.'

'And he told you to keep silence, and gave good reason for it.'

Sulkorig inclined his head. 'And so I will.' But his voice was unsteady.

Conrig smiled. 'Don't be troubled. All will go well. Come – let's rejoin the others. You must tell them of the new boar.'

Later, a second enormous animal was found and chased and dispatched with wild panache by the Lord Constable of the Realm, Tinnis Catclaw, who had proved his courage during the Battle of Holt Mallburn. Conrig lavished praise on the youngest member of his Privy Council, then took him aside for a quiet word while the other nobles shared wine, and the retainers prepared the dead boar for conveyance to the palace.

Tinnis Catclaw had been a minor baron of the Dextral Mountain country when he first served as an officer in Conrig's victorious small army. He was famed for his fighting prowess, however, and for his unfashionably long golden hair, in which he took a naive pride. When other nobles teased him for keeping it shining clean and dressed with perfumed unguents, he shrugged and pointed out that, when braided, the stuff made perfect helmet padding. After Didion's surrender, Tinnis became one of several redoubtable warriors invited to Cala Palace to help reform Cathra's standing army, which had fallen into a sad state during the reign of Conrig's late father, Olmigon. There the baron showed such outstanding organizational ability that the king eventually named him Lord Constable, in spite of the fact that he was not yet forty years of age. Together with Earl Marshal Parlian Beorbrook, he supervised the land forces of the Sovereignty.

But Lord Catclaw's prowess as a general was not what Conrig needed at the present time.

'Tinnis,' the king said, 'do you love me enough to follow any command of mine without question?'

'Sire, you know I do,' the Lord Constable replied. 'There is no man in the Sovereignty more loyal. I would lay down my life for you.'

'I require that you take life.'

'Even so, I'd fight for your cause to the last drop of my blood.'

Conrig turned his head away, looking at the torn and gory forest undergrowth where the constable had slain the boar. 'There are two persons who pose mortal threats to my life and crown. One is very far from here, in the Tarnian stronghold of Cold Harbor, on its arctic coast. Earlier, I hoped that another agent of mine would be able to deal with this enemy, but now that's become impossible. So I'd send you – alone, save for a troop of trusted retainers of your choice – if you would consent to it. A fast ship will carry you north this very day, and every resource will be placed at your disposal.'

'Sire, I'll rid you of this Tarnian foe gladly. Only give me particulars on where he's to be found, and I'll be off –'

Conrig lifted a gloved hand. 'Wait. There's a second villain, whose perfidy only came to light recently. He's here in Cathra . . . in this very woodland clearing not six ells away from us. He must be killed so artfully that it appears an accident. I care not how you arrange it, so long as the deed is done by yourself alone, before you leave the kingdom.'

Tinnis Catclaw's pale blue eyes glittered. 'Name the whoreson!'

'Vra-Sulkorig Casswell.'

'Futter me blind!' the constable whispered. 'A Zeth Brother?'

'And the one you must kill in Tarn is my former wife, Maudrayne Northkeep, who is alive and conspiring with her countrymen to ruin me and break up the Sovereignty. Tell me plain, Tinnis, whether you're prepared to ease both of these persons from this life, only because I ask it.'

The Lord Constable of the Realm pressed his right fist against his heart. 'My liege, I will.'

No, Ansel. You may not return to the peel and Maudrayne, nor may you bespeak your cousin Ontel and warn him of the danger from Duke Feribor. My foresight counsels against it, although I don't understand why.

'Feribor will take them, Source! He'll use Maude and Dyfrig against Conrig! What will become of our plan to have the king defend High Blenholme against the Salka hordes?'

We can only hope that our plan will succeed, as Feribor fails in his evil purpose.

'Why can't we make sure that he fails? Let me return to the peel and carry Maudie and Dyfrig to a safer place! Or at least let me defend them with my sorcery.'

No. She is shortly to have an important meeting there. With someone else. You would interfere. You may not go to her.

'So. A meeting, is it? With the Royal Intelligencer, I presume! I know he's on his way to Tarn, and I also know that Conrig all but commanded the spy to kill Maude and the child if there's no other way to save his damned crown.

Are you still prepared to sacrifice Maude and the boy for the sake of Blenholme's Sovereign?'

Dyfrig will certainly live. He's to be enlisted in the Conflict – as you knew full well when you rescued his suicidal mother from the sea. Maudrayne's fate is up to her. She will choose life or death by her own response to a proposal that will shortly be made to her.

'What proposal? Do you mean to say that a compromise might still be arranged between her and Conrig?'

Yes.

'When will you put the proposal to her?'

I will not. I cannot. Another will do that, provided he survives his incautious use of Subtle Gateway.

'Source! Did you give that Great Stone to Deveron Austrey? Is he already in Tarn, near Maude's hiding place?'

The Green Man Odall gave him the sigil, at my direction, during an encounter that I engineered with marvelous precision. But the young spy was rash in using the stone. I never expected him to carry numbers of his companions with him through the Gateway to Skullbone Peel. He should have gone alone to lighten the pain-debt. Poor fool! Now he lies senseless at his destination, his flagging body enduring an extremity of torture for the past two days. He may survive. You must pray that he does, and so will I, for the proposal he'll make to Maudrayne may yet solve our problem.

'Prayers?! You might have warned Deveron of the danger!'

I thought I had. He must have misunderstood. I can't think of everything. I've been so long Denied the Sky that both wisdom and resolve begin to crumble. And I also suffer, you know.

'Great God, and now you whine! I wish I'd never known you.'

Go to Donorvale, dear soul. Force the Company of Equals to wait until Maudrayne's choice is made before revealing her secrets to the world. Will you do that for me, at least?

    . . .

Ansel Pikan, will you do that?

. . .

The hunt supper was winding down, having been served in the palace rose gardens between two fountains that filled the perfumed air with cooling spray. King Conrig and most of the others at the high table settled back to drink and listen to ballads sung by a remarkable Forailean bard, brought to court especially for the midsummer festivities.

The Lord Constable excused himself to the king, left his seat, and went to speak to Vra-Sulkorig, who sat near the other end of the board. Tinnis Catclaw's handsome features bore an expression of diffident concern. 'Brother Keeper, it was made plain to me during today's sport that you are one wise in the ways of horses, as well as in arcane matters. You may have noticed my own fine stallion, Windhover, a beast of high spirits that I love like a child. Of late he has puzzled me with a strange and annoying mannerism that neither the stablemaster nor the horse-leech can explain. I wonder if you would be so kind as to stroll with me to the royal stables now, while all is quiet there, and perhaps advise me on what might ail him? The odd quirk is not easily described, but I'm sure we can provoke the animal into demonstrating it to us.'

Sulkorig smiled. 'Why not? Puzzles amuse me, and one involving a horse might prove more diverting than most.' He addressed the king. 'With Your Grace's permission, I'll withdraw with Lord Tinnis.'

'Go, by all means,' Conrig said, catching the eye of the constable for the briefest instant.

As they left the gardens and circled round to the rear of the palace, Tinnis Catclaw questioned the Brother casually about how talented persons made use of the so-called 'wind' to scry and to bespeak one another. Sulkorig did his best to simplify the arcane technicalities for this interested layman, making what he thought was a good job of it by the time they reached the stableyard. Only a few grooms were still about the building where Windhover was stalled, the animals having been settled for the night some time ago.

'That was a most fascinating explanation, Brother!' Tinnis said, as he unlatched the stall door. The powerful sorrel, who stood at least eighteen hands high, whiffled and snorted as his master caressed his cheek. 'Now let's hope your talent – or perhaps your horse-sense – is able to penetrate the brain of this recalcitrant beast and fathom the motive behind his peculiar behavior. Be pleased to enter the stall with me.'

The enclosure was good-sized, as befit such a large animal. Windhover stood placidly enough as Tinnis fed him a carrot from his large belt-wallet.

'Now be so good as to stand at his left shoulder, facing his rear and resting your own left hand on his withers . . . Excellent. Is he shuddering faintly at your touch?'

'I feel nothing unusual,' Vra-Sulkorig said.

'Soon you will. Tap him a little with your fingers.'

The constable stepped behind the other man, pulled a horseshoe from his wallet, and smote Sulkorig a mighty blow on the right temple with the iron. With a groan, the Brother fell into the straw. Windhover shied away, rolling his eyes. Tinnis knelt, then took from his wallet a harness-maker's awl, thin-shafted as a quill and sharply pointed. This he drove with great force into Sulkorig's right ear. The Brother's body gave a single convulsive jerk, then went limp, its sphincters relaxing in death.

Windhover let out a shrill scream and retreated stamping to the far side of the stall, frightened by the smell of the fast-pooling blood and effluvia. Tinnis wrapped the tools of murder in a piece of wash-leather and replaced them in his wallet.

Then he took hold of Sulkorig's robe and began hauling him out of the stall, shouting for help at the top of his lungs.

'So he is dead, with his poor skull cracked by a startled horse!' Tears spilled from Stergos's eyes as the king told him of the dreadful accident. They were together in the bedchamber of the Royal Alchymist, who had not yet retired, seated in a large window-seat that overlooked the now-deserted gardens. 'And he loved the animals so.'

'Vra-Sulkorig was attempting to advise the Lord Constable on some crochet of his stallion's behavior when the beast lashed out with his forefeet for no good reason. The Brother died instantly. There was nothing the alchymists and physicians could do. Tinnis is devastated by sorrow, but there's no question of his remaining in Cala for the funeral. He must take ship for Tarn on the morrow. I need him to talk some sense into the sealords in Donorvale before going in search of Maude and the boy.'

'Help me into bed, Con,' Stergos said. 'This death on top of the ominous disappearance of Deveron has drained me sorely. Aside from losing a dear friend and colleague in Sulkorig, we are now deprived of our confidential windvoice. I shall have to shoulder that task again myself, I suppose – at least when we deal with the miserable shaman Bozuk. Do you think he told us the truth about Maudrayne's place of captivity? When Duke Feribor's windvoice Vra-Colan bespoke Sulkorig with the tidings, there seemed to be a tinge of reservation in his windspeech. Sulkorig spoke to me about it and was anxious. If only he were still alive, Con! We could have analyzed his memory of the message's nuances. Perhaps compelled Colan to repeat it –'

The king drew fine net midge-curtains around the bedstead after Stergos was composed for sleep. 'We can talk of that later, Gossy. For now, you must rest. The Lord Constable will sort matters out when he reaches Tarn in a few days.'

'Yes. I'm sure he'll do his best – for one not possessed of talent.' Stergos lay back on his pillows. His next words were weighted with grief. 'Sulkorig might have discovered the truth much quicker. He was an extraordinary adept and a *good* man, steadfast and loyal for all that he was deeply troubled by the secret knowledge that he learned so inadvertently.'

'You think he would have kept silent about my talent, as you advised him?'

'I explained to him at length the dire political ramifications of revealing it, and also the strong moral arguments in favor of keeping the secret. He seemed fully convinced.'

The king went to the chamber windows and drew the drapes to shut out the twilit sky. 'Well, the question is now moot. The only ones who can still attest to the truth are Maude, Ansel Pikan, Ullanoth . . . and you, Gossy. My former wife can accuse me, but has no sure proof. Ansel's testimony may impress the sealords, but it would never sway a Cathran tribunal. Ullanoth, even if she lives, would never betray me – and neither would you.'

His brother said nothing.

'Gossy?' Conrig felt ice stir in his vitals and hastened to return to the bedside. 'Would you, Gossy?'

But the Royal Alchymist was already asleep.

TWENTY-TWO

The heavy rain returned, and all that the king's men could do was huddle beneath the rock ledge, share tales of their exploits, sing bawdy songs very softly, and consume endless cups of tea improved by their fast-dwindling supply of spirits. It was early in the morning. Their leader had been unconscious for two days now. Radd Falcontop, who had the most experience with ailments and was the closest they had to a physician, was growing apprehensive.

'The chills and sweats are worse,' Radd confided to Sir Gavlok. They were in the deepest part of the overhang, where the ground was driest and Snudge lay beside a tiny fire. 'That's not all. He almost never moves. I can't rouse him enough to get water down his throat, and he gags at swallowing mush. His piss is scanty and orange in color. If this was anything but a sickness brought on by sorcery, I'd fear he was dying of poison.'

'He warned me that doing the magic would provoke awful pain, but said nothing at all about these other things. Perhaps he didn't know.' Gavlok bent over the figure shrouded entirely in blankets, uncovered his friend's face, and laid a hand on his forehead. 'Shite! His brow's like ice. And if he

won't drink, he's surely in a bad way. Have you tried plying
him with a bit of liquor?'

The Swordsman shook his head. 'It'd do harm to one in
his state, that I'm sure of. Sweet warm tea and broth are the
best drinks for Sir Deveron – if we could only get him to
swallow. But what our commander really needs is a doctor
and some stronger remedies. The map shows a wee village
not far south of here. It might have a resident herb-wife, if
nothing else.'

Gavlok winced at the thought. 'Do we dare risk it? They'll
be wary of strangers. They're bound to report us to their
overlord in Skullbone Peel. We'll be captured, perhaps killed
if they suspect we're after Princess Maude. At the least, our
mission might fail.'

'As it will in certainty if Sir Deveron never awakens,' Radd
said starkly. 'None of us can use these magic amulets to
rescue the lady and her son. You must make the decision.
But if we're to try the village, it's best we do so at once,
before Sir Deveron gets any worse. We'd have to bring the
healer here. Gold would provide incentive enough in a poor
region like this. Maybe gold would stop the healer's gob,
too – at least for a little while! We could say our boat's
pulled up in the ravine cove for repair of a sprung garboard
strake. We were taking on water so fast we couldn't make
it to the village harbor. Our sick shipmate that we were
hoping to bring to the shamans at Fort Ramis took a turn
for the worse.'

Gavlok bowed his head, either in thought or prayer. After
a long moment he looked up and held Radd's eye. 'It'd have
to be you and me who go. We can't leave the armigers alone.
They might betray themselves to the enemy with some incautious action. Hulo must stay with them.'

Radd climbed to his feet. 'We're off, then, right now! You
find some money and put on clothes that aren't so grand.

I'll talk to Hulo about how to care for Sir Deveron, and fetch the things we'll need.'

Induna was vexed with her grandfather.

After two days aboard Duke Feribor's speeding frigate, Bozuk was in misery from seasickness and the strain of generating favorable winds. The ship had made a splendid rate of knots until reaching the area of the Icebear Channel off the upper Lavalands Peninsula. There the natural wind fell off and thick fog closed in. More ominous, there were many icebergs. The captain had immediately demanded that the shaman either push away the bergs and melt the fog with sorcery, or else use his scrying ability to guide them through the treacherous waters. All this while keeping the ship's sails filled.

Bozuk had already worn himself out generating the wind. Moving drifting mountains of ice was impossible, and as fast as he dissipated the fog, more rolled in from the Barren Lands to the north. So he was obliged to search out their route, which meant huddling on the cold, damp quarterdeck for hours on end, giving orders to the steersman. Unlike weaker magickers such as the Zeth Brethren and the Glaumerie Guild wizards of Moss, a top-notch shaman such as he had no difficulty performing two acts of sorcery at once – provided neither was too strenuous. So he kept a breeze blowing in near dead-calm conditions as he oversaw the ship's course, shivering in a cocoon of woolen shawls and calling down curses on Duke Feribor or anyone else who had the temerity to interrupt his work.

Including Induna.

You've got to bespeak me, Eldpapa. It's important. I won't wait until later. Listen to me!

Damn the wicked jade! Why wouldn't she let him be, stop breaking his concentration? It was too hard to hear her from so far away whilst scrying and wind-whistling together. Let her wait until the ship rounded the tip of Lavalands and escaped the cursèd fog and ice.

Eldpapa! Someone else is here. Five men – maybe six. They're hiding near the peel. I think they might try to rescue the princess and her son.

He gave it up. 'Lower sail,' he commanded the first mate, who stood on the other side of the helmsman. 'Drag an anchor – or however you slow the bloody ship down. Have your own men watch out for ice. I must cease this work for a time and go to my cabin.'

The mate began to protest. 'But my lord duke has given orders –'

'Futter Feribor and his orders!' Bozuk shrieked. He threw off the wrappings and tottered to the companionway. Before he entered his little cabin, he told an amazed seaman: 'If any man dares to disturb me, I'll turn him into a toad! Give warning – and be sure you tell the damned duke!'

He slammed the door, shed his damp robe, and flopped onto his bunk, rolling himself in the feather-tick he'd insisted on bringing and making sad moan until he finally felt warm and dry and fit to bespeak Induna.

'Granddaughter, respond to me at once! Tell me everything you know about the men you've found. Everything – or it'll be the worse for you.'

More nasty threats, Eldpapa? Will you never learn?

'You young ingrate! Why can't you show respect? I've a good mind not to share the second part of the bounty with you. Why should I? Our agreement was for you to get a third of the five thousand. It's quite enough. What does a young wench like you need with more? You'd only squander it on baubles and gowns –'

Stop it. You'll waste what little strength you have left. Now listen! I only just located these interlopers, and I don't think the talented ones at the peel have taken note of them yet. They're encamped in a seaside ravine about half a league from the peel. Five of them are hale and sturdy and well armed. The sixth man – if he is indeed a person and not merely a heap of blankets and gear, lies unmoving and may be sick. It's impossible for me to scry him clearly, covered up and hidden beneath a rock ledge as he is. The style of the men's garb is Cathran, and I believe they've surely come for the princess and her son.

'Did they arrive by sea? On horseback? How could they have eluded the oversight of Lord Ontel as well as your own?'

I know not. There's nary a trace of boat or mounts. As to why they weren't scried, I can't say, except that I never thought to look for such persons earlier, as I rode toward the whaling village from the Mornash track. Perhaps Lord Ontel didn't think anyone would come looking for his prisoners so soon. The men are very craftily concealed from oversight down in the ravine. The true mystery is why Red Ansel never spotted them. What do you want me to do?

'Slay them!' Bozuk cried in a frenzy.

Eldpapa, be sensible. I'm a healer! I don't use my talent to harm people. Only in self-defense would I even consider smiting another with my sorcery.

'We're stuck in the damned fog up here,' the old man raged. 'We won't sail out of it until tomorrow, at least, and then it's another eighty leagues to the cove below Skullbone. Our arrival might be delayed until day after tomorrow. These mysterious fellows must not be allowed to leave their hiding place. If Lord Ontel is alarmed, he may remove the prisoners to another place. Then my plan to coerce him with the ship's guns and tarnblaze will be ruined – and God knows what Duke Feribor would do! The man's temper smolders like a volcano, Induna. He ordered a seaman flogged to death for a petty bit of insolence this morning. The day before, he smote a clumsy steward senseless for spilling the soup. The poor knave's jaw was broken! What if Feribor turns against me?'

Freeze him solid. Fling a ball of lightning at him. Send him mad with frightful visions . . . Why do you ask me what to do, you silly thing? Aren't you Blind Bozuk, the mightiest renegade shaman in all of Tarn?

'Feribor could attack me before I realized the danger. And I'm so weary, Induna! Too old and decrepit to perform the magical feats that have been demanded of me. I thought I'd only have to create a little wind. The God of the Heights and Depths knows that this ship of the duke's is a marvel of speed even without my pushing its sails. But in a dead calm, such as we have in this miserable fog . . . is there much wind where you are?'

There was yesterday. Today the sea is flat and it rains straight down.

Bozuk gave a croak of despair. 'Do what you can to keep the strangers away from Skullbone Peel. Will you promise me that, lass?'

Certainly. I'll think of something. Take care of yourself, Eldpapa. Farewell.

The old man groaned again. And then there came a strong rapping at his cabin door. 'Master Bozuk! It's Feribor. Open to me! What's this nonsense about toads?'

'Coming, my lord,' the shaman said. Slowly, he unrolled himself from the feather-tick and shuffled to the door.

Induna sighed as she cut the wind-thread. Rain tapped on the slate roof of the cottage, but her little loft chamber was cosy enough. It was almost time for the mid-day meal: whale stew. She shuddered.

Well, perhaps she ought to scry out the lurking men again and give serious effort to reading their lips. They might furnish useful information.

She sat on a stool and covered her eyes.

Five minutes later, with her face gone very pale, she pulled on a pair of stout boots, grabbed up her cloak and a leather sack of herbal medicines, and was off into the pouring rain before the affronted goodwife of the cottage could object.

Radd Falcontop beckoned Gavlok to join him. Both lay prone amidst a dripping patch of willowherb and dwarf birch on a seacliff overlooking Lucky Cove. Rain beat down on them, and on the anchored boats and bleak little houses and factory buildings of the whaling station. Smoke from the chimneys hung low, and an odd, pervasive stench filled the air. There was not a flower or a patch of greenery to be seen anywhere within the muddy precincts of the hamlet. Three men in oilskins worked on the hull of a careened sailboat, hauled up on a shingle slope just below the cliff. Aside from them, not another soul was to be seen.

'What a hellhole,' Gavlok murmured. 'And this is high summer! Imagine what it must be like in wintertime, when the sun peeps over the horizon for scarcely two hours a day and the arctic tempests roar.'

'Folk live where they can find work,' Radd said mildly. 'We are not all belted knights attending upon a king and dwelling in a palace.'

'I didn't mean –'

'Hush!' The veteran Swordsman had wrenched his body about about and stared in narrow-eyed alarm at the rolling plateau behind them. He muttered a curse. 'I hear someone coming up the path from the village. Crouch down in the weeds and don't move.'

Gavlok obeyed. After a few moments, he heard the footsteps, too, splashing and crunching and now and then dislodging a loose stone, becoming ever louder. But no one came into sight.

'Where is he?' Gavlok whispered frantically. 'God knows, he makes enough noise – but I see no one.'

A female voice said, 'Because I don't wish to be seen.'

Both men gave great starts. Still acrouch, Radd drew his long dagger and assumed a fighting stance. Gavlok was too bemused to do anything save sit on the wet ground and stare wildly about.

'Who are you?' the voice said. It was high and clear. 'What do you want?'

Radd said, 'We're Cathran mariners in trouble, beached a few leagues to the north. One of our number is taken ill. We hoped to find a healer in yonder village, but we hesitated to approach, not knowing how we'd be received. Some folk hereabouts don't welcome strangers.'

'Put up your blade. As it happens, you're in luck.'

Wondering, Radd sheathed his dagger. He and Gavlok were now on their feet, looking this way and that for the unseen speaker.

She appeared, and even as they exclaimed in surprise, they realized that she'd been there all the time – but somehow their minds had refused to admit the fact. Small of stature, she was nevertheless a woman full-grown, sixteen or seventeen years of age, with a round pretty face and steady dark eyes. Strands of curly red-gold hair stole from beneath the hood of her raincloak, and she carried a bulging leather scrip and a walking staff.

'I am Gavlok Whitfell and this is Radd Falcontop.' The tall knight bowed politely and touched his brow in salute. 'Madam, are you a sorceress?'

'I'm an apprentice shaman and a healer,' she said. 'My name is Induna of Barking Sands.'

Gavlok cried out eagerly, 'Will you come and look to our sick friend, Mistress Induna? We fear he may be dying. We'll gladly pay for your services –'

'I'll come, and no payment will be necessary.'

Radd's eyes went slitty as he studied her with a slow smile. 'We're indeed lucky to have met you, all dressed for travel and willing to accompany us with no ado. It's almost as though you were expecting us! Do you carry medicines in your bag?'

'Yes.' She was unperturbed. 'And I can but hope they will be the proper ones to give succor to your friend. Perhaps you had better describe his ailment in detail as we walk along. As I said, I am yet an apprentice, but my studies are far advanced. Perhaps I can help.'

They started along the clifftop path. Gavlok gave a halting description of Snudge's symptoms without saying how the illness came upon him. When she inquired whether the sick man might have eaten tainted food or some poisonous plant, or if he had suffered a blow to the head, Gavlok denied it.

'So your friend Deveron is the only one among you who is ill,' she summarized, 'and all of you ate the same meals, and he did not sample any strange mushrooms or berries, nor suffer an injury to the skull. And he is a man of twenty years who has always enjoyed excellent health.'

'Aye, mistress.' Gavlok's reply was uneasy.

'Such persons may be suddenly laid low in the way you describe, without obvious cause,' she said. 'But this happens only rarely, perhaps due to the abrupt failure of some vital body part that was overfragile from birth with no one the wiser. If this is the case with your friend, I regret to say that his outlook is very grave indeed, and I probably can do nothing to cure him . . . But there is one other thing that might be wrong, and for this I might have remedy.'

'What?' Radd asked.

She paused on the path, her calm gaze sweeping over them. 'You must be honest. Is it possible that your friend Deveron is bewitched?'

Gavlok's face had gone ashen, but he pressed his lips together and shook his head, intending to keep the secret of the sigils as he had solemnly promised. But Radd had no such scruples when his leader's life was at stake, and the success of his mission as well.

'Mistress, you may have hit on it,' the Swordsman said. 'Deveron is a petty trickster, able to perform only a few simple conjurations. He attempted a more serious piece of magic, and it was after this that he fell into the mortal swoon.'

'Ah,' said Induna. 'I would not be surprised to hear that a hedge-wizard of Didion was so afflicted. But I had thought that all Cathrans possessed of talent were forced to join the Mystic Order of Zeth.'

'In most cases, they are,' Gavlok admitted. 'But Deveron's magical abilities are so very slight that no one in authority took note of them. He reveals them only to his closest friends. We refrain from exposing him, since a free spirit such as he would pine away in a life that was both regimented and celibate, such as the Zeth Brothers must embrace.'

'I can only be thankful that Tarnian shamans are not treated that way,' Induna murmured. 'This Deveron sounds like an interesting young man. With all my heart, I pray that I can restore his health.'

Three hours later, she and her companions arrived at the ravine. She said not a word about the nonexistent 'boat' the men were supposed to have arrived in, nor did she comment on the unusual quality of their weapons and equipment. After a brief examination of the sick man's face, without removing his body coverings, she asked for as many candles as they possessed, and had them lit and placed round about Snudge's pallet. Then she commanded the five to leave her alone with the patient. When they had withdrawn as far away as possible, while keeping to the shelter of the ledge, she turned down the blankets and opened Snudge's shirt.

'By the Icebound Sisters!' she gasped, lifting the golden chain with its softly glowing amulets away from his bare flesh. 'So that's it!' She eased the chain over his head, being careful not to touch the stones herself, and laid them aside on the dry dust of the shelter floor. For an instant, the internal light of the one shaped like a tiny door flashed a brighter, baleful green. Then it was as dim as before.

Induna sat back on her heels, thinking furiously. She knew what the amulets were: moonstone sigils of the Coldlight Army. She'd even seen one once, years ago, a quaintly carved translucent octagon that her mother Maris, who was also a healer shaman, had found washed up on the Barking Sands after a tremendous winter storm. That sigil possessed no glowing heart; it was not alive, as were the stones of her patient. Mother was deeply afraid of the moonstone she had found, and when Induna timidly suggested that they give it to Eldpapa, Maris had slapped her shocked little daughter and screamed that she must never, never tell Bozuk of the thing's existence.

Later, Mother had gone off secretly in a small boat to visit the terrible sea-hag Dobnelu, and had given the sigil to her. When Maris returned, she explained to Induna that the moonstone was a thing accursed and supremely perilous – not only to humankind, but also to Green Men and Salka and Morass Worms and Small Lights. Only the sea-hag and a few other great shamans such as Ansel Pikan had the power to dispose of them safely. As for using their sorcery –

Maris told her daughter the story of Rothbannon of Moss, and how he tricked the Salka monsters into giving up the legendary Seven Stones, and how he alone had managed to use them without harming himself or losing his soul. Then Maris related the histories of Rothbannon's royal successors, who were not quite so lucky, ending with the gruesome fate of Queen Taspiroth, who had managed to offend the Great Lights and was cast into the Hell of Ice. Young Induna had suffered nightmares from those tales until her mother laid on her an ameliorating spell.

As a young woman and an apprentice shaman herself,
Induna learned about the fate of Taspiroth's insane husband
Linndal and the rivalry between their son Beynor and
daughter Ullanoth. But like the other low-status wonder-
workers of Tarn, she had believed the Mosslanders were the
only humans to use sigil magic.

So what was this young Cathran adventurer doing with
two of them?

Did he intend using them to take Princess Maudrayne and
her son away from Ansel Pikan, the almighty Grand Shaman,
who evidently didn't even know that Deveron and the others
were here?

Induna came close to the unconscious man and studied his
countenance. He was good-looking in an unexceptional way,
pallid and blue-lipped and with dark circles about his eyes
from the arcane illness. It was not a face belonging to a person
who had surrendered his soul to evil – nor even come danger-
ously close to doing it, as Eldpapa had. She touched his
clammy brow and he stiffened. His eyes flew open. They were
black, the pupils so distended that the color of the irises could
not be perceived. After a moment, he relaxed again and his
eyes closed. He let out a long, sighing breath. His heartbeat,
which had been irregular, overslow, and weak, quickened
minutely as he partook of a small portion of her vitality.

'Tell me who you are, Deveron. Tell me what you are!'

Her insight, which was one of the keenest aspects of her
talent, now informed her that he was one who sought the
good and tried to shun wickedness, but was sometimes torn
between duty and conscience. He was, her perception assured
her, a ranking agent of the Sovereign of Blenholme, Conrig
Wincantor. But he also served another, much greater cause.

What cause might that be?

But there was no answer to that, save the one that might
come from his own lips, were he to be healed.

'Shall I cure you, then, Deveron?' she whispered. 'Shall I
share with you my own most treasured gift, of which I possess
only a limited amount, in order to learn your story? Is it possible,
after all, that you've sought out this beleaguered princess and
her child without evil intent, even though you possess two
moonstones that take power from the Great Lights?'

The thought came to her unbidden: Was he a rescuer rather
than an abductor?

Induna had been deeply confused by the implications of
Bozuk's messages, those she had relayed over the wind to
the Sovereign. She was unable to decide whether Maudrayne
was victim or villainess or political pawn. Conrig Wincantor,
on the other hand, was beyond doubt a ruthless man with
a heart of stone. All of Tarn knew he'd cruelly cast this once-
cherished wife of his aside because she seemed unable to
have children. He'd deceived his people about his secret
talent. But he'd also unified the four nations of the island
and saved them from being invaded by Continental oppor-
tunists eager to take advantage of the late Wolf's Breath
disaster.

Induna felt she had two clear choices. She could obey
Eldpapa and keep these men away from the mother and
child until Duke Feribor seized them, or she could try to get
to the bottom of this strange situation and do what was right
and just.

Once again, she placed her hand on the unconscious young
man's forehead. 'Will you tell me the whole truth of it if I
remove your pain and heal your tortured body?'

She waited, and after a long time, the answer came.

Yes.

He knew that the price exacted by Gateway would be terrible,
but never expected that it would overwhelm him so
completely. For one thing, the agony was part of his sleep,

a condition so contrary to the natural order of things – when unconsciousness always brought relief from suffering – that his mind screamed at the injustice of it.

The Lights laughed at his resentment, and fed.

In all his short life he'd had little experience of excruciating pain. The debt owed for his few uses of the minor Concealer sigil had been insignificant. He'd suffered far worse while enduring toothache and a broken arm when he was a child. The more eldritch tortures of Iscannon and his master, Beynor, had introduced him briefly to the horrors of the icy sky-world inhabited by the Lights; and the price he recently paid in order to activate Gateway had been severe but easily forgotten – as though the Lights didn't want to frighten off a fresh victim with juicy potential.

This pain was very different, being both physical and mental, combining bodily hurt with the wrenching terror of nightmares. It was relentless and all-consuming, and Snudge was certain it was going to be the death of him.

He accepted this for a fact; and the fury and despair he felt, knowing that his loyal companions would soon find themselves abandoned in the shambles of his failed mission, gave a fresh dimension to his misery. His only prayer was that he would die soon. He saw the way to eternal peace, strove with all his willpower to follow it, but was denied.

Live on! the Lights said, laughing, *for as long as we choose. And suffer.*

Then he saw her, coming toward him in the bright abyss of woe: a young woman with curling red-gold hair, slender and spare of stature, with a round face that shone confident and serene. Was she only a fever-dream, a device to magnify his torture? She asked him many questions, but he hung mute in hideous Light, unable to reply.

Finally, she said, *Will you tell me the truth of it if I remove your pain and heal your tortured body?*

He forced the word from his numbed mind: *YES!*

The Lights howled their frustration, drawing away from him as the woman approached. He saw her reach into her own heart and take out a pearl-colored thing like a girl-doll or a tiny statue, no larger than a finger-joint. As she did this, her own body shimmered like an image reflected in water and was diminished in some subtle manner. She reached out to him, smiling, and pressed the pearly homunculus into his own breast. He saw its minute arms and head move before it disappeared, and knew that the thing was alive. She had taken part of her own soul's substance and donated it freely to him.

The pain vanished. The wrathful Lights vanished. His ordeal ended.

The Source said, *Now let me tell you the rest of it, so you know what is at stake when you put your proposal to Maudrayne, and so that she knows it, too.*

He listened. And then he opened his eyes.

Induna's transfer of vital energy effected a perfect cure. Snudge was instantly restored to consciousness and his damaged body was rendered whole again. For all that, he was like a fine clock or other delicate mechanism new-made, which must not be allowed to work at full capacity until its parts are tuned and lubricated.

He would have risen at once from his pallet, but she forbade it, as she also forbade him to speak. First he must drink little but often from a decoction of warm water infused with centaury, melissa, rosehip, and honey. Then, every hour, all throughout the rest of that day and all night long, he must sup a few spoonfuls of thin oatmeal gruel. The next morn, she allowed his squire Valdos to wash his body and dress him in fresh clothes. After dismissing the squire, she herself anointed his limbs and back with a mild monkshood

liniment to invigorate the muscles, then felt for the pulse in
his neck.

'It's good and strong,' she pronounced, 'but to be safe,
we'll physick you with a modicum of foxglove.' She let fall
two drops of liquid from a glass phial into a cup of water
and had him drink it down. 'Now, Sir Deveron Austrey,
Knight Banneret and Royal Intelligencer, you may sit up at
last and speak if you wish, for you are very nearly as whole
as you were before undertaking your rash experiment with
sigil sorcery.'

Snudge's voice was at first hoarse and weak, but he grinned
at her as he said, 'You're a benevolent tyrant, Induna of
Barking Sands, but I thank you heartily for healing me. May
I ask you some questions?'

She nodded. 'And I'll answer – provided you also respond
to mine.'

Gavlok and the armiger Valdos, their faces shining with
relief, had been helping as they could during the final hour
of Snudge's treatment and still hovered near. Induna now
turned to them with kindly firmness. 'Please allow Sir
Deveron and me to speak privately.'

Gavlok blushed, for he, like both squires, was already half
in love with the winsome shaman. 'Certainly, mistress. If you
need us, only call.' They went to join Hanan, who was
watching the Swordsmen play a game of draughts using
stones and squares scratched into the earth.

When they were out of hearing, Deveron's smile faded.
'What have you done with my sigils, Induna?'

'They are safely buried somewhere in this shelter. An
important part of your cure involved removing the stones
from contact with your bare flesh. However, I'll be frank: I
came here not only to heal you, but also under orders from
my grandsire, the shaman Blind Bozuk. He has commanded
me to prevent you from apprehending and harming Princess

Maudrayne and her son Dyfrig. Duke Feribor Blackhorse has delivered your king's gold to Bozuk. But the duke has also offered my grandsire an equal additional sum to guide *him* to Maudrayne.'

'What?' Snudge gaped at her.

'I won't let you have your sigils back, or allow you or your men to leave this place, until the princess and her child are safe in the hands of the duke. At this moment, he is approaching Skullbone Peel in a great ship. It will arrive before this day ends.'

Snudge was aghast. 'Induna, you don't understand why I've come here! I hope to help Maudrayne and the little boy – not harm them. They'll hardly be safe in the hands of Feribor. Just the opposite!'

She inclined her head, as if this was the response she'd expected. 'If that's true, you must explain everything to me. Everything! For I confess that I'm both perplexed and worried by my grandsire's actions. I came here from Northkeep thinking only to help him obtain the rich reward that would ensure his comfortable retirement. He's a rascal, but he loves me in his own way. However, since my arrival here, the situation has changed drastically. I'm troubled by his new alliance with Duke Feribor, who appears to be a blackguard. Eldpapa may have been too clever by half, agreeing to assist this man. He's frightened.'

'And well he might be, mistress. Feribor's only purpose in rescuing Maude and her child is to use them against High King Conrig.'

She gave him a level look. 'Who is himself no paragon of virtue – and no good friend to the lady.'

Snudge groaned and lay back against the pack that served as a pillow. 'Shall I tell you the whole tale, as I understand it?'

She sat beside him, poured more warm herb tea into his

cup, and proffered it. 'Please do. Drink this as you speak. It will help your voice. And as you relate the story, be sure to include mention of the great secret cause that you serve, which commands more of your loyalty than does your liege lord Conrig.'

He froze with the cup halfway to his lips. 'How do you know of that? I've told no one of it!'

She tapped her temple. 'One of my talents is that of insight. It's not mind-reading, but it does reveal to me the bent of a person's temperament, and suggests what things are most dear to him in life.'

'Good God.' Snudge looked at her more intently. 'What manner of archwizards does Tarn breed? And you're so young!'

'And so are you,' she retorted, 'to use the sorcery of the Coldlight Army when you are but a wild talent and a spy. Tell me all.'

So he did, not knowing why he felt impelled to trust her. It had nothing to do with her empty threats. He knew instinctively that if he called out to his stolen sigils they would respond to him, and he'd find them easily enough. Once they were in hand, this girl's magical restraints would be impotent against him. His urge to confide in her was motivated by something else, which he did not understand.

He poured it all out: his early years, his unwitting use of his wild talents, his recognition of Conrig's magical taint and the uneasy relationship they had shared ever since. He told Induna of his fear that the king intended him to kill Maude to eliminate her threat to the Sovereignty, and his knowledge of Feribor's numerous criminal actions and his craving for a crown. Then he told her about the Source and the New Conflict and his own voluntary enlistment in a battle between inhuman forces.

Last of all, he explained the compromise proposal he intended to put to Maudrayne and to Conrig, in hopes of resolving their antagonism without bloodshed, and how the Source had encouraged him to deal with the princess as best he could.

'And now I must go to her at once,' he concluded, rising up again from his pallet and reaching for his boots. 'If, as you say, Feribor is shortly to arrive on the scene, there's no time to waste. Will you try to prevent me, Induna?'

She slowly shook her head. 'Nay. For as you told me all of this, my insight sifted through it and concluded that you mean well. Your proposal is a wise one that might succeed . . . if this lady's bitterness and ill will are not so strong as to override her good sense.' She paused, then continued almost shyly. 'If you think I could help – either by bolstering your shaky strength with my magic or by lending my own support to your words as you beseech the princess – then let me come with you.'

He considered it. 'I'll have to use my sigils again. The one called Concealer, which is a minor stone not demanding much pain from me in its use, will allow me and my men to creep close to the peel unseen, enter through some subterfuge, and slay the guards. You might easily be included within the sigil's shield of invisibility, which extends for about four ells in each direction as I command. There is no pain inflicted upon my companions, of course. But Concealer's magic does derive from the Great Lights. Are you willing to compromise your integrity by making use of it, as I do?'

She shrugged. 'If necessary. However, I myself am able to move about without being seen through use of my own sorcery. Furthermore, I can easily bewitch the guards at the small fort to open the sallyport, then forget what they've done. They need not be slain, and my integrity thus remains intact.'

He chuckled, climbing to his feet and offering a hand to assist her rising. 'Mistress Induna, I'm glad we've decided to be friends, rather than foes.'

She waved that off, deep in thought. 'Had you anticipated any magical assaults inside the peel? Shaman-Lord Ontel's sorcery isn't very strong, but he has three other magickers attending him who could prove difficult if they scry us. Your Concealer sigil will give protection as we all make our way to the princess's chambers. But you can hardly put your proposal to her while invisible. And someone might chance to scry you as you converse with her.'

Snudge said, 'No one can scry me. This is *my* unique talent! And so while the rest of you stay safely hidden, I'll emerge and present myself to her. If it seems safe, you might also appear.'

'And if she agrees to your proposal?'

Snudge told her what he intended to do then.

'Oh, no!' she cried. 'It would be too perilous! There must be another way. Let's discuss –'

'There is no other way,' he said flatly. 'I've considered the options long and hard. Maude must survive if God wills and she herself does also. Her son *will* survive, for I have the Source's own word on it. But equally important is that no harm come to Conrig Wincantor and his Sovereignty – either through the vengeful princess, through her Tarnian friends, or through the perfidious Feribor. We will do it my way.'

She lay a hand on his upper arm and studied his face with a whimsical frown. 'Are you always so stubborn?'

'Others have asked the same question,' Snudge said, 'and one of them a king.'

TWENTY-THREE

'Are you ready?' Snudge asked his men. They were all armed, but the rest of their equipment was to be left behind. Whatever transpired at Skullbone Peel, they would not be returning to the ravine shelter.

'Ready,' they replied, but their doubt and hesitancy were still evident. Lengths of thin leather strapping fastened to their belts linked them together and to their leader like some bizarre Tarnian dog-team hitched to a sled: but the sled – which was Snudge – would draw the team along after him. Two men were to follow on his left and two on his right, the pairs keeping close, while a longer center strap allowed the sixth man to bring up the rear. They had been warned that when Concealer's spell enveloped them, no man would be able to see the other, nor would he easily know how far distant he was from the boundary of the shielding bubble emanating from their leader's sigil.

'At first,' Snudge said, 'we must move along very slowly until you become accustomed to being invisible. It'll be difficult. We'll have bumps and tangles. If one of you somehow becomes separated from the rest and pops into clear view, stand utterly still and give a soft whistle. I'll bring you back under cover as quickly as I can.'

Hulo Roundbank, the tailman, fingered the strap that attached him to Snudge. 'This is a bloody awkward way to travel. And how can we fight, lashed together like this?'

'You won't,' Snudge told him. 'When and if our situation demands violent action, you men must forgo the safety of invisibility. By then, we should be inside the peel and carrying out our plan of attack.' He turned to Induna. 'And you, mistress, being the only one of us unencumbered, will scout out the path for us and otherwise serve as advance guard until we reach the gates of the fort.'

She nodded, her lips twitching from a suppressed grin. 'I will. And I give fervent thanks that I need not creep through rocks and brush on a leash like you poor lads.' She folded her hands, closed her eyes, and disappeared from their sight. 'And now, Sir Deveron, show me how your Concealer works.'

He pulled it from his shirt and gripped it, then spoke the Salkan words. 'BI DO FYSINEK. FASH AH.'

Curses and gasps came from unseen mouths. Somebody said, 'Swive me! I'm gone!'

'Up the side of the ravine,' Snudge commanded, and they were on their way.

They approached the peel with irritating slowness, hindered by the inadequacy of the exiguous little path, which was severed completely at one point by the collapse of an undercut part of the cliff. The result was a sheer drop-off to the heaving sea, and no easy way to proceed across the gap because of the nature of the shore rocks. They were thus forced to detour inland, picking their way cautiously for two hours through trackless brush, before they were able to turn back in the direction of the shore. They made better time then, hiking down a watercourse that skirted the peel's partially wooded hill.

The sky was still overcast, but the hard rain had ceased, leaving the air humid and abuzz with hungry midges who were undeterred by invisibility. The men were out of temper and simmering from their constraint, having to halt frequently to restore their disrupted marching order when one or another came to grief. Induna, who ranged ahead more freely, was the one who first reached the beach that rimmed Skullbone Cove. She surveyed the little harbor, where only a few small boats were tied up at the docks, and was relieved to see no one about. The long flight of steps leading to the block-shaped peel was still wet, another welcome development. No one inside the fort would see their footprints as they ascended.

Then she thought to scan the hazy northern horizon with her talent, and scried the approaching ship.

Quickly, she dashed back up the stream to the invisible men, who were perceptible from the weird depressions their boots created in the shallow waters. 'Stop!' she hissed.

There were splashes and profanities as several of them came up short and collided with one another. Radd Falcontop's voice grumbled, 'I hate this.' Someone else said, 'Mind your damned sword, whoever you are.'

'Silence!' Snudge commanded. 'What is it, Induna?'

'Feribor's ship is coming. It might be nine or ten leagues distant. We have a little over an hour to act, if my estimate of its speed is correct. Even though the air is still, my grandsire Bozuk is creating wind to propel the vessel.'

Radd asked, 'What manner of ship, mistress?'

'It's plainly Cathran by its rigging, although it shows no flag. It has three masts and is of a goodly size.'

'And is probably armed with goodly guns,' the Swordsman muttered.

'Let's get down to the water,' Snudge said. 'I need to scry into the fort more closely and see what kind of opposition we might expect.'

They moved on as fast as they could. Snudge paused to
fill a spare sock with sand from the beach, then ordered the
group to continue to the small quay at the foot of a long
flight of stone steps. There he had the other men sit or crouch
near him, while he concentrated on looking through the
stone walls and ironbound oaken doors of the peel that
loomed on the knoll above them.

'Can you count the guards, Induna?' he asked softly.

'Oh, yes.' Her tone was tart. 'I also can scry through stone,
sir knight.'

They took note of four warriors at the main gate and fifteen
others posted in other parts of the peel or at work in the
armory. Ontel, his three associate magickers, and a man who
might have been the captain of the guard were huddled
together on the ramparts, staring anxiously out to sea. They'd
spotted the ship, too.

'Can we find a way to keep them up there?' Induna
wondered. 'I see two trapdoors giving access to the roof.'

Snudge said, 'Open wooden steps lead from the armory
in the south-western corner of the upper level, and from the
adjacent guards' dormitory in the north-western corner. The
other rooms on that floor, a library and two smaller chambers that may be laboratories used by the resident shamans,
give only onto the corridor and main staircase. It may be
possible to trap the men on the roof if we act quickly.'

The peel was simply constructed, having three levels and
a cellar. On the lowest floor were the gate vestibule and
guardroom, the great hall, the kitchen, washrooms, cramped
dormitories for the housecarls and maids, and some small
offices. The middle floor had a solar, the master sleeping
chamber, three other fine bedrooms, and sleeping cubbies
for the lord and lady's bodyservants.

'I see ten or a dozen servitors here and there,' Snudge
said, 'and two well-dressed older boys in a chamber near the

kitchen working at some manner of woodcarving. Perhaps they are part of the shaman's family. And up in the library is a much younger lad who must be Prince Dyfrig. But the woman with him is not Maudrayne. She has the look of a servant. Where can the princess be?'

'Look to that low annex building at the right of the main keep,' Induna said. 'The lady is in the uppermost part of the windmill turret, also watching the ship. But she uses a spyglass, not talent. How beautiful she is! One would know she was once a queen, even though her dress is plain.'

Snudge oversaw the tall, proud figure crowned with unbound fiery hair. Her gown was unadorned light-green linen, but she wore a magnificent necklace of opals mounted in gold. After a moment she set the long brass instrument aside and seated herself. Her lovely face was unreadable, but she would surely know that the ship was Cathran. Did she speculate that rescuers might be aboard – or would she make a more realistic judgment and think that Conrig's agents had found her at last, and she and her son had not long to live?

'Comrades,' Snudge said, 'the presence of the ship, and the fact that the princess and her son are so widely separated, complicates our mission. The little prince is in a room close to the armory, where at least eight guards are at work, and Ontel and his shamans are also very near to the boy. I had hoped to avoid fighting, but now it may be inevitable. This is what we're going to do.'

Once Induna's compulsion had forced the four guards at the gate to open the sallyport, Snudge and his men, come out from Concealer's spell and freed of their hated straps, made short work of the ensorcelled defenders. The four stood silent and as docile as lambs while being bound, gagged, and stripped of their livery and armor. The captives were then consigned to a dark nook in the guardroom while Gavlok, Hanan, Radd, and Hulo assumed their identities.

Valdos had to wait briefly while invisible Induna sought out and bewitched a household lackey of appropriate build, then conducted him to the guardhouse. This fellow's garb provided a suitable disguise for the task assigned to Snudge's squire.

While his men were changing their clothes, Snudge took Induna aside. 'I'd be more easy in my mind if you'd accompany me to Princess Maude's turret, rather than sharing the more perilous work.'

'I might be sorely needed,' she said, 'if Ontel or one of his magickers comes down from the roof before the steps can be destroyed, or if a mêlée ensues. And I can protect little Prince Dyfrig better than your men can.'

Snudge scowled. 'Very well. You've persuaded me. But take care. You must all be with me and the princess inside the turret before the ship comes within cannon range of the peel. Feribor will surely threaten to bombard it as a ploy to obtain the prisoners. He may even lob a shell or two for emphasis – and only heaven knows how Ontel will respond. He's probably thinking of using one of those catapults from the armory. I scried some guardsmen tinkering with them. It'll be devil catch the hindmost if Ontel tosses a bombshell at the ship, and it fires back. The peel will have the worst of it. I doubt a backwoods Tarnian castellan like Ontel has any notion of the power and range of a modern frigate's guns.'

'We're ready, Deveron,' Gavlok said. He and the others who had put on the guards' helmets, mail shirts, and surcoats formed up and smote their breasts in mock salute. Valdos hung behind them, smirking. He'd been forced to give up his sword but had hidden two daggers under his servant's smock.

Induna said, 'I'm going with you soldier boys. But don't give me a second thought. I can take care of myself – and I may even be able to make myself useful in a pinch.' She vanished.

'God go with you all,' Snudge said, and took up Concealer.

There was a single workman in the annex, making some repair to the water-pump machinery at the base of the turret. The rest of the stone building comprised a stable, a byre for two milch cows, a fowl-coop, and a warren of miscellaneous storerooms.

Snudge crept up on the kneeling engineer while invisible and hit him a tap just above the ear with the sock he'd filled with beach sand. The man fell over, moaning, and was quickly trussed and put out of the way. Then Snudge mounted the turret's spiral iron stairway, moving slowly. The initial pangs resulting from his use of Concealer had sapped some of his strength, but the worst of it would come the next time he slept, and would no doubt be submerged in the greater pain-price he anticipated paying later . . .

When he reached the top of the tower, making no sound, the princess was looking through the spyglass again, standing with her back to him. He cleared his throat and spoke low.

'Lady Maudrayne, please refrain from turning around.'

She could not help flinching at the unexpected voice, but displayed no fear. 'Why should I not?' she asked sharply, and lowered the spyglass and began to turn anyway. 'Who are you? How dare you accost me here? Lord Ontel gave me this place for a private sanctum. Where are you hiding, you impudent knave?'

'Lady, the shamans may be scrying you as you speak. I beseech you to compose yourself! You must not rouse their suspicions. Go back to the window and resume your study of the sea or else sit quietly on the bench. Please show no excitement, and cover your mouth with your hand if you must speak. I'll explain myself. I've come to free you and your son.'

She plopped down on the circular seat surrounding the

shaft housing, eyes wide and lips parted in astonishment as she realized she was being addressed by one who was invisible. An instant later she lowered her head and allowed her thick auburn tresses to veil her face. 'Are you a wizard, then? Perhaps come here from yon ship?'

Snudge intoned, 'BI FYSINEK.' He appeared, sitting beside her.

Her blue eyes blazed behind the gleaming curtain of hair. 'You,' she whispered. 'Deveron Austrey, my husband's strangely talented spy! I think you've come not to liberate us, but to put an end to us.'

'Not so, my lady. These days, I serve not only the High King, but also another master – whose commands supersede those of Conrig, and who wishes no harm to befall you.'

'So you say,' she jeered. 'Aren't you afraid the shamans will scry you talking to me?'

'You called me talented, and so I am, and *very* strangely. No one can scry me. But we must not bandy words, for there's little time. The ship you observed approaching the peel carries Duke Feribor Blackhorse. He intends to steal away you and your son and force you to serve his own purposes before disposing of you both.'

'No!' she cried.

'It's true. Whereas I hope to transport you to the safe custody of your uncle, High Sealord Sernin, after making to you a proposal that may insure your future safety – and give to your son some of his birthright.'

'What are you saying?' she breathed, leaning closer to him. 'What sort of a proposal? Who is your master, if not the man who is my greatest foe?'

'Lady, there's no time to speak of this now. He is a person of great power, that is all I can tell you about him. He knows how you were taken away and safeguarded by Ansel Pikan, but also knows that Ansel is no longer able to protect you from those who would deny your destiny. He's the one who permitted me to come to you, when Ansel would have tried to prevent it. Most important . . . he is one who knows that only Conrig Wincantor can save our world from the terrible catastrophe that threatens it. Only the Sovereign will be able to defend our beloved island from an impending invasion by Salka monsters.'

'Salka?' She was skeptical. 'But they hide in Moss's fens.'

'No more! These inhuman fiends have already murdered the entire royal family of Didion. They are poised to take over the kingdom of Moss, now that Queen Ullanoth is gone. After that, they'll attack Cathra and Tarn, using the same moonstone sorcery of the Beaconfolk that confronted Emperor Bazekoy when he conquered Blenholme on behalf of humanity. No other ruler living has the military prowess of Conrig. He is a flawed man: in many ways, a wicked man. But he is the only one who can save our island. And for this reason you will not be permitted to destroy him.'

'I . . . will not be *permitted* . . .' Outrage robbed her of speech.

'Lady, you have been cruelly wronged. You thought yourself justified in avenging yourself and your son by revealing Conrig's two great secrets to your brother and to the other sealords. Perhaps you believe that the king's fate is already sealed. It's not. He won't be deposed because of what you've done. He will not lose his Iron Crown. But he *will* be distracted, and his energies will be diverted from more important matters as he defends himself against you. His human enemies will also assail him if he seems vulnerable. Thus he may be prevented from defeating the monsters . . . if you do not recant your accusation.'

'Never!' She was ashen with reined-in fury. 'Never never never will I take back my words, because I have spoken only the truth!'

'Let me tell you what you would receive in exchange,'
Snudge said. 'First of all, your son Dyfrig would be given
special status by the king. Since you cannot prove absolutely
who his father might be –'

She drew a breath to scream an imprecation, but Snudge
covered her mouth with a firm hand and said urgently,
'Listen! Listen, for the love of God. We have no time for
your temper!'

She slumped forward as though he'd struck her. He felt
hot tears on his hand and she shuddered, shaking her head.

He released her. 'There is no proof that Dyfrig is Conrig's
first-born, but neither is there proof that he is not. And so
by royal decree he can be placed third in the line of succession, behind the king's young twin sons by Queen Risalla,
Orrion and Corodon. Dyfrig will be adopted by the Earl
Marshal of the Realm, Parlian Beorbrook, a nobleman of
impeccable character. He will be styled Prince. If Dyfrig
shows competence, he will eventually inherit Lord Parlian's
familial office and the great Duchy of Beorbrook. The
marshal's only surviving son, Count Elktor, cannot in justice
fill his father's boots, and he already has lands of his own.
Should Parlian die untimely, the office of earl marshal will
remain vacant and its perquisites held in abeyance until
Dyfrig is of a suitable age to take them up. If for some reason
he cannot do this, he will still be provided for as a prince
royal.'

'Third in the succession?' Maudrayne said tremulously.
'Adopted by dear old Parli?'

'This is my proposal. As for yourself, you will live in Tarn
under the protection of your uncle, who will be responsible
for your good conduct. You'll have no physical contact with
your son until he has reached his majority. He will know
you are his mother, however, and you will be permitted to
write to him – although not secretly.'

'And to attain all this, I must say I lied when I revealed Conrig's secret talent.'

'You must *convince* the sealords of it,' Snudge corrected her gently. 'There can be no half-heartedness, no sly winks, no mental reservations or future denials or treasonous schemings. Or else Dyfrig will suffer the ultimate penalty, while *you* will live on.'

She wiped away her tears. 'This is hard. Harder than you know. Conrig betrayed me with Ullanoth –'

'He never will again. She is as good as dead.' Snudge waited, but Maudrayne only raised her head and stared out to sea. The ship was perceptibly closer. 'Well, my lady?'

She sighed. 'I agree to all of it . . . But how will we now escape from here? You said you would carry us safely to Donorvale, but that seems hardly possible.'

'It is possible, and it will be done. But first I must put the proposal to the High King and obtain *his* agreement.'

'What! He doesn't know?'

Snudge's expression was rueful. 'I could say nothing to him until I successfully reached your side, and heard from your own lips that you would agree. I am a wild-talented windvoice. With your permission, I'll now bespeak Lord Stergos in Cala Palace, and he'll put the matter to His Grace.'

She was trembling with shock and anger, and for a moment it seemed her fierce pride would overturn everything. But then she threw back her head and laughed. 'Go ahead. But oh – how I wish I could see Con's face when he's told!'

'I've sent for him,' Stergos told Snudge on the wind. 'He's at a meeting of the Privy Council and the Lords of the Southern Shore, attempting to quash the rumors that already filter out of Tarn. But I've informed him that the message is crucial – and that you're alive.'

But not that I'm with Princess Maudrayne, I hope!

The recuperating Royal Alchymist lay in a long chair on a shaded balcony of the palace. He had dismissed the Brother Secretary who was assisting him with his papers as soon as Snudge bespoke him, and now carried on their wind-conversation with one hand shading his eyes. 'No, no, I've said nothing to the king about Maude – but I couldn't contain my happiness and my relief at your survival. How in Zeth's name did you ever get to Tarn?'

Through sigil magic. I was given a Great Stone called Subtle Gateway by the Source, who also told me where Maudrayne and the boy were being held. Gateway is able to carry me and my companions anywhere, at a price. We're in a small place on the eastern coast of Tarn, near Fort Ramis.

'But the shaman Bozuk told Duke Feribor she was imprisoned at Cold Harbor, far to the north! The Lord Constable was sent in search of her when it seemed you might be dead.'

Bozuk lied, my lord. And Duke Feribor has played our king false. He bribed Bozuk to take him to Maude, thinking to use her in support of his own claim to Cathra's throne. At this minute, Feribor's ship is only a few leagues distant from us. The situation is tricky, but I believe we'll surely be able to escape before he arrives.

Stergos groaned. 'My royal brother would never believe ill of the duke, no matter how we two sought to persuade him. Perhaps now he'll listen.'

Your windvoice falters, my lord. Are you strong enough to continue? Perhaps Vra-Sulkorig should relay my message to the king while you stand by.

'Oh, Deveron! Of course you don't know. Poor Sulkorig is dead by misadventure, his head broken by the hoof of the Lord Constable's horse. The beast took fright for some reason while the two men were examining it in its stall.'

I regret to hear it. Sulkorig was an able man, and an honest one.

'Although he did give me much cause for concern,' Stergos

admitted in all innocence. 'His conscience was troubled by his inadvertent discovery of the king's talent, but I convinced him that he had no moral obligation to report it to the Royal Tribunal.'

And His Grace knew of this?

'Well . . . yes. But you can't think that –'

'Gossy! What is it?' Conrig strode out onto the balcony, his face shining with excitement. 'Is it really Snudge bespeaking you?'

The Royal Alchymist's hand flew away from his eyes and he stared at his brother with a mixture of consternation and fear. 'Con! Oh, how you startled me!'

'Are you well?' the king asked in concern. He lowered himself to a padded stool.

'Yes, yes.' Stergos forced a smile. 'I'm well, and Deveron is *very* well. Con, he's found Maudrayne and the boy! And he says he's managed to convince her to recant her accusation concerning your talent. There are some concessions required, but I do believe we've found the solution to your terrible dilemma.'

'Great God,' Conrig murmured. 'Snudge talked Maude around?' He scowled. 'What concessions?'

'Just a moment, while I let Deveron know you're here. Then he can tell you everything himself.' He spoke on the wind, then pulled himself to a sitting position. At length, he presented to the king a verbatim account of Snudge's proposal and Maudrayne's acceptance.

Conrig listened, thunderstruck. When Stergos finished, the king said, 'But how will Snudge get Maude and the boy to Donorvale? For that matter, how in hell did Snudge get to Tarn?'

'He has a new sigil named Gateway,' Stergos admitted with reluctance. 'Acquired from some . . . some wizard he met along the way. I still have to get the straights of it myself.

The thing is able to transport a number of persons from one place to another through sorcery.'

'God's Teeth! Our Snudge is a veritable wellspring of surprises. The proposal is ingenious. I quite like the notion of having Parli Beorbrook adopt the lad. But can we trust Maude's word? I must think hard about this.'

'Deveron says there can be no delay. Your friend Feribor has deceived you and is about to attack the place where Maude is being held. If you accept Snudge's proposal, he'll carry the princess and the boy Dyfrig to Donorvale, using the Gateway sigil. The sealords can witness her recanting and her acceptance of the agreement. If you decline or withhold a decision, Deveron says he'll take Maude and Dyfrig else-where and – er – find them a new home.'

'Damn him for a treasonous whoreson!' Conrig bellowed. 'He dares to bargain with me?'

Stergos stiffened. 'His proposal is a good one, Con. Without Maude's accusing testimony, there is no cause for any tribunal, here in Cathra or in Tarn, to look into the matter of your talent.'

The king gave him a mutinous glare. 'It's lèse-majesté! I'm the Sovereign!'

'For now you are,' his brother said sadly. 'Con, agree to it. You gain much and lose nothing but Maude's bitter enmity and the threat to your throne. I implore you! So much lies in the balance.' More than you know, the Royal Alchymist thought, but I can say nothing to you about the Source and the New Conflict, for you would never believe me!

Conrig said, 'Very well.'

'What?' Stergos leapt like a trout, recalled from his abstraction.

'I'll do it. Our Tarnian ambassador can be one official witness and the Lord Constable the second. I draw the line at facing that hellcat myself. Let it be part of our agreement that I never see Maude again. Tell Snudge to get her and the boy to Donorvale without delay.'

'I will!' Stergos covered his eyes and sent the message on the wind, weeping for joy all the while.

Conrig Wincantor, the Sovereign of Blenholme, turned away from his brother and helped himself to the wine that was on a small refreshment table near the balcony railing. Then he looked out over the expanse of Cala Blenholme Harbor, sipping from his crystal cup and smiling. Tinnis Catclaw's ship was speeding to Tarn. He was already commanded to stop at Donorvale to confer with the sealords, and now there was no need for him to proceed further. He would witness the agreement.

And then, if Conrig thought it was for the best, he might fulfill his original task.

No one in the peel challenged the squad of bogus guardsmen as they marched up the grand staircase from the gate vestibule to the third level, trailed by a youthful servant. Many of the residents had already learned that a strange warship had hove into view, causing the shaman-lord much anxiety. A timid-looking housemaid clutching a feather-duster even ventured to ask the passing king's men if Skullbone Peel was in danger.

'Nothing to concern you, wench!' Gavlok told her sternly. 'Back to work.'

At the armory door, the armiger Valdos whispered to the others, 'Can you give me a minute or two to get the child out of the library before you raise a ruckus in there?'

'Only that,' came the voice of unseen Induna. 'Take the prince to the turret as fast as you can.'

Valdos trotted to the library at the far end of the corridor and pulled open the door. The four-year-old boy sat at a long table amidst the shelves, reading very slowly from a book while pointing out the words with his finger. A homely, big-boned woman, evidently his nursemaid, sat across from him mending a shirt.

'Prince Dyfrig!' Valdos called out. 'Your lady mother has urgent need of you. You must come with me to the turret at once, where she awaits.'

Dyfrig said, 'After I finish this sentence. Is there such a word as ee-num-russ?'

'You must come now!' Valdos crossed to the table.

The maid scowled at him. 'Is something wrong?'

'No. Yes!' Valdos spluttered. He held out his arms to the boy. 'Here, I'll carry you.'

Dyfrig was patient. 'Rusgann can't read. Can you? Look – what's this word? Ee-num-rus? I never heard of it.'

Outside, there were shouts and a sudden metallic clash. The maid surged to her feet with a squawk of alarm and dashed to the open door.

'Don't go out there!' Valdos cried. 'Laddie, come to me!'

'The word,' came the implacable demand.

Frantic, Valdos peered at the place indicated by the small finger. '*Enormous!*' he shouted, and scooped Dyfrig up.

'Thank you,' said the little prince.

Induna appeared, pushing Rusgann back into the room and slamming the door behind her. 'It's going wrong, Val. Come close to me and we'll make a run for it. I can probably shield you and the boy with my magic while still going unseen –'

'What's happening?' Rusgann demanded.

'We're rescuing the boy and the princess,' Induna snapped. 'Stand aside, woman. There's fighting in the corridor.'

'I won't go without Rusgann!' Dyfrig shrieked. 'I won't!' And he began to squirm and flail his limbs like a mad thing, so that Valdos nearly dropped him.

'Stop it!' the armiger pleaded. 'We'll take her, we'll take her!'

Dyfrig was instantly still in his arms. 'Good.'

Induna cracked the heavy door open, then closed it again, cutting off the sound of a loud affray. Her expression was bleak. 'There's a shaman out there. He didn't see me. He must have come down the stairs in the guards' dormitory just across the hall. He's creeping toward the armory, probably sent by those on the roof to investigate the fighting. A scrier wouldn't make any sense of it – guard fighting guard. We've got to take down the magicker, Val. Give the boy to the maid and grab that big book. I'll go invisible and trip him up, and you swat him with the book when he's down.'

'Swat him? I'll carve out his lights!' the squire blustered, fumbling for his dagger.

She slapped him roundly. 'Do as I say,' she hissed.

Valdos took up the huge tome from its stand, muttering. A moment later he and Induna were out the door.

'Are we really being rescued, Rusgann?' Dyfrig was safe in her strong arms, an expression of keen interest on his face.

'God only knows. Hold onto my neck, Dyfi.'

The sound of a tremendous explosion rocked the room. Induna flung the door open. 'Come with me! Go carefully and don't trip over anything.'

The corridor was filling with smoke that poured from the armory. Shadowy figures moved about in it, yelling and cursing. Swords clanged. On the floor lay a man in a shabby brown gown, his head hidden beneath a book. Radd Falcontop, with a sinister black iron sphere in one hand and a sword in the other, came running toward them. He cleared the fallen shaman with a single leap and darted into the dormitory, shouting at Rusgann. 'Get the hell out of here, wench – down the stairs!'

'This way!' said Induna's voice. The strapping maid felt an invisible person tugging at her apron, drawing her into the smoke. She clung tight to Dyfrig, was momentarily blinded by the swirling fumes, heard coughs and screams, stumbled

over a guard's bleeding body. Then she saw the small woman
beckoning to her, pointing out the way of escape.

'Over here! The stairs. Go down. Go to the windmill turret.
Take the boy to his mother!' The witch vanished again.

Another explosion shook the peel, coming from the dormitory. A thunderous voice called out in the murk, 'It's done!
Both sets of steps to the roof gone. All you king's men – fall
back. Fall back and run!'

Rusgann said, 'Hang on, Dyfi,' and plunged down the stairs.

'We're within range of Skullbone Peel, my lord duke,' the
captain said to Feribor. 'You, wizard! Keep light airs blowing
so we can maneuver. Quartermaster! Raise the colors of the
Sovereignty and the duke's pennon.'

Feribor used a spyglass to survey the peel from the quarterdeck of the frigate, which lay broadside to the shore.
'They've finally got the catapult set up on the fort roof, and
it's loaded with a sizable tarnblaze shell. The silly damned
fools! That engine couldn't fling a bomb more than a hundred
ells . . . I wonder what the two columns of smoke are all
about? Think it might be a signal of some sort?'

The captain shrugged. 'I can't say, my lord. Shall we fire
a dummy charge to attract their attention?'

'Not yet. But see that the guns are readied.'

'It's already done.'

Feribor turned to his windvoice, a slope-shouldered older
man with a long, sardonic face. 'Vra-Colan, bespeak Shaman-
Lord Ontel. Tell him who we are and present my personal
compliments.'

The Brother pulled up his hood so that his face was shadowed, except for the mouth. After a few minutes had passed,
he reported, 'Ontel also conveys the usual sentiments of
greeting to you, my lord. He asks what brings you to the
Desolation Shore.'

'Say we have come to take away Princess Maudrayne Northkeep and her son, who are his unwilling guests. Have him be so good as to send them out to our ship in a small boat. He has exactly one half-hour to comply.'

Vra-Colan spoke on the wind, paused, then gave the reply. 'Ontel asks what you will do if he declines.'

'Tell him that my ship's guns will pound his wretched little fort to rubble. And assure him that I care not whether the lady perishes along with him and his people, since she is already under sentence of death for having threatened grave harm to the Sovereign of Blenholme.'

The message was sent, and Feribor waited impatiently for the reply. When the minutes continued to drag by in silence, he finally barked, 'Colan! Demand that they answer!'

Blind Bozuk sat slumped in a chair a few paces away from the duke, the windvoice, and the captain, close beside the helmsman at the wheel. He called out feebly. 'They're preparing their answer! One of them is lighting the fuse of the great bombshell in the catapult.'

The captain burst into derisive laughter. 'Tarnian lunacy!'

'Let's hope so,' Bozuk wheezed.

An instant later the arm of the engine threw the missile high into the air. As it soared to the top of its trajectory, Feribor sneered, 'Far short! Even I can see that it – God's Bones! Look! It can't be!'

The shell was not falling, as all logic said it must, but instead continued on toward the ship as though it were an airborne balloon rather than a heavy ball of steel loaded with explosive chymicals.

'The three shamans.' Bozuk's tone was oddly apologetic. 'They're pushing it with their overt talent. Quite an impressive meld of magical power. Who knew they had it in them?'

The captain shouted, 'Helm, hard aport! Wizard, all the wind you can muster!'

'I have no strength left in me,' Bozuk admitted, 'not even enough to lift a feather. Nor am I able to divert the projectile from its path. It may yet fall short or miss us.'

'She don't answer the helm, cap'n!' cried the man at the wheel. 'We're flat becalmed.' His eyes were wide with terror, fixed on the rushing sphere that trailed sparks and a thin plume of smoke. It came at them a few ells above mastheight, giving hope that it might indeed pass over the ship. But the magic of the shamans halted it in midair, where it paused and plummeted straight down.

The helmsman screeched, 'Cap'n, it's coming right at us! Cap'n!'

But that officer was already dragging Feribor forward toward the quarterdeck stairs. Both men tumbled down them as the hissing, smoking ball struck the ship's wheel, causing it to disintegrate into a hail of lethal fragments that shredded the flesh of the helmsman and the ancient shaman cowering in his chair, killing both of them instantly. Vra-Colan was left moaning in a small pool of his blood, only slightly injured. The missile penetrated deck after deck as it fell, demolishing the ship's steering mechanism and finally ending in the bilges of the aft hold with all of its momentum spent.

There it exploded.

Bruised and battered, Duke Feribor felt the tremendous jolt and heard the smothered roar of the detonation as he lay on the upper deck beside the captain. A few seamen had fallen but most were on their feet, dashing about in response to orders screamed by the mates and petty officers. The guns of the starboard battery crashed out a single broadside. The captain stirred, groaning, and clutched at his left arm.

'Broken, curse it! Lord duke, can you haul me up?'

But Feribor was still too shocked to move, and it was the quartermaster, leaking blood from a gash in his scalp, who pulled the captain to his feet and helped sling his broken arm inside his jerkin.

'Arlow! Belay firing the guns and get the pumps going,' he said. 'Bendanan, find Chips and survey the damage to the hull.'

Other officers were crowding around the captain as he issued further orders. A seaman helped Feribor to arise, and at his request led him to the starboard rail where he might survey Skullbone Peel. The blocky white fort was un-damaged, although two black columns of smoke still issued from its roof, where tiny figures seemed to be dancing on the battlements. Only a single cannonshell had found its mark: the windmill turret was a ragged stub, its top half missing save for twisted fragments of its spiral iron stairway.

'Well, that's small loss,' Feribor said. He stumbled back to the captain. 'Get me a small boat and a squad of marine warriors! I've got to go ashore and hunt out Princess Maudrayne.'

'You may eventually hunt your pathetic quarry, my lord,' the captain snarled, 'but not until I've secured my ship from sinking – if that's possible. Go to your cabin. Now! And don't set foot outside it until you're sent for.'

'My lord?' a weak voice inquired.

Crimson with rage, Feribor whirled to find Vra-Colan standing there, his robes ripped to shreds and his face a mass of small cuts. A youthful sailor supported the windvoice, who said, 'I think she was in there. Princess Maudrayne, in the room atop the blasted turret. I oversaw her only briefly and then she eluded my windsight – a woman very beautiful, with auburn hair, amidst a group of other people. I said nothing to you at the time because I was unsure of her iden-tity, and you were engrossed with your spyglass.'

Feribor clutched the windvoice's upper arm, causing him to flinch in pain. 'Scry the place now! See if you can find her!'

'Do it from the duke's cabin,' ordered the captain tersely.

None of Feribor's protests or threats availed, and so he and Colan went below. For hours the debilitated Brother did his utmost to see through the stone walls of the peel, hindered by smoke. He reported small fires and damage to two chambers on the upper level, and wounded men being cared for, and even numbers of dead bodies. Toward the end of his long surveillance, the persons trapped on the roof were finally rescued with ladders. But nowhere in any part of the fort was there a tall woman with auburn hair, or a very small boy.

Finally Feribor permitted the exhausted Brother to abandon the windsearch and sleep. He sat brooding in a chair until well after midnight, when the captain came at last and told him that an improvised patch on the hull was holding, and they were not in immediate danger of sinking.

'But we're a long way from home, my lord duke, in hostile waters, with our steering shot to hell. So if you know any good prayers, start saying them.'

Rusgann ran like a deer with Dyfrig in her arms when she finally reached the ground floor of the peel – through the kitchen and the scullery, along a covered passage to the annex building, past the half-enclosed animal shelters and the storerooms, and into the pumproom below the turret. No one pursued them, nor did the young witch or her servant-lad confederate or any other person follow after.

'Let me catch my breath,' the maid gasped, setting Dyfrig down at the foot of the iron stairs leading up into the tower. 'I've got a fierce stitch in my side.'

A woman's voice called faintly from above. 'Rusgann? Dyfi? Are you there?'

The boy squealed, 'Mama!' And before Rusgann could stop him he was up the stairs and out of sight, and she heard people approaching through the barn rooms, their low conversation punctuated with coughs and an occasional moan. Hastily, she ducked out of sight behind a huge piece of wooden machinery, all cogs and shafts and lever-arms shining with grease, but unmoving because a piece of it had been detached and lay on the floor along with scattered tools.

Three men dressed in the uniforms of peel guardsmen, with helmets and mail shirts missing, entered the pump-room. All were filthy with soot and blood. A stocky youth and a tall skinny fellow half-carried a much older man whose head lolled on his breast. Rusgann recognized him as the fighter who'd run at her carrying a tarnblaze grenade and sword, who had warned her to flee.

At the foot of the iron stairs, the skinny man yelled, 'Deveron? Are you up there?'

'Gavlok!' The reply echoed off the turret walls. 'Thank God. I tried to scry you but the smoke got too thick. The princess and her son are here, safe! And she's agreed to the proposal.'

'Hanan and I have Radd with us,' the one named Gavlok called. 'He's badly bashed up but we're fine. Poor old Hulo's dead. We had a nasty fracas in the armory. I don't know what's become of Val . . . or Induna.' Laboriously, the uninjured pair began to pull their comrade up the narrow steps.

Rusgann waited until they reached the top, then climbed up herself. The small tower room seemed crowded wall to wall with people. Through the window on the seaward side she saw a three-masted man o'war lying not far offshore.

'My lady!' she cried, pushing past the youth called Hanan, who was tending to the wounded man. 'Have these knaves harmed you?'

'They're friends. It's all right.' Maudrayne held Dyfrig in her arms. Both of them had wet cheeks, but they were smiling. 'Come sit beside us on the bench and I'll explain.'

Snudge stood with Gavlok, staring at the frigate. 'There's

some kind of a parley going on between the shamans on the peel roof and the warship. I can't decipher it but the direction of the bespoken wind-threads is plain.'

'The castle people had the catapult up at the battlements before we arrived at the armory,' Gavlok said. 'We demolished both sets of stairs with small bombshells. It'll be a while before Ontel and his wizards get down. We're safe here for awhile.'

Snudge turned his attention to the roof of the keep. 'What the devil do they think they're doing over there? Look – the pan of the catapult is loaded and they're cranking down the arm. The ship's far out of range.'

'Its starboard gunports are open,' Gavlok pointed out. 'If the cannons let loose, we're finished. But Feribor wouldn't really dare endanger Maudrayne and the boy, would he? I mean, it has to be a bluff.'

'Does it?' Snudge gave an edgy little laugh. 'Cathran naval gunners are well-trained. They could pepper Skullbone with shells, putting the pressure on. Unfortunately, this windmill turret is a perfect target for a demonstration of marksmanship. We've got to get out of here soon, Gav. Let me try to scry Induna and Val again.'

He covered his eyes. After a few minutes, he gave a cry of distress. 'I see them, just entering the kitchen. Val's hurt. Looks like he's senseless. Induna's holding him up with her arms and her talent and moving him along, but the squire's heavy and she's tired.' He opened his eyes and flashed a look of desperation at his friend. His next words were delivered in a whisper. 'I don't dare leave here. If things fall apart, I'll have to use the Gateway sigil to take these people away at once. Maude and her son *must* reach Donorvale safely, and the others deserve to go as well.'

'So many?' Gavlok was incredulous. 'Has that been your plan from the beginning? You'll kill yourself! Look what happened to you the last time! And with me and two others as well –'

'But no heavy equipment. Donorvale's only a hundred and fifty leagues away – a third of the distance we traveled before. I ought to be able to do it, even carrying seven adults and a child. But I'll probably have only one go at it. The sigil will strike me down and I won't be able to come back. So . . . will you try to fetch Induna and Val? I'll wait for you until the last minute.'

'Oh, shite,' said the lanky knight. 'Of course I'll go.' He spun about and vanished into the stairwell.

With a sinking heart, Snudge focused his windsight on the quarterdeck of the ship. Bozuk looked a complete wreck, the evil old bastard. It was his fault that Feribor had come here. The sight of the duke, so debonair and merciless, almost choked Snudge with rage. Of all the people King Conrig might have sent to Tarn . . . He seemed to be waiting now, glaring at his hooded windvoice and tapping his foot on the deck. Waiting –

Bozuk was pointing at something, speaking. His withered lips were hard to read. *Answer . . . lighting fuse . . . catapult . . .*

Snudge caught his breath. From the roof of the peel soared a missile that was surely fated to fall into the sea. Uncannily, it did not. At the top of its arc it seemed to hesitate, then continued onward in an unnaturally straight path toward the warship, moving much more slowly than before, gradually losing altitude as though it were rolling down a smooth incline.

The mad Tarnian buggers were pushing the thing along with sorcery.

'Look!' Rusgann cried. She'd seen the smoking shell – and an instant later most of the others did, too. All save prostrate Radd Falcontop rushed to the eastern side of the tower to watch, exclaiming in wonderment and morbid speculation.

When the shell made its dramatic halt above the ship and began to fall, Maude screamed, seized Dyfrig, and turned away with the boy howling his disappointment in her arms. The others cried out in horror at what happened next, so that Snudge almost missed hearing the sound of voices rising from the base of the tower.

He shouted down the stairs. 'Gavlok? Induna? Hurry, for the love of God!'

Can I use my talent to help them up? he asked himself. It was not a type of magic he was good at, but the situation was desperate. He sent out a shout on the wind: *Source, help me if you can!*

He reached out to the slow-moving climbers, took hold, and pulled with all the soul-strength he could command.

The tall knight and the tiny woman and the collapsed squire shot upward and knocked Snudge over. They all skidded into Radd's body, and he uttered a great groan. 'All of you!' Snudge cried from the squirming heap. 'Come quickly to me. Come close.' He pulled Subtle Gateway from his shirt and gripped it in his fist. Gavlok got to his knees and dragged Maudrayne and Dyfrig to him.

'Oh, look!' Rusgann said. 'The ship's cannons are firing back.'

'Right at us,' Hanan said. He and the nursemaid stood frozen at the window.

Were the two close enough to be carried? Snudge cried out, 'EMCHAY ASINN – to the High Sealord's palace in Donorvale!'

The white flash of the sigil's sorcery and the golden blast of the tarnblaze cannonshell coincided.

TWENTY-FOUR

He was adrift in darkness again, only this time there were
no stars. Neither were there any malignant auroral lumi-
nosities taunting him. He was sure that the Lights were there;
but they were in eclipse, almost but not quite ignoring his
presence, as though he were a distraction from more important business. They spoke to one another in their unique and
peculiar manner, and he listened.

> *Calamity may happen. What was postponed in the Old Conflict.*
> *The abomination made by the One Denied . . .*
> *When debased, he made it.*
> *An abomination then called Unknown Potency, lost then stolen.*
> *And now in a stupid brute's gizzard, renamed! So what?*
> *He is not stupid. And he goes to Rothbannon's castle.*
> *The wise thief! He wrote down the means of activation in a book.*
> *But never dared to bring the Potency to life.*
> *It may yet live. Calamity may happen, and a New Conflict.*
> *Look: the one we cursed goes to meet the brute.*
> *Cursing a mistake. He now may be our one hope!*
> *Shall we not convert the Wrong-Named, then?*
> *Snudge? He is not ripe and may never be. Rethink the one cursed.*

The One Denied the Sky is half-free. Think of that!
Better to think of the brutes. And the Moon Crags.
BEST to think of feeding! Amusement! Irony! Paradox!
Best for now.
There's time. A lot of it.

He heard them laughing, laughing. The pain and fear took hold of him and he fell –

But not far. He forced his eyes open and saw the bodies.

Rusgann and Hanan standing upright, looking about them in stunned disbelief. Gavlok and Induna crouching protectively over Valdos and Radd, who still lay unconscious. Maudrayne on her knees, cradling Dyfrig, whose eyes were still squeezed tightly shut. All eight of them surrounding him as he sprawled on the flagstones of the forecourt of Sealord Sernin Donorvale's riverside palace. A squad of household guards were running toward them, shouting.

Snudge chuckled weakly and murmured, 'All of us here. That wasn't so bad, was it?' He felt the pain blossom hideously, saw Induna crawling toward him with her face intent. 'The bad stuff starts now, I guess,' he told her. His eyes, black and deep as wells, began to close again as he surrendered.

'No, you don't!' cried Induna of the Barking Sands. She ripped the chain holding the two sigils from his neck and flung it aside, warning the others, 'Don't touch those stones. They'll burn you.' Then she plucked forth a pearly little female image from her breast, and for the second time gave away a part of her soul. '*Now* you may sleep. For as long as you like.'

His eyes opened again, and she saw that this time they were a vibrant, glinting blue, full of unasked questions. But before he could speak, he succumbed to the warm, quiet dark.

*   *   *

Beynor watched them come with his windsight, wave after wave surging up the Darkling River estuary, over ten thousand monsters, armed with the most effective minor sigils still in the race's possession. They had already laid waste to Moss's second-largest city, Sandport, and crushed the sealing town of Balook. They sank the six frigates and twelve fighting sloops of Moss's Navy. They overwhelmed Salkbane Fortress and slaughtered its conjure-lord and defending wizards, and then the victorious army of amphibians closed in on Royal Fenguard itself. They expected to find Beynor waiting for them there, expected their human ally to lead them through subterranean passageways into the bowels of Rothbannon's castle, straight to the tomb that secured Ullanoth's sigils. There Beynor would activate the Known Potency for the Salka, initiating the reconquest of their ancestral home. That's the way it was supposed to happen – but would not.

He sat on a tall black horse, cloaked head to toe from the rain and unrecognizable to the monsters' relatively puny windsight, amidst rocks on a lofty hill above Fenguard Castle. From that vantage point, Moss's one-time Conjure-King oversaw the teeming invaders, led by their Supreme Warrior, Ugusawnn. He also saw Moss's uprisen population of native Salka converging on the capital from the Little Fen and the Great Fen, making casual slaughter of humans as they rejoiced that a new era had begun.

Beynor saw it all taking place. As he saw his own cleverly crafted scheme in ruins.

It was not until he had nearly reached Fenguard, and his long journey's end, that he had finally been able to scry through the castle's thick granite walls and bedrock-shrouded cellars to perceive the debacle: Beynor discovered that Rothbannon's tomb held only Rothbannon's ashes. The platinum casket that should have secured his sister's living sigils was gone, as was her enchanted body.

He had planned to destroy that body (as he once planned to kill the living woman by stealth), and by doing so render her truly dead, and her sigils dead as well. Then, when the Salka arrived, met him, and followed him to the tomb, they would believe that the box still contained moonstones that were alive, deadly, and useless to them – until touched by the activated Potency. It was impossible for the Salka to scry out the truth about Ulla's stones: sigils could not be seen through talent. And no one save a descendant of Rothbannon could enter his tomb.

Beynor would have declared himself ready to fulfill his part of the bargain. He would have asked his mentor Kalawnn to disgorge the Potency and hold it up, then he would have coached the Master Shaman in conjuring the spell that activated the Stone of Stones.

Kalawnn would never have suspected that his human protégé contemplated a magical coup. (Although Ugusawnn might have!) The Master Shaman, like the other Eminences, believed that Beynor could not touch or use the activated Potency. He thought, erroneously, that the sigil would bond to the person who activated it, as others of its ilk did, and burn or kill anyone who tried to steal it. But Beynor had discovered that the Potency bonded to no one; and he had hoped and prayed that its sorcery transcended the Lights' curse as well.

Beynor had planned to invite Kalawnn alone to enter the opened tomb with him. After all, there was hardly room inside for more than one of the huge amphibians! He had been confident that he could snatch the Potency from the clumsy Salka shaman, open the platinum box, and activate Ullanoth's Concealer and Interpenetrator sigils within a split second.

He'd planned to vanish with the box of moonstones, scathelessly penetrate the Salka mob in the passage, then activate Subtle Loophole to spy out the best escape route.

And all of it would have been accomplished without a debt of pain . . .

But now it would never happen. The best he could hope for was to retrace his path before the monsters overran all of Moss, make his way into northern Cathra, and retrieve the last remnant of Darasilo's Trove that luckless Brother Scarth had concealed in the bear's den: another Weather-maker, an Ice-Master, and a Destroyer. Three inactive Great Stones that would become, when activated by the incanta-tions contained in the book hidden with them, superlative and hazardous weapons . . . but not for him.

It was enough to make the most stalwart sorcerer weep! On the hill in the rain, windwatching the monster horde encircle doomed Fenguard Castle, Beynor ground his teeth together and cursed the God of the Heights and Depths and the most peculiar of the deity's creatures, the Coldlight Army.

Beynor! Beynor, where are you? Respond to Master Kalawnn!

No, he wouldn't respond – just in case there was a chance, sometime in the dubious future, of getting the Known Potency back. It would be good if Kalawnn thought he'd been prevented from making the rendezvous through some misfortune.

Beynor of Moss, you groundling conniver, respond to Ugusawnn the Supreme Warrior! Respond – or suffer the dire consequences!

He whooped with caustic laughter, startling his horse, which gave a nervous whicker and stamped its hooves. The dire consequences were already at hand! Since the Lights' curse prevented him from using those three hidden Great Stones, he'd have to give them up to someone else. With luck, he'd find a way to retain some vestige of control over the surrogate wielder.

That person would *not* be Kilian Blackhorse.

The traitorous alchymist was already secure in King

Somarus's new court, along with his cronies, stirring up
trouble for Conrig Wincantor. No, Beynor would need to find
one who was both loyal and none too clever. It was a problem
that would keep until later.

*Beynor! Respond to Kalawnn. We have begun our assault on the
castle. Come and join me without fear, young human. The Supreme
Warrior shall neither insult nor abuse you, for I am the designated
Master of the Potency, not he. Beynor!* . . .

He could hear human screams and death-cries on the wind
now, and the triumphant roars of the monsters. With a
shudder he sent his thread of oversight winging far away to
the southwest, beyond the Dismal Heights and the Dextral
Range to the upland moors of Cathra where the bear's den
was. The remains of Scarth and his mule had long since been
scattered by scavengers, and the great brown predator himself
was not at home. But the leather saddlebag was still on the
rock shelf, besmirched a little now by bat droppings and
mold, but safe for all that.

Beynor banished the vision. Once again he erected the
ingenious spell of couverture he'd learned from Kilian. Then
he backed his horse out of the rocks and set off down the
hill toward the Moss Lake road.

Stergos heard of the Salka invasion from the High
Thaumaturge Zimroth, as she and most of the other members
of the Glaumerie Guild barricaded themselves in a castle
tower in a last stand against the attackers. Even as she related
the frightful events then transpiring, her windvoice was
abruptly stilled. No other Mossland magicker bespoke Stergos
after that, nor was he able to scry so distant a scene himself.
In haste, he bespoke the new head of Zeth Abbey, Abbas
Bikoron, and begged him to learn what he could of the
disaster.

It was very late. Stergos had been reading in bed when

he was bespoken, and most of Cala Palace had retired for the night. It would not be appropriate to summon the High King to him, and yet Stergos felt he could trust no one to pass on such politically sensitive tidings. So he rose from his bed, took a walking stick, and limped to the royal suite, brushing aside the Knights of the Household standing guard and pounding on the door with the silver knob of his stick.

'My liege! Sire, open to me, your own brother!'

After a few minutes the sitting-room door flew wide. Conrig yanked the Royal Alchymist inside and shot the bolt. 'What the devil d'you mean by this, Gossy? Risalla and I were fast asleep.'

Stergos tottered to a chair and dropped into it. 'Moss has fallen to a huge army of invading Salka. I had the news from Lady Zimroth, trapped with other ranking conjurers in a Fenguard tower. I believe she perished even as she bespoke me.'

'Bazekoy's Blood! So the rumors were true after all.' The king perched on the edge of another chair. He'd thrown on a light robe but wore nothing else. 'Lord Admiral Skellhaven heard from fishermen that a vast pod of the brutes had been sighted on the high seas off the Dawntides, but I'd hoped it was some mistake.'

'Master Ridcanndal besought the aid of our navy,' Stergos said, staring at the floor. 'He feared this was coming.'

'And I could not send the navy!' Conrig said. 'My promise was made to Ullanoth, and she's dead – if not before this, then surely now, after the Salka have despoiled her unbreathing body. Our navy, and our armies as well, must stand ready to quell a rebellion in Didion. That bastard Somarus has "postponed" coming to Cala Blenholme in order to tender his oath of fealty. He'll come in two weeks, he says! The uproar in Moss will now give him an excuse to put the thing off indefinitely. Our fleet will take to sea, Gossy, but it will sail to Didion Bay, not Moss, to remind that saucy kinglet whose vassal he is.'

'What will you do about Moss?' Stergos asked, without much hope.

'The only thing possible for now: contain the monsters there. The fens are ideal places for them to dwell, and they may not wish to move into drier lands. But we must learn what set them off. And if it seems that they show signs of expanding beyond the miserable corner of Blenholme they now occupy, we must look more closely into the weaponry at their disposal.'

'Zimroth said the assault forces used minor sigils. It was long thought that the Salka had only a few of the things, but perhaps the supposition was wrong.'

'Beynor was exiled to the Dawntide Isles,' Conrig recalled. 'He could be the instigator. Zeth knows he wanted revenge against his sister and the others who would not support his pilfered kingship. Ulla believed him to be as mad as their slain father Linndal.'

'The earl marshal warned of warclouds building in the north, Con, but I doubt he foresaw anything like this. Do you really think Somarus will disavow fealty and challenge you?'

'Oh, yes,' the king said wearily 'Once I would have thought he'd come charging headlong over Great Pass with no more thought than a stampede of wild oxen. But now that Kilian has become his adviser, Somarus may learn more of generalship than any of his barbarian ancestors. If so, he may become a formidable adversary.'

'And large numbers of his people love him,' Stergos said, 'as they did not love Honigalus.'

'A more serious worry of mine, now that we know the Salka threat is real, concerns a possible alliance between them and Didion. *Why* did the creatures kill Honigalus and his family? No one professes to have a clue. My Privy Council dismisses the notion of a human-nonhuman alliance as unthinkable. But is it?'

'We'll have to find out the truth, Con.'

The king rose, stretched, and yawned. 'And so much more! Is our Lord Treasurer a villain? Will the Lords of the Southern Shore oppose my naming Dyfrig third in the succession and hold out in favor of Feribor? Will the Sealords of Tarn remain loyal to the Sovereignty with Maude in their midst to remind them of how close they came to casting off vassalage?'

'The Princess Dowager has meekly recanted and signed the document,' Stergos reminded him. 'We can hope this will defuse the situation in Donorvale. Arrangements are already made for Dyfrig to go to Beorbrook, and the earl marshal has pledged to welcome him. And yet . . . I'm loath to admit it, Con, but I can't help but wonder whether long years of separation from her son might eventually harden Maude's heart. She's a woman of strong Tarnian passions, as we both know.'

'She'll not break her word.'

'Can you be sure?' Stergos asked.

'Oh, yes,' the Sovereign said. 'I'm very sure.' He took his brother's arm, helped him up, and led him to the door. 'One of the knights will see you safely to your chambers. Try to put all troublesome thoughts from your mind now and sleep well. That's what I intend to do.'

It was always this way at the end of a complicated mission: Snudge felt let down, at a loose end, restless and moody. In a few days, he and his men would sail back to Cala Blenholme in the Lord Constable's fast frigate *Cormorant*. Until then, he diverted himself in the High Sealord's palace doing what he did best: spying. Rendering himself unnoticeable in the usual way, with his talent, he prowled about eavesdropping and snooping in a desultory fashion, at first learning nothing much.

His men spent their time eating, drinking, hashing over the great adventure, or indulging in pure relaxation. Their hero-worship of him was intensely embarrassing.

Princess Maude was understandably morose and subdued in temper, since Dyfrig would also be departing in the ship of Lord Tinnis Catclaw. The mother and son were constantly together, and she had engaged a local artist to paint a portrait of the boy and also of herself, so that each could have a lasting memento of the other.

Rusgann attended her mistress in glum silence and seemed to harbor formless apprehensions; she'd boldly asked Snudge whether he felt uneasy, too, and he'd been unable to deny it.

The Lord Constable, whom Snudge had had little to do with before, proved jovial, friendly, and eager to please. He ordered a special refit of *Cormorant* to accommodate the crowd of civilian passengers in comfort, and provisioned the ship with the best of food and drink for the voyage home.

Induna stayed on in the palace as an honored guest of the High Sealord, who had conferred upon her the largely symbolic title of Sealady of Barking Sands in recognition of her efforts. She intended to return to her home in the northland after the others had sailed away, having been thoroughly bemused by two messages sent her on the wind within a day of her abrupt arrival in Donorvale. The first, from Shaman-Lord Ontel Pikan, informed her that Bozuk, her grandsire, was indeed dead, buried at sea with a length of anchor-chain weighting his corpse. The second message, from the Northkeep banker Pakkor Kyle, requested instructions for the investment of her new inheritance – ten thousand gold marks. She had no notion what to tell him, but Sealord Sernin was giving her sound advice.

Snudge had almost taken Induna's sacrifice for granted, not really understanding what she'd done for him until one of the palace's resident shamans explained it. Then he was abashed and a little angry, as the recipients of some great benevolence often are. *Why* would she do such a thing for a stranger? What did she expect in return? But he found himself strangely unwilling to ask the questions of her, nor had he any wish to spy on her. After congratulating her on her marvelous legacy, Snudge avoided her company, although he saw her each day at dinner in Sernin's great hall and made polite conversation as a courteous knight should. Yet his thoughts returned to her at odd moments, and this both puzzled and disturbed him.

Snudge's fit of somber self-absorption came to an abrupt end when he found the three forged suicide notes.

He'd come again to the guestroom of the Lord Constable, wondering why it was always kept locked, intending to examine his portfolio of official papers more thoroughly for clues to the man's character. (Locks had never deterred Snudge's investigations.) The forged notes, together with an undeniably genuine short letter of Maudrayne's, were stuffed in Lord Tinnis's briefcase any old way, as though he'd been interrupted while perusing them . . . or more likely, penning them. Each suicide note was the same, and each mimicked the handwriting of the princess with more accuracy.

My dearest Uncle Sernin: Without my beloved son, life is no longer worth living. The potion I have taken will lead me to the peace I can find in no other way. Forgive me for causing you sorrow. Tell Dyfrig I will always watch over him.

Snudge felt his heart turn over in his breast, then a tidal

wave of fury and grief smote him with such force that he almost cried out aloud.

Conrig was responsible for this. What Snudge had balked at, Tinnis Catclaw was all too willing to do. The High King, believing his intelligencer dead, had beyond doubt dispatched the Lord Constable to Tarn to apprehend Maudrayne and Dyfrig and slay them. Later, with the circumstances altered, the death-sentence of the little boy was rescinded – but Maude's was not. Conrig was not ready to risk that she might someday withdraw her recanting.

With shaking hands, Snudge replaced the parchment sheets as he'd found them and slipped out of the room. His first thought was to track down Lord Tinnis on the Donorvale docks and slip a dagger between his ribs – but Conrig would only send another assassin. His second thought was to warn Maudrayne and Sealord Sernin that she was about to be poisoned – but this might provoke the very calamity the Source had been trying to prevent. The princess could not be allowed to testify to the High King's talent. Conrig Wincantor must keep his Iron Crown.

Distraught to the point of incoherence, Snudge stumbled to his own small guestroom and locked himself inside. Then he cried out on the wind for the Source.

'Why did you forbid Deveron to do anything at all?' Red Ansel asked.

He was in the eerie place of icy imprisonment on other business, consulting with the One Denied the Sky about the fall of Moss, and the near-certainty that Master Shaman Kalawnn would soon find in Rothbannon's library the book containing the incantation that would activate the Known Potency.

Because Maudrayne must make her own choice in the matter.

'I see no choice! There's only death awaiting poor Maudie!'

The Source was calm. *You don't foresee far enough, dear soul. She will still choose freely, and so will Deveron. As for Kalawnn, his discovery was inevitable. Rothbannon always possessed the means to activate the Potency. He was only afraid to do it – as his successors were – because he knew not the purpose of the enigmatic stone.*

Ansel sighed. 'So this, too, is part of the New Conflict: an empowered Potency in the possession of the Salka.'

Yes.

'The monsters will go after the two Crags, you know. They'll hunt them down one way or another and manufacture new moonstone sigils.'

Perhaps. I can't tell. The Potency can either activate such stones or abolish them – remember that! We must ask ourselves how the Lights will react to the presence of sigils that draw power from them, while vouchsafing no satisfaction of their hunger. The Likeminded and I are still mulling over the matter, and its possible effect upon the New Conflict.

Ansel Pikan gave a tired little laugh. 'Mull away! I must leave you to it and go to Thalassa Dru. But be sure that I'll be windwatching my dear princess all the while. And doing some mulling of my own – over my personal role in your great game.'

When he failed to come to the farewell feast held for the departing voyagers, Induna went looking for him, thinking he might have suffered a delayed reaction to his healing, which had been unexpectedly rapid. She found him in the palace stables, strapping saddlebags onto a powerful blue-roan stallion. He was dressed in traveling garb.

'Sir Deveron! What are you doing here?'

'Do you like my new steed?' he inquired archly. 'His name is Stormy, and he's supposed to be a holy terror. But we'll get along. I've a talent for dealing with horses.'

Induna glanced swiftly around the stableyard. None of the grooms were near. She spoke softly. 'Aren't you leaving for Cala tomorrow with the others, sir knight?'

Snudge fastened a buckle, then began to lash on a bedroll wrapped in waterproofed leather. 'No. I intend to stay and seek my fortune in Tarn . . . and I'm no longer a knight, although my royal master hasn't heard the bad news yet. I've given up being the Royal Intelligencer of Conrig Wincantor. My heart tells me that I can never again serve him in good conscience, since he has ordered a shameful act to be committed. The king will probably be livid when he finds out I'm gone for good, and he may put out a death warrant on me. But I'm unscryable, and Tarn is a large and lonely place.'

Induna watched him work. 'There is a long, somewhat perilous track I know, that leads to Northkeep and then to a tiny place called Barking Sands.'

He froze, catching her gaze. 'What are you saying?'

'Only that I admire and respect you, sir,' she said in a low voice, 'and even more so now, after you've confided your crisis of conscience to me. I'd welcome your enduring friendship. I would also welcome you to my home' – she smiled slyly at him – 'which, as you know, will soon be much more commodious than before. My mother is a superior healer-shaman, and she'd welcome you, too. The lot of Tarnian magickers is an interesting one, with many challenges. Do your talents include healing?'

'I don't know. I'm self-taught. There may be things within me that I never suspected.'

'Yes, as one matures, they sometimes manifest – not always as one might wish. Perhaps Mother and I together can work with you. To help you control and enhance your talent, if you should wish it.'

He cocked his head to one side and lifted one eyebrow.

'And will you also show me how sands can bark, if we ride up there together?'

'Oh, yes!' Her face shone with eagerness.

'Mind you,' he added more soberly, 'I intend to be away within the hour, before a certain Cathran lord notices I'm missing. But if you're serious, I'll secure a horse and tack for you while you fetch what you intend to bring.'

'I agree.' She nodded judiciously. 'Give me half an hour, sir.'

'You must now call me Deveron, for that is my name.'

'Very well – Deveron. I'm glad we are to be friends.' She turned and ran off lightly, her red-gold hair gleaming in the lowering sun.

He'd acted impulsively, perhaps foolishly. But the feeling of oppression that had earlier haunted him and the later pangs of anger, hatred, and sorrow were no longer so intense.

Induna! His previous experiences with women had been brief and casual and few. Perhaps this would be different.

The evening was still very warm. Feeling a sudden thirst, he strolled to the well that supplied both the stable and the laundry. As he bent over the stone rim to note its depth, he felt the two sigils slip out of his open shirt and dangle at the end of their chain.

The waters below gleamed darkly and deep.

He took hold of the glowing things, slipped the chain over his head, and let the moonstones dangle in space. Perhaps it was time, now that he was ready to begin a new life . . .

Not yet.

The voice was regretful, sad, and utterly compelling.

He sighed, hung the chain around his neck again, and went off to find the stablemaster. He had quite forgotten to take a drink of water.

Maudrayne was gowned in her favorite emerald green, wearing her opals and a little matching tiara that Sernin had given her as a homecoming gift. When the Lord Constable invited her to walk with him on the shining black marble esplanade beside the river, she readily agreed. It had been overwarm inside the great hall. Most of the visiting sealords and other highborn palace denizens were still in there with Sernin and his lady, drinking vast quantities of mead and spirits, not quite celebrating and not quite mourning her recantation and her agreement to what they thought was Conrig's proposal.

'It's blessedly cool out here, isn't it?' Tinnis said to her. 'And quiet as well, with no one about. Would you like to take a short stroll to the docks and cast an eye over my ship? It would please me to show you the fine accommodation the carpenters have wrought for Prince Dyfrig.'

'I don't fancy a tuppence tour given by groveling officers,' she said shortly.

He only laughed. 'They're all ashore, as are most of the rest of the crew. Come, a little air will lift your spirits.'

So she took his arm and they walked to the palace landing stage where the tall ship was berthed. The two guards at the gangplank's foot saluted them but made no comment as they went aboard. Maudrayne dutifully admired the small luxurious cabin, and was particularly appreciative of the nautical books that had been collected for Dyfrig's pleasure, and the colored charts pinned to the bulkhead that showed both the sea route to Cala Blenholme and the land route from there to Beorbrook.

'Dyfi will enjoy these greatly.' Maudrayne was sincere. 'I thank you for your consideration, my lord. He's a clever lad, but so very young – and he'll be afraid.'

Tinnis Catclaw chuckled. 'That one? Not for long! He'll be up in the rigging before we're out of Gayle Firth and bedevilling the officer on watch wanting a chance to steer.'

'Shall we return to the palace?' she said. 'I feel a small headache coming on.'

'Ah! I have the very thing in my own cabin. It's just next door.'

He ushered her to it, found a crystal decanter and two silver cups, and went to rummage in a hanging locker above the washstand.

'Here it is, my mother's own remedy for all manner of megrims. I never travel by sea without it.' He lifted a small glass phial that gleamed ruby-red, removed its stopper, and put four drops into a cup. Then he filled both cups with wine and handed her the one with the physick. 'Drink up, my lady, and by the time we're back at the palace, I guarantee that all your suffering will be gone.'

'Truly?' She met his eyes. 'And tell me, Lord Tinnis: will it even banish my anguish at losing Dyfrig?'

'It will,' he said very quietly. 'In a short hour.'

She looked into the cup, her lips tight. 'Has my former husband, the King's Grace, ever made use of this medicine?'

'No . . . but I've heard him recommend it most highly for distress such as yours.'

She said, 'I know he sent you north to search me out, when Deveron Austrey was thought lost.'

'Yes.' He lifted one hand and gently touched the long tress of fiery auburn hair that spilled over her shoulder. 'I came eagerly, as was my duty. But I would have come even more swiftly, had I recalled how beautiful you were. I saw you only three times when you dwelt in Cala Palace, for I was then a callow young mountain baron with small reason to visit the capital.'

'Ah.' With delicacy, she turned and stepped back, so that his hand must fall away. 'Yet now I must drink.'

She lifted the cup, but before it could touch her lips he took hold of her wrist, staying it. 'We – we could talk. I may have another remedy that would better suit you.'

'Even though I'm prepared to take this one? Lord Tinnis,

you perplex me. I'm weary and bereft and in need of peace.'

'My dear lady – Princess Maudrayne! It could be done. Not easily – but if you choose, it could be done.'

They stared each one at the other for a long moment, and then she told him her choice.